What Will Survive

MARK GARTSIDE

What Will Survive

MACMILLAN

First published 2012 by Macmillan
an imprint of Pan Macmillan, a division of Macmillan Publishers Limited
Pan Macmillan, 20 New Wharf Road, London N1 9RR
Basingstoke and Oxford
Associated companies throughout the world
www.panmacmillan.com

ISBN 978-0-230-75989-3

1 3 5 7 9 8 6 4 2

A CIP catalogue record for this book is available from the British Library.

Typeset by CPI Typesetting
Printed and bound by CPI Group (UK) Ltd, Croydon, CR0 4YY

For Mum and Dad, with love

Part One

1.

2009: Home Again

I suppose I was looking for signs that something was out of the ordinary; normally I wouldn't have noticed that the light next to the front door was on at ten in the morning, nor that the gate at the side of the house was open. But I'd been stuck in Paris for the night, my flight cancelled without warning or explanation, and my fifteen-year-old son had been home alone.

A semi-circle of cigarette butts surrounded my front door. At least fifty, if not more. That meant ten teenagers smoking five each; or twenty smoking fewer. Say half the kids smoked. That put it at between twenty and forty teenagers unsupervised in my house. Quite impressive, given that Michael had only found out he'd have the house to himself when I'd called at eight o'clock the night before.

I shook my head in frustration. He'd promised not to have a party. Twice. I'd made him repeat it in the hope that a double promise would somehow loom larger in his conscience than just one. It was the final triumph of hope over experience.

Next to the front door, a white Adidas trainer was wedged in the milk bottle holder. The toe was stained yellow by the residue oozing from a Bacardi Breezer that someone had stuffed inside it. For a second, I imagined taking the shoe and finding the owner by forcing Michael's friends to try it on, like the Prince when he's trying to find Cinderella. I glanced around the front garden. There was a clutch of beer cans in the roses and an empty vodka bottle lying by the potted plants. Thankfully, there was no sick.

At least, not outside. I opened the front door and gagged, smelling the yellowing patch of vomit by the side of the stairs before I saw it. It was ground into the carpet. A vacuum cleaner lay on its side a few feet away, a crust of teenager sick on the base. A brilliant idea to hoover it up. It had Michael's stamp all over it.

The smell must have distracted me, because it was a few seconds before I heard the noise. It was a rhythmic creaking, coming from the room above the lounge. My room. Where my bed was. I listened harder. It couldn't be. Michael was fifteen, for God's sake. He was a minor. It was illegal.

And the girl. If she was his age then she too was a minor. It was rape, technically. The creaking got faster. I took a deep breath.

'Michael?' I shouted. 'Are you home?'

The creaking stopped. I heard the thud of running feet and the shuffling sounds of what I assumed were people struggling into their clothes. Michael's voice came from the top of the stairs.

'Dad? Hang on, I'll be down in a second. Wait there. I just need the loo.'

I heard the flush of the toilet. *That'll be the condom*, I thought. *At least he's using one.*

He came down the stairs, barefoot and wearing a pair of football shorts and a T-shirt. He looked a lot like his mother; the same intense dark eyes and curly brown hair. Now though, those eyes had dark circles underneath them, and the hair was greasy and plastered flat to his head.

'You're back,' he said. 'I thought your flight was screwed up. I didn't expect you for ages.'

'I got lucky. What's all this mess?'

He glanced left and right, up and down, unable to look me in the eyes. 'Er, I had a few friends over last night.'

'A few? Well, you'd better start cleaning up.'

'Sure. But, er, I was going to go out this afternoon, meet some mates in town. Can I do it later?'

I shook my head. 'No. Start here with the sick.'

'Have you been in the kitchen?'

'Not yet.'

The hope that swept his face suggested the mess was bad. 'Look, Dad, why don't you go out for an hour? When you get back, I'll have this place cleaned up.'

'Michael, I've just got back from the airport. I've got no intention of going out again.' His tongue licked the corner of his mouth. He'd always done that when he was nervous, ever since he was a little boy. 'And you might want to put your T-shirt on the right way round.'

He looked down at his chest. 'Oh, yeah.'

'That's what happens when you get dressed in a hurry. Were you alone upstairs?'

'Yeah, 'course. I was having a kip.'

'Michael, you're in a lot of trouble already. Don't make it worse by lying.' He was a terrible liar, like most teenagers. You catch them out, their faces pale and they put on a strained tone of voice as they babble some excuse. It's incredible that they don't see how transparent they are. What they do have going for them is persistence. Once they've told a lie they'll stick to it, until eventually you just give in.

Not this time though. This time it was too easy to get to the truth. I gestured to the stairs. 'I'll just pop up then, get changed.'

Michael blocked my path. 'No. Let's go in the kitchen, or something. I'll make you a cup of tea.'

'It's all right. I want to freshen up.' I put my hand on his shoulder and levered him aside.

'Ok,' he said. 'You're right. Well done. There's someone up there.'

'Really? A friend? Why don't you introduce us?'

He closed his eyes in resignation. There was a cluster of spots with yellow heads in between his eyebrows. 'All right. I'll be back in a second.'

He ran upstairs. I heard some muttered conversation, and a few minutes later he returned with a girl two steps behind him. She had dyed black hair that had been scraped into a pony-tail. She was pretty in a generic kind of way, although she had large, bright eyes, of a striking dark green, almost marine, colour. Thank God she was about his age; it might still be illegal, but at least she wasn't much older, or, heaven forbid, younger.

'This is Carly.'

'Hello, Carly.'

'Hello, Mr Melton.'

'Graham,' I said. 'All Michael's . . . friends call me Graham. Did you attend the party last night? Did you stay over?'

She nodded. She looked terrified.

'Do your parents know you're here?'

She shook her head. 'They think I'm at me mate's house.' She had a strong Warrington accent, a hybrid of Mancunian and Scouse. I hadn't seen her before. I wondered whether she was at Michael's school, or if she went somewhere else.

'Well,' I said. 'You'd better get back before they find out where you really are.'

Michael took her hand. 'I'll walk you to the bus stop.'

'Then straight back here,' I said. 'You've got a lot of tidying up to do.'

I watched him walk down the drive with Carly, his arm around her waist and his fingers dipping into the pocket of her jeans. From the back they could have been in their twenties. Michael kissed the top of her head protectively, and I saw for the first time that even if he was not yet an adult, he was no longer a child. He was like a loaf of bread fresh from the oven, fully risen, but not yet cooled and hardened.

The kitchen was a mess: beer cans, chip wrappers and crushed cigarette packets littering every surface. The sink was full of dirty water, the plug hole blocked with the remains of a pizza. The paint on the windowsill above the sink was scorched, sticky and bubbly where someone had left a cigarette to smoulder. They must have lit it, put it down and walked away, a long cylinder of ash testament to their forgetfulness.

Michael sloped into the room, his hands in his pockets.

'It's all right, Dad,' he said sheepishly, 'I'll clean it up.'

'Damn right you will. Have you been smoking?'

'No. It was some of the others.'

'You better not be. You know how I feel about smoking.' He should have done. We'd talked about it often enough. My dad had been a heavy smoker all his life, fond of saying that it had never done him any harm, until he went for a check-up and found he had late-stage lung cancer and three months to live, at best. He lasted six more weeks. 'How do you know Carly?'

'She's the cousin of one of the girls from school.'

'And you met her last night?'

'Yeah.' He seemed oblivious to the implication that he'd been in bed with a girl he'd met the night before.

'How old is she?'

'Dunno. Fifteen. Summat like that.'

'Michael, be careful. She's not old enough to have sex. It's illegal. And I hope you're using condoms.'

He flushed bright red. 'Dad! Shuddup! It's none of your business!'

'It will be when her father calls me, or you bring a screaming baby back from the hospital. We need to talk.'

'No way! I don't mind clearing up this shit, but I'm not talking to you about . . . that stuff. What do you know about it, anyway?'

'A bit. How do you think you got here? Dropped off by the stork? Bought from the baby shop? There's more to it than that, Mikey. You see, Daddy and Mummy, they do a special thing together and nine months later—'

'Shut up! You're grossing me out.' He grabbed a bin bag from under the sink and started throwing the bottles and cans in it.

'Don't forget to recycle,' I said. If there was one way of getting teenagers to do something, it was to make the alternative even worse, like talking to your dad about sex.

He marched outside with the bottles and I went upstairs for a shower. Michael and Carly had hastily arranged the pillows and duvet on my bed, although it had obviously been slept in. I stripped it down, shaking my head. I would never have slept with someone in my parents' bed, would never even have considered it. It was only twenty-odd years ago, but things had been very different when I met Michael's mum.

2.

1985: Meeting Charlotte Marshall

1985. I was fifteen, living in Thatcher's Britain. My dad worked at the Greenall's Brewery on Wilderspool Causeway – long gone now, replaced by a supermarket, of course – and my mum was a nurse at the General Hospital. We lived in a terraced house on Miller Street in Latchford. I remember them buying it, fretting over a mortgage of twelve thousand pounds. It was on the market the other day, for a hundred and twenty grand. If Dad was still alive, I think he'd have laughed.

Nowadays it's easy to forget, looking at all the cut-out-and-keep politicians, how ideological life was in England in the eighties. It felt like there was something at stake, as though there was a choice to be made about what kind of country we would become. Tory or Labour? Maggie or Kinnock? They looked different, thought different, spoke different. If you liked one, by definition you hated the other.

And we hated Thatcher. Her name was a dirty word in our house. Dad had been on the side of the miners during the strike, and the defeat still rankled. He was a trades unionist, like his dad had been, and like I was planning to become. It was the only way to stand up to the power of Big Business, to make sure that the little man had his say. Either way, that was what my dad told me, and I believed him.

I believed it all. Unilateral nuclear disarmament? Bring it on. Nationalized industries? No doubt about it. From each according to his means, to each according to his needs? Not quite – I wasn't a commie – but if pushed I agreed with the sentiment, and it was better than the alternative: Thatcher's bloodsucking capitalism.

I took all this for granted during my childhood. It was all so obvious. Of course Labour were right: Labour, good; Tory, evil. *Maggie Thatcher, Milk Snatcher. Maggie, Maggie, Maggie, out, out, out.* It was the gospel where I lived. No one I knew questioned it, ever.

And then I met Charlotte. She went to private school. *Entrenching privilege*, my dad thundered. *Too good for the common people. Keeping standards low for everyone else.* And there was no doubt how her family voted.

She was also the most beautiful girl I'd ever seen.

Tommy, my best friend ever since the first day of junior school, was having a Christmas party. His parents were going to his aunt's place and wouldn't be back until the morning. His aunt, Meredith, was having her third baby, and Tommy's mum was going to the hospital with her. Tommy's dad was looking after the other kids while she was in labour, as the father-to-be had vanished a few days after he found out Meredith was pregnant.

The party had been arranged at the last minute, the usual crew leaping on the chance to get together in a free house. This time, though, there was a difference; Lainey, a girl from the swimming team Tommy had been in since he was a kid, had asked if she could bring two of her friends: Charlotte, and a girl called Stephanie Twigg.

Had they been private school boys we would have refused to have anything to do with them. We had only one mode of interaction with the private school boys when we saw them coming home from school, later than us and dressed in their uniforms, briefcases swinging from their arms, and that was to shout abuse at them. But private school *girls*? Well, as they were the fairer sex we thought we'd be able to hold our noses. The demands of class war crumbled in the face of an opportunity to meet some chicks. Besides, Tommy told me that posh girls put out more. I hardly dared believe him.

When they knocked on the door I opened it as coolly as I could, given that I was holding a box of twelve cans of Skol lager. I had to keep it with me; unattended, it would've been empty within minutes. That's the problem with socialists; they have no concept of private property. Either that or Thatcher was right when she said there's no such thing as society.

Charlotte was on the left; I knew because Lainey had described her to me. To be honest, I can't remember the other girl, Stephanie, all that well, but that first sight of Charlotte is burned into my memory. She was wearing a white jacket, white boots and a pair of baggy white trousers that billowed around her legs when she walked. I think someone famous popularized them. Whoever it was had a lot to answer for: a generation grew up thinking that was how to look cool. It must have left some scars. I wasn't much better dressed. I was wearing shiny grey trousers and patent leather shoes. I think I'd put on my white shirt with thin red stripes and I was almost certainly wearing my thin black tie. I wore it everywhere. Oh, and I had a mullet. Why did nobody stop us? If ever there was a case for the introduction of the fashion police it was teenagers in Warrington in the mid-eighties. Without adequate adult supervision of our clothes choices we went wild. It was like a fashion version of *Lord of the Flies*.

I let them in and offered them both a can. Only Charlotte

accepted. She smiled at me, her eyes half-hidden by her curly brown fringe. I grinned back, wondering what to say.

'Thanks,' she said. 'For the beer.'

'It's ok, I've got loads. There's another ten in the box. You can have more, if you like.'

She sipped the warm, cheap lager and her lips tightened. 'One's enough for now.'

'So, Charlotte. Nice to meet you.'

She frowned. 'How do you know my name?'

Oh, shit. Why had I said that? Now she knew I'd been talking about her. It made me look a bit weird. 'I heard one of your friends say it,' I babbled, then stupidly corrected myself. 'Tommy mentioned it to me. His cousin told him.' I stopped talking. *Put your spade away, lad*, I said to myself in my dad's voice. *Stop digging*.

She broke the silence. 'What's your name?'

I felt the cold shiver of disappointment. Lainey hadn't told her, or if she had, she'd forgotten. 'Graham,' I muttered. 'Do you want to sit down?'

We sat on the couch, looking at each other in silence over our cans of Skol. Who knows why we find one person attractive and not another? Who knows why her combination of freckles and snub nose, unruly brown hair and near black eyes was irresistible to me? But it was, and from the moment I saw her I was smitten. A few months later she told me that she didn't like her looks, that she thought she was unconventional and weird. I couldn't believe it. I tried to convince her how beautiful she was by flicking through the pages of a fashion magazine, pointing out all the models I thought she was prettier than.

'Do you like music?' I asked. 'What do you listen to?'

'Paul Young, stuff like that.'

Of course. They all loved Paul Young. I hated him; I liked to think it was because his songs were garbage, but mostly it was jealousy.

'I listen to UB40,' I said. 'You know, they got their name off the form you get when you claim the dole? Unemployment Benefit, Form 40. "Red Red Wine" was on the charts for over a hundred weeks.' The facts spilled out like precious gifts. I assume I thought that girls liked informative chats.

'It's a good song. You know, it was originally by Neil Diamond.'

I snorted. 'Nah. Can't be.' There was no way that UB40 listened to Neil Diamond, let alone covered his songs.

'I think it's true. That's what my dad said, anyway.'

Uh-oh. I was caught between saying her dad was wrong and accepting that there was a crack in the edifice of UB40's, and hence my, cool. I grunted a maybe and left it at that.

'I also like classical,' she said.

Classical? Jesus. But if she liked it, so did I. 'Me too!' I said with as much bright-eyed enthusiasm as I could muster.

'Do you? What do you like? What's your favourite?'

Bloody hell. What kinds were there? I took a stab in the dark. 'Opera.'

'Really? I *love* opera. Dad takes me once a year to Manchester to see one. What's your favourite?'

I gave the only name I knew of a classical musician. 'Mozart.' Did he even do operas? I held my breath.

'I *love* Mozart's operas. I'm going to see *The Magic Flute* at Christmas.'

'That's a pretty good one, *The Magic Flute*. One of his best.' I was on thin ice but I seemed to have got away with it. It was time to change the topic. 'I also like Joy Division and the Pistols. Punk stuff, you know.'

'Oh. I hate them. They're so depressing.'

Depressing? They were my idols. I'd just spent all my savings on a rare 12-inch vinyl copy of a Joy Division B-side at Afflecks Palace in Manchester. I bit my lip. 'I only like them a bit. I know what you mean about them being depressing. Some people *really* love them but I think they're a bit overrated.'

She smiled. 'I suppose they're all right. I'd better go and find my friends.' I loved her voice. She sounded like a newsreader on the BBC.

'Why?' I sounded too desperate. 'I mean, they'll be ok. There are loads of other people here.'

'It was nice to meet you, but I think I'd better go and see them.'

She disappeared with a smile and, despite my best efforts to corner her again, I didn't see her until nearly midnight, when she was on her way out.

I managed to intercept her at the door. She looked a bit startled. 'So,' I said. 'Cool.' I was a bit drunk.

'Right. Cool.' She looked at her watch. 'My dad's here. I have to leave.'

I stared at her. It was now or never. 'Do you want to go out sometime?' It was a bit of a blurt, but at least it was out there.

'Yeah, sure. That'd be great. You're funny.'

'I'll call you soon,' I said. 'Maybe tomorrow.'

'Ok,' she said, looking at me in a strange way.

'Speak to you tomorrow.' I was speaking too quickly, the words running into each other. I'd nearly pulled. This was as good as.

Charlotte leaned forward. 'Aren't you missing something? How are you going to call me? You don't have my number.'

My mouth fell open. 'Oh, shit, yeah. Write it here.' I grabbed a pen from the table by the phone and held out my hand.

She leaned forward and kissed me on the cheek. The spot where her lips touched me burned. She whispered a number in my ear. 'See if you can remember it.'

I repeated it to myself. She was saying something but it was hard to concentrate when I had the number running round my head. I had to keep it there, but I didn't want to write it down. It wouldn't look cool, but what if I remembered it wrong? I might never see her again. I scribbled it on the wall when she wasn't looking.

I walked outside with her and waved goodbye. Her dad had parked on the other side of the street in a large, dark car. I caught a glimpse of the leaping cat on the front. Her dad drove a Jag.

Shit. This would never work. Private school, Jags: these people were rich, which meant they were Tories, which meant they were the enemy. He'd never let me see her.

I weighed up my political affiliation. Could I convert? Would the Tories have me? *I'm a Tory*, I'd say, when she asked me. *My folks aren't, but screw them. I'm blue, through and through.*

First my musical principles had been sacrificed and now my political ones. There wasn't all that much left. I had no backbone when it came to girls, none.

As I watched the Jag glide away, Tommy shoved me in the back. 'Nowt,' he said. 'I talked to Stephanie Twigg all night. She wouldn't even give me her number.' He shook his head bitterly. 'I wasted all me best jokes on her.'

I showed him the six digits inked on the wallpaper. 'Charlotte's number.'

'Fucking hell!' Tommy slapped me on the back. 'How did you do that? Did you get off with her?'

'A bit. She kissed me.' I touched my cheek where her lips had met it. The burn had faded to a tingle. 'Here.'

'On the cheek? That doesn't count. Still, it's not bad seeing as you just met.' His face brightened. 'I told you posh birds are dirty.'

'She's not,' I said. 'It was just a peck. Don't talk about her like that.'

He raised his hands in mock defence. 'Don't talk bad about a bird? You've changed your tune.'

'I haven't. It's just . . . I don't think it's nice.'

Tommy snorted and handed me a can of Skol. 'Here. Drink that. You sound like you need it.'

I called Charlotte the day after the party. Tommy suggested that I play it cool to avoid seeming too keen, so I waited until the afternoon. My fingers shook as I dialled the number. Twice I put the phone down before it started to ring, my hand shaking and my mind blank. More to the point, my breath was short and I didn't want her to think I was a heavy breather.

I wrote down the words I planned to say, and let it ring. A man answered; it was probably her dad, the owner of the Jag. My throat tightened. I had been hoping for Charlotte or, if not her, her mum.

'Charlotte Marshall phone answering service.'

He was joking. What was I supposed to do? I was too nervous to depart from the script I had prepared, so I ploughed into it.

'HellocouldIspeaktoCharlotteplease?' Mum had told me what to say. *Don't just say 'Is Charlotte in', say 'Could I speak to Charlotte, please?'* First impressions mattered, according to her.

'Sorry? I didn't catch that.' Her dad sounded confused. I'd said it in one breath. It was too quick for a human ear to decode the sounds.

I closed my eyes and focused on each word. 'Hello. Could. I. Speak. To. Charlotte. Please?' That was it. Much better.

'You certainly can.' The phone thudded onto whatever table or windowsill it lived on. The voice called in the distance. 'Charlotte! Phone for you, believe it or not.'

She evidently got a lot of calls. That was good, she was popular; but bad, they might be from boys.

'Hello?' Stars reversed their spin, galaxies were born. It was her.

'Charlotte. It's me. We met last night. At Tommy's.'

'Gordon! How lovely.'

'Graham,' I said, as my heart shattered. 'It's Graham.' Gordon? Was there a Gordon, or was it a mistake? Gordon. I'd kill him if I met him, the bastard.

'Of course. How silly of me. How are you? I've been thinking of you.'

My heart reassembled.

'I've been thinking of you too.' How tender a sweet nothing can sound; what balm for my aching teenage soul.

'It was fun last night, wasn't it? Tommy's a nice guy.'

I relaxed. This was going as well as I could have hoped. 'So, I asked you about going out. How about Friday?'

'I can't. I'm going to Chester with Mum.' She sounded like she regretted it, so I tried again.

'Saturday? We could go to the pictures.'

'Not Saturday either. My aunt's coming round. We've not seen her for ages.'

That was a lame excuse. An aunt? When mine came round, I ran a mile. 'Ok,' I said. 'Well, maybe another time.'

'Hang on,' she said. 'Wait there.' The phone thudded down again. A minute later she was back. 'How about Sunday? Mum says you can come round for Sunday lunch.'

If there was a world record for fastest acceptance of an invitation, I have no doubt it would still be mine.

The following week was the longest week of my life. I thought about her all day, every day. I was trapped in a swamp of long seconds and tedium. Finally, Sunday arrived. I told my dad where I was going and asked him for a lift.

'Lunch, eh? Dinner, you mean.'

'Whatever. Can I have a lift? She lives in Lymm.'

He whistled. Lymm was a smart commuter village a few miles away. 'Lymm? Posh, is she? Don't bring her round here. She'll think you're a scrubber.'

The words pierced me; the truth can have that effect. 'Can I have a lift or not?'

'All right lad, all right. But mind your p's and q's while you're there. And don't use the fish knife for the butter.'

He dropped me off in the driveway of a massive house. It was three storeys high, the perfect lawns that surrounded it were edged with trim flowerbeds. I don't know when it was built, but it was a lot longer ago than our house. In fact, it was so different to our house that the word 'house' didn't seem capable of describing both.

To the left was a detached, two-storey garage. For a second I wondered whether they lived above it, then the front door of the house opened and a man came out.

He saw us and sauntered over. He was dressed in chinos and a blue shirt, open at the neck. His thinning hair was swept back, lines of grey stretching out from his temples like fractured glass. 'Hello,' he said, putting out a hand for me to shake. 'You must be Graham? Charlie said you were coming for lunch.'

'Hello, Mr—' I realized with horror that I didn't know Charlotte's last name.

'Stephen,' he said. 'Call me Stephen. And you must be Graham's dad? Nice to meet you.'

Dad shook his hand. 'That I am, for my sins. Eric Melton.'

'He's staying for lunch, isn't he? I can run him home later, if you like. I'm going out to play tennis anyway.'

Out of the corner of my eye, I saw Dad raise an eyebrow. Tennis was like golf. An effete sport for the soft middle classes.

'Thanks,' Dad said. 'I'll be watching the Wires later. I normally have a few pints after, so it'll be handy if you can drop him back.'

'The Wires?'

'Warrington Rugby League. They're known as the Wires.'

'Oh. Do you go often? I've never been. I'm a Union man.'

If only he'd meant trades unions. That would have been ok. But Rugby Union? He couldn't have said anything worse. If Thatcher had been a man, Rugby Union was the sport she'd have played. It was number two on the list of things we hated in our house.

'You'll have to come along one day,' Dad said. 'See some real rugby. Some running and handling. It'll be a treat for you after watching all that kick 'n' clap.'

Stephen nodded enthusiastically. 'Sounds lovely. Especially if there's a few pints on offer afterwards.' He had a relaxed, easy charm that I found myself wanting to imitate. My dad was always on edge, always campaigning about something. 'And we might be seeing a bit more of young Graham if what Charlie says is anything to go by. She's been talking about him non-stop.'

I nearly died. I almost wish I had. I'd have died happy, that was for sure. She'd been talking about me! About me!

The front door opened and Charlotte appeared in the porch. She was wearing high-waisted blue jeans and a fluffy pink sweater. I couldn't take my eyes off her.

'You must be Charlotte,' Dad said. 'Nice to meet you. Be kind to him, would you? He's been like a lost puppy since he came home last Friday.'

Charlotte laughed. I jabbed Dad in the ribs with my elbow and glared at him.

'Come in,' she said. 'Mum says we're nearly ready to eat.'

As I moved to follow her, Dad's hand settled in between my shoulder blades and his thick fingers gripped my neck. It was a shock; he'd not touched me so affectionately for years.

'Have a good time, son,' he said.

'So,' Dad said, when I got home. 'How was lunch at the palace?'

'Eric,' Mum said. 'Give over. It's only Lymm. How was it, love? Did you have a nice time?'

I did in the end, but it hadn't started well. As soon as we sat down for lunch Stephen – it was a real effort not to call him Mr Marshall – poured me a glass of wine. He didn't ask, he just poured it. Wine! We never had wine at home. It was a point of principle. Once, when Charlotte and I had been together a while, we were having dinner at our house and Dad told us that he didn't drink wine. Charlotte asked him what he drank when he ate in restaurants. *Restaurants*? he said with a laugh. *I don't eat in restaurants. They're full of the kind of people who drink wine.*

I took a sip as Mrs Marshall – or Georgina, as she told me to call her – loaded my plate with roast beef, potatoes, Yorkshire puddings and thick, dark gravy. She looked a lot like Charlotte, but with blonder hair, done up in a perm. She was wearing a silky blouse that hung open a bit at the front so I could see her bra. I fought not to look. I didn't want to be caught staring down my new girlfriend's mum's top.

'So, Graham, Charlotte tells me you live in Warrington?' Stephen said.

'Yeah. Miller Street.'

'Miller Street? Where is that, exactly?'

'You know the hardware store opposite Viccy Park? You turn left there. It's up that street, in the estate.'

'Where do you go to school?' Georgina asked. I told her, and she frowned. 'Isn't that the school that's closing?'

I nodded. My school was condemned, scheduled to be destroyed and merged with another one. We were the last year that would be educated there. It was eerie, having the entire school for one year group. It isn't hard to imagine how motivated we, and our soon-to-be-unemployed teachers, were.

'It must be a bit depressing,' Stephen said. 'To know the place is going to be knocked down as soon as you leave. Hardly conducive to school spirit.'

I didn't reply. I was examining the beef. I pointed at it with my knife. 'Is this done?'

Georgina looked puzzled. 'I think so.'

'It's a bit red, in the middle.' I was used to it being a lot darker when Mum made it. Perhaps Georgina wasn't that used to cooking. 'It might need a few more minutes.'

'Ah, I see. Well, some people like it like this. Would you like me to pop yours in the frying pan?'

There was a tense silence. I wasn't sure what I'd done but I knew it wasn't good. I decided retreat was the best option. 'Nah. It's ok.'

Stephen topped up my wine. I was the only one with an empty glass. I'd have to slow down; I was used to beer. 'Charlie said you like classical music? Opera?'

'Er, yeah. Mozart.' That was the name I'd used last time and it'd worked. Stick to what you know, my Dad always said.

He stood up and went to the stereo, rifling through a stack of records in a cabinet underneath it. 'I like Mozart's operas, but they're not really music to eat by, are they? Shall we listen to something else? Do you like other composers? Bach? Beethoven?'

My forehead was prickling with sweat. 'Nah. I don't really like them.'

'Oh.' He looked over his glasses at me. He seemed a bit surprised.

'I mean, they're ok, but . . . they're not my favourites.'

'Well, let me know if you like anything in particular.' He picked out a record. 'We can try some Sibelius, for now.'

After that we talked about other things: Charlotte's school work, which O levels we were taking, what my parents did for jobs. It was bloody hard work, and I was glad when it was over.

Charlotte stood up. 'Thanks for lunch, Mum,' she said. 'Graham and I'll be in the back sitting room.'

'Thanks,' I said, wondering exactly what a sitting room was. Was it full of chairs? 'It was really nice.'

'If a bit underdone,' Stephen said with a wry smile.

'No, no,' I said. 'I like it like that now.'

'Stephen,' Georgina said. 'Leave him alone.' She turned to me. 'Don't worry. He's just teasing you.'

I followed Charlotte to a small room with a TV, a couch and loads of books. 'This is me and my brother's sitting room. He's not here; he's at university.'

So this was a sitting room. It looked a lot like a lounge. And they had two of them. It seemed almost a waste. We sat together on the couch and she put the television on. There was an old black and white film on BBC2. I held her hand, and, after she didn't move it, I put my arm around her. Gradually, we inched closer to each other until our heads were touching. I don't remember exactly how – the memory has been erased by the joy of what followed – but after a few awkward turns and near misses, we kissed.

The wine had left me light-headed, and I was further intoxicated by the sweet smell of it on her breath. She wasn't the first girl I'd kissed, but she was the first I'd kissed like that. It felt like we really meant it.

When her mum knocked on the door to say it was going-home time, it felt like we'd only been in there for a few minutes. Charlotte called that we were coming, and we kissed once more, for as long as we dared, then emerged into the hallway where her dad stood jangling the keys to the Jag.

'It was good, Mum,' I said, with a teenager's gift for understatement. What I meant was that it was the best day of my life, and until Michael was born, nothing else came close.

3.

2009: Michael in the Jungle

When I woke from my nap Michael was gone. It was typical. He was always out with his friends at the weekends. I missed him, missed the day trips we used to take together, back when Chester Zoo with his dad was still an exciting prospect. We'd sponsored an animal there, a parrot of some kind. He'd loved it, an obsession with parrots displacing dinosaurs for a while. I'd bought him a parrot costume that he wore everywhere. It had been a real struggle to stop him wearing it to school. We still sponsored that parrot – the zoo still sent me the renewal form each year and I paid the dues. I doubted Michael thought about his parrot very much these days; I doubted he even knew it was still his, but I couldn't bring myself to cancel it.

I swung my legs out of bed. It was still light, just about, but the sun was low in the sky. The kitchen was clean; well, cleaner. Most of the bottles and cans were gone, presumably now in the bulging bin bag propped up against the back door. Michael had outdone himself by wiping the counter top and the kitchen table down, but my bare feet still stuck to the tiles. Still, if I was honest, it was a better effort than I had expected. Michael was above cleanliness; as far as he was concerned it was a vague and unknowable religion that the foolish adult world followed. Had they but taken his approach they would have wasted a lot less time.

I made a cup of tea and went into the garden. Michael and I lived in a barn conversion on the edge of the village of Stockton Heath. At the end of the garden, the first fields of the Cheshire countryside stretched away. When I'd bought it, in 1993, the place had been a wreck. The bedroom had been a mattress in the front room, next to the only working radiator. Dad and I had more or less rebuilt the place from top to bottom. I'd supplied labour and funds, but my dad had been the real driving force behind it. It had given him something to do after he'd been made redundant in the recession in the early 1990s.

The side gate banged open and I heard the scrabbling of dogs on the flagstones.

'Graham? You there?' Tommy appeared round the side of the house, four large dogs straining at their leads. He had hardly changed since we were teenagers; a bit thicker round the middle, the unruly blond hair a bit thinner on top, but still the same wiry, sinuous build. He thumped into the chair beside me and freed his dogs. They surged and tumbled into the garden, their barking shattering the quiet evening.

'They've got lots of energy,' I said. 'Not been keeping them busy?'

Tommy had set up a dog-walking business, convinced that he could just let them play in his garden. He had discovered that four dogs could make a hell of a mess of your lawn and reluctantly started taking them for walks.

He rubbed the back of his neck and grimaced. 'They're lovely dogs, but they're a lot of work. Pat's sick of them. You want one for the night?'

'I've enough on my plate with Michael. He's growing up.'

'That's a no, then?'

'It is.' I sipped my tea. 'This morning I found him in bed with a girl from Orford. Fifteen years old.' I shook my head. 'I don't know what to say to him sometimes.'

'Tell him to double bag it.'

'It's not so much the practical advice I'm missing, but I'll bear that in mind.'

We chewed the fat for a while longer. After Tommy left, I went inside and checked my emails. There were loads, as usual, but most of them could wait. I frowned and opened one from the bank – you never expect good news when the bank gets in touch – but it was just informing me that interest rates were staying low. I yawned; despite my nap I was still tired, so after watching some TV I went to bed.

I was woken by the phone ringing.

'All right, Dad.' It was Michael. His voice was thick. A twist of anger roused me. I hated the thought of him drinking at his age, but whatever I said I was powerless to stop it.

'Michael?'

'Were you sleeping?'

I glanced at the alarm. It was one in the morning. Despite the anger I was worried. 'Yes, I was. What's wrong?'

'I'm in Orford. I can't get home.'

'Orford? What on earth are you doing there?'

'It's where Carly lives.'

Christ. I didn't want him stuck on the streets of Orford. It wasn't the Bronx, but it was bad enough that a fifteen-year-old shouldn't be there at one in the morning.

'Where's Carly?'

'Home. Her dad threw me out when he got back from the pub.'

The caring sort, obviously. 'Can't you get a taxi?'

'I've got no money.'

'Tell the driver I'll pay him when you get here.'

'They won't do it. They make you pay up front, so you don't do a runner.'

'So you're saying I need to come and fetch you? Jesus, Michael. Where are you?'

'Dunno. On some estate.'

I snorted. 'Michael! Use your initiative. Look for a street name, or a pub, or something.'

After a second he gave me the name of a street. I jotted it down and grabbed my car keys.

He was sitting on a low wall in front of a terraced house. It was one of a row of 1950s terraces, built in a hurry and wearing their age badly. The pavements were cracked and uneven and the street-lighting was patchy and dim, pools of darkness encroaching on the struggling light. He was dressed in a thin T-shirt, and he had his arms wrapped around himself. When he got in the car he was shivering. I turned the heating up.

'This has got to stop,' I said. 'Last night you wreck the house and tonight I have to pick you up drunk on a street corner.'

'I'm not drunk,' he said, his words heavy and hard to make out.

'Really? Then why are you speaking like that?'

'I'm not drunk! And I didn't wreck the house! I tidied it up, all right!' He glared at me, and I saw tears glistening in his eyes. I also saw the dark bruise on his right cheek. No wonder Carly's dad had thrown him out. He looked like a ruffian.

'Michael, have you been in a fight?'

He looked away, out of the window.

'Michael, what happened?' We pulled up at a red light and I turned him to face me. In the pale light I could see that as well as the bruise he had a swollen lip and two angry red welts on his neck where someone had gripped him. That was why he sounded drunk. A wave of anguished concern for my child washed away my anger.

'Who did it?'

He shook his head. 'No one.'

'Come on, Michael. It must have been someone.'

He bit his lip, trying to stop it quivering. 'It was no one.'

The lights turned green and we set off. I put my hand on his arm and spoke softly. 'Michael, let's not have this farce. It must have been someone. Tell me who.' I took a deep breath. 'Was it Carly's dad?'

'No! . . . Promise not to tell anyone, especially not the police.'

'I promise.' It was not a promise I was sure I could keep.

'You mean it? You promise?'

'I'm on your side, Michael.' I was worried now; the depth of his fear was alarming. 'What happened?'

'It was Carly's ex. Him and his mates saw us in the park.'

'And they beat you up?'

'No! They just pushed me around a bit.' He sniffed and fell silent. When he spoke again his voice was low. 'They said next time they're really going to kick my head in.'

Despite his distress, I felt a sense of relief. It wasn't Carly's dad; it wasn't some kind of drug deal gone wrong. It was just teenagers messing around. 'Don't worry about that,' I said. 'You'll be fine.'

'Dad! You don't get it! They're Orford! They said if I don't stop messing with Carly they'll kill me!'

'It can't be that bad. Stay away from them for a while and they'll forget about it.' I'd got into plenty of scraps as a teenager and they'd always resolved themselves. It was just part of growing up.

'It won't work!' He sounded miserable. 'You don't know what they're like.'

'Then maybe you should think about not seeing Carly again.'

'But I want to see her.'

'You've only just met her. Anyway, if this is what happens, are you sure she's the kind of girl you should be hanging around with?'

'What do you mean? You're just saying that because she's from Orford.'

'It's nothing to do with that. I'm saying it because she's the kind of girl who has ex-boyfriends who beat people up. You don't need to get involved in all that.'

'I like her, Dad. A lot.' He shuddered. 'But those lads. I don't want to mess with them.'

The poor kid. Caught between fear and love. It was going to be a rough ride for him.

4.

1986: Sweet Sixteen

In March 1986 we'd been together four months. Four short months, which already felt like the whole of my life.

I looked at my parents over my cornflakes. 'It's got to be good,' I said. 'I want my present to be the best one she gets.' It was Saturday morning, and later that day Charlotte was having a birthday party. She was turning sixteen. I'd been thinking about it for weeks. It was my chance to impress her, and I wanted to get it right. 'I'm going to get her a necklace. I'm going to Ratner's later.'

'Why don't you make her something?' It was Mum's way of telling me not to waste my money. She probably remembered the presents teenage boys had bought her. 'Write her a poem.'

I rolled my eyes. Mum had clearly never read any of my poems.

Dad looked up from the paper. 'Why do you need to get her anything? And, if you have to do, why does it have to be some crap from Ratner's?'

'Ratner's is all right.' I hesitated. 'Do you think I should go somewhere else? I want to get something expensive.'

Dad shrugged. 'Why do you think that value is judged purely on monetary grounds? Is a present worth something only if it cost lots of money? It's typical Thatcherite rubbish. I thought I'd brought you up better than that.'

Thatcherite? In my family, that was the worst thing you could be accused of. It wasn't a term bandied about lightly. Was I being Thatcherite? Should I buy nothing, and show her family the error of their ways? I pictured myself explaining to Charlotte that I'd not bought her anything because birthdays were a materialist, commercial fallacy created by capitalists to persuade the workers to hand over their cash in return for meaningless baubles. I pictured her telling her parents what I'd said. My blood ran cold.

'Can you give me a lift to town, Mum?' I said, avoiding my dad's look. I couldn't help but hear his snort, though. I felt a sudden anger at his principles. 'So what would you do, then?' I said. 'Give her a subscription to the *Daily Worker*?'

He nodded, as though considering it. 'Not a bad idea,' he said. 'Or, you could take her for a walk. Show her something of nature. Give her a book. Something of lasting value. Tressel, for example, *The Ragged Trousered Philanthropists*. You both might learn something.'

'Right. And I'll be single until I'm sixty.'

He folded his paper. 'You know, there's more to life than impressing people with expensive presents. If she's the kind of girl that needs that kind of thing, then you ought to think twice.'

That was enough. He was suggesting that I sacrifice Charlotte, the love of my short life, for a political principle. It was out of the question.

'Would you have done that with Mum?'

'Your mum and I agreed on those things.'

Mum looked at me and rolled her eyes. 'I wouldn't have minded a nice present though, Eric. To you it's about principles, but Charlotte might not understand that. Graham doesn't want her to think he's stingy.'

Dad looked at her sharply. 'Did you think I was stingy?'

'No, but it was a different time then, and I understood your principles. I could hardly fail to. You told me about them all the time. I'm just saying that Charlotte might not. She's only young yet.'

Dad put his toast back on his plate. 'What did you want? What presents did you want that I didn't buy you? I'll buy 'em for you. I'm not stingy.'

'I know you're not, love. You're very generous.'

Dad shook his head and took a bite of his toast. I left the table and went up to my bedroom. It was the first real argument we'd had. We'd disagreed on little things, like curfews and pocket money, but we'd never argued about something so fundamental. I'd taken it for granted that what he said about politics and society was true. When he'd said that Tories weren't all evil, that a minority were stupid instead, I'd believed it. But now, I wasn't so sure. I liked Charlotte. I *loved* Charlotte. I liked her family. I liked drinking wine at dinner – which at their house was the meal served in the evening. Most of all, I liked that they never talked about politics.

Later that day, Mum dropped me off at Charlotte's. The drive was full of cars. I was introduced to a bewildering range of uncles, aunts, cousins and grandparents.

'You must be Graham,' they said. 'We've heard so much about you.'

'All of it good, I hope.' It sounded lame but it was the only way you could respond when someone said that. Anything else and you risked sounding like a smartarse.

I was wearing my best clothes, which meant my grey school trousers and an old blazer of my dad's. On my way out he'd looked at me, his lips pursed, and declared that it was time we went shopping for some decent clothes. It was a peace offering after our argument, but it was bloody badly timed. It was hardly what I wanted to hear on my way to my posh girlfriend's birthday party.

The small packet I'd bought earlier sat heavily in my inside pocket. Every time I moved I felt it bumping against my ribs, reminding me that I hadn't yet given it to its soon-to-be-proud owner.

I saw Charlotte leave the lounge and seized the opportunity. I followed her out and put my arms around her. 'I want to show you something,' I said. 'It won't take a minute.'

'I've got to get Aunt Shirley a drink. Can it wait?'

'No. Quickly. I can show you here.' I reached into my pocket. 'I got you a present.'

'Graham,' she said. 'You didn't have to. What is it?'

The box was wrapped in red paper with gold diagonal bands. I'd chosen that pattern from the three they'd offered me in the shop. It seemed the classiest and I wanted this present to show how grown up I was. Ratner's had a lot of choice, and there was some really good stuff. I'd ummed and ahhed for ages about what to buy her, but in the end I settled on two options. One was a silver bangle twisted to look like a rope; the other was a pendant with an emerald surrounded by rubies. I couldn't decide. The bangle was nice, and the shop assistant recommended it – she said it was more versatile – but in the end I turned against it. I didn't want versatile, I wasn't looking for everyday. I wanted special, and the emerald and ruby necklace had more about it. She might not be able to wear it as often, but when she did she'd think of me.

I thrust it at her. 'Open it.' She undid the ribbon and peeled back the red paper. The box was covered with dark purple velvet, the name of the shop stamped on it in gold letters.

'Ratner's,' she said. 'Oh.' She opened the box. She looked at it for a long time, soaking up its magnificence. 'Graham,' she said, after a pause. 'It's beautiful. Thank you. I love it. I love you.'

I love you. I stared at her. She looked shocked. I wasn't sure she'd planned to say it, which made it all the better.

'I love you too,' I said.

'Do you? Really? You're not just saying it because I did?'

I was saying it because every cell in my body believed it. 'No,' was all I could say. 'I really do.'

Neither of us spoke for a minute. I gestured to the necklace. 'Put it on.'

'I will, but not now. I'm wearing Grandma's necklace. She'll be upset if I take it off.'

I looked at her neck. She was wearing some kind of snowflake, studded with diamonds. It was nowhere near as striking as the emerald and ruby flower. Still, I didn't want to upset her grandma. She grabbed my hands and kissed me on the lips. I tried to make it last. I wanted to stay out there forever.

'It's lovely,' she said. 'You're so thoughtful. That's one of the reasons I love you so much. Come on, you can help me get the drinks.'

Charlotte's dad had arranged for a photographer – a *photographer* – to take some pictures, and after about an hour he called for people to assemble.

'Family first,' he said. Charlotte's parents, Charlotte and her elder brother Richard gathered in front of the fireplace. After he'd reeled off a few shots, her dad held up a hand.

'Let's take a few with Graham in,' he said. 'Come on, Graham. You're nearly family.'

I could have fallen over with happiness. I was *nearly family*. I walked over and stood next to Charlotte's elder brother, Richard.

Richard was a law student at university in Durham. He'd started there in September, a few months before I met Charlotte, so I hadn't seen that much of him. He'd been around at Christmas and Easter, but he mostly kept himself to himself. He didn't have many local friends because he'd gone to boarding school, so in the holidays he tended to visit people or go off inter-railing for months on end. When he was at home, he wasn't very interested in me, so our interaction was limited to a few nods and smiles. To be honest, I was happy that way. I found him quite intimidating.

As the photographer prepared the camera Richard leaned over and whispered four words in my ear, four words that killed my happiness dead.

'Nearly,' he said. 'But not quite.' I've still got a copy of those photos and he isn't smiling in any of them. Not a single one.

Lady Charlotte, Dad called her. *Lady Charlotte on the blower*! he'd shout when she called. *Lady Charlotte, no less*, he'd say when she turned up at the door. I hated it, but she thought it was funny.

'Right,' he said. 'Does Lady Charlotte eat bacon butties?'

Mum was working a weekend shift at late notice, so he was cooking Sunday lunch. At least, he was cooking lunch on Sunday, and it was going to be his speciality: bacon sandwiches.

'Of course,' Charlotte said. 'Normally for breakfast, though.'

'Then this'll be a special treat,' Dad said. 'I'll even give you the recipe.'

'What, bread, bacon and brown sauce?' I said. 'I think we could guess it.' As usual for a teenager, I had no sense of humour when it came to my parents.

'And butter,' Dad said, winking at Charlotte. 'See, it's not as easy as you think, Graham. Good job it's me making these. We don't need you messing them up. You two go and sit in the lounge. I'll bring them out.'

Dad's bacon sandwiches consisted of about six rashers of bacon crammed between two inch-thick slices of brown bread. There was very little variation. Sometimes the bread was thinner, but that was the extent of his experimentation. We never had white bread. He was very suspicious of it, like frozen food, which he refused to eat. He claimed to be able to tell whether something had been frozen, although I knew that Mum used to serve it all the time without telling him.

I ate mine – I was used to them – but Charlotte only managed half of hers. Dad looked at her in fake horror. 'Bloody 'ell, Lady C. You'll waste away.'

'I know, Mr Melton,' Charlotte said. 'That was only about a quarter of a loaf.'

Dad took the sandwich from her and wrapped it in a paper towel. 'I'll take it to the match. No point in it going to waste. You two behave yourselves while I'm out.'

The Wires were playing at home that Sunday, and with Mum at work that meant we'd have the house to ourselves. We'd chosen the day a few weeks earlier and made all the necessary preparations: we were going to have sex.

Charlotte had turned sixteen in March; my birthday was coming up, and we were both virgins, which, in 1986 was not uncommon for kids of our age. I knew of one or two lads in my year who weren't, but they were a tiny minority. I was going to be one of the first in my group of friends, and I was very nervous.

We watched from the front window as Dad walked up the street.

'So,' I said. Suddenly the house was very quiet. We sat on the couch and I hugged her. It felt like we were on the back row of the cinema trying to find a way to kiss.

'Let's just cuddle a minute,' she said. 'I love you.'

'I love you too.' It had never seemed so important to say it.

We sat there in silence, holding each other close. We were on the threshold of something important, and we needed each other to get through it.

'Let's go upstairs.' She said, looking a little pale.

I nodded, my tongue sticking to the roof of my mouth, and stood up, taking her hand in mine. We walked silently upstairs and sat on my bed. Not sure what to do, I opened my bedside drawer and took out the packet of condoms I'd bought, stammering with embarrassment, the day before. I'd taken a bus to Runcorn to use a chemist there, so that no one I knew saw me.

'Do you know how to use those?' she said.

'I think so.' I didn't have the faintest idea. 'You just kind of roll it on.'

She took the packet. Inside there were instructions printed in small writing on a piece of thin, folded paper.

Charlotte read them for a long time. 'Ok,' she said, finally. 'Pinch the tip to expel the air and roll the condom down the penis. Make sure it goes all the way to the base.'

'If it's big enough,' I said, in a reflex, nervous return to the jokes I made with my friends.

'Do you think it will be?' Charlotte said, suddenly anxious.

'Yeah. I think so,' I said. 'But what if it's not? What if it splits? Maybe we shouldn't . . . you know. Maybe we should wait for another time?' In truth, I was ready to stop. I was terrified, and worse, if it didn't work out it could ruin our relationship.

She shook her head. 'It'll be fine. I want to. I love you. I want it to be with you.' She ripped the top off the foil packet and handed it to me.

Getting the condom on was horrible. I'd practised the night before but it was much harder with an audience. It was awkward and fumbling and I was full of fear. Once it was on, I looked at her, my heart racing and my hands trembling. If I could have run away then, I would have, but Charlotte lay down and pulled me on top of her. I pushed around frantically, aware of her positioning herself underneath me, and then it was done, that first moment was over, and we were doing it, actually doing it, actually having sex.

Afterwards we lay together in silence, half content, half shocked. We knew, somehow, that things had changed. In the end, relationships are made of shared experiences. Before you meet you're following your own path, but the more you spend time together, the more your paths become intertwined. The more you share, the more you become bound up together. When you're sixteen this happens very quickly since there's not much there to get in the way. For two adults it's harder; your hinterland is a lot more dense, so it's harder for another person to insinuate themselves into it. Getting under each other's skin is harder when the skin is covered in scar tissue.

Not that I thought that at the time. Then I was just glad it was over and done with.

When we weren't together, I saw and heard her everywhere, echoing through the voices and silhouettes of every woman I encountered. Even the female teachers reminded me of her, and I found myself wondering if they loved someone, if there was a man somewhere behind a desk dreaming of them.

I spent my time counting the minutes until the next time I saw her. Whole lessons passed by and I didn't remember a single word the teacher had said. I envied my friends whose girlfriends were at our school. They saw them all the time. For us, even though our houses were only five miles apart, it was far enough that I couldn't just pop in. We had to rely on parental permission, which meant that we mainly saw each saw each other at the weekends, except for a brief few hours on Wednesdays, when I cycled round after school and stayed until her parents kicked me out after tea. On the weekends we were inseparable, selecting whichever house was free of adults to go and spend our time in. I did woodwork at school, and

I made her a wooden box, lined it with red velvet and filled it with reminders of things we'd done together: postcards, cinema tickets, a piece of paper with the date we'd met written on it. Every time something important happened we put a memento in that box. I still have the box in the attic, although I don't look at it. I thought it was lost but I stumbled across it a few years ago when I was trying to fix the water tank.

My mum and dad loved Charlotte. In particular, my mum loved having another girl around. I was an only child, and I think she would have liked a daughter; Charlotte filled that gap.

I was pretty sure that her parents felt the same way about me. If I was there on a Saturday and there was cricket or football on the television, her dad would pass me a beer and chat to me about the game. He advised me on what qualifications to pursue: I wasn't planning on staying on at school after O levels and trying for university, so he talked me through the other options, the technical qualifications and apprenticeships.

One Sunday, Charlotte and I were curled up on the couch watching a video. Georgina came in and handed us a plate of poached eggs on toast.

'So, are you coming next Saturday?' she said.

'Where to?' I asked.

'The Duck Race. I'm on the organizing committee.'

'Mum,' Charlotte groaned. 'We were going to go to town. To see a film.'

'It'll be fun. You can watch a film anytime.'

'What is it?' I liked the idea of racing ducks. I wasn't exactly sure how you'd do it, but it sounded interesting. More interesting than racing frogs, which Tommy and I had tried one summer. They just hopped off in any old direction, even when we put some food at the finishing line for them to eat. Perhaps they didn't like corned beef.

'You put your duck in the dam, and they race down the river to the weir in the village centre. The winner gets a prize.'

'We should go, Charlotte,' I said. 'It sounds fun. Can anyone come, Georgina? Can Tommy come?'

'Of course. It's a public event. The more the merrier.'

I smiled. Tommy was going to love this. It was right up his alley.

It was the morning of the day of the Duck Race. Tommy and I stood on the canal towpath, watching a small flotilla of suspicious-looking ducks float by in the warm spring sun. Tommy was holding a cat-carrier, a small plastic box with a metal grille on the front.

'How're we going to get one? They won't come to the side.' He bent down and made a succession of strange noises. It sounded like a record jumping on a turntable.

'What are you doing? You'll scare 'em off.'

'I'm tempting them with a series of clicks and whistles. I've seen it on *Flipper*. That's the language they speak.'

'Flipper's a dolphin. So even if you were making the right noises, ducks wouldn't understand.' How he came up with these ideas was beyond me. Tommy's thought processes were a total mystery. Sometimes I wondered whether he was a misunderstood genius or an idiot, although if he was an idiot, he was a happy one: the thing with Tommy was that he always came up smiling.

'You'll have to get in,' he said. 'It's the only way.' He handed me the cat-carrier. 'Just swim over, and then, when it's not looking, shove it in the carrier.'

'Me? It's your idea. You do it.'

'I can't swim.'

'Yes you can. You're in the town swimming team.'

'I mean, I can't swim now. I've got an ear infection and I can't get my head wet.' He looked at me and shrugged. 'Sorry.'

I looked at the canal. It was grey and lifeless, and it stank. Plastic bags and bottles drifted by amidst the tangled weeds and surface insects that made up most of its flora and fauna. On the far side, the ducks eyed us warily.

'Come on,' Tommy said. 'We can't go to a duck race without a duck. Everyone'll laugh at us. Charlotte'll think you're a geekburger.'

'A *what*?'

'Geekburger. It's what they say in America. I saw it on the TV. That new lad from London's got a satellite dish in his garden. He can get TV from everywhere. He told me he's got a hundred channels so I went round to have a look.'

I sighed. 'All right. I'll go.' I stripped down to my underpants and sat on the edge of the canal. The water bit at my feet, the cold shocking. I could see the dirt swirling around. I closed my eyes and slid in.

It wasn't that deep. The water only came up to my chest, which was a relief as it meant I didn't have to swim. The downside was that my feet sank into the soft mud of the canal bed. I didn't want to know what was oozing between my toes. Occasionally I stepped on something hard. In my imagination, it was a skull, or a knife, or a dog's rotting skeleton. I forced the thoughts from my mind and waded slowly towards the ducks.

Every time I got near, they drifted away. They never went a long way, never far enough so that the hunt was off; they were too interested in the idiot with the plastic box that was following them to do that. They kept themselves just out of reach.

'Try this,' Tommy shouted, and threw a plastic bag at me. 'It's bread. Ducks love bread.'

I caught the bag, and turned to look at him with what I hoped was a frosty expression. 'You had this all along? We could have attracted the ducks to the side. We could have at least *tried*.'

Was that a look of amusement in his eyes? His expression didn't change. 'Forgot,' he said. 'I was busy thinking of other ways.'

'Like me getting in the canal.'

He nodded. 'Exactly.'

The ducks showed some interest in the bread and came closer to get the chunks of Warburton's finest that I sprinkled in front of them, struggling to keep my arms above my head. The cat-carrier floated next to me.

'Put some in the carrier,' Tommy said. 'Lure 'em in and then spring the trap.'

'It won't work,' I said. 'Unless these are the stupidest ducks in England.'

'It will,' he said. 'Stop thinking like a human. You've got to think like a duck.'

'And what does a duck think like, Tommy? Are you an expert on duck psychology, all of a sudden?'

He sighed. 'It'll see the food in the carrier and think it's a free meal in a nice dark cave. It won't know that it's a cat-carrier, because it's never seen one.'

It turned out that Tommy *could* think like a duck. A green-headed mallard ventured into the carrier to peck at the bread I had cunningly placed at the back, and I closed the grille on it. We had our duck.

Once we were away from the water the duck went quiet. It'd made an almighty racket for the first few minutes, and we were lucky no one had seen us. People get funny about ducks, for some reason.

After a shower and a change of clothes – the canal water stank – we bought our bus tickets and took a seat. Tommy put the cat-carrier on the seat in front of us. At the next stop an old lady tottered onto the bus, balancing on her stick. She looked at the empty seat next to the duck.

'Can I sit here?'

''Course,' Tommy said. 'Let me give you a hand.'

He stood up and helped her into the seat. She rested her shaking hands on the cat-carrier. 'You've got a little pussy cat, have you?'

'Er, yeah, sort of,' Tommy said.

The duck quacked, as ducks do.

The old lady's face took on a puzzled expression, and she adjusted her hearing aid. 'I thought I heard it quack,' she said. 'This hearing aid keeps on packing in. I'll have to get a new one.'

I looked helplessly at Tommy. *Do something*, I mouthed. He shrugged. What can I do?

The duck quacked again, loudly. A few heads turned to look at us.

'That *was* a quack,' the old lady said. 'Have you got a duck in there?'

'It *was* a quack,' Tommy said. I could almost hear the cogs turning. They clicked into position. 'But it's not a duck. It's a cat that quacks.'

'Really?' The old lady looked uncertain, as well she might. 'I've had a few cats, and none of them quacked. One made a sound like my late husband clearing his throat – I wondered if he'd come back as a cat for a while – but it was nothing like a duck.'

'That's because it's not an ordinary cat. It was raised by ducks. Its mum abandoned it, and the ducks looked after it. I found it a few months later,' Tommy said.

We'd studied the founding myth of Rome recently in which Romulus and Remus are abandoned and raised by wolves. It seemed that it had made an impact on his imagination.

The old lady raised her sparse, white eyebrows. 'Well,' she said. 'Wonders never cease, eh? Even at my age you can still see something new. Can I have a look?'

Panic flashed across Tommy's face. How was he going to explain that the cat also looked like a duck?

'I'm afraid not,' he said. 'It doesn't like new people. It spits on them. 'Cos of growing up with ducks, see? It didn't see many people, so now it doesn't like them.'

The bus pulled up to let some people on.

'This is our stop.' Tommy grabbed the carrier and jumped to his feet. 'Nice to meet you.'

It was still a few miles to Lymm. I sighed and followed him off the bus.

'That was close.' He was sweating. 'We'll have to walk the rest of the way.'

When we arrived, there was already quite a crowd of people at the start line of the duck race. Georgina was behind a desk handing out papers and things. Stephen and Charlotte stood to one side, looking out over the dam. I shouted and waved, and they waved back.

As we approached them the duck started to make a lot of noise, quacking and beating its wings against the cat-carrier. It must have sensed that it was nearing water.

'Shhh!' I said. 'Calm down! Don't waste your energy for the race. You'll be free any second. Just hold on.'

The duck ignored my pleas. If anything, the noise level rose. By the time we reached Charlotte and Stephen it was squawking and banging about frantically. Everyone in the vicinity was staring at us.

'What've you got there?' Stephen said. 'It's making a hell of a noise.'

'It's our duck,' I said. 'We trapped it this morning.'

There was a long silence.

'You did what?' Charlotte looked at me like I'd just offered her a dolphin sandwich. 'You've brought a real duck?'

A horrible chill gripped me, despite the warm sun. I looked around at the crowd. They were all holding small, yellow, plastic ducks, with black numbers painted on the sides. In the cat-carrier our real, flesh-and-blood duck continued to protest.

Stephen burst into laughter. 'Brilliant,' he said. 'That's the first time I've heard of anyone bringing a real duck to the duck race. I must say, I'm quite impressed you managed to do it. It can't be easy catching a duck.'

'It wasn't,' Tommy said. 'Can we enter it in the race anyway? It seems a shame to waste it now we've gone to all the trouble of catching it.'

'I don't think that would be appreciated,' Stephen said. 'My suggestion is that you slip off to a quiet spot on the banks of the dam and let it out without anyone seeing.'

Before Tommy could argue, I snatched the carrier from him. 'We'll be back in a minute.'

We opened the cat-carrier and the duck waddled to the water's edge, where it turned and glared at us. It didn't seem to want to go in. It should have been happy. The dam was much nicer than the canal. All that, and the bloody duck wasn't even grateful.

In June 1986, we sat our O levels. I hated them, not because of the exams – I didn't care much about them, as I had a job lined up as a trainee finance clerk at a gearbox manufacturer in St Helen's – but because I didn't get to see Charlotte. She was locked away, revising. I pictured her as a fairy-tale princess, locked in a high tower by a tyrannical king and queen, and fantasized about freeing her, but it was to no avail. I just had to wait until the exams were over.

When they were finally finished, I forgot all about them. I was starting work at the end of August, and my results didn't really matter. In the end I did ok. I got an A in Maths, passed sciences, scraped by in English, and got an A in, of all things, French. Charlotte was the opposite, harvesting As and Bs in English, History and Geography, and squeezing over the finishing-line in Maths. In any case, she got the grades she needed to go to sixth form and do her A levels.

Things carried on pretty much as before. She went to school, I went to work. My job was to enter the orders we got and make sure the invoices went out on time. It was pretty routine stuff, but I enjoyed it. My dad had worked on the shop floor all his life, so it felt like a step up, working in an office. He laughed at me for it, though. He used to ask me how my nails were, from messing about with paper and a calculator all day. Don't worry, he'd say: if you break one you can always call in sick.

He was proud of me, though. I knew it. I heard him boasting to one of his friends about how good I was at maths one night. 'He works hard,' he said. 'And he's a smart lad. Always has been. Must get it from his mum.' They were having a drink in the yard, and I was in the room upstairs. I could hear them through the window. My heart swelled until I thought it was going to burst. He never praised me, my dad, never.

Charlotte and I kept on seeing each other every Wednesday and every weekend. My parents wouldn't let Charlotte stay over, but her mum and dad were ok with me staying there. I protested to my dad, but he wouldn't budge. As far as he was concerned, if her parents allowed it, that was their business, but it wasn't for him to allow a girl to sleep in a bed with a lad. He had nothing against me staying at hers; he just wasn't prepared to let her stay at our place. In the end, I didn't mind. She had a three-quarter bed so there was more room, which was useful given what we got up to every time we were in it. So, with the instinctive disloyalty of a teenager, I abandoned my parents for a new, improved family.

It stayed like this for months. The first inkling I had that there might be trouble in paradise came in May 1987.

The General Election was set for 11 June of that year. It was the first election that I had really taken an interest in, even though at seventeen I was still a year away from having a vote. Even though I didn't talk about it with Charlotte, I was gripped by the election, and I believed fiercely in the issues that were in play. In 1983, Michael Foot had led the Labour Party to a catastrophic defeat, and the party had realized that it had to change if it was to be elected. Now, under Neil Kinnock, Britain was ready for a bright new dawn.

How could it not be? After what Maggie had done to the miners, after the three million unemployed, how could the country not want to change? It was inevitable. Some were talking about this election as a chance for Labour to re-establish itself as the main opposition in the face of the SDP-Liberal Alliance that had challenged for that spot in 1983, but I knew different. The Alliance was a waste of time, and the Tories were on borrowed time. Labour was on the march to power.

Late in May, I was eating Sunday lunch at Charlotte's. Richard was back for the weekend, for some reason, and he was gracing us with his presence at lunch before driving back up to Durham.

'God,' he said. 'I'll have to put up with the bloody socialists for the next few weeks. They're everywhere in Durham. It's the one downside of the place. It's full of militant miners and commie students. I can't wait until it's over and Maggie's safely back in Downing Street.'

'That's if she makes it,' I said coyly. 'I think Kinnock might win it.' I was deliberately toning down my language. I was *sure* that Kinnock would win it.

He snorted, one of the peas he'd half-chewed forcing its way past his lips. 'Good God, the pinkos are everywhere,' he said. 'Even in our house! You didn't say he was a red, Charlie.'

'I don't care,' Charlotte said. 'Politicians are all the same anyway.'

'They're not,' I said. 'The Labour party believes in fairness and justice. The Tories believe in helping the rich. Look at the miners. Look at what Maggie did to them. It's a disgrace.'

'You would have preferred the country to be held to ransom by Scargill? God, you're a good example of why I sometimes wonder whether we should let everyone have the vote. If you're going to waste it on Labour, you don't deserve it.'

'Scargill was right about the issues,' I said. 'He got the tactics wrong. He should have had a national ballot.'

Richard laughed. 'Is that what your daddy told you? Forget it. We shouldn't talk about this. You haven't got the faintest idea about the real world. If it was left up to people like you we'd be following the Communist International.'

'Now, Richard. There's no need to be personal,' Charlotte's mum said. 'We all have a right to our opinion.'

'Thank God that's all he's got the right to. Maybe by the time he gets the vote he'll see sense. Let's talk again when you've grown up, Comrade Graham.'

My hands were shaking under the table. I could feel my cheeks burning. 'At least I work,' I said. 'At least I earn money, in an industry that makes things. That's the real world, Richard, not a big house and a law degree and a car that Daddy bought for you. You should come to my workplace someday. You wouldn't last five minutes.'

Richard shook his head and placed his hand protectively on his sister's forearm. 'When do you finish school, Charlie? The sooner you get to university and dump this fellow the better. Leave him in Warrington to wallow in his class hatred.'

'You two!' Stephen said, frowning. 'That's enough. You can keep your arguments away from the dinner table.'

Richard got to his feet. 'Come on, Dad. We all know that if you thought this was a serious relationship you'd stop it. You know that it'll fizzle out when she gets to university and meets some real men, some men with prospects.'

If he'd stayed, I think I'd have hit him, but he turned and walked out. I looked round the table at the shocked faces and I felt tears prickle my eyes. I got to my feet and left. I couldn't have stayed there a second longer.

I closed the front door behind me and marched down the drive. What the hell had I done? I'd blown it, arguing with Charlotte's brother in front of the entire family. They were not my kind of people. I should have known it all along. I think I had known it, but I'd dared to think that it wasn't true for me and Charlotte.

At least I'd have the consolation of Kinnock's victory, of seeing Maggie turfed out. As I walked to the bus stop I pictured Richard, his face in his hands as the election results flooded in and his heroine was sent packing. I rehearsed what I'd say to him – magnanimous, but mocking – as the superiority of my arguments was made clear by the choice of the electorate. I almost pitied him.

5.

2009: Family Affair

'Hello again, Carly.'

Michael and Carly had just walked into the kitchen. His bruise was darkening and turning yellow at the edges. In the week since the fight he'd grown almost proud of it, but when I'd mentioned the attack I'd seen the fear still in his eyes. For another thing, I'd noticed that he made sure to go and meet Carly in town and not near her house.

'Hello, Mr Melton.' She was prettier than I'd remembered, although there was a dull, powdery look to her skin. Like most girls her age, she wore far too much make-up, applied with far too little skill.

'Are you here for tea?'

'If that's all right.'

'No problem. I'm making pizza.'

Michael put on his most casual expression. 'Are you going out tonight?'

'No. Why?'

'Nothing. Just wondered.'

Just wondered. How could he think I didn't know what he was

up to? One of the many blind spots teenager suffer from is the failure to realize that their parents were teenagers once, so for the most part we've done whatever it is they're trying to do. I decided to have some fun.

'Do you *want* me to go out for some reason?'

'No. Just thought you might have plans. It *is* Saturday night.'

Carly was blushing beneath her make-up. 'We wanted to watch a DVD, Mr Melton. We don't want to get in your way.'

Ah. Much more like it. They were doing *me* a favour. Still, I remembered being that age. Time alone with your girlfriend was precious.

'Well,' I said. 'I was thinking I might pop in on Grandma. I'll only be gone a couple of hours, though.'

Michael glanced at Carly. 'That's fine. That'll be long enough. To watch the film.'

I couldn't resist one more tease. 'You could come if you like. Grandma would love to see you.'

'Er, maybe tomorrow. We've been wanting to see this movie for ages.'

'Ok,' I said. 'I'll say hello from you.'

I could have been saying hello from Prince Charles for what it was worth. That's the strange irony of Alzheimer's: there's this person you love, confused and helpless, often scared, and all you want to do is reassure them. *It's me, Mum, Graham. It's your son. I'm here.* But the very thing that leaves them needing reassurance stops them getting it: the disease means that they don't know who you are. Who anyone is.

She'd wanted to die when she found out what she had. Dad was already gone, and she knew what it meant. A few years' slow decline on her own, then moving into a home for an anonymous twilight.

It would have been better if she had died, in many ways. To all intents and purposes she was already dead. Her mind was gone, and the person she'd been was no longer living in the scarred shell of her body. What are we, if not our memories? When you lose every memory you ever had, what's left? She didn't recognize me, so my presence gave her no pleasure. It just worried her. She could tell from the way I acted that she was supposed to know me, she was supposed to be reacting in a certain way, and her failure to do so was painful. I'd changed my will, leaving instructions that if it ever happened to me, I'd want to find a way to end it. I knew it wasn't legal now, but perhaps society would have moved on by then.

Mum lived in an old Victorian house that had been converted into a care home. I parked in a visitor space and walked up the stone steps to the front door. The place had that institutional smell of old age, a combination of bleach and baked beans.

A smiling nurse – or care assistant, as I think they were now called – passed by. 'Hello, Mr Melton. Come to see your mum? She's upstairs in her room.'

Mum was watching television. I say watching; she was looking at the screen, in the state of permanent semi-confusion that was her normal condition.

'Hi, Mum.'

She turned round and frowned. She didn't recognize me; she never did, but she knew I'd called her Mum, so I must be her son.

'Hello. I'll put the kettle on.' She still had her manners.

'Sit down. I'll make it. How are you?'

'I'm fine. Fine.'

'Michael's got a girlfriend.'

'Michael?' Her voice quavered, like it did when she knew she was getting something wrong.

'Your grandson. My son.'

For a second she looked at me as though she understood, and then it was gone. Those patches of lucidity were the worst part of the disease, the moments when she returned to herself for an instant. The thrill of being whole again was crushed by the realization of the horror of her plight. It broke my heart every time I saw that flicker of understanding in her eyes. Watching her slip back under was almost a relief.

It was pointless telling her, she wouldn't remember, but the doctors said it was best to be patient and explain. 'She's called Carly.'

Mum looked at me, uncomprehending.

'We're going to come and see you tomorrow,' I said. 'Michael and me. We'll bring you some flowers for your room.'

'That'll be lovely.'

We drank our tea. I had brought her a new pair of gloves, and she laid them beside the other pairs in her drawer. She'd developed an obsession with gloves, and although she never wore them she loved to look at them. It was the only thing that made her happy. At first I had seen it as a sign of the disease and tried to stop it, but now she could have every pair of gloves in Warrington, if it helped.

She grew tired quickly. It's a strain to have guests at the best of times, but when you don't know who they are and you know you're supposed to it's even worse. I took her cup and kissed her.

'Love you, Mum. See you tomorrow.'

She turned away and walked over to her bed. Other than the Alzheimer's she was in fine condition. I had no idea how it worked, this disease, how something so destructive could be so selective. It had taken her self, erased the last vestiges of her personality, but left her with a healthy, functioning body that could sustain her shattered mind for years to come.

*

'Why don't you get a bird, Dad?'

We'd just dropped off Carly at her house. Michael had mentioned – casually, just so that I knew – that he was taking Carly home on the bus. I'd taken the hint and offered them a lift. I was pretty sure that Carly's ex would forget about her after a while, but in the meantime I didn't need to see my son take another beating. From the darkness of the car I'd watched him kiss her on the doorstep. Presumably he thought that because he couldn't see me, I couldn't see him, like an infant that hides behind its hands.

He looked at me. 'So, why don't you?'

'I . . . it's not the kind of thing I really think about. I mean, it's not the kind of thing you can just do.'

'It is. You just have to meet someone.'

'Easier said than done, Mikey. I don't meet that many single women of my age.'

'What about internet dating? You could try that. Loads of people do it nowadays.'

'Michael, I don't think so. I'm not so desperate that I need to meet people online.'

'It's not desperate, Dad. Everyone's doing it. You should try it.'

'No. It's not my thing. I'm happy as I am.'

'What about when I leave home? You'll be lonely.'

'You've got plans you're not telling me about? I'll survive, Michael.' I changed the subject. 'Carly's nice.'

'Yeah. She's cool.'

'Everything ok, with her ex?'

When he replied, he sounded distant. 'Yeah. I've not seen him since.'

'You know, your mum and I met when we were your age.'

He sat up in his chair. I didn't talk about her much, but when

I did he loved hearing about Charlotte. 'Yeah? How did you meet?'

'At a party. Tommy knew her cousin and he invited them to a party at his house. She was a private school girl.'

'Was she rich?'

'Quite, by my standards anyway. Grandad Stephen had a Jag.'

'He still does. Or he did last time we saw him, anyway.'

We didn't see Charlotte's parents often enough. They lived in Dorset in a village by the sea. I'd only taken him down there once, so I suppose the fault lay with me as much as them. They loved Michael and they had a right to see him. They had also put a substantial sum of money in a trust to be given to him when he was twenty-five. Michael didn't know it, but he was quite a wealthy young man.

The change of topic seemed to have relaxed him. 'By the way, Dad, I've got a surprise for you. Me and Carly have been working on it.'

I tensed. Experience had taught me that it was better not to be surprised by Michael, even when he had the best of intentions. 'What is it?'

'I'll show you on Sunday, when Carly's round.'

'How about now? Now works for me.'

'It'll hardly be a surprise if I tell you now, will it? And it's not fair on Carly. She helped, so she should be there when you see it.'

'I think I'm past the age of surprises, Michael. What is it?'

He laughed. 'You're like a kid before Christmas. Be patient.'

This was another thing about teenagers. There came a point when they started treating you like the child. I started to protest, but Michael interrupted.

'I'm not saying, so don't ask again. You'll have to wait, but not for long. You'll find out on Sunday.'

*

Six rashers of bacon in between two inch-thick slices of brown bread, a thick layer of brown sauce, and my addition to my dad's bacon sandwich recipe: a sprinkling of cayenne pepper and a handful of pine nuts.

'Here you go, you two,' I said, handing over the plates. 'Sunday brunch.'

Carly stared at the doorstep on her plate. 'Thanks, Mr Melton. I'm not sure I can eat all that.'

'Eat what you can. I'm sure Michael will help you out if it's too much. He's a bottomless pit.'

I sat at the table and took a bite of mine. 'This was your grandad's recipe,' I said. 'He made them—'

'Every Sunday. I know. You always tell me,' Michael said. 'Now, are you ready for your present? You're going to love it. It'll change your life.' He gave me a meaningful look that made my blood run cold. 'Literally change it.'

'All right. Hit me with it.'

He grimaced, and looked apologetically at Carly. 'Don't say that, Dad.'

'What?'

'Hit me with it. It's not cool.'

'Not according to you.'

'Not according to anybody.'

I knew when I was beaten. 'Just go and get the present.'

'All right.' Michael shot out of the kitchen and came back seconds later with his laptop. He switched it on, tapped on the keys and spun it round to face me. 'There you go.'

I stared in disbelief at the screen: 'Dating Harmony: The Upmarket Internet Soul Search.' 'Michael. What's this? I told you. Internet dating's not for me. Anyway, I don't have time.'

'Dad! It's easy. Just give it a try. We've set you up a profile.' He came and stood next to my chair. 'Your log-in name is GraMel. I put my name as your password for now.'

'Forget it. I'm not interested. Delete the account.'

'It'll be a laugh. Look, here's your profile. What do you want to put?'

'Nothing. I don't want to put anything. I'm not joining.'

He ignored my protests. 'Age, forty. Profession. What's your job? Accountant? You can't put that, it sounds boring.'

'That's fine by me. Put what you want.' I looked at the screen. Accountant did sound boring. 'Put "Finance Professional".'

'What's your target age range? Twenty-six to thirty-five?'

'No! That's too young. Anyway, you can stop it. I'm not signing up.'

'Thirty-five to forty-five, then. Hobbies? I'll put reading and music. That's all you seem to do.'

'Michael! That's enough. I'm not interested. Now go and do something else.'

Michael closed the laptop with a shrug. He and Carly disappeared upstairs, and I cleared the table and washed up. When the last plate was put away, I sat down to read the paper. As a rule I preferred not to check my email on a Sunday, but my Blackberry was on the armchair and was flashing. There was a pile of emails from colleagues about the usual stuff: finance calendar, travel plans, past dues. There was also one welcoming me to Dating Harmony. Michael had bloody well gone ahead and signed me up, and he'd used my work email address.

I had to change it. The last thing I needed was a flood of emails from a dating agency flashing up on my screen while I did a presentation. Michael's computer was still in the kitchen, open at the Dating Harmony website. I clicked on the link at the top, *My Profile*, and changed my email address to my personal one. As I did so, a message flashed up. *You have new mail.*

I clicked on the inbox. *One user has viewed your profile and would like to make contact. Click here to see her profile.*

She was thirty-eight, with sculpted blonde hair and the shadow of a double chin. Jenny Wilson, a care worker. Underneath her picture were two buttons. I clicked *Reject.* I did *not* want to get into this. I had neither the time, nor the inclination, nor, for that matter, the need. If I wanted to meet women I didn't need the internet.

Over the next few days, I noticed the occasional email from Dating Harmony, saying that someone had viewed my profile and wanted to get in touch. I ignored them all. Then, one evening, there were seven messages, all arrived that day. When I got home, I logged onto the site.

'Nice one, Dad.' Michael appeared at my shoulder. 'You've got loads.'

'And I don't want them. I'm going to shut this thing down. I should have done it before.'

'Hang on. You can at least check them out. Look at that one.' He grabbed the mouse and clicked on a thumbnail of a dark-haired woman. 'Pippa. She's fit. And she's a doctor. Come on, Dad, fit and rich. You can't ask for more than that.'

'Is that what you think matters? Looks and money? Where did my son learn to be so shallow?' I looked at her picture. It looked like it had been cropped from a bigger photo, taken in a city somewhere. She had her head tilted to one side and was laughing. Her dark hair was full, falling around her face. She had an angular nose, pinched in above the nostrils, which gave her a hint of severity, like a school teacher, but she was beautiful, I had to admit it. A doctor, thirty-six. Interested in rock-climbing, aerobics and yoga. What the hell she was interested in me for, I couldn't imagine.

Michael manoeuvred the mouse around. I watched the cursor move over the *Accept* button.

'Michael!' I grabbed his hand, but it was too late. The mouse clicked and the screen changed. *Congratulations! Pippa will be in touch.* 'Bloody hell. What are you doing?'

'There you go,' he said. 'She'll be in touch to make a date. Nice one, Dad!'

I shook my head. I was going to stop this. I'd explain the situation when she got in touch and then that would be the end of this whole, stupid experiment.

6.

1987: Not Yet on the Scrapheap

The day after my row with Richard I sat at my desk, staring at the phone. I couldn't get started at work; it was impossible to concentrate. Things Charlotte had said or done kept popping up and I couldn't stop myself analysing them from every possible angle. In the end, though, it all came back to the same thing: I knew it had been doomed from the start. Girls like her didn't stay with guys like me.

I fought to convince myself that it was time to move on. *You'll be fine. There's plenty more fish in the sea. She was good to practise on, but think what's next!* It was a fight I had little confidence I would win.

As I was getting ready to go home, Tommy called. He had some good news which he thought would cheer me up after the debacle at Charlotte's the night before. He'd bought a new car. A Mark II Jag.

'I need to pick it up,' he said. 'I've agreed the price with the owner, but I need someone to fetch it with me. Will you come?'

'Where is it?'

'At Traynor's.'

'Traynor's? Traynor's, the scrap yard? What the fuck have you bought?'

'Come and see. She's a beauty.'

'She' was a piece of shit, twenty years old and barely functioning. Matt black, which meant she had been hand-painted, and with more modifications than original parts. We had no idea what exactly those modifications were, because it had no log book, which was no surprise, and which made no difference because it was a wreck. It didn't even have a starter motor, so we were going to have to tow it to Tommy's parents' house.

'Where are you going to park it?'

Tommy shrugged. 'Dunno. Out the front.'

'You can't park it on the street. It needs a lot of work.'

'Nah. I'll have her up and running in a couple of weeks. It'll be fine.'

'But you know fuck all about cars.'

'It can't be that hard. Stop worrying.'

I gave up. Once Tommy got an idea in his head you couldn't stop him. He didn't know how to back down. And he had got it into his head that the guy in the yard had the log book but wasn't giving it to him.

'You sure you've not got it?' he said, after he'd handed over fifty pounds, not a single one of which the rusting hulk was worth.

'Sure. Why would I not give it to you?'

Tommy coughed. 'There might be something in its past that you don't want me to know. That might affect the price.'

The yard guy squinted at him. The muscles in his arms rippled. 'What? It's a fucking wreck. What's to conceal?'

'A bad crash? There might be some structural problems. It might not be safe to drive. I don't want to find something like that when I've done it up.'

'Are you fucking me around, son? Of course there's structural problems. It's more rust than metal. This is a scrap yard, not a fucking Jag dealership.'

Two of the workers in the yard heard his raised voice and stopped what they were doing. The banging of metal on metal ceased as they stared at us. An Alsatian prowled out of the back room of the portakabin that served as an office.

'Come on, Tommy,' I said. 'Let's go. I think it's all right.'

'I want the log book,' Tommy said. He really could be a total idiot.

'Get the fuck out of here,' the guy said. 'Or you'll be picking your teeth out of your shit for the next week.'

I pulled Tommy outside. He would have happily taken a beating. He had no sense of when to give in, none at all.

'Wanker,' he said. 'Right. Let's get her home. You steer the Jag.' He grabbed a piece of rope from the boot of his 1.3 litre Escort and attached it to the two cars.

I looked at the rope in horror. 'Is that it?'

'Yeah. What's wrong?'

'It's too short. It's only six foot long.'

'That's loads.'

'Tommy, that Jag weighs about two tonnes. When you brake I'll need the reaction time of Superman to avoid slamming into the back of you.'

'Better keep alert then,' he said. 'Right, Superman?'

We fixed the rope on, and I climbed into the Jag. As we pulled away I watched the back end of the Escort shudder. I thought it was going to come apart, but gradually we picked up momentum. With no power, the steering and braking were ridiculously heavy, and every time Tommy slowed I nearly had to pull the steering wheel off to get enough force to press the brake pedal. After a few minutes I was bathed in sweat.

We were coming to a set of traffic lights on a hill. They were green, and I watched them, praying for them to stay that way. With a few yards to go, they turned orange.

'Keep going!' I screamed. I didn't fancy my chances of stopping that Jag on a slope.

For the first time in his life, Tommy erred on the side of caution, and his brake lights went on. I slammed the brake pedal as hard as I could, but the Jag barely slowed. It cannoned into the back of the Escort.

Tommy leapt out.

'What the fuck are you doing?' he screamed.

'Me? What the fuck are you doing? Why did you stop? On a hill?'

He looked at the back of his car. It was staved in. There wasn't a scratch on the worthless Jag.

'You're paying for that,' he said. 'I don't have insurance.'

'Forget it, Tommy. I'm paying nothing.'

'It's your fault.'

'How is it my fault? It was a stupid idea in the first place. You had the wrong rope and I told you it wouldn't work.'

'You said you'd need the reactions of Superman.'

'And I'm not fucking Superman! Jesus, Tommy. Be reasonable, for a change.'

'From the way you said it, I thought you were saying that you could do it.'

'No! I wasn't! Look, I've had enough. Is it any wonder Charlotte's family think I'm a scally when I get into this kind of thing? I mean, who does this, really?'

'Well, I'm fucked now,' Tommy said. 'Both my cars are useless.'

He looked at the crumpled rear end of the Escort and I saw what a man looked like when his dreams were crushed.

'Look, mate, we'll sort it out. We'll fix the Escort. One of my dad's mates has a body shop. He'll do you a deal. I . . . I dunno about the Jag. That might be a stretch.' A car pulled up behind us and beeped. I turned round. 'Oh, shit. This is just what I need.'

Charlotte's dad opened the door of his Jag, which was shiny and new, and stepped onto the street. He was wearing a blue suit and a striped tie. I was in the grease-stained jeans I'd worn to go to the scrap yard.

'Hi, boys,' he said. 'Everything ok?'

Tommy's eyes devoured his Jag. 'Nice motor. You're a man of taste.' He gestured to the rusting hulk buried in the back of his Escort. 'Like me.'

For the first time I saw Stephen's impeccably calm facade crack. 'Yes. I suppose so. That's yours, is it?'

'Just bought it. Graham crashed it into my Escort, but I reckon I can fix 'em up all right.'

'I admire your optimism. I suggest you push them to a safe place and I'll give you a lift home. I think you might need to get the services of a tow truck.' He put his hand on my shoulder. 'I'm glad I ran into you. I've been meaning to talk to you.'

We dropped Tommy off, and Stephen gave him the name of a garage he knew. In the end they managed to fix the Escort, although the passenger door never shut properly again. His dad made him move the Jag onto a piece of waste land at the end of the street, where it sat for the next eight years, until the police made him take it back to the scrap yard.

At my house I invited Stephen in for a cup of tea. The front door opened directly onto the lounge in the style that was typical for two-up, two-down terraces. I wondered whether he'd ever been in one before. He sat on the couch and I sank into the armchair. It was old, and the springs had gone. You kind of disappeared into it, like being hugged by a sponge.

'Graham, I wanted to talk to you about yesterday. Charlotte said she tried to call you after you left but you wouldn't come to the phone.'

I'd come home the night before and gone straight to my bedroom. When the phone rang, I shouted down to my mum that if it was Charlotte I wasn't in. When she hung up, she came upstairs.

'Everything all right, love?'

I shook my head. 'They don't want me to go out with her. They think I'm not good enough.'

'I don't think so,' she said. 'Charlotte and you are a lovely couple. Her mum and dad know that.'

'That's not what her brother said. He said they were waiting for her to go to university so she'd break up with me.'

Mum's eyelids flickered. She looked pained. I think she'd feared it all along. Mums know that boys get their hearts broken easily. 'Look, love. Why don't you get an early night. Things'll look better in the morning. The only thing between hope and despair's a good night's sleep.' It was her favourite saying. It may have been true, but I didn't find out that night. I barely slept a wink.

I looked at Stephen. I couldn't think of a suitable answer. I reached for my Dad's solution to all awkward situations. 'Brew? I'll put the kettle on.'

I went into the kitchen. I didn't want to know what he was going to say. Didn't want to know that Richard was right, that he had just been saying what the rest of her family had been thinking all along.

When I could avoid it no longer, I went back in and handed him his tea. As his hand closed over it I saw that I'd made in it in a big, chipped red and yellow Labour mug. *Vote Labour. 1983*. Shit. Another mistake.

He didn't seem to notice. 'You left rather hurriedly last night. I think that you felt unwelcome, after what Richard said?'

I didn't reply. I just shrugged.

'Well, you weren't. What Richard said was wrong, both in the sense that he shouldn't have said it and in the sense that it's factually incorrect. Georgina and I don't think that at all. As a father, all I want to see is my daughter happy, and she's happy with you. Last night when you didn't talk to her, she was terribly upset. That tells me all I need to know.'

I couldn't speak. My throat was constricted, and I knew that if I'd tried to make a sound I would have choked.

'Graham. Georgina and I like you and admire you, and we don't think, and never have thought, that you're not good enough for our daughter. Just because I voted for Maggie and you think she's one step down from the Devil himself doesn't mean I think you're a bad person.'

'You don't care that I'm Labour?'

'Life's not about how you vote. It's about how you live. Charlie's our daughter, Graham. Our job is to help her be happy, not to throw pointless prejudices in her path.'

I nodded. It was all I could do.

'Although it might be better if you stick to plastic ducks in the future.'

I was too miserable to see that he was joking. 'I will.'

'Anyway, that's all. How about you come round tonight for dinner? Charlie would love to see you. We can relax the rules about schoolwork for one night, I think. I'll give you a lift.'

I leapt to my feet. 'Thanks, Stephen.'

He looked me up and down. 'You might want to have a quick shower, though. I'll be in the car.'

7.

2009: Hug a Hoodie

This was stupid. I didn't want to go on the date in the first place, so what did it matter which shirt I wore? Michael didn't agree, and after hijacking my account to set me up with this Saturday afternoon meeting in a coffee bar, he was now critiquing my dress sense.

'Don't dress like an accountant, Dad. She'll think you're boring. You need to look cool.'

'I am an accountant and I don't care if she thinks I'm boring. I'm only going because it would be rude to cancel.'

Michael sniggered. 'Yeah, right. You could pull out easy, if you wanted. She's fit. That's why you're going.' He looked me up and down. 'The jeans are ok, but you need to change those shoes. Carly said you should wear the black suede ones and the black shirt.'

I had a little more confidence now that I knew it was Carly's opinion and not his. A teenage boy who wore baggy jeans and a hoodie ninety percent of the time was not a reliable fashion guide. Carly, on the other hand, might know what she was talking about. Whereas Michael cultivated the image of having thrown on the first clothes he grabbed by throwing on the first clothes he grabbed, she at least seemed to choose what she wore.

We climbed into the car. Michael was due at Carly's house, and I had promised to drop him off on my way into town.

'Now,' he said. 'Have a good time, but don't be back too late.'

'Right,' I said, laughing. 'I'll be a good boy, Dad, promise.'

'And don't do anything I wouldn't do.'

'That leaves me with a pretty wide field, unfortunately. Any more words of advice, son?'

Michael nodded. 'Yes, as it happens. If you can't be good, be careful. Remember that one, it's an important one. And if you get an opportunity, lunge.'

'Thanks. That'll do for now, I think, but if I need any girlfriend advice in future I know who to ask.'

'Anytime. Oh, shit.' He slumped in his seat, keeping low.

'Michael? What's wrong?'

'It's them, at the lights.'

Up ahead, three teenage boys were standing on the street, hunched forward with their hands buried deep in their pockets. Their faces were hidden by grey hoods. I guessed that these were the ones who had beaten him up over Carly. As we approached, the lights turned from green to red.

'Don't stop,' Michael said. 'They'll see me.'

'I have to stop. I can't jump a red light, it's illegal. Anyway, you'll be fine. You're with me.'

We braked to a stop. Michael slid further down in the passenger seat. The boys paid us no attention, stepping in front of the car to cross the road.

One of them glanced through the front window, and stopped. He stared at Michael. Front on, you could see his face. He had narrow eyes and bad acne.

'It's that fuckin' wanker who's knobbin' Carly,' he said to his friends. He leaned on the bonnet and waved his hand, his thumb touching to his forefinger. 'Wanker!' he shouted.

His friends joined him, one on either side. The one to his left banged repeatedly on the bonnet and then spat on the windscreen.

'Hey,' I shouted. 'What the hell do you think you're doing? Piss off.'

Next to me Michael groaned. 'Dad, don't make it worse.'

'What do you mean? I'm not going to take this. It's ridiculous.'

'Dad! Don't do anything! Please! It'll just make it worse.'

'Michael. They're just kids. I'm not scared of them.'

I sounded the horn loudly and revved the engine. The lights were back on green. 'Come on! Bugger off!'

They didn't move. All three of them stared at me.

'Right. I've had enough.' I undid my seat belt and climbed out, shielded behind the car door. 'You three, get lost. Go on, scram.'

The acned one walked round the car and stood in front of me, defiantly close. His two mates lined up behind him. 'What are you gonna do about it, you fuckin' wanker?'

What *was* I going to do about it? Beat them up? My dad would have whacked one of them and sent the others packing, but I wasn't my dad. I was a product of Blair's Britain, a fully paid up member of the freshly minted New Labour middle classes. Violence was not on the agenda; aggression was an admission that sophistication had failed; use of physical force was a sign of weakness. This was the other side of Blair's Britain: a generation of teenage boys with nothing to do and nowhere to go, other than a job selling mobile phones or taking orders for flowers in a call centre. I noted with shock that my legs were shaking.

'Are you his dad?' one of the others said. 'Are you a fuckin' pussy as well?'

'Get to fuck,' the acned one said. He pushed the car door hard and I stumbled backwards, grabbing the frame of the car door to keep my balance. One of them flicked a cigarette butt against my face. It didn't hurt, but the sting of the hot end shocked me. I scrambled upright and glared at them.

They stared at me, tensed and watchful. They were like animals; any sudden movement on my part and they would uncoil, fighting and hissing. I pointed at them. 'You three are in a lot of trouble. I know your faces.'

The acned one barked a laugh. ''Course we are.' He jerked forward, his fist raised, and I flinched. He laughed again as I climbed back into the car and onto the front seat.

Michael was looking at me, his face white. I grabbed the door to pull it shut, but the boy had grabbed it and was holding it open with one hand, smiling mockingly at me.

'Go on,' he said. 'Shut the door and run away, you soft cunt.'

I jerked the door, hard, and it swung in a few inches, but he was too strong. He pulled it slowly open again. He leaned over the door until his face was inches from mine.

'Fuck off,' he said, and hawked. His cheeks and lips pulsed as he moved the spit and snot around in his mouth. 'You can take this with yer.' He tilted his head back slightly and spat at me. I lowered my face and it hit me on the back of the head, spreading wetly down my neck. 'You're next, you prick,' he said, pointing at Michael. He slammed the door shut and walked away, his friends laughing and patting him on the back.

'Nice one, Dad,' Michael said. 'That was Connor and his mates. You showed them.'

I struggled to turn the key in the ignition. My feet were shaking so violently that I could barely release the clutch, and the car kangarooed as we moved off. I ignored the spit running down my back, too shocked to acknowledge it.

'We have to call the police,' I said, eventually, a feeble anger returning. 'They can't get away with that.'

'No!' Michael said. 'You don't get it! They don't give a shit about the police. They'll batter me! You've caused enough trouble as it is. Just leave it alone. Please. You're no use. You've just shown that.'

His words twisted in the wound the yobs had opened. I was ashamed, humiliated in front of my son. What was I thinking? Images began to play in front of my eyes in which I ran them over, crushing them mercilessly under the wheels of my car.

I was brought back to myself by a loud horn. I had pulled out to turn right without seeing an oncoming lorry. It swerved to miss us, the driver waving his fist.

'Dad! Concentrate!' Michael slapped his face into his hands. 'For fuck's sake! Can't you even drive?'

I pulled into the side of the road, my heart thumping. I closed my eyes and took a few deep breaths. When I was calm, I turned to look at him.

'Ok,' I said. 'I'm sorry. I'll take you to Carly's.'

When we reached her house, he didn't get out of the car. Normally he was unbuckling his seat belt as we approached, and had the door open and his feet on the tarmac before the car was at a standstill.

'Are you ok?' He was worried for me. I saw the man in the boy. How had we come this far? How had he changed from the baby I'd cradled in the small hours into an adolescent on the cusp of adulthood? It felt like it had happened overnight, like I'd looked away for an instant and when I looked back I had a grown up son.

'I'm fine,' I said. 'Call me. I'll pick you up tonight. I love you, Michael.'

'Thanks,' he said. He paused, and then got out of the car. 'See you later. Enjoy your night out.' The door swung shut as he vanished into Carly's house.

8.

1988: Students

We were standing in the queue for The Haçienda nightclub. It was all over the press, *the* place to be seen: home of the Happy Mondays, Madchester, and, as far as I could tell, loads of wankers. Tommy and I had gone to see Charlotte at her halls of residence. She'd moved in a few weeks earlier to start her English degree at Manchester University. She'd passed her A levels with good grades, and could have gone pretty much anywhere, but she'd chosen Manchester as it wasn't that far. At first she'd been planning to live at home so we could see each other, but my dad had persuaded me that it would be better for her to live at university.

'Don't let people make sacrifices for you,' he'd said. 'Or they'll become martyrs. Tell her to bloody go and live there. It's only Manchester. You'll see her at the weekends.'

Tommy was all for it. As far as he was concerned, it was a guaranteed ticket to the Eldorado of student muff. He worked with his dad, labouring in a builder's yard, and he was convinced that students were all (a) good-looking, and (b) desperate for a bit of rough. If Charlotte lived in halls, he would have unfettered access to her desperate student friends. On the way to Manchester in his

Ford Escort, he'd regaled me with tales of what went on after lights out in student halls. Most of his stories seemed to have come from the pages of *Men Only*; he appeared to believe that when students weren't sleeping with another student, they were sleeping with two other students. *Except Charlie*, he added, patting me on the shoulder. *She's a good girl*. I could tell he didn't believe it.

Fortunately, I'd stayed with her a few times and the reality of student life was far more mundane. Most of the lads suffered from the same awkwardness around girls that everyone else did; most of the girls spent their time pretending not to notice that the lads were trying clumsily to flirt with them. Of course, there was plenty of coupling, but no more than in any other place where you put lots of young human animals in close confinement.

We'd been queuing for a while. Tommy was telling Charlotte's neighbour, a dark-haired girl from Taunton called Henrietta who hardly said a word all night, about a guy he worked with who'd served time for murder. It was the kind of thing he thought would impress her, I supposed. At least he wasn't telling her about Billy Ocean. He loved Billy Ocean, whose songs provided much of his personal philosophy, such as it was. He derived particular insight from Billy's song *When the Going Gets Tough*, an insight which was complicated and given more time and respect than I thought it merited, but then I didn't claim to understand. Besides, I spent most evenings listening to Chris de Burgh singing *Lady in Red* – so much for Joy Division – and agonizing about whether to put it first on a mix tape I was making for Charlotte.

As we stood in the queue, Henrietta looked more scared than impressed. Tommy was flagging in his efforts to chat her up, and I was holding Charlotte's hand and thinking about how I really wanted just to go back to her room and get into bed with her. She'd just finished her period, and it had been a while since we'd had sex. I was thinking of suggesting it when someone ducked under the rope and pushed into the queue.

'Hi, Charlie,' he said. 'Mind awfully if I join? It'll be *ages* in the queue.'

'Hugh.' Charlotte said. 'Hi.'

There were some mutterings from the people behind us and a few shouts. Hugh turned round. 'They were holding my place,' he said. 'It's all right.'

Hugh was tall, with floppy, wavy brown hair. He was wearing chinos and a dark blue rugby shirt. It was not a very Madchester look.

'Thanks, Charlie.' He kissed her on her cheek, then turned to Henrietta and kissed her. 'Henners, you look gorgeous. You must be Graham,' he said. 'Nice to meet you.'

I shook his hand. His grip wasn't as limp as I'd expected. 'This is Tommy,' I said. 'A friend of mine.'

'Tommy,' he said. He started to put out his hand, but Tommy made a point of shoving his hands deep into his pockets and he pulled it back. 'Nice to meet you.'

'All right,' Tommy grumbled.

'Charlie, before I forget.' Hugh said. 'Can I borrow your essay on *Paradise Lost*? I'm behind with mine.'

'Of course,' Charlotte said. 'Although you won't think much of it.' She turned to me. 'Hugh pretends not to know what's going on, but don't believe it. He's read all the classics. Everyone knows already that he's on for a First.'

'First in the biggest shithead competition,' Tommy muttered.

If Hugh heard he didn't react. 'Not at all. Beginner's luck. We'll see what happens when the exams come round.'

'Come on, Hugh,' Henrietta said. 'You got three As at A level and turned down a place at Oxford. Compared to the rest of us you're a damn genius.'

Hugh smiled. I'd never seen anyone look so smug. 'Strange you need to copy Charlotte's essay, then,' I said. 'From the sounds of it, you should be teaching her, not the other way round.'

'I know, I know,' Hugh said, lifting his hands in a gesture of theatrical resignation. 'You're right. I'm a lazybones. It's all a fraud.'

'Graham!' Charlotte said. 'If Hugh wants to see my work, that's fine. I'm just glad he thinks there's something worth seeing.'

We had reached the front of the queue so we paid and went in. I noticed that Hugh borrowed the entrance fee from Henrietta.

When we got in, he offered to buy us a drink. At the bar, he ordered three pints. When they came, he patted his pockets. 'Bugger. Seem to have left my wallet,' he said. 'No chance you could help me out? It's most embarrassing. I'll get you back next time.'

Tommy threw a note on the bar. From the look on his face, I doubted there'd be a next time.

The Haçienda was better talked about than experienced. Over the years the legend would grow and the memories would become tinged with nostalgia and affection, but the reality was that it was just a nightclub. If you were one of the in-crowd – the musicians, the owners, the dealers – no doubt it was wonderful, but for the punter? You sweated like a miner, couldn't hear what anyone said and paid twice pub price for a pint of watery beer.

On the way home I sat on the night bus, my arm round Charlie. A few seats behind us Tommy and Henrietta were locked in a long and noisy kiss. Either she'd drunk too much or given into some kind of *Lady Chatterley* fantasy, or both. Miraculously, Tommy's vision of easily available 'student muff' was solidifying into reality.

'Hugh's a character,' I said. 'Bit of a chancer.'

'What do you mean?'

'Well, Tommy had to buy his drinks. He didn't have any money on him. And he borrowed a tenner from Henrietta to get in. I guess that's how the rich stay rich. You have to prise their cash from their iron grip.'

'He's a nice bloke, Graham. He's the younger brother of one of Richard's friends, from Durham. That's how I know him.'

I laughed, as sardonically as I could. 'Fucking Richard. Your brother still trying to break us up?'

'No he's not! And Hugh's just a friend. For God's sake, Graham.'

'Your brother's a snob. That's why he wants us to break up, because he thinks I'm common.'

'You know, I'm sick of your class war. You've been like that ever since we met, judging people by their jobs, or their accents, or the school they went to. You accuse the rich of looking down on you, of judging you because you're working class, but they aren't. You're the one who's doing the judging, not them. Most people don't care, Graham. They just get on with their lives.'

I stared out of the window.

'Why are you so insecure that you take it to heart like that? Why do you get so jealous of someone like Hugh?'

'I'm not jealous. I never said I was. I was just saying that he didn't buy his round.'

'Which, according to the pub folklore you and Tommy are so proud of, is a sign that someone is lower than a snake's belly. Yes, I know. Well, I'm sick of it. It's time you grew up. And before you ask, I don't fancy Hugh. He's a nice bloke, but he's not my type. My type's more like, oh, I don't know, like you. Which is why we've been going out for three years.'

She looked out of the window. I could see her face reflected in the glass. It was set hard and unsmiling. Behind me I heard the flare of a lighter and the crinkling sound of a cigarette being held to a flame. I turned round to see Tommy passing the cigarette to Henrietta. He caught my eye and winked.

Henrietta knocked on Charlotte's door at the crack of dawn and deposited Tommy in her room. It hadn't turned out like he'd expected. Her passion on the bus had evaporated when we got back to the halls, and he'd spent the night on her floor, shivering in his clothes. It hadn't gone much better for me. Charlotte hadn't kicked me onto the floor, but she might as well have done. After the argument we'd fallen into silence – hers thoughtful, mine drunk and stubborn – and slept back to back.

'You'd better go,' Charlotte said. 'I'll call you later.'

'I was going to stay for the weekend.'

'I've got work to do. I have to hand in an assignment on Monday.'

She hadn't mentioned that until now. 'I'll come back tonight. Or Sunday.'

'Graham, please. I'm . . . just accept it, I'm busy. I'll call you.'

I could see there was no point arguing, so we got in the car and left. Tommy pulled into a greasy spoon just off the motorway and we ordered the full English.

'Frigid,' he said. 'I couldn't fucking believe it. On the bus she was all over me. That was it, though. Turned frigid as soon as we got in the room. All she'd do was let me kiss her. She wouldn't even let me feel her tits, not that she's got much. In the end, I fucking gave up and kipped on the floor. Fucking students.'

'I know,' I said. 'I'm going out with one. For the moment, at any rate. I don't think I will be by Sunday night, though.'

He looked up sharply at me, a forkful of egg and beans halfway to his mouth. 'Bollocks,' he said. 'You two are solid. Everyone knows that.'

I shrugged. I'd not slept, and my eyes felt raw. I swigged my tea. 'Try telling that to Hugh.'

'Nah,' he said. 'He's a cunt. There's no fuckin' way she's interested in him, no fuckin' way. She totally loves you. God knows why, but she does.'

I wasn't so sure. I told Mum when I got home. She took a deep breath, and thought for a few moments.

'Well,' she said. 'Here's what I think, for what it's worth. She's in a new place, meeting new people, and she's probably all caught up in that. You should let her get on with it for a while.'

'What do you mean? Don't go and see her?' And leave her to Hugh? I didn't like the sound of that.

Mum sighed. 'I know, love,' she said. 'It's hard. If you're scared she's slipping away, you want to chase harder. But sometimes – most times – that just makes people run away all the more. If she loves you, she'll snap out of it. If not, then at least you know.'

I was alarmed to feel tears sting my eyes. 'So you're saying I should leave her? Don't even call?'

'You know, love, sometimes you have to lose a little now to win a lot later. Listen to her: she said she'd call you. Take her at her word. Let her call.'

Twice that afternoon I picked up the phone and started to dial the number of the call box in her corridor. Twice I put it down. It was the same on Sunday. If I was still for a few minutes I'd be taken by an overwhelming urge to call her and I'd snatch up the phone and begin dialling. Each time it was harder and harder to put the receiver back in the cradle. Once, I let it ring until someone answered. I think it was Henrietta. I slammed the phone back down.

Images of Charlotte in bed with Hugh tortured me. I looked for ways to keep busy: I went for a run, something I'd not done since compulsory cross-country at school, watched the rugby with Dad, read a book and chatted to Mum after dinner. Anything to postpone the moment when I'd have to go to bed and be assailed by the thought of Charlotte, crying out in ecstasy in bed with that posh fucker Hugh.

On Monday morning, I went to work, dark circles around my eyes. After morning break, my boss, Peter Drury, told me that his boss wanted to see me.

'Graham,' his boss said. 'Take a seat.' He was leaning back in his swivel chair. A cigarette burned in an ashtray on his desk, next to a shiny wooden sign: *Terry Sprocton, Finance Director.*

He rubbed his thick black moustache and took off his glasses.

'How long have you been with us now?' He had a strong Lancashire accent. Now came out as two syllables: *nah-oo*. 'Two and a bit years, isn't it?'

'Yes,' I said. He had a reputation as a ruthless bastard, and my mouth was dry. *Why today?* I was thinking, *when I've had no sleep and my girlfriend's about to leave me. If he's going to fire me, why today?*

'Well,' he said. 'You've done well, Peter tells me. You've an eye for detail, you work hard and you've a calm temperament. He says he can rely on you, which is a skill in itself, I can tell you. Anyway, lad, I've spoken to the MD and we've decided to offer you the chance to do a qualification. The firm'll pay, don't worry. If you're interested, we'll sponsor you to do an accountancy course.'

'Really?' I said, all the emotion of the weekend welling up to the surface and making me babble. 'I thought you were going to fire me.'

He tilted his head to the side and raised an eyebrow. 'Not unless you want me to.'

'No,' I said. 'No, not at all. That's not what I was saying.'

'So, are you interested then?'

'Yes,' I said. 'Yes, I am. When do I start?'

'Not for a while yet. HR will sort out the details with you.' He reached into a drawer under his desk and pulled out two thick books which he slid over the desk to me. 'But you can start by reading these. It'll give you a flavour of what's to come. One more thing. The MD decided to give you a bonus. He likes to look after our people. It's not much, but it's nice to have. There'll be an extra thousand pounds in your pay packet this month.'

I think my mouth fell open. I babbled my thanks, and he packed me off out of his office with a grin. A thousand pounds. I'd never had that much money at any one time in my life. I was going to be a thousandaire and I was going to be an accountant.

Peter came over to my desk. He was my dad's age, with immaculately neat salt-and-pepper hair and a dark green bow tie. He always wore a bow tie. 'Congratulations,' he said. 'The work starts here, mind.' He opened one of the books. 'Depreciation schedules. I remember all that. You've got it all to come, my boy.'

The books were unintelligible, full of tables of figures and symbols I didn't understand. I imagined myself explaining the contents to my parents or to Charlotte. It was an intoxicating picture. 'Thanks, Pete,' I said. 'I can't wait to get started.'

'You've earned it. That young lady friend of yours'll be pleased. You can take her out with the bonus.'

'Yeah.' My stomach shrivelled. 'She'll be dead chuffed.'

'Congratulations again. And if you need any help with the books, just let me know. I can still remember most of it. I hope so, at any rate.'

When he left I picked up the phone. Surely this was a legitimate excuse to call Charlotte? She was still my girlfriend, after all. I dialled the number. The phone rang and rang. I let it carry on. It often took a while for someone to answer it. My mind drifted as I imagined the conversation. My gravel tones, her excited shrieks, a dinner date at a posh restaurant.

I was interrupted by someone picking up the phone. 'Hello?' A male voice. Posh, and deep. I was pretty sure I recognized it. I would have sworn it was Hugh. I shoved the phone back into its cradle.

By Friday I was coming to terms with the fact that she was going to dump me. After putting the phone down when Hugh answered, I hadn't called again, and I'd not heard from Charlotte. To my mind, there was only one explanation. I already knew what I'd say to her when she did it: I'd explain, in a calm, generous tone, that I loved her, but if she wanted to go her own way, she should do so and she should do so without feeling guilty about me. All I wanted was for her to be happy, even if that meant I couldn't be her boyfriend. It was my fervent hope that such a display of selflessness would cause her to see the error of her ways and realize, in a flash, that I was the one for her. If that didn't work, I planned to resort to the last of the last hopes: begging.

Of course, since I wasn't going to call her, to dump me she'd have to call. If she didn't, then technically, I realized, I'd be her boyfriend in perpetuity. It wouldn't be the most rewarding of relationships, but it was something.

I was about to leave work for the weekend when the phone rang. We finished at 1 p.m. on Fridays, so I was meeting Tommy for a pint and some lunch.

'Hello, Graham Melton speaking.'

'Graham. It's me.'

I wasn't expecting it to be Charlotte. By now I'd almost given up hope of her calling, and besides, she never called me at the office.

'Hi. You all right?' I muttered.

'Yeah. You?'

'Busy. Lots going on at work.'

'That's great.' She sounded nervous. She sounded like someone who was going to dump her boyfriend. I started to stall.

'I'm doing a course. The firm's sponsoring me to become an accountant.'

'Graham, we need to talk.'

'And I'm getting a bonus. A grand.'

'That's wonderful.' I heard her take a deep breath. 'We need to talk.'

'What about?'

'Us.'

My legs were weak and I felt a kind of ache in my lower back. The world loosened and seemed to slip around.

'What about us?'

'Graham. This is the hardest thing I've ever had to say. I need a break.'

'A break? What do you mean?' Perhaps if I made her spell it out it would not be what I knew it was.

'I need some time to myself. Some time apart.'

'How much time? A week? Two weeks?'

'I don't know. For as long as it takes.'

'Takes to what? You're dumping me, aren't you?'

'No . . . no. Not exactly.'

'Have you met someone else? That wanker Hugh?'

She sighed. 'There's no one else. I just need a chance to find myself.'

'You're in Manchester,' I said. 'You're not lost.' It was a feeble joke and she didn't laugh. She didn't say anything. 'Don't you love me?'

It was the longest and deepest silence I'd ever not heard. 'I'm not sure.'

'Which means no. At least be honest with me, Charlie.' I spat out her name. I never called her Charlie. It was what other people called her, posh people, people from her tribe. I called her Charlotte. Besides, it was a boy's name, for fuck's sake.

'It doesn't mean no. Really, it doesn't.'

Great. So now I had hope to contend with. That was almost worse. 'Well,' I said, angry and hurt and wanting to hurt in my turn. 'It's been nice knowing you. You can fuck off now, and fuck your new posh fucking boyfriend.'

'Nice one, Graham. That's the way to charm the ladies. I'm regretting it already. God, I love being insulted. Keep in touch.'

What the fuck had I done? That was not what I'd planned at all. Where was the selflessness? I'd been planning selflessness, and *that* had happened. Christ. All I'd done was upset her. I splashed water on my face and looked in the mirror. My face was all blotchy. I couldn't go back to my desk like this. I slipped out of the loos and walked to the bus stop. I'd pick up my stuff on Monday. It'd be fine until then.

By the time Tommy got to the pub I was three pints deep and sinking fast.

'What happened?' he said, thumping onto the seat next to me.

'She dumped me.'

'Fuck. I'll get you another.'

He returned with two pints and two shots of whisky.

'So what the fuck happened?' He lit a cigarette and handed me the packet. I hardly smoked, but I lit one and sucked in the smoke. My head started to swim.

'Dunno. She just said she needed some time.'

He shook his head. 'That's what they all say. Nah, she's fucking that posh bloke, whatsisname.'

I looked at him in disbelief. I may have thought that but I didn't need him to tell me it. 'Thanks a lot, mate. Shit, it makes me want to go and kick his head in.'

Tommy looked at me. 'Do you want to? We could go later. It's not like you've got owt to lose now anyway. She's already fuckin' dumped you.' He shook his head. 'Bitch.'

We drank hard for the next few hours. By the time we left the pub to get some chips we were convinced that Charlotte was womanly perfidy personified. On the way to the chippy, we passed a phone box.

At the sight of the phone all the hatred fell away. It was a portal to her. I just wanted to hear her voice. If I could just speak to her, maybe I could convince her. 'I'm going to phone her. I need to talk to her. Tell her how I feel.'

Tommy squeezed into the phone box alongside me. 'Here. I've got some ten pence pieces.'

'Thanks. You're a mate. I know I can count on you.' I fed them into the slot and dialled the number.

'Hello?' A girl answered the phone. She had a London accent.

'Hello? Is Charlotte Marshall there?'

'Dunno. I'll have a look.'

The credits ticked down on the phone. I could hear people talking and laughing. Faint voices; male voices.

'Hello?' It was Charlotte.

'Charlotte,' I said. 'It's me.'

'Graham. I can't talk right now. Perhaps another time.'

'I wanted to speak to you. There's something I wanted to say.'

Tommy nodded and gave me the thumbs up. He twisted the phone towards his lips. 'You fuckin' slag!' he shouted. 'Get to fuck, you dirty bitch!'

'Tommy!' I grabbed the receiver from him. 'Charlotte, that wasn't what I wanted to say. I'm sorry. Charlotte.' The line was dead. I shoved Tommy out of the phone booth and into the street. 'Tommy, what the fuck was that? What were you doing?'

'Shit,' he said. 'I thought that was why you were calling her.'

I held my head in my hands. 'I was calling to make it up with her.'

'Sorry, mate. I wouldn't have done it if I'd known. Anyway, someone had to tell her. Let's get to the chippy before it shuts.'

9.

2009: Black Shirt and Jeans Day

I was late but I stopped in a pub to clean up. I didn't want to have to explain why I had a gob of dried spit in my hair. I also needed a few minutes to get my bearings. The incident had shaken me up. I had not been ready for the level of aggression of the yobs. Was this what Michael had to deal with? No wonder kids were so defensive. No wonder they put on such swaggering poses. It was the only way of surviving.

Was there something I could do about it? If a group of lads had beaten me up when I was fifteen my dad wouldn't have hesitated. He'd have gone round to their house and told their dad to sort them out, and if they'd done it again he'd have taken them to one side and given them what he called a hiding. The thought of a group of teenagers swearing and spitting at an adult was unimaginable. They'd have been thrashed for something like that.

I'd always accepted that corporal punishment was a bad thing, that the use of violence as a punishment was a relic of a brutal age and a failure on society's part to come up with anything better; it was a comfortable, progressive orthodoxy. Now, I couldn't help thinking those hoodies would have benefited from it. It would have made me feel better, that was for sure.

As soon as I entered the coffee bar, I recognized her. She was sitting on a stool at a bar table. I'd wondered whether the photo was misleading and I wouldn't know who it was, picturing some awkward greeting – *Oh, it's you? I was expecting someone different, from the photo . . .* – but the photo didn't do her justice. She was wearing her hair up, pulled back from her face, but I recognized the full mouth and subtle beauty. In person she was more than the sum of her parts; she radiated a calmness which was both reassuring and intoxicating.

I waved from the door, and she slipped off her stool and held out her hand. She had a firm grip. The muscles in her forearm rippled as she shook my hand. She was wearing a black shirt with the sleeves rolled up and a pair of tight, dark blue jeans that showed off her legs. I was glad I'd made an effort.

'I'm Pippa. Nice to meet you.' Her eyes glittered. They were very dark, almost black, like her hair. It was hard to see what was going on in there.

'Graham. Likewise. Sorry I'm late. I had to drop my son off somewhere and we had a delay.'

'Looks like it's black shirt and jeans day.'

For a second I didn't understand, then I realized our clothes matched. 'Great minds think alike.'

'Like minds think alike. It could just as well be simple minds as great minds.'

Her smile looked a bit forced. I think it sounded harsher than she'd meant, so I laughed reassuringly. 'I think I prefer great minds, although it was my son who recommended the outfit, so I wouldn't be too sure.'

'He dresses you, does he?'

'He likes to help. That's how I got on the internet dating thing, to be honest. He set up my profile, all that. I'm a bit of a Luddite when it comes to computers and the like.'

'No need to be embarrassed.'

'I'm not. I meant . . .' The waitress rescued me. I ordered a coffee.

'White wine,' Pippa said. 'Sauvignon Blanc. You don't want to share a bottle? It *is* Saturday evening.'

'I have to pick Michael up later. And I don't drink much. At all, really. Not for the last twelve years or so.'

'Wise. I love the odd glass, though.' She smiled. 'I have to say, your profile was very interesting. I couldn't resist finding out more about you.'

'Really?' I wondered what had so grabbed her attention about a thirty-nine-year-old accountant. 'I didn't think it was that exciting.'

'Come on! What kind of planes do you fly?'

'Sorry?' I thought I'd misheard. 'Planes?'

'Commercial flying, military? Or is it just a hobby?'

'I'm sorry, Pippa. I'm not sure I understand.'

'You *are* a pilot, right?'

'No. I'm a terrible flyer. Nervous as hell.'

'But your profile said . . . I think perhaps there's been a mix-up?'

I realized what had happened. There was no mix-up. It was Michael. So that was why I'd suddenly had seven messages. Bloody Michael had changed my profile.

'I think there might have been. Just out of interest, what else did my profile say?'

She frowned. Exaggerating – or worse, outright lying – on your profile was a big no-no in the world of internet dating. Even someone who knew as little as I did knew that. My cheeks reddened.

'You need me to tell you? It's your profile, isn't it?'

'Kind of,' I said. 'I think my son may have . . . helped with it.'

Her face softened and she laughed. 'Oh, I see. Helped without your knowledge?'

'Yes. As I said, he can be very helpful, can Michael.'

'So you're not a pilot?'

I shook my head.

'Not a classically trained pianist?'

'Nope. Tone deaf, in fact.'

'Not interested in extreme sports?'

'Not that either.'

'And the dolphin training? I rather liked that.'

'Never been near a dolphin in my life.'

'Oh,' she said. 'Well, it seems like I might be here under false pretences.'

I finished my coffee and started to get to my feet. 'Sorry about this. It was lovely to meet you.'

Pippa smiled and put her hand on my forearm. 'Stay. Tell Michael it worked. I couldn't resist your profile. I did wonder about the dolphin training, though. He's very creative.'

'That's one way of putting it.'

'He sounds like quite a character.'

'He is. It's been quite exciting with him, over the years. Not always pleasant, I have to say, but rarely dull.'

'Oh? Nothing too bad, I hope?'

'No, I suppose not. Just the usual.'

We lapsed into silence. There's a moment when you meet a new person where the momentum of the initial conversation you're having fades. When it restarts you either continue the small-talk, never to meet again, or chemistry takes over and you draw subtly closer to each other.

'He's a good lad, at heart. I'm lucky to have him. You? Any children?'

''Fraid not. I've been a bit career focused, really. All the marriage and kids stuff rather passed me by.'

'You're a doctor?' She nodded. 'It must be nice to have a vocation, even if it takes up all your time.'

'Oh, you can be a doctor and have a life outside work, like with any job, but for me it was just work, work, and more work. I qualified, did a stint as junior doctor, specialized. Suddenly, I look in the mirror, I'm thirty-six and a life on the shelf is beckoning.'

Her candour was refreshing, but a bit forced. It was too smooth a narrative, too practised an answer to what, in the end, was a simple question that a woman of her age must have been asked often. *Do you have kids? No, never got round to it.* It sounded rehearsed. Still, it wasn't my place to press.

Besides, she was pretty – no, beautiful – obviously intelligent, and charming. There must have been loads of men interested in her. I couldn't say that, though. I tried to think of something non-committal. 'Well, good job you signed up for the website then, I suppose.'

'I guess it is. I have to say, it's not really worked. Most of the men I've met weren't exactly what I was hoping for. That's the problem with this kind of thing, I suppose. You can never be sure that what's advertised is what you'll end up with. You can put whatever you want in your profile.'

'Like dolphin-training.'

She laughed. 'I didn't mean it like that. Most of them had *some* relation to reality. Yours is the first that's a total fabrication. I'll have to warn the website, you know. We're supposed to report breaches of the policy.'

'You needn't bother. I'll be deleting my profile. It's too dangerous with Michael around.'

'Surely it wasn't *that* bad meeting me?'

'No, that's not what I meant.' My cheeks reddened again. 'It's just not for me.'

Pippa looked at her watch. 'It's getting on. Do you want to get something to eat? There's a Thai place round the corner.'

'I can't,' I said. 'Thanks for the offer, but I have a lot of things to do and I have to pick up Michael later.'

'Another time, maybe?'

'Sure.' I avoided the question and picked up the bill. 'I'll get this.'

'Please. Let me pay my share.'

'It's only a drink. I think I can pick this one up.'

'Ok,' she said, getting to her feet and picking up her bag. 'Then, thanks for the drink, Graham. I enjoyed meeting you.'

I stood up and nodded. We'd been there over an hour; it felt like minutes. 'You too.' I lifted my hand in a little wave, hoping to avoid the awkwardness of a kiss goodbye, but she leaned forward and brushed her lips against my cheek.

'Bye,' she said. 'And thanks again.'

10.

1988–89: New Year

The world was leached of colour. Everything seemed grey. I couldn't enjoy anything. It all reminded me of Charlotte. I stopped listening to the radio after I heard the Human League singing *Don't You Want Me, Baby?* It was suddenly more than a pop song: I felt his pain. As the words echoed around my mind I examined them, weighing their significance. Was the placing of *baby* at the end a deliberate attempt to highlight his loss? Other songs were the same. However banal the sentiment, however saccharine the words, everything reminded me of Charlotte. I'd lie in bed at night, lyrics whirling around my skull and keeping Charlotte front and centre in my sleepless mind.

I hoped to see her over Christmas out in town, but she stayed away. On New Year's Eve, Tommy and I went to the Cavern Club in Liverpool. *Wall-to-wall fanny*, Tommy promised, *guaranteed.* After a few beers, I was in the mood to find out.

A red-haired girl pinched my backside on the dance floor. I winked at her and grabbed her hand to dance. Five minutes later we were snogging amidst the heaving bodies.

She was the first girl, other than Charlotte, that I'd kissed since I was fifteen. It was strange. I was so used to the way Charlotte kissed, to the little routines that we had, to the way she reacted, that I was constantly reminded of her when the girl, Michelle, did something different.

When the slow songs came round, the DJ played The Beatles' *Michelle* and she wrapped herself around me, whispering something in my ear. I couldn't work out what it was until she'd said it a few times. *Sing it to me*, she was saying. *I'm your Michelle*. But she wasn't. The whole sorry charade just reminded me of Charlotte and how much I missed her. I was glad when Tommy tapped me on the shoulder and said it was time to go. He hadn't pulled, and we drove home in his freezing car, the wind whistling in through the partly closed passenger door. The damn thing had never shut properly since the Jag had crashed into it.

New Year's Day dawned cold and miserable. At least I had a hangover to distract me from Charlotte. 1989 stretched out like a desert. I thought back to the last few New Year's Days when I'd had dinner at Charlotte's place. Her family always had a big meal to see in the year. It was a tradition I'd hoped to be part of for years to come; now, I pictured them all around their dining table without me. I wondered whether they missed me, or whether there was a replacement. I imagined Hugh and Richard laughing together, Richard telling him that Charlie used to have a local boyfriend but he was glad it hadn't worked out.

I couldn't take it. In the evening I called Tommy. 'I need you to drive me to Lymm.'

'What?'

'To Lymm. I need a lift to Charlotte's. It's the New Year's Day meal.'

'Has she invited you round?'

'No. It's a long story. Can you give me a lift or not?'

Tommy showed up half an hour later. We drove through the darkness until I told him to stop, a hundred yards from Charlotte's house.

'So,' he said. 'What's the plan? Gatecrash the party?'

'No. I just want to see who's there. See if Hugh's there. I'm going to climb the gate and go round the back. I'll have a quick look. I'll be back before you know it.'

Thankfully, Tommy is not at all a sensible person, or he would have tried to stop me. As it was, he nodded his approval. 'They won't be able to see owt,' he said. 'You can't see out of a window when it's light inside. You'll be able to get right close up.'

I knew the house well, and I was soon over the gate and into the side passage that led to the back garden. Once in the garden, I kept my distance from the house, skirting the edge to a large tree from where I could see the back of the house.

They were sitting at the table, the lights blazing. Four of them: Charlotte, Richard and her parents. There was no one else there. I looked for evidence of a guest – an extra chair, a plate – but there was nothing. At least it seemed that Hugh was not worthy of a place at the New Year's Day meal.

My heart ached. Even at a distance Charlotte looked as beautiful as ever. She'd had her hair cut into a bob, the curls beaten out of it by some hairdressing witchcraft. It couldn't be over between us. It just couldn't.

I studied her, still as in love as I had ever been. I knew, with a terrible certainty, that whether it was over or not, this feeling was never going to go away.

I heard a noise from the side passage. Tommy's head appeared over the fence. 'Graham.' A low hiss. 'Where are you?'

Shit. I'd told him to stay in the car. I waved. 'Here!'

I saw his shadow move along the back of the house towards the patio. 'Tommy!' I called, as loudly as I dared. 'Stop! Don't go that way!'

The shadow halted. 'Where are you?'

'At the back of the garden. Be careful! There's a security light!'

Charlotte's dad had had a light installed. It was activated by motion. The sensor didn't reach around the edges of the garden, but if you got too close to the house you'd set it off. He was very proud of it; it had the latest halogen bulb. He'd once boasted that you could play football at night, it was so bright.

'A what?' Tommy hissed. 'Stay there. I'll come to you.' The shadow carried on its journey along the back of the house.

'No! Tommy! Don't move!' It was too late. The switch clicked on and the garden was bathed in a blue light. I slid behind the tree.

Tommy froze. He was right in the middle of the lawn.

At the table, the conversation stopped. All four of them stared at Tommy. He raised his hand in a greeting. Charlotte said something, then stood up and opened the patio door.

'Tommy?' she said. 'What are you doing here?'

'Er,' Tommy glanced around. 'Just, er, just came to say Happy New Year.'

'Happy New Year.' She smiled. 'You could have rung the doorbell. Do you want to come in?'

'No. That's all. Just thought I'd say hello. Cheerio. I'll be on my way.' He waved to her parents. 'Happy New Year, Mr and Mrs M. See you, now.'

He waved again, and walked across the garden and down the side passage. There was a loud scraping as he climbed the back gate. Charlotte didn't move. She stood by the open door, looking out at the lawn.

'Graham? Are you coming in?' she said. 'All the heat's getting out.'

I stepped out from behind the tree trunk. 'Happy New Year,' I said.

Richard looked at me like I was the shit from his shoe. I didn't care. I was used to it. Stephen poured me a glass of wine. 'How's Tommy?' he said. 'Sure he doesn't want to come in?'

'No,' I said. 'He's probably a bit embarrassed.'

He chuckled. 'It is a somewhat irregular way of introducing oneself. Effective, though, if you want to make an impression.'

Under the table, Charlotte put her hand on my knee. I got the stirrings of an erection. 'Can we talk?' she said. 'When you've had your wine?'

'It's fine. We can talk now.'

She smiled, and we went into the back lounge. It was all so familiar. We sat side by side on the couch.

'You're such a gonk,' she said. 'What were you thinking, lurking in the garden?'

I shrugged. 'It was New Year's Day. I wondered if you were having dinner. I miss you.' I didn't mention Hugh. It didn't seem worth it. Every time I had in the past we'd had an argument.

'I miss you too. I've been thinking about you a lot.' She leaned forward and kissed me softly. 'I'm glad you came. It means I can give you this.' She stood up and opened a drawer in the sideboard. She handed me a letter. 'I was going to post it.' I started to open it. 'Not now. Read it at home. You'd better go. Tommy'll be worried.'

'Charlotte,' I began. There was so much I wanted to say.

She put a finger to my lips. 'Call me.'

She showed me out. Once I was past the end of her drive, I broke into a run.

In the car, I held the letter up to show Tommy. 'She gave me this.'

He switched on the wan internal light. 'Go on. What's she say?'

I tore it open.

Dear Graham,

I've written you this letter because there's a lot I want to say and I want to make sure that I get it right. If I phone you I know that I'll miss some of it. It's like writing an essay: I've got a list of notes surrounding me, ready to be turned into a finished product.

First, I'm sorry. Sorry that I treated you so badly. It was unfair of me just to drop you like that, with no explanation. I know it must have been awful for you. When Tommy called me a bitch on the phone I agreed with him. I was a bitch, but it was the only way I could have done it. If I'd spoken to you and seen you I would never have been able to go through with it.

I needed some time, Graham. We've been together since we were fifteen and I needed the chance to have a look at our relationship from a distance, to see if it was right for me. Right for us. A lot of things have changed since we met – we've grown up, our lives have taken certain paths and I needed to be sure that you were the right man for me.

You are. I missed you from the moment you left that Saturday after we went to The Haçienda. It was torture not calling you – I think we've talked nearly every day since we met – but I forced myself not to. When you didn't call that made me wonder if you'd forgotten me, and I just missed you all the more.

So that was why I did it the way I did. If I'd come and seen you to explain I would never have managed to make the break, and it was important for me that I gave our separation a chance. I needed to see if I could live without you. If I could, then maybe we weren't right for each other. If I couldn't, then that was that. I gave myself until the New Year to decide.

Well, the New Year's come and gone and I miss you as much as ever. I love you as much as ever.

There's one thing I need to tell you before we get back together. I had a fling. It wasn't much, and it wasn't the reason we split up, but I want you to know. I don't want any secrets between us. Don't ask me for the details, I won't tell you. All I will say is this: you should be glad, because it was boring and tedious and it made me realize just why you're the one for me.

I hope you can forgive me. I know that if you can then things will be better than ever.

I love you,

Charlotte.

'Shit,' I said. 'I don't fucking believe it.' I jumped up and down in delight. 'She wants me back! She fucking wants me back!'

'Women are weird,' Tommy said. 'Why did she dump you in the first place?'

'It's a long story.' I bit my lip. 'Wait here. No, go home. I'll be a while. I'll walk back or something. I have to go back to her house.' I paused. 'The only thing is, she had a fling.' Saying the words in front of Tommy was embarrassing, and a tiny hatred for her flared in my stomach.

Tommy nodded his head knowingly. 'Typical. Fuck that. You can't trust her, mate. If she's done it once, she'll do it again.'

I tried to ignore him, but at the back of my mind I feared he was right. 'It was after the split,' I said. 'At least she's been straight with me.'

'You believe that if you want to. Me, I wouldn't touch her with yours, after she's been at it with some other bloke. I'd leave it. Let's go for a pint.'

'I dunno.' The thought of her in the house, available after all this time was irresistible. 'I think I'm going to go and see her now.'

Tommy blew out his cheeks. 'Look. Why don't you sleep on it? If you still want to see her in the morning, call her. She's goin' nowhere. It'll do her good to sweat a bit.'

'No,' I said. 'I can't. Thanks, Tommy. I'll call you to tell you how it went.'

I climbed out of the car and walked back up the road, a newly restored vision of a future with Charlotte dancing before my eyes.

11.

2009: One Step up from Porn

After I left the cafe I drove through town to pick up Michael. As I pulled into the estate where Carly lived, I realized that I couldn't remember the journey. I'd been thinking about Pippa.

I was surprised by our date. I'd been planning to have a coffee and apologize for wasting her time. It wasn't that I didn't want a girlfriend, or that I didn't find women attractive; of course I did. The issue was that I didn't need a girlfriend. I didn't feel the lack of anything. My life had settled into a comfortable equilibrium and, for better or for worse, a relationship could only disturb that. Frankly, I no longer had the taste for drama.

I parked outside Carly's house and texted Michael to tell him I was there. At the far end of the street was a Bargain Booze, a group of teenagers moving in and out of the pool of light outside the shop. The red tips of their cigarettes glowed, and I could see them swigging from cans, drinking aimlessly and cheaply and destructively. They were like circling hyenas, ready to mass into a pack. I switched off the headlights. I didn't want to draw their attention.

God, it was ridiculous. I was an adult, and I was scared, genuinely scared, of these kids. It was the sense of the unknown that was so disturbing. I'd grown up in Warrington, in a similar place to this, but I didn't recognize it, didn't remember the atmosphere of lawlessness, the lack of respect and disregard for authority. I was glad I'd already done my growing up. I didn't envy Michael his.

The front door of Carly's house opened and Michael stepped onto the pavement. He climbed into the front seat and slammed the car door. He was apparently incapable of closing it gently. It was as though he wanted to weld it to the frame.

'How was the date?' he said.

'Fine.' I turned and looked at him. 'Although somehow she had the impression that I was a musical pilot with a sideline in dolphin training.'

'Not bad, eh?' He didn't appear to be on the verge of apologizing. 'The dolphin training was Carly's idea. She loves dolphins. She said that if she ever met a dolphin trainer she'd consider finishing with me.'

'Then you'll have to keep her away from aquariums. So she was in on this as well?'

'Yeah. And her dad suggested being a pilot. Birds love pilots.'

'Her *dad*? He knows about this debacle?' I groaned. 'I've never even met him.'

'He said it was a bit sad, using the internet to meet girls. He reckons it's one step up from porn, but I told him you've been doing it for ages.'

'I haven't! It was all your idea! Christ, when we get home, I'm cancelling this whole thing. It's over. You're not to set any more dates up, or modify my profile, or anything like that. Understand?'

He ignored the question. 'I bet she thought you were cool, though, eh?'

'Perhaps she did, until I set her straight.'

He whirled round, his mouth open. 'Dad! You didn't tell her the truth, did you?'

'Of course I did! I can't have her going around thinking that kind of thing!'

'But you're an accountant. You don't want her to know that.'

'What's wrong with accountants? You might be one some day.'

He snorted. 'Yeah. When I've had a personality bypass. I told you, I'm going to be a TV news reader. You get paid loads, and all you have to do is read some stuff a few times a day. It's a piece of piss.'

'Well, when reality finally intrudes on your life, you might find that those jobs aren't that easy to come by.'

'Well, when reality finally intrudes on my life, I still won't be an accountant. There're loads of other things I'd do before that.'

'Anyway, Michael, that's not the point. The point is that you can't go around lying to people.'

'Yeah, but it's not really lying, is it? It's just telling a bird something to impress her. Not proper lying, anyway.'

'Of course it's lying. Telling her I'm a pilot isn't lying? How's it *not* lying? What kind of a basis for a relationship is that?'

'You're going to have a relationship?'

'No! But if we were, how do you think she'd feel when she found out I'd been lying from the start?'

'I dunno,' he said. 'Cross that bridge when you come to it. But the thing with birds, see, is that it's all about first impressions. You can sort the rest later. Once you hook 'em, the rest is cake.'

'Jesus,' I said. 'Where this rubbish comes from I've no idea. Anyway, I told her the truth, so there's nothing more to discuss.'

He groaned. 'You've blown it. She'll never go out with you now. You'll have to start again. Find one who's not as fit. One who doesn't mind going out with an accountant.'

'Have I blown it? Really? As it happens, she wants to see me again. And *she* asked *me*.' I shook my head. Was I really having this conversation? It was pathetic.

'Really?' He sounded genuinely surprised. 'So you gonna see her again?'

I hadn't been planning to but my son's goading had provoked me. 'Might. Not made up my mind yet.'

'You should.' We pulled up at the house. 'Nice one, Dad.' He sounded almost impressed.

I spent the rest of the weekend with my mum and it was a few days before I logged on to Dating Harmony. There were a lot of messages. Dolphin trainers were clearly in demand. There was one from Pippa. I deleted the others and opened it.

> **Hi Graham. Lovely to meet you. So you are a pilot after all? Of course I would like to see you again, but I think Michael might have been helping. Love, Pippa.**

I scrolled down. The messages were in a thread, so you could see what had been written so far. There it was, a message sent two days before, the evening I'd told Michael that I'd confessed to being an accountant.

> **Hi Pippa. So, let's do it. Another date, that is. Let me know when UR free. By the way, forget all that stuff about being an accountant. I was just saying it to see if you like me for who I am and not for all the cool stuff I do. Graham.**

I put my head in my hands. The little shit. I replied:

> **Pippa. Graham here. It's actually me this time. Look, sorry about this. Michael means well, but he's, well, he's a teenager. You can ignore his ravings. Cheers, Graham.**

The next morning there was an answer.

> **Shame. I was looking forward to dinner. I'm game if you are? Thai, this time? Saturday 8 p.m.? Pippa.**

I drummed my fingers on the desktop, hesitating over what to reply. Just do it, I thought, what the hell. Anyway, it would be rude not to.

Michael was unbearable all Saturday. He had endless advice about how to deal with Pippa – play hard to get, split the bill, tell her she looks nice – and in the end I gave him a handful of cash and dropped him off at the cinema with Carly.

I met Pippa at the restaurant. She was wearing a black knee-length skirt and a red woollen roll-neck. I told her she looked lovely; she smiled and I thought I detected a slight flush. Perhaps Michael was on to something.

The waitress led us to a dimly lit table in the corner and handed us a menu. Pippa ordered a Singha beer; I stuck to water.

'So you really don't drink? Not even a beer with this spicy food?'

'No, I gave it up. With a young kid you can't afford the hang-overs.'

'You brought him up on your own?'

I nodded. 'Pretty much.' I didn't want to expand.

'So he must get the persistence from you? He's quite a character, sending me those messages.'

'He's going through an annoying phase at the moment. He thinks he knows best, and so he's constantly telling me what to do. About you, about the house, about my job. I suppose it's part of growing up. You suddenly realize you're nearly an adult so you start trying to act like one, but you don't know anything, so you just give out useless advice.'

'I remember being just like that. I told my mum what to wear, how to get her hair cut, what she was doing wrong behind the wheel. I thought I was being helpful, but I must have been such a pain.'

'Probably. Well, now that Michael has a girlfriend he's developed a particular expertise in women. Apparently, lies to impress a woman aren't lies as such. They're operational necessities that you can reverse later. The important thing is to get 'em on the hook.'

'Sounds like good advice.'

'You think?'

She shrugged. 'Worked with me, didn't it? I clicked on your profile.'

'But now you know it was all rubbish—'

'I've still come out for dinner with you.' She leaned forward. 'You can tell Michael that his strategy worked, at least on this occasion.'

'Only because it wasn't me doing the lying.'

'Don't let's split hairs here, Graham. The basic principle holds: you got my attention.'

She looked me in the eyes, a slight smile on her lips. In the light from the electric candle on the table I could see the faint hairs on her forearms and the curve of her breasts.

The waitress came over holding her pen and paper.

'Anything in particular you want?' Pippa said. 'I could order, if you like.'

'Sure. Go ahead.'

Pippa ordered a pile of stuff: a papaya salad, some kind of spicy grilled chicken, a red curry and a glass noodle salad.

'You know the food well.'

'I lived there for a while, in Chiang Mai.'

'Doing what?'

'*Medecins Sans Frontières*. It's a kind of charity that doctors can give time to. I was with them for a year. Most of the work was in Laos, but we were based in Thailand.'

'Very impressive. My dad would have approved. He was all about working for the community.'

'My dad hated it. He thought it was a waste of time.' She took a sip of wine. 'I could have done with a dad like yours. A bit of support.'

'Maybe. My dad was a great guy, but he was a bit opinionated when it came to politics. I had a very left-wing childhood. He was a socialist, through and through.'

'How about you? Are you a socialist?'

'I'm not really anything. No one is these days, are they? I mean, if you are a socialist, where do you go to be one? The Labour Party's full of clones, the trades unions are emasculated. There's nothing left of all that now. It's sad, in a way.'

'There's just lots of shops and as many plastic baubles as you can find space for.'

I smiled. 'My dad *would* have liked you. You're speaking his language.'

The waitress brought the food. It smelled delicious. I put some curry on my plate and took a bite. 'The food's spicy.' My eyes started to water. 'My mouth's burning.'

She took a bite and nodded. 'The hotter the better, for me.'

Was that an innuendo? Or was it just an innocent comment on food preference? We had crossed some threshold into a place where things were suddenly uncertain. It was not a place where I was used to going, and the unfamiliar geography was disorientating. I felt as though I was dancing with a skilful partner and I couldn't hear the music. Was I supposed to respond with an innuendo of my own? Did I even *want* to start exchanging innuendos? Where was Michael when I needed him?

I decided to keep it neutral. 'I can live with it quite hot,' I said. 'I'm pretty flexible.' Shit. That hadn't come out as I'd hoped. *I can live with it quite hot? I'm pretty flexible?*

She didn't seem to notice. Either the flirting was all in my head or she was better at it than me.

'Try this.' She handed me her fork. 'It's som tam. A papaya salad.'

As soon as I put it in my mouth my eyes started to water. I swallowed without chewing. 'Jesus. No more of that one.'

'I'm impressed. Lots of men would say they liked it. Wouldn't want to appear a wimp, and all that.'

'It's not some sort of courageous honesty,' I said. 'I just don't want to have to eat it again.'

'Here. You stick to the curry. I'll take care of the som tam.'

'Now I do feel like a wimp.'

After we'd finished, Pippa beckoned to the waitress and ordered a glass of wine. When the waitress brought it she asked if she could book a taxi in forty-five minutes.

'Where are you going?' the waitress asked.

'Appleton Thorn.'

'Look,' I said. 'That's not far. I can give you a lift home. I'm not drinking.'

'Are you sure? I don't want to impose.'

'That's fine.' I smiled at the waitress. 'It's ok. We don't need the taxi.'

We split the bill, and walked out to my car. She lived about fifteen minutes out of the village, in a cottage on the edge of some fields. I pulled up outside and put the car into neutral. I left the engine running; I was on the point of turning it off but I worried it might give the impression that I expected to be invited in.

I pointed north-west across the field. 'That's where I live. If you walked across those fields you could get there, probably without going on any roads.' I said some stupid, boring things.

'Well, thanks for dinner. I enjoyed it.' She unbuckled her seat belt. 'Can I offer you a drink? Coffee? Tea?'

'It's ok,' I said. 'I'm fine.'

'Right.' She stayed in her seat, looking at me with her faint smile. 'Well, see you soon.'

She leaned across the handbrake and kissed me on the cheek. She left her face close to mine. I could smell the sweetness of the wine and the spice of the food on her breath. Her hand brushed my other cheek and she gently turned my face until our lips met.

The kiss was long and slow and uncertain. Her hand stayed on my cheek, her fingers spreading behind my ear and into my hair. I reached out and put my hand on her hip, running it down over her thigh.

She pulled away and looked at me, her hand caressing my cheek.

'Do you want to come in?'

'I can't. Michael's at home on his own.'

'You know, he *is* fifteen. Your concern for him is touching, but I'm sure he can look after himself. It is sweet though, to see such a doting father.'

'It's not that,' I said. 'I just can't trust the little bastard. You've seen first hand what he can do, and you've not even met him.' Another stupid thing to say. Why not just go in, have a cup of tea? Before I could change my mind she sat back in her seat and patted my leg.

'True enough,' she said. 'Call me.'

I watched her open her front door and disappear into her house. A light went on somewhere in the back. A faint smell of perfume lingered in the car. For a second I was desperate to be in the house with her, and I had to stop myself getting out of the car.

Next time, I told myself. Next time.

12.

1989–94: Qualification

Once Charlotte and I were back together things quickly got back to normal. The spectre of her fling – I always wondered if it was that foppish wanker, Hugh – receded. I was glad that I'd kissed that bird in the Cavern. It somehow made up for it. When, in the spirit of honesty, I told Charlotte, her face turned white.

'Was it just a kiss?'

'I'm not going to say. Let's just say that I met someone and we spent some time together.' I put a heavy emphasis on 'time', giving a not too subtle hint that there were some sexual shenanigans that had gone on. I remembered what her letter had said. 'But be glad. It made me think of you.'

She pouted and claimed that she needed to know. One night stands, apparently, were worse than flings. She needed to know if I was the kind of person who had them. I graciously refused to answer. I couldn't really. Having hinted that I'd gone through half the positions of the *Kama Sutra* with an experienced woman of the world, I could hardly confess that it was just a drunken snog and that I'd turned down an offer of anything more because I was still maudlin over Charlotte. I would have looked like a right plonker.

In her second year, she moved into a student house with three friends: Gemma, Tash and Raquel. That made things much easier for us. I'd always felt like an outsider when I stayed in the university hall, which was like a members-only club for excited teenagers. It was much better when she was in the house; I could stay there most nights.

When she moved there, her dad made a proposal. Why not buy the house and charge rent to the other three to pay a mortgage? He offered to put up the deposit, if I took out a mortgage against my salary. My dad was unhappy: he hated the idea of me being a landlord, but I agreed. Why not get a foot on the property ladder? Everyone else in Thatcher's Britain was making out like bandits, so why not me?

I was doing well at the firm. Peter, my boss, was nearing retirement, and they'd offered me his job if and when I passed my accountancy exams. The course had another eighteen months to run, which meant I'd be finished at the same time as Charlotte.

At the end of her second year, the other three girls moved out. Since I was making a decent wage, we didn't need the rent to pay the mortgage. I moved in full time. It was a long commute in the mornings to St Helens, but it was worth it, and it was only for a year.

I was glad of the peace and quiet in the house. At times we felt as though we were locked away in our own world, but I was struggling with all the work and I needed a lot of time to make all the information stick.

It wasn't like Charlotte's degree. She seemed to be able to get by with a few hours of reading and a lecture or two. She told me that no one ever failed English. After all, it was mainly about expressing your opinion and being able to justify it. That was not true of accounting. What you recognized as operating revenue, and what accruals you made for warranty exposure were a matter of rules and considered judgement, not opinion.

I was putting in ten hours a day at the firm, then another few hours' revision in the evening. By the time I handed over that last paper I'd just about had enough. I almost didn't care whether I'd passed or not, as long as I didn't ever see the textbooks again.

Charlotte's exam results came through towards the end of June. She'd got a 2:1, the result she was hoping for. I asked about the friends I knew; it seemed that most had passed. Henrietta had a 2:2. Hugh, it turned out, had failed.

'Was he the guy?' I said. 'The one you had a fling with?' Now that he had been revealed as a fraud I felt as though I could cope with knowing.

'Hugh? God, no. Is that what you thought? No wonder you were upset. Look, I suppose it doesn't matter now. He was in the third year, a Londoner called Al. Just some random bloke.'

Just some random bloke. Hugh had been revealed as a clown, I could finally look down on him, and it turned out that it wasn't him after all. It was some faceless southerner. 'Poor Hugh,' I said. 'It must be tough to fail, after all that work.'

I didn't think I'd find out how tough, but a few weeks later I got a letter from the exam board. Apparently, I'd misread one of the questions and scored zero on that section. I'd done ok elsewhere, but that one fuck-up had been enough to keep me below the pass mark. The board regretfully said they couldn't pass me. They did, however, suggest that I re-sit later in the year. There would be another round of exams in December, and after a few days in the pub drowning my sorrows, I wrote back asking them to sign me up.

'Jesus,' I said. 'This is terrible. There's soot and dust and shit everywhere. There are probably dead birds up there.'

That summer, 1991, we'd sold the student house and made ten grand profit, which we'd put towards buying a barn on the outskirts of a village called Stockton Heath. It was on the edge of Warrington, the town centre on one side and the Cheshire countryside on the other. It was a tip. The building was sound, but it needed to be renovated from top to bottom: walls plastered, floorboards ripped up and replaced, new plumbing and electrics. We were starting in the room that was going to be the lounge, eventually, but in which we were going to sleep while we did the work. We were still young enough that a mattress in the corner of a barn was an adventure. It was a good job we were: since I was working and revising full-time for the re-sits, and Charlotte had started on a graduate HR scheme, there wasn't much time for renovations, and that mattress was going to be our bed for a while.

We were cleaning out the chimney. She held a bag open beneath the opening. 'It's horrible,' she said. 'You think there's dead birds? If there are, I'll scream.'

I raised my eyebrows. 'Close your eyes then,' I said, reaching up the chimney with a brush. 'It'll be best not to look.'

She needn't have worried. There were no dead birds up there, or at least not that she was going to see in the next few minutes. She didn't know, but I'd checked it all out the day before.

I rattled the brush around, banging it against the chimney walls. A stream of thick black soot shot down. Some of it went in the bin bag, but most burst onto the hearth and rose up in clouds around us. As I rattled, I reached into a gap in the brickwork and pulled out a parcel, which I let drop onto the floor.

'What's that?' Charlotte said. 'Hold on. Something fell out.'

I stopped as she picked it up. It was a small, square object wrapped in an old cloth.

'Hmm,' I said. 'Take a look.'

Inside the cloth was a jewellery box, dark red velvet with the name of the jeweller stamped on it in gold letters: Ratner's. Charlotte looked up at me without opening it. 'You kept the box?'

'Of course. I was proud of that present.' I took the box from her hands, crouched on one knee and flipped open the lid. Amongst the dark soot of my hands, the ring glistened.

'Charlotte,' I said. 'Will you marry me?'

She smiled, her face streaked with soot, and dived on me, pushing me to the floor. 'Of course,' she said, her mouth finding mine. 'As long as you promise me that only the box is from Ratner's.'

When I look back, the next few months seem almost dream-like, as though they took place in a fairytale castle which has since disappeared, never to be seen again. We were young, living in our own place, madly in love, both in good jobs: the possibilities seemed endless. As far as I could see, life couldn't offer much more that what we had at that moment.

The only grit in the oyster was the exams. The first time round, I'd hated them, but at least I'd been confident I'd pass. This time, I didn't have that certainty. I responded by throwing myself into the revision, hour after hour. I could have recited those textbooks chapter and verse. When I wasn't working, I was revising. In the few hours left each week when I wasn't revising, I was knocking down walls or plastering or wall-papering or fitting a new shower. The shower taught me one of the key lessons of DIY: some things are fair game, like decorating or putting up shelves, but some are better left to the professionals. There's a reason why plumbers and electricians go on long training courses, and I learnt it when the shower leaked through the ceiling and brought it crashing down into the kitchen.

December came round in a flash. The days shortened, the nights drew in, the inadequacies of our heating became clear, and the exams loomed large. The morning of the first one, Charlotte kissed me goodbye and wished me luck.

I read the questions ten times. There was no way I'd misread them this time. I did the workings, made my conclusions, checked and re-checked the answers and handed in the paper. If it didn't work this time, then I'd have to accept I wasn't going to be an accountant and call it a day.

The letter came on the twenty-third of December. We were lying on our mattress when we heard the flap of the post falling to the floor. I walked into the hall in my boxer shorts, the cold floor chilling my feet. It didn't matter. I wasn't going to be out in the cold for long. In a few seconds I was either going to be back in bed being comforted or back in bed celebrating.

The envelope was thin. Just one sheet of paper, then. Like last time. My mouth was dry and my hands were clumsy, pawing at the envelope. In the end, I ripped the top off, tearing a piece of the letter. I unfolded the paper, glancing at it sideways, afraid to read the contents, scanning it for clues as to what it said.

I saw only one word.

Congratulations.

I pumped my fist and shouted, holding the letter above my head. Charlotte appeared in the hall.

'What is it? Did you pass?' I didn't need to answer. She ran downstairs and hugged me, grabbing the letter from my hands and reading it aloud. She kissed me, her lips and tongue warm in the chill winter air, and dragged me towards the bed.

'Come on,' she said. 'I've never done it with an accountant before.'

*

1992. Another election year. This time I could vote, and it was finally going to be Labour's year, I just knew it. My constituency, Warrington South, was a bellwether seat, and it was going to fall.

I was especially confident now that the scourge of Labour leaders, Mrs Thatcher, was gone, condemned by the treachery of her party. If ever there was proof that you couldn't trust the Tories, it was there for all to see in the way they had disposed of the woman who'd brought them three election victories and allowed them to run rampant, enriching themselves by selling off the nation's assets. Thatcher, the creator of the yuppie, had been eaten by her own offspring. If it wasn't so sickening it would have been poetic.

Having had Maggie's technicolour leadership, the Tories went to the other extreme when they replaced her. John Major? Even *Spitting Image* couldn't satirize him. They just made a grey puppet that spoke in a monotone. It was funny the first time, but after that the joke wore thin. A bit like Major himself.

So how could Kinnock lose? Up against a man whose party was tired and unpopular and who had the charisma and personal charm of a dusty cupboard? It was impossible.

Dad and I stayed up to watch the election results flood in. The exit poll had it as a hung parliament. How we laughed. They were normally quite accurate, but this was another example of the Tory media trying to bias the election. Those polls were wrong and there was going to be a clear winner.

There was. By 2 a.m. it was clear that John Major was prime minister of Great Britain. Great Britain? Great? What kind of second-rate country would elect the Tories for a fourth time? After what they'd done? What would it take to get a Labour government? At that moment I was convinced we'd never win, ever.

At least Mike Hall won Warrington South. A small victory for common sense.

Major's government was limping into its second year when Charlotte woke me one morning with a smile on her face and a little white stick in her hand. We weren't really trying for a baby, but she'd stopped taking the pill and we were letting nature take its course. That plan lasted about a week. When she knew she was ovulating I became irresistible, morning and night. I had a brief insight into what Mel Gibson must have felt like all his life, although if I'm honest, I knew it wouldn't last.

'Is that what I think it is?'

She bit her lip and nodded, tears running down from the corners of her eyes.

I wondered how I'd explain it to my parents; they were traditionalists, and the wedding was still a way off. We had no money for it, and we didn't want our parents to pay, or rather, Charlotte didn't want her parents to pay. She'd decided it was an outdated tradition with its roots in the dowry. I pushed the thought away. Now wasn't the time.

Yelping, I grabbed her and dragged her onto the bed, kissing her and stroking her hair. My thigh slipped in between her legs and she pushed against it.

'Can you still, you know, have sex, when you're pregnant?'

'Let's find out,' she said. And it turned out you could.

When Charlotte was fourteen weeks pregnant, we went on holiday to France for a fortnight. I enjoyed the seafood and white wine; she stuck to mineral water and well-cooked steak, but we had a fine time. We came back and I had a busy week at work, then had a business trip for four days in Birmingham. By the time I returned, the holiday seemed a distant memory, but Charlotte had barely budged along the pregnancy time scale. How could so much time have passed without anything changing? She was now eighteen weeks pregnant.

If that was what it took to get from fourteen weeks to eighteen weeks, then how would we ever get to the full nine months?

And yet, the time came. One afternoon, the phone rang in the office and she told me to come home. I left to cheers from my colleagues and cries of 'Good luck' and 'Don't faint.'

When I got home I found out that all there was to do was more waiting. I tried to fill the time with useful activities. I started a 'contraction log', noting the time, duration and intensity of each contraction on a piece of A4 paper. They were irregular, and varied in strength, and by the time 10 p.m. rolled round we were starting to get anxious.

'Let's go to the hospital,' I said. 'It's been hours.' Charlotte had already phoned them up and they'd said not to bother, but I wasn't convinced.

'There's no point. The contractions have to be regular.'

Her mum stroked her head. 'Why don't you go? Set your mind at ease. Then at least you'll know.'

Charlotte gave in, and I grabbed the bag we'd packed with her overnight stuff. This was it. We were on our way.

We were at the hospital less than an hour before we were on our way back. It was a 'false labour', a term that I instantly hated. The doctor, a tired-looking young man with a BBC accent, told us that the contractions were doing nothing to open the cervix; they were just tiring Charlotte out, and it would be for the best if she went home and got some rest. They gave her a pill to calm the contractions down and sent us on our way.

She was pale and drawn, the flush of expectation drained by the disappointment. As we left, I took the doctor aside.

'Is she ok?' I said. The worst thing about pregnancy is the worry. You just want the baby – and the mother – to be ok. It stays like that for years afterwards. Once you're a parent you live in perpetual fear. 'Is there something wrong?'

'It's perfectly normal,' the doctor said. 'It's just the body's way of getting ready.'

'So the baby's on the way, then?'

'It'll come when it's ready. Could be tonight, could be a week from now. I can't give you any guarantees.'

A week from now; I couldn't wait that long. Not after all the waiting I'd already done. 'But if you had to pick a day, what would you say? Is it more likely tonight or in a week?' I lowered my voice further. 'Look, I know you can't give any guarantees because you don't want to get our hopes up, and I won't tell her what you say, but between you and me: is the baby on its way tonight?'

'Probably.' He smiled. 'If I had to lay a bet, I'd say that by midday tomorrow you'll be a father.'

'What were you talking to the doctor about?' Charlotte said when I came into the corridor outside the maternity ward.

'Just understanding the process. Let's get you home.'

It was a strange car journey. She was silent, her hands resting on the bump, her labour over before it had really begun. I was pretending to share her disappointment and to console her, but inside I was leaping from roof to roof singing the joys of the world.

'The baby'll come when it comes,' I said. 'Let's just go home and relax. The main thing is that everything's ok.'

'I just hope it comes soon. I don't want another false labour. How are you supposed to know when it's the real thing, anyway?'

'Oh, you'll know,' her mum said from the back seat. 'Trust me. It's unmistakable.'

And so it was. At 3 a.m., Charlotte woke me. She was on all fours on the bed, groaning deep, wild groans. They were so dramatic that

I thought for a second she was acting. One look at the pain on her face cured me of that illusion. Thank God I hadn't asked her. She relaxed and slumped onto her side. 'This is it,' she said. 'It's started.'

I grabbed the contraction log and noted the time. For the next six minutes she was quite normal, then she tensed. 'Another one's coming. Oh, God. Here it comes, oooohhh.' She climbed back onto all fours and clutched the head of the bed. 'It hurts, God, it fucking hurts.' She closed her eyes and I heard her teeth grinding. Slowly the noise died down.

'That was sixty-five seconds long,' I said, and noted it on the log. 'What was the intensity?' When I'd started the log earlier in the day I'd asked her to estimate the pain based on a scale of one to ten. Some had been as high as six.

'Is there a category for "fucking agony"?'

'I'll make that a ten.' I didn't ask about any of the contractions that came later. They all looked as bad, to be honest.

By six a.m., we were back in the hospital. I was frantic. At one point the doctor asked for an oxygen mask, which he put over Charlotte's mouth. I asked if she was ok. *Fine*, he replied, *just making sure the baby gets enough oxygen*.

My legs went weak. The baby needed oxygen. It was being starved of oxygen. He had to *do* something! An emergency caesarean! Anything!

The doctor told me to relax. I hadn't realized I was talking out loud.

I held Charlotte through the contractions, rocking her back and forth on the bed to ease the pain and telling her I loved her. She gripped my biceps so hard that her nails drew blood. I made a mental note. If anyone ever asked me for tips on assisting at your child's birth I'd tell them to make sure their girlfriend/partner/wife cut her fingernails. A small thing, but important, I'd say.

When the pushing phase began, I wondered whether Charlotte

was going to burst, she was so red. In between pushes her legs were shaking, like she'd run a marathon. I could see that she was at the end of her strength.

'One more,' the midwife said. 'Tell her one more. It's nearly here. You can see the head.' Her hands were cupped underneath Charlotte's vagina and I looked at the slick, bloody, hairy, crown of my first-born's head.

'Come on,' I whispered. 'One more push. One more. You can do it. Atta girl.'

I wrapped my hands around her shoulders and buried my face in her neck as the contraction came and she tensed. 'Come on, you can do it. I love you,' I shouted, the words audible only to her amidst her screams.

She gave a cry, then slumped in my arms. 'Is it here?' she whispered. 'Is it over?'

The doctor leaned forward, a grin on his face and a baby in his arms. He placed it gently on Charlotte's chest, its face against her skin. 'Congratulations. You're parents.'

I stared at the wrinkly pink body lying on my girlfriend. The doctor lifted its leg. 'Do you want to tell her?' he said. I looked at him, not understanding. 'The sex.' He lifted the leg again, to reveal a pair of tiny testicles and a shrivelled penis.

'It's a boy,' I said. 'We've got a son.' And then I started to cry.

I've never cried that way, before or since. I lost it. I dissolved into a sobbing wreck. I couldn't look at them. I stumbled into the antechamber to the delivery room where I leant with my hands on the wall and tried to compose myself. When I went back in, Charlotte held my hand and asked me if I was ok, as though I was the one who'd just given birth.

The midwife came over and congratulated us. 'It's nice to see a father so emotional,' she said. 'A lot of them try to hold it in.'

'You certainly weren't doing that,' Charlotte said. 'I can't wait to tell him one day how much his dad cried when he was born.'

'God,' I said. 'He's bound to think I'm totally uncool anyway. That'll just put the icing on the cake.'

'Are we sticking with the name? Now you've seen him?'

We'd tentatively chosen names for boys and girls, but were waiting until the baby was born to make the final decision. He was lying on her chest, wrapped in a white towel, fast asleep. A clutch of tiny pink toes poked out of the bottom of the cloth. 'Michael,' I said, trying out the name. 'Michael. I think that's right.

He looks like a Michael.'

Charlotte kissed the tuft of black hair on his head. 'Hello, Michael. I love you already.'

13.

2009: Dinner Interrupted

'How's your new bird?' Michael smeared Marmite on his toast, in a thick, glistening black layer. The smell made me feel ill. I didn't know how he could eat the stuff, never mind in the quantities in which he managed to consume it. I always bought the biggest jar available, but every time I checked it was empty. Sometimes I wondered what he was doing with it. He couldn't be eating it, surely, and if he was, it couldn't be good for him. What was Marmite, anyway? What was it made of? Did anybody know?

'She's not my bird, Michael. And don't call her that. It's disrespectful. She's not a teenager.'

He did that fake offended thing where you shake your head and whistle as if to say 'Ooh, you're very touchy.' He folded the entire piece of toast into his mouth. When he spoke his voice was muffled. ''Specially seeing as she's not your bird.'

I ignored him and checked my BlackBerry. Even though it was Saturday, I had thirty-nine emails since last night. Thirty-eight of them pointless, no doubt. People seemed to think that they needed to respond to every email they received, even if they had nothing to say. Particularly on Friday nights. It showed how dedicated they were. That was the main impact of making communication cheap and easy: the volume increased massively. I wasn't sure there had been a consequent increase in the quality of work done or information exchanged, in fact it was probably worse. I had to sift through all the crap, panning it for the gold. Before email, most of the memos, faxes or letters I got were important. You didn't bother sending them if they weren't; it was too much effort. That's why complicated application forms existed. The work to fill them in deterred speculative applicants.

'Have you given her one?'

I looked up sharply. I considered telling him off, but that was what he wanted. To wind me up by overstepping the mark. I decided to play the same game.

'One what?'

He stopped munching on his toast and looked at me, a sheepish grin spreading over his face.

'What do you mean, "given her one"? One what?' I persisted.

He blushed, his eyes flickering from left to right.

'Do you mean, have I made love to her? Have we made sweet, glorious love?'

'Dad, please! That's lame. No one calls it that.'

'Calls what that?'

'You know, doing it. No one calls it making love.'

'What do they call it then?'

He wiped his top lip with his index finger and rubbed his chin with his thumb. 'You know. Shagging. Banging.'

'We are talking about sex, aren't we? Lovemaking, right? That's the same as banging or shagging?'

'Yeah. So have you?' He was trying to regain control of the conversation.

'Well,' I said, tapping my nose with my forefinger. 'That's for me to know and you to wonder about.'

He thrust his fingers down his throat in a simulation of vomiting and put his plate heavily in the sink, toast crumbs spraying all over the kitchen floor. He swept them lazily under the counter with his foot while dusting the plate with water and stacking it in the drying rack, streaks of Marmite still clinging to the rim like skid marks in the toilet.

'That's not washed. Do it properly.'

'It is. It's fine.'

'Michael! Do it properly.'

'I have. To *me* that's properly.'

'Well, it's not to me. Or to any sensible person. It's filthy.'

He shrugged. 'We'll have to agree to disagree. You think it's dirty, I think it's clean. Never mind.'

'Michael! It's not a question of what you think. The plate's dirty.'

'Then why did you ask me?'

'What?' I was losing the thread of the conversation, if you could call it that. Ridiculous arguments; hallmark of life with a teenager. I'd had enough. 'It was a mistake. I mistook you for a rational human being. Now clean that up.'

He gave it a cursory rinse and walked out, mumbling that he was going to Carly's house, where people weren't so anal about everything. It was a small victory for parenthood: I still had to clean his plate properly, but at least the smears were gone.

I showered and changed, getting ready to go and see Mum. On my chest of drawers I kept a few old, framed family photos which I never looked at, but that morning they caught my eye. There was one of me and Mum and Dad at the lido in Morecambe, me in shorts, my hair wet from swimming, Dad in trousers and an open-necked shirt. Mum was wearing a dress with a kind of polka-dot pattern. I remembered that dress well. I'd heard them arguing about it when she'd bought it. Dad thought clothes should be practical, worn until they fell apart and then replaced. Anything else smelled of luxury, a sin of which he was particularly scornful. It showed moral weakness of the highest order.

There was another of my dad when he was a little boy, with his dad. I had fond memories of Grandad, a gruff old man who smelled of pipe smoke and dust, and who was always affectionate towards me. He was such a loving grandparent that it was hard to reconcile him with the stern-looking man in a flat cap in the picture, his hand resting on his son's shoulder, neither of them smiling. It looked like he hadn't shown much affection for Dad, but that was probably a generational thing: back then parents were less in awe of childhood. I wondered how their relationship was when Dad was fifteen. Somehow I doubted that he was asking Grandad if he'd given one to his bird.

I opened the top drawer. At the back was a small, oval silver frame, the metal tarnished. In it was a Polaroid photo of Charlotte and Michael, the edges cut off to fit the shape. I hadn't looked at it in years, hadn't looked at any photos of Charlotte. This was the only one I kept in the house. All the others were in a box in the garage. I didn't want to look at them, but I couldn't bring myself to throw them away.

I ran my thumb over the image. Charlotte was sitting in an armchair at her parents' house, holding him. She was totally focused on him, her love for her son expressing itself in that moment as an intense fascination, her concentration so intense that there was no space for any other emotion to register on her face. I'd taken the photo without her knowing, and she'd snapped up to look at me, protesting that she didn't look good, that she was tired that day, that

I shouldn't do that to her without her knowing. I'd smiled, humbled by the bond between mother and son that I was happy to be part of, but could never understand.

The phone rang and I put the picture back. It was Pippa. I hesitated before picking it up. My mind was filled with Charlotte.

'Pippa,' I said. 'Hi.'

'I made a reservation at that new place on London Road. Half-seven ok?' Of course. We'd agreed to go out for dinner.

'Great, that'll be fine. Thanks.'

'Do you want to meet there? Or go for a drink first?'

'Whatever you want. You decide.'

'I thought perhaps the London Bridge? We can sit on the terrace by the canal.'

'Sounds nice.'

'So shall we say six-thirty?'

I realized I didn't know where she meant. I'd not been listening. 'Sorry, Pippa, where was it again?'

'The London Bridge.' There was a silence. 'Are you ok, Graham? You sound a bit down.'

'I'm fine. Long week. Michael being a pain in the backside this morning. You know how it goes.'

'If you want to cancel, that's fine with me. We can reschedule for another time.'

'No, no. Tonight's fine. I'm looking forward to it. Sorry, Pippa. I've just got a lot on. See you later.'

I got there early, guilty that I'd been so off with her, and ordered a sparkling water. Six-thirty came and went with no sign of Pippa. It was unusual; the other times we'd been out together she'd been punctual. I was the one who arrived at the last minute, having been late leaving work, or stuck in traffic after dropping Michael off somewhere.

I fiddled with my BlackBerry, sent a few emails, played the little ball-bouncing game on it, sipped my water. By seven my glass was empty, and I went to the bar to get another.

I detected a hint of sympathy in the barman's smile. He must see loads of people stood up. If it happens one in every one hundred times, then he would have seen a person every few nights, sitting at their table alone for half an hour then finishing their drink and leaving. What did you do in these situations? How long did you give it before you called them, or left? No doubt Michael would have had some advice for me.

When I sat down again I called her. Her phone was switched off so I decided to finish the water and leave. As I drained the glass, the phone went.

'Graham. Sorry, I got called into work. An emergency. I hope you've not been waiting too long.'

'Since six-thirty. I was starting to think you'd stood me up. The barman's giving me funny looks, sitting here on my own.'

'God, I'm so sorry! Leave, if you want. Otherwise, I can be at the restaurant in twenty minutes. I'll be in my scruffs, but it's the best I can do.'

I left the pub, to sympathetic looks, and walked to the restaurant. When Pippa showed up she was dressed in jeans and a black fitted jacket. Her hair was pulled back and she was wearing little if any make-up. Despite the shadows under her eyes, her skin had a healthy glow, as though she'd just stepped out of the shower. She looked fabulous.

'I'm not normally this late,' she said, kissing me on the cheek. 'I've been at the hospital since this morning. There was a rail accident near Wigan and it was all hands on deck.'

'Don't worry. So you're a bit late. At least nobody died.' As I said it I realized how it sounded, given where she'd been all day. Perhaps some people had died. 'Sorry. I didn't mean it like that. I didn't think. It was just a figure of speech.'

'I know. It's fine. Let's order something. Apart from anything else, I'm starving.'

We were sitting by the window. As we looked at the menus I became aware of a tapping on the glass.

'Graham. There's a boy and a girl waving at us.'

I looked up. 'That,' I said, 'is my son and his girlfriend.'

'Excellent!' Pippa beckoned them inside. There was a triumphant smirk on Michael's face as they walked in.

'Hello,' she said, standing up and shaking their hands in turn. 'I'm Pippa. Do you want something to eat?'

'We already had something, but thanks anyway,' Michael said.

'Michael,' I said. 'How did you know we were here?'

'Saw it on the pad by the phone.'

'Ah. You should think of becoming a spy.'

'It was hardly that difficult, Dad. You'd left it by the phone in our house. It wasn't as though I had to break into the Tower of London to get it.'

'I was just making conversation. It was a joke.'

'Oh. A joke. Normally people signal jokes by saying something funny. Yours are harder to spot.' He had a cheeky grin on his face. The only time he really reminded me of when he was a little boy was when he grinned like this. He'd done it then as well, whenever he'd been caught doing something he knew he shouldn't be doing, which was most of the time.

Pippa laughed. 'You should think about it anyway. It'd be a fun job.'

'What do you do?' Michael said.

'I'm a doctor. A surgeon.'

Carly's mouth dropped open. She did not have a talent for disguising her feelings. 'A doctor? Really?'

'Really. At Warrington General.'

'Do people always ask you for medical advice at parties?' Michael said. 'I bet you get sick of it.'

'I don't mind that much. A lot of the time people need reassurance.' She sipped her wine. 'Why do you ask? Is there something you want to talk about?'

'No.' Michael blushed. 'I just wondered.'

'Well, if there is, let me know.' She had a gentle way of speaking. Even though she was teasing him she stayed on the right side of the line. There was no nastiness, just a gentle nudge in the ribs. The famed bedside manner. It was impressive: she had the measure of Michael immediately.

And of Carly; Michael's girlfriend was on edge, standing straight and slightly away from the table. Pippa reached out and fluttered her fingertips on her arm, resting them there. Carly visibly settled. 'Are you sure you two won't join us?' A calm, genuine offer.

Carly hesitated, drawn to Pippa, tempted to stay with her and soak up whatever it was she gave off. Michael glanced at me and the spell was broken. At the end of the day, what was on offer was Saturday night with his dad.

'It's all right,' he said. 'We're meeting Danny and the others.'

Pippa folded her napkin onto the table and stood up. 'It was lovely to meet you both. Another time for dinner, maybe?'

They shook her hand and left. As Carly went out of the door she looked back, her face stamped with admiration.

'You've made some friends,' I said. 'Kids seem to like you. You've got the golden touch. You'll have to tell me the secret sometime.'

'I don't think there is one.' She shrugged. 'Just treat them with respect, like you would anyone else.'

'If it was that easy we'd all do it. I struggle terribly to connect with Michael. Sometimes we seem to occupy different worlds.'

'You do occupy different worlds. The thing is not to judge his. You were probably the same with your parents. I know I was.'

'Have you got siblings?'

'None. I'm an only child, I'm afraid. I think my dad wanted a boy, but it never happened. He put all his hopes in my cousin. When I qualified as a doctor he was dismissive, but when my cousin qualified . . . it was as though destiny had fulfilled itself. Dad wanted me to be like Mum; a traditional, stay-at-homer. He mentioned it the other day. *If you hadn't been so bothered about your career you'd be married with children now.* He's right, as well. And that's my point. I don't try and tell him he's wrong, I just accept that we have totally different views of the world.'

I thought of my parents, of my mother's unquestioning assumption of all the household duties, of my father's unbending socialism. I'd always wanted to battle it, although I'd never really dared to argue with my dad. Perhaps that was the difference between me and Pippa, the reason why she managed to project such an effortless charm: she could accept, where I wanted to battle. That, in the end, was my father's legacy.

'No comment?' she said.

'I was just thinking, about my mum and dad. It was kind of the same between us as it is between me and Michael. I'm not sure that I want it to end in the same way. What's that poem? *They fuck you up, your mum and dad / They may not mean to, but they do*. Was that Larkin?'

She shrugged. 'I'm a doctor. We don't go in for poetry, or at least I don't, but it seems to me that it's just the same as saying *they make you great, your mum and dad.* If they're responsible for what's bad then they're responsible for what's good, right?'

'I just wonder if I'm doing the right thing with him.'

'And I wonder if I'm doing my job well, or if I'm a good daughter. That's just the human condition. If you care about something you worry about it. But for what it's worth, he seems a nice lad. Cheeky, but it could be a lot worse. Some of the kids his age we get in the hospital – on drugs, with knife wounds, abused by their dads or uncles or neighbours – it breaks your heart.'

She was right. It could have been worse. And you can't protect them forever. That's possibly the hardest lesson for a parent to learn.

14.

1994–95: Parked up

A few weeks after Michael was born, the MD called a meeting on the shop floor and told us that a large American corporation had bought the industrial conglomerate that owned us. The conglomerate specialized in chemicals, and it was the chemical businesses that the new owners wanted. The gearbox division was of no interest to them, so we were up for sale. If no buyers could be found, there was a risk we'd be shut down. Most of us left the meeting convinced we would soon be out of work.

I sat at my desk and rubbed my eyes. I was now the Financial Controller since Peter had retired and I'd passed my exams. With the extra work and the baby, I was exhausted. Michael was not a good sleeper. Fortunately, Charlotte was breast-feeding him, so she bore the brunt of the night feedings, but I was still lucky to get four straight hours of sleep. It felt like it would never end.

My phone went. It was Terry, the Finance Director. He wanted to see me in his office. When I got there, the MD, Andy Norris, was sitting on his desk. He was an ex-rugby player in his fifties with a growing belly and a florid complexion.

'Hello, Graham,' he said. 'I hear you're a father. Congratulations.'

He looked at the dark circles under my eyes. 'You certainly look like a new father. Don't worry. It gets easier.'

'Thanks, Mr Norris. He's like a vampire. Sleeps in the day, awake at night.'

'And he'll soon be sucking you dry!' Norris was pleased with his joke. I laughed politely. I was feeling quite sensitive at that moment. Jokes about money and babies when you'd just been told your job was at risk weren't that funny.

'So,' Terry said. 'Here's why we wanted to see you. As Andy said earlier, we're up for sale. At the moment, there are no buyers, but there may be a solution. We're thinking of an MBO.'

A management buy-out. They would buy the business and run it.

'If we do it,' Norris said, 'we need to retain key staff, which is why we're talking to you and a few others. Given the uncertainty, people will start looking for jobs. We want you to know that we're working on this. If it goes through and you stay around you'll get a loyalty bonus of five thousand pounds.'

A bad day was getting brighter. 'Will it go through, do you think?' I asked, sounding bolder than I felt.

'A good question. The key question, in fact,' Norris said. 'It's all about finance. We've got some backing, but we're still short.'

'How short?'

Terry stroked his moustache. 'A couple of hundred thousand. We've got the capital we need, that's not the problem. What's missing is the cash flow. We need a couple of hundred k working capital for the first three months. It's a short-term funding issue. As you know, Graham, in business, "cash is king".'

I nodded. I still found it thrilling that I understood the language of finance. I felt as though I was a member of an exclusive club.

'So,' Norris said. 'Here's a retention contract with the details. We hope you stick around, Graham. You're one of our rising stars.'

I blushed, mainly because I found his salesman's patter embarrassing. 'Thanks. I'll take a look.'

'There is one other thing,' he said, suddenly serious. 'There will be changes here. We can't run the business as it is.'

'Some people will have to go,' Terry said. 'Downsizing. It's the only way to stay competitive.'

'No,' I said. 'We can't do that.' *It's Thatcherite*, I wanted to add. I would have added, if I'd had the courage. If I'd been my dad.

'I understand your concern,' Norris said. 'But we're dealing with the harsh realities of business here.'

They're always harsh, the realities of business. No one ever says *the pleasant realities of business*, or *the gentle and accommodating realities of business*. You couldn't justify all the things you planned to do if you said that.

'We'll have to get rid of all the non-core activities and focus the business on where the value is – the precision manufacture of parts, the engineering. The other stuff'll have to go, the casting and machining.'

I knew the numbers and did a quick calculation. 'That's about half the workforce.' A thousand people. A thousand families.

Terry nodded gravely. 'We know. It's sad, but it's that or all of the workforce.'

Was it? Or could we have carried on, employing everyone but making less money? As it was, we made a profit. After the downsizing, we'd be leaner, making higher margins, more profit for fewer people. Was that better? As long as you were making a profit, paying your bills and paying people's wages, surely that was all that mattered? Wasn't it better to keep more people in jobs, but have less left over for the owners, than to fire half the workforce so that those owners could get richer? If ever there was an example of Thatcherite greed, this was it.

'The thing is, Graham, we need someone to manage the transition and we'd like you to do it. You know the business, know the workforce. It'll be better coming from someone like you than some outsider. They trust you.'

They trust you. They'll let you put the knife in. I was about to say no and march out of the office when Terry applied the *coup de grâce*.

'In return, we'd offer you a share of the business. It wouldn't be enough to retire on, not yet, but your future – and your family's future – would be secure.'

It was a betrayal of every principle I'd ever believed in, but I owed it to my family to at least consider it before I rejected it out of hand. I picked up the contract.

'I'll think about it.'

Norris smiled. 'If you could let us know on Monday. We need to get started.'

Stephen's words rang in my ears as my dad shook his head. *It's an excellent offer*, he'd said. *You should definitely consider it. These things tend not to come round more than once in a lifetime.*

He was right. But Dad did not see it that way. Not at all.

'There's no way you can do this. You're putting the workers out of a job so you can get rich. It's appalling. You'll not be able to sleep at night.'

'It's a good offer, Dad. It's a fair offer.'

He put the contract on the kitchen table and looked me in the eyes. 'Don't say you're considering this, son. Don't tell me that you think this is an ok way to behave, that the thought even enters your mind for a second. You should be out on the barricades with the workers, not inside plotting their downfall. You don't belong there.'

'Dad, I belong wherever I fit. Just because I grew up a certain way doesn't mean I can't change.'

'So you *are* thinking about it?'

'I'm considering it.'

'Then we've nothing to say to each other. We have no common ground, Graham.'

'Dad, come on. It's just politics, just ideas. Can't we agree to differ? I'm still Labour. It's hardly like I'll vote Tory, ever. But I have to make the best of my life.'

'Just politics?' His voice rose. 'Is that what you think? Just ideas? Those ideas matter. They make a difference in the real world, to people's jobs, people's livelihoods. People's lives. Some of the men you put out of work will never work again. Some will turn to drink. Some will lose their families. Children will grow up without their fathers. Remember the miners? I've seen it and you'll see it too. So, if you want, we can agree to differ. The difference is, I fought against it, and you took part in it. The difference is, I'll have a clear conscience and you won't. You'll always know that you put money before your fellow men.'

'So what do you suggest, Dad? That we follow the Russians? That's hardly been a success, has it? The problem with your ideology is that equality is all that matters. We should all be equally poor. Capitalism might not be the perfect system, but it's the best of a bad bunch.'

There. It was said. I was a capitalist. A Labour-voting one, for sure, but one none the less. I felt light-headed.

'Well, you make your own choices,' Dad said. 'Enjoy the cash, son.'

Being a father was incredible. I know that's no great insight and I know I'm not alone in saying that. Ask most parents and they'll say the same. The things people say sound like clichés because you hear them so much – it'll change your life, best thing that you'll ever do – but they're true.

You love the child in a way that you can't imagine beforehand. You watch every move they make, analyse every sound in case it's a word – and you hear words where there are none, I was convinced Michael said 'it's there' when he was six months, but Mum said it was wind – and muse on who they look like. You re-examine your own life to see what's really important, you think about your wife or fiancée or girlfriend differently, and you finally understand your parents.

The first few weeks were chaos, of course, and all we could do was try to survive. Michael ate every two to three hours, which meant, since she was breastfeeding, Charlotte was almost constantly awake. I did what I could: I brought him to her in bed, settled him down afterwards, but your role is pretty limited when you're a new father. You just do whatever you can to make it work.

After those few weeks some kind of pattern emerged and the fight for survival eased into something which was at least manageable. Not easy, but manageable. I remember the first time I felt as though we had it under control. One day, when Michael was about three months, I came home from work, put the key in the lock, opened the door . . . and nothing. The house was quiet. No beeping toys, no crying, no Charlotte dashing about trying to get stuff done while Michael slept.

I checked the porch for the buggy; it was there, so they were in. At that time Michael was sleeping in a Moses basket by our bed, so I climbed the stairs and opened the bedroom door.

Charlotte was lying on her side, her head resting on her outstretched arm. Her eyes were closed and she was breathing deeply. She was wearing a nursing top which was open, exposing her breast. Latched on, and fast asleep, was our son, a peanut in a bundle of blankets.

I studied her. Her mouth was half-open, her curly brown hair spreading out on the pillow beneath her head. In her sleep she looked like the girl I'd met when we were teenagers, and I wondered how we'd done it: how we'd made it this far as a couple, how we'd made each other happy for so long, how we'd made a baby.

Her eyes opened.

'Hi,' she said. 'How long have you been there?'

'Not long. A few minutes.'

'What are you doing?'

'Thinking how lucky I am. How much I love you.'

She smiled. 'I love you too. Come and lie with us.'

I lay on the other side of Michael, facing Charlotte. 'Can you believe it?' I said. 'We're parents. We're Mum and Dad. We're going to have to bring him up. Make him behave. Teach him manners. How do you do that? How are we supposed to know what to do?'

'I don't know. Just love him. Be there for him.'

'If you'd said we'd end up like this the night I gave you a can of warm lager at Tommy's I'd have laughed.'

'I know. I'm glad you did though, even though the lager was horrible and you had such an awful haircut.'

'You can talk. I remember the perm you got before you went to university. You were really proud of it.'

'I wonder what fashion disasters Michael will fall prey to?' She stroked his thin black hair. 'I doubt they'll be as bad as ours. The eighties were pretty spectacular when it came to terrible clothes.'

'Who knows? They might be back in when he's a teenager. He can borrow my shiny suits.'

'Whatever they are, I'm looking forward to finding out.' She lifted Michael's hand to her lips and kissed his wrinkly fingers. 'It's weird. I want him to stay like this forever. I don't want him to grow up, but I can't wait to see what he's like as a boy and a teenager and a man.'

Michael must have heard us and decided to register a protest because his eyes flickered open and he let out a loud cry, followed by a rumble and the smell of a full nappy.

Charlotte rolled on her back. 'Your turn, Dad,' she said. 'Wake me up when he's hungry.'

When Michael was one we had a birthday party which carried on long after he'd gone to bed. It was also a kind of house-warming for the barn, which finally resembled a house, with central heating, a new kitchen, carpets and an acceptable level of cold draughts. Where those draughts came from baffled me. I'd insulated every inch of the place, but still there were currents of cold air nibbling at your ankles.

Tommy was there with Pat, a girl he'd been seeing for a few months. Henrietta had come with her girlfriend, Jess. Stephen and Georgina had brought a case of champagne. My dad had brought sandwiches and cans of mild, and Mum was tipsy on Buck's Fizz.

That was what Dad did now. He refused to eat food and drink beer bought with the money I'd made by exploiting the workers, so when he showed up it was with his own food and his own drink. That was the accommodation we'd reached on our political differences. I was still his son, and that would never change, but he refused to share in the fruits of my immoral labour. It was infuriating, especially when we had other people there (mainly Charlotte's parents), but in a way I admired the stubborn old bastard.

'So,' he said, sipping his mild from the can. 'When are you two lovebirds going to tie the knot? You've been engaged for a while now. Engaged does mean "engaged to be married", you know.' He nudged me with his elbow. 'Or is she having second thoughts? Wouldn't blame her, myself.'

'Nice one, Dad. A joke.' I blushed. I still couldn't handle being teased by my parents. Friends, Mum, Charlotte, the in-laws: no problem. Mum and Dad? Forget it. We're eternally teenagers with our parents.

Charlotte put her hand on his shoulder. 'Soon. When Michael can walk.' She smiled. 'We want to hold his hand walking down the aisle.'

'Oh, petal,' my Mum said. 'That's lovely.'

We'd decided this a few days before the party. Charlotte didn't want Michael to be excluded from anything, so the wedding was on hold for another eighteen months or so.

The party ran late so we were feeling less inclusive when Michael chose the next morning to wake up at six a.m. Charlotte kicked me in the ribs. 'You get him,' she said. 'I don't feel well. I've got a headache.'

'So have I. It's called a hangover.'

'Fine.' She rolled out of bed. 'I'll go, you lazy git.'

I'd buy her some flowers later and beg forgiveness. It was better than getting out of bed.

It felt like ten minutes later that she woke me up and handed Michael over. I looked at the clock. It was ten minutes.

'I feel dizzy. Will you take him? I need to lie down.'

I looked at her. She was very pale and her eyes were dull. She fell over me into bed, shivering. It was a bad hangover. I hadn't realized she'd drunk that much.

'Mummy had too much to drink,' I said, swinging my legs out of bed and picking up Michael. 'The problem is, so did Daddy. Come on. Let's leave her to sleep.'

I carried our son into the kitchen and made a cup of tea. It was torture playing with him when you had a hangover. He was becoming a little boy, which meant that everything was either something to be thrown or something to be banged. The noises echoed around my battered skull.

After a handful of paracetamol and another cup of tea, my ravaged body began to settle down. I dressed him and put him in the buggy. A bit of fresh air and an hour with the paper would complete the cure. I'd pick one up at the newsagent's and bring it back. Charlotte could look after him for the rest of the morning.

I bought a loaf of bread, a packet of bacon, two bottles of Lucozade and the *Sunday Times*. The lead article was on the new Labour leader, Tony Blair. He was fast becoming my hero, although I wasn't about to fall into the trap of hoping he could bring power. I'd been burned too many times in the past. Dad hated him. As far as he was concerned, Blair could do what he wanted, but he wasn't Labour. Dad wanted the means of production in the hands of the workers. Nothing else would do.

Back at the barn, I made two bacon butties and a pot of tea.

'Come on, Mikey. Let's wake Mummy up with breakfast in bed.'

I went upstairs with the tray in one hand and Michael under the other arm, and kicked the door open.

'Wakey, wakey, Mummy,' I said. 'Mikey's made you something.'

I flicked on the light. She didn't look good. She was grey, a cement grey that I had never seen before. Beads of sweat clung to her temples, and her hair was stringy and dark. She looked at me, one eye seeming bigger than the other, and shook her head.

'Turn the light off. I can't eat. I feel awful. I think it's a migraine.'

'It's quite a hangover. Must be because you've hardly drunk anything for so long.' While she was pregnant and breast-feeding, she had steered clear of alcohol. Her tolerance must have plummeted.

Michael wriggled out of my arms and I put him down on the bed. He half-crawled, half-fell across to her, his arms and legs snagging in the tangled duvet. He flung himself on her, planting his face against hers and wrapping his arms around her neck. 'Mama,' he said. 'Mama. Mama.'

Charlotte groaned. 'Not now, Mikey. Mummy doesn't feel well.' She pushed him away and he fought to get close to her.

'Are you ok?' I was starting to worry. This seemed worse than a hangover.

'Yeah. Just get me a drink and some paracetamol. Thanks, darling.'

She stayed in bed for the rest of the day. I left the phone near the bed so she could call, and took Michael to see my parents. We got home around six. Half an hour later, she came down the stairs in her dressing gown.

'You look better,' I said. 'A bit more colour in your cheeks.'

'The headache's gone.' She picked up Michael. 'Sorry, baby. I missed you.'

'What was wrong, exactly?'

'Just the most awful headache, and a feeling of being on the edge of throwing up all the time. Thank God it's over.'

'Do you want to see a doctor? We can call the weekend surgery.'

'No, I'm fine now. It was probably just a bug. The drinking didn't help.'

I stood up and hugged her and Michael. He looked at me, then her, and smiled the smuggest smile I'd ever seen.

'I love you,' I said. 'And I love our family. It's a shame you're not feeling well. I was going to suggest that we think about making it one bigger.'

Charlotte laughed. 'How can you think that now? Look at me. I'm a mess.'

'Like I said. I was *going* to suggest it. I'm not now, though. Although, if you had a shower—'

She pushed me away. 'Are you serious?'

'Why not? You're feeling better, you said.'

She bit her lip. 'You give Michael his dinner and put him to bed. I'll jump in the shower.'

I watched her climb the stairs. Poor Michael must have wondered what was happening as the next ten minutes unfolded. He'd never eaten so fast in his life.

'Right, Michael,' I said. 'Can you kick this ball?'

On a whim, I'd bought a plastic football at a garage on my way back from work. I couldn't stop myself buying him presents when I was out: a huge Tonka truck, a farm set, a life-size stuffed monkey. I'd see them in a shop and picture his eyes lighting up when he saw it. Charlotte said I was spoiling him, but why not? Life had enough disappointments. You might as well enjoy the start.

He ran up to the ball, picked it up and tried to eat it. Then he put it in the corner, ran back to me and bit my knee. I picked it up and put it in front of him. 'Kick. Like this.' I mimed the action. Michael laughed and repeated the actions he'd just done: eat the ball, put it in the corner, bite my knee. He must have done it twenty times.

Mum came in with a cup of tea. She and Georgina looked after Michael while Charlotte was at work. Charlotte had started back on three days a week just after his first birthday. It was tough for her. She was used to seeing him all day, and it was a wrench to leave him, but she was settling into it now.

'Good day?' Mum said.

'Not bad. Usual, you know. You?'

'Oh, lovely. He's a treasure. He's an easy child. So affectionate.'

I smiled and looked at him, biting the ball in the corner. 'I don't think he's going to be a footballer.'

'Your Dad'll be pleased. He thinks he should play rugby. League, that is. Don't, for heaven's sake, let him play Union.'

The phone rang in the hall. It was Charlotte.

'Graham.' She sounded weak. 'Can you pick me up? I don't feel well.'

'Where are you?'

'Near Walton Gardens. In the phone box at the side of the road where you turn up towards the park. I feel awful.'

'Is it a headache again?'

'Yeah.' Her voice was slurred, indistinct. She was having trouble speaking.

'I'll be there in five minutes. Hold on.' I put my tea on the coffee table. 'Mum. Can you hang on a little while? Charlotte's not well and I need to pick her up.'

'Of course. What is it?'

'A headache. A migraine, I think. It's the second one.'

Mum frowned. 'Has she seen the doctor?'

'No. She's been busy.'

'She should see someone, Graham.'

'I'll talk to her. Look, I have to go.'

Charlotte's car was parked carelessly on the grass verge by the side of the road. She was bent over the steering wheel, her head in her hands. I pulled up beside her and yanked open the door.

'You ok?'

'I can't see.' Her voice trembled with fear and panic. 'I can't see. I'm blind.'

'You're not blind.' She couldn't be. People didn't just go blind like that. 'It's just a very bad headache. Let's get you home.' I took her hands and pulled them away from her face.

She tilted her head upwards and my legs went weak. Her eyes were unfocused and bloodshot, one pupil much bigger than the other. 'Graham, what's happening? Help me.' Her eyes flickered from side to side. It was clear she couldn't see me.

'Jesus.' I picked her up and put her in the passenger seat. 'We need to go to the hospital.'

I pulled out and put my foot down. Next to me, Charlotte groaned and shifted in her seat. 'I can't see. I don't want to be blind. Help me, Graham.'

'Charlotte.' I spoke loudly. 'Hold on. We're nearly there. You'll be fine. Listen to me. Just hold on.'

She shivered and wrapped her hands around her knees. 'I'm cold.' Her voice was whining and pitiful. 'I'm cold.'

She fell back in her seat, her mouth lolling open. 'Where's Michael?' She was mumbling now, her words thick in her mouth. 'Tell him I love him.' I looked at her, struggling to keep my eyes on the road. Her eyelids flickered and her head slumped against the car door.

'Charlotte! Charlotte!' She didn't respond. I slammed the brakes on and stopped the car in the middle of the road. There was a squeal of tyres, and the cars behind sounded their horns. I leaned over and titled her head upwards, holding her face between my hands. I lifted her eyelids and a wave of nausea hit me. Her eyes were bloodshot and unseeing.

'Charlotte! Wake up! Listen! Can you hear me?'

I slapped her cheek, harder than I'd meant to, and it bloomed red. At least that was some kind of response; even if she couldn't talk then at least her body was still working. I had to get her to the hospital.

Cars were backed up behind me, their horns beeping incessantly. In the mirror I saw the door of a blue Fiesta open and a man climb out. Before he could reach me, I slammed my foot down, my tyres screeching as I pulled away, the road ahead open. The man threw his hand up, his fingers in a V.

The hospital was on the other side of town, past three major sets of traffic lights. As I approached the first one I saw it was on red.

Come on, I thought, *change. Just change.* It stayed red. I jammed my hand against the horn, flicked the lights on full beam and shot straight through it, barging into the traffic coming from the other side of the junction. A grey delivery van braked sharply to let me in, the driver waving a tattooed fist at me out of his window. *If you only knew*, I thought, *you'd forgive me.*

A few minutes later I pulled up outside the hospital's A&E department and flung the double doors open. The receptionist looked up from behind her desk.

'Somebody! Help!' The people waiting on the rows of seats fell silent and looked at me. I pointed to my car. 'Quick!'

A nurse stepped in front of me and put her hand on my elbow. She was Mum's age; they'd probably worked together. 'What's the problem?'

'It's my fiancée, Charlotte. She's unconscious. In the car.'

The nurse called to a colleague, a young Asian woman, and they ran outside. The car door was open and the older nurse leaned in. When she emerged again she was as white as her uniform.

'Is she ok? Tell me she's ok.'

'Step back, sir.' She looked at her colleague. 'We need a trolley. Right now.'

The nurse leaned back into the car, holding Charlotte's head in her hands as her colleague ran into the hospital. I peered over the nurse's shoulder, trying to see what she was doing. She didn't seem to be doing much.

'Give her something,' I said. 'She needs something.'

'Please, sir. I'm doing all I can.'

There was a clattering of wheels on the tarmac and two orderlies skittered towards the car with a trolley. One went round to the passenger side, and with a deft strength they lifted Charlotte's limp body onto the mattress. One of them clipped up the metal sides of the trolley and they disappeared through the double doors.

The nurse put her hand on my forearm. 'You can wait in one of the offices. Come with me.'

I didn't want to wait in one of the offices. I didn't need special treatment. I didn't *want* to need it. 'I'll be all right in reception.'

She ignored me and steered me away from the main desk and into a room with a desk and an overhead projector. I slumped in a chair.

'I'll make you a cup of tea.' She stood in the doorway. 'Someone'll be along as soon as they can.'

'Do I need to fill in a form?' I was filled with an urge to make sure the paperwork was correct; I suppose it was the only thing I could do to help.

'No. We can sort that out later.'

She shut the door, and a silence settled in the room. I got to my feet and walked to the door, then back again, then to the window. A young girl with a baby in a pram was standing outside smoking. She saw me looking and scowled. She must have thought I was a disapproving doctor. I wished I was. I wished there was an alternate world where I was here to work, and not here with my sick fiancée.

My sick fiancée. I should have known something was wrong when she had the headache after the party. Charlotte never complained. I should have realized it was serious. All the evidence had been there; I'd just ignored it. I should have made her go to the doctor. If I had, then all this could have been avoided.

I felt myself spinning into a panic and took a deep breath. I was getting ahead of myself. It was probably nothing, just a combination of some bad bug and new parent fatigue. After all, she was tired. She was back working and Michael still wasn't sleeping; it was hard.

Anyone could get ill. I relaxed a little. At heart, I had faith in the universe. She'd be ok. We'd be ok. Michael and I didn't deserve to lose her.

I distracted myself with a wall-chart showing the anatomy of the inner ear. The pictures were alien, the words incomprehensible. I was examining something called the organ of Corti when the door opened.

The nurse handed me a cup of tea. 'I put milk and sugar in,' she said. 'It's a good idea to have something sweet.'

'How is she?'

'The doctor is with her. He'll be here soon.'

'Is it serious?'

She looked at me, blinking. 'I can't say; I don't know. The doctor will be here any minute.' She paused. 'Is there someone you can call to come in? You can use the phone on the desk.'

'Call? Why? Why do I need someone to come in?' I tugged at my neck. 'Is it because there's a problem?'

'I don't know that. I just think it's good to have support, that's all. I'll be back soon. Try not to worry.'

Try not to worry? Was she joking? I knew it was her job to reassure people, but still. First they put me in this room, then they tell me to call someone for support. I took another deep breath and picked up the phone.

My dad answered after a few rings. 'Yup?'

'It's me. I'm at the hospital.'

There was a pause, and then he spoke, his voice alarmed. 'The hospital? Is it Mike?'

'It's Charlotte. She's ill.'

'Ill? What do you mean, ill?'

'I don't know. She collapsed. I don't know what's going on.'

'You want me to come?'

'Please. Thanks, Dad.'

I couldn't stay still. I walked from the window to the door and back again; read the ear chart and the hygiene requirements and the evacuation plan over and over. All the time my mind raced, weighing the possible causes and outcomes. It was like when you're falling in love and you constantly try and second-guess the other person, find clues to how they feel in what they do or say. You can never know for sure until the glorious moment when they look at you and smile and say they love you.

I'd done that with Charlotte when we were schoolkids. On weekdays, when we were apart, I'd held on to every detail of the weekends together, weighing and sifting them for meaning. I used to imagine her watching me at school, being proud of me as I answered a question right or scored a goal, or whatever. It was a comfort to pretend she was always there.

It still was. Whenever anything happened she was the first person I told; whenever I did anything it was with her and Michael in mind. Going to work, building a house, saving for the future. All for them. They – she – were everything to me. Everything. Which was why she'd be back home soon. Any alternative was too awful to contemplate. There couldn't be anything wrong with her. There just couldn't.

The door opened.

An Indian doctor came in. He was in his fifties and had thick black hair swept back from his forehead. The nurse followed behind him.

'It was your wife who was brought in just now?' he said.

'Fiancée. We're not married yet. We're planning it soon.'

He nodded. I waited for him to congratulate me. That's what people did when you said you were engaged. I'd become used to it.

He folded his arms, then put the tips of his fingers on his bottom lip. He glanced at the nurse and gave a small nod. She pulled out a chair and pushed it towards me.

'Take a seat.' The doctor looked at me from behind a pair of gold, half-moon spectacles which did not hide the sadness in his dark eyes. 'I'm afraid I have bad news. I'm sorry.'

'What kind of bad news?'

'There was nothing we could do.'

He started to explain but I didn't hear it; I didn't need to. The world was reduced to one fact; there was nothing else to know.

Charlotte was dead.

Part Two

1.

1995: A Helping Hand

The church was full for the service. I stood at the lectern, took out my notes and looked at the congregation: a chessboard of black cloth and white faces, silent with an instinctive respect for my grief. It had been four days since that dash to the hospital, four days that had passed in a blur of uncomprehending pain. Somehow I'd got through them. I'd not been to work, not even thought about it. Not even started to think about it. It was somewhere in the uncharted badlands, way off the map of my consciousness. I was a long way from working again.

Dad had picked me up at the hospital. I sat in the car tapping my fingers on the dashboard as though deep in thought.

'She's gone,' I told him, although he already knew. 'Not alive.' Being not alive sounded somehow better than being dead. It sounded like it was one side of a coin you could flip over at will: alive / not alive. Not alive / alive.

She'd suffered a massive brain haemorrhage. The doctors had no real explanation. It was just one of those things that sometimes happen to an otherwise healthy human being. There was nothing anyone could have done. I told them about the headaches; could we have found it earlier? They said that it would have made no difference. They said that the doctor would have thought it was a hangover, like we had, and sent her away. Were they telling the truth? I didn't know. Perhaps it would have saved her if we'd gone to the doctor the first time, perhaps it wouldn't. I suppose they said it to stop me feeling guilty.

If that was their goal, it was pointless. I blamed myself completely; of course I did. Was it my fault? Not really, but so what? Someone had to be to blame, and I looked at myself. Although even if I'd not felt guilty, I wouldn't have felt any better. There's a point so low that you can't get any lower. The guilt was just another shade of agony, another texture of pain. I had no idea that you could hurt this much.

I looked down at my notes, struggling to bring the words into focus. I couldn't remember what I'd written the night before, and as I read them now I saw that my notes were patchy at best, and rambling and incoherent at worst. In any case, they were mostly illegible. I set them aside. There was only one thing I could say that meant anything.

'Thanks for coming,' I said. 'You don't need me to tell you what Charlotte meant to us all.' I looked at the front row: at Michael, sitting on his Grandma Georgina's knee as she dabbed her eyes with a handkerchief. At my mum, her eyes cast down at the stone floor. At my dad, facing forward, his face set and expressionless, while tears ran down his cheeks. 'I . . . I tried to write something about what a wonderful partner she was, what a loving mother, what a devoted daughter and loyal friend, but nothing I could think of could do her justice.' My voice was breaking, and I looked at my shoes, rubbing away the tears with my sleeve. I started to speak, but the tears came again, and I sobbed, once – a deep heave that shook my whole body – and then I dissolved. I looked at the coffin, and at the congregation, and at the coffin again. 'I'll miss you, Charlotte,' I said, forcing the words out. 'We all will.'

The next morning I was woken by the sun: sweating, dry-mouthed and with my head banging. I fought to stay in the half-dream, but a growing awareness of an urgent need to piss dragged me to consciousness and I stumbled from my bed.

Charlotte was dead.

It was the same thought that greeted me every time I woke up, every time my mind wandered from whatever short-term task I had imposed on it to distract it. It was the thought that made me dread the day, dread wakefulness, dread the condition of being alive and without her.

I was never free of the pain; it never left me alone to get over it. It was a physical presence, a muscular ache that made me want to curl up and forget the world existed. Everything looked subtly changed, as though I had been born again into a world that looked like mine but was of a changed colour. The only time I forgot the pain, for the briefest of moments, was when I awoke and was thoughtless; then, with the first thoughts it came back, and my chest tightened, the day darkened, my heart broke anew.

The days were endless. I couldn't escape her. I willed myself not to think of her, but in the act of doing so I thought of her. If I heard a song, I thought of times we'd sung it together; if it was a new song, I thought of how she would have liked or disliked it. If I saw something on the news, I'd picture myself discussing it with her. I imagined her watching me, and I held a silent conversation with her spectre, explaining what I was doing, sharing the details of my life. No great thoughts, or declarations of love; just the comfort of the humdrum. And so I was reminded, constantly, that she was no longer there.

I didn't see how it would end: I felt constrained by everything I saw and everything I did, like a hot-air balloon held down by a thousand invisible silk threads, tiny ropes that bit into my flesh.

I would have killed myself, no question, if it hadn't been for Michael. On more than one occasion in the days that followed I decided to do it, to end it, but each time I imagined someone explaining to my son what his dad had done – telling him not to think badly of me, that I wasn't a coward – and I pulled back. It was close, though. I craved obliteration.

Downstairs, I heard Michael in his walker, zipping from wall to wall. He was nearly on his feet, but while he was still unsteady he used the yellow plastic contraption that allowed him to move around. Charlotte had bought it. She dealt with those kinds of things, what foods he was ready to eat, what clothes he needed. I shuffled downstairs, picked him up and went into the kitchen.

'Morning.' Mum was making him some breakfast. Her face was lined with worry. She'd aged years in the last few days. 'Would you like some tea, love?'

'I'll do it. You sit down. What are you making for him?'

She looked at me, almost pityingly. 'Don't worry, love. You take a seat. You've plenty of other things to deal with.'

Michael put out his arms for my mum. 'Mama,' he said. 'Mama. Mama.' It was one of the few words he knew, and he used it often.

My mum took him and kissed his forehead. 'I'm not your mama,' she said. 'I'm your grandma. But I love you very much, just like your mama does.'

Did, I thought. Like your mama did. The fist lodged in my chest tightened and I turned away. In the living room I filled a glass with soda and added a slug of whisky, just to unclench that fist. A weak one. That would do for now. Just take the edge off the pain. Just to make sure, I took a slug from the bottle, the hot liquid burning through the fist. When I turned round, Mum was in the doorway.

'You shouldn't drink in the morning.' Her voice was flat and blunt. 'It's not good. I know you're sad, but that's not the answer.'

'I know. And I'll stop, soon. As soon as the pain dies down.'

She bowed her head. 'I hope you do, love. You've got this lad to look after. He needs his dad.'

By lunch, the whisky had worn off. Mum had gone to the shop to get some food for the week and I was feeding Michael his lunch. We alternated mouthfuls: him of mushed up vegetables, and me of white wine. By the time we were done, I'd had most of the bottle. I left him in his high chair while I washed up and put the bottle back in the fridge.

It was so obvious on the bottom shelf. Mum would see it and know that I'd had the best part of a bottle of wine. It'd be better to tip the rest down the sink and throw the bottle out.

At the sink, I hesitated, the bottle nearly horizontal, the liquid ready to pour out. What difference did it make if I tipped it away or drank it, as long as the bottle was gone? I lifted the neck of the bottle to my lips and sucked the rest of the wine down in one.

The back door opened and my dad walked in.

'Though I'd pop in to see how you've been,' he said. He looked at the empty bottle in my hand. 'You drinking?'

'Just a few glasses with lunch.'

'You've done nothing but drink since she died, Graham. It's time to get a grip.'

'Dad, I'm fine. It's nothing. It'll pass.' I was slurring my words.

'You're pissed as a fart,' he said, his face covered in disgust. 'Where's that boy? I'll look after him until your mum gets back. Go to sleep, son, and when you wake up, think on what kind of a man you want to be.'

'Dad,' I began. 'It's not that easy. I miss her. I don't know what to do without her.'

If anything, the look of disgust hardened. 'Listen. We all of us have sad things, tragic things, to deal with. All of us. What matters is how you react. You can either wallow in self-pity or you can shut the fuck up and get your nose down.'

I knew he was right. It didn't help much.

When I woke up, I heard them playing downstairs, Michael, Mum and Dad, a family missing a generation. Perhaps they'd be better that way, without me and my grief messing things up even more. My head was throbbing and I closed my eyes, hoping to recapture the dream I'd been having about the time Charlotte had taken me back.

If I had known how bad this was going to be, I'd never have gone round that New Year's Day. It would have been better to have lost her then, before we wrapped our lives together. The worst of it was the sense of an unbridgeable gap between us, the feeling that she was still there, but that I couldn't connect with her. We aren't prepared for the feeling of loss when someone dies; we don't even have words for it. We say things like *gone*, *departed*, *deceased*, *passed away*, all of which have the sense of moving from one state to another, as though the person has gone somewhere, as though they have a continued existence. We don't say that the person has turned back into carbon atoms, and if we did it wouldn't mean much, because we don't think in that way. We think of the person as still existing.

Which makes it worse. Your entire being is reaching out to the person you've lost – there's another one, *lost*, as though you can find them – but at the back of your mind you know it's hopeless. You'll never see them again. Never hear their voice. Never see them kiss their son. And it makes you want to stop existing yourself.

Over the next few days I collapsed to my most basic core, found the minimum requirement for survival. I did as much as I could: fed and changed Michael, read to him, hugged him, told him I loved him, broke down in tears, but that was it. Once he was asleep, I hit the bottle, drinking hard and fast until I fell into unconsciousness. It wasn't sleep; for starters, it was dreamless. I learnt early that you had to drink enough to stop the dreams, because they were the worst. In them, she was alive, and you woke up only to lose her again.

I can understand all those myths about people going to the underworld to rescue the dead or even just to have a chance to say goodbye, even though they know the consequences will be terrible. I would have done it, in a heartbeat. It's like that Stephen King book about the Indian cemetery that brings animals back to life. The father buries his dead kid there, hoping that it'll work, even though he knows it'll end in tears. But if there was a chance, any chance, how could he have resisted? How?

So what do you do? Where do you look? You can't look to the past, the memories are too painful. You can't look to the future, it's too bleak. So you stay in the moment, trying to ignore what's happening. Which is where the drink comes in.

Alcohol is about the only thing that can get you through. It's your best friend, your only friend, the one friend that never judges you for spending time in its company. It gets you through the worst of the disaster, holds your hand while you cross the road. What I didn't know then was that once you're on the other side it wants to be paid, and the price is a piggy-back for the rest of your life.

2.

2009: Nine Stitches

The sun was nearly set, the last vestiges of its orange halo winking out over the horizon. I watched it go, sitting on the deck I'd built in the back garden with an open book balanced face down on my knee. Pippa had recommended it, *The Rotters' Club*, by a guy called Jonathan Coe. I was enjoying it: the depiction of the UK in the 1970s reminded me of my childhood. It was a vanished world, even though it was hardly that long ago. The weird thing was that the change wasn't uniform. It went in bursts. Between 1980 and 1990 everything seemed different – technology, manners, politics – whereas what had really changed from 2000 to 2010? The eighties were the ancient past. Today's world would have been science fiction to people in the eighties; to those in the nineties it was their birthright.

My BlackBerry buzzed and I picked it up. 'Hello,' I said, cheerfully. I was expecting a call from Pippa, so I didn't look at the number.

'Is that Graham Melton?' A man's voice, a Scouse accent, sounding angry. I sat up.

'Yes. Who's speaking?'

'Billy McAndrew. Carly's dad.'

What had Michael done now? The fact Carly's dad was calling on a Saturday night was not a good sign. The fact he sounded angry was even worse. I braced myself to apologize on Michael's behalf, and got ready for a fresh bout of humiliation at the hands of my son.

'Hello, Billy. Is there something wrong?'

'Damn right there is. Your lad's causin' trouble again.'

'What do you mean, causing trouble?'

'Fightin'. And draggin' our Carly into it.'

'Look, I'm sorry, Billy, but I'm sure Michael's not the one causing the fights. He's been having some trouble with some lads – Carly's ex-boyfriend, or something.' I pictured the hoodies we'd run into. 'Is he ok?'

'He's all right.' It sounded like he didn't want him to be. 'Listen, mate, I don't care who's startin' it. I don't want my girl involved.'

I started to feel angry at Billy McAndrew. Who did he think he was, blaming Michael? It was those thugs who were behind all this, but I bit my tongue. Michael wouldn't thank me for falling out with his girlfriend's father. 'Ok, I'll have a word with him. Thanks for calling.'

'First, you can pick him up. He's at ours. I'd throw him out, but he won't leave.' The line went dead.

Billy McAndrew was in his early thirties, red-haired, about six-foot tall and with wide, thick-set shoulders. The beginnings of a paunch were filling out his T-shirt. I shook his hand; his fingers were like sausages and his skin was rough. I guessed he was a labourer of some sort.

'Nice to meet you, Billy.'

He nodded and gestured for me to come inside. The door opened directly onto the living room. A woman stood in the doorway. I assumed she was Carly's mum. She looked just like her: dark-haired, petite, pretty, too much make-up. If I hadn't known different I would have thought she was her sister. She couldn't have been much older than thirty. Billy introduced her; she was called Kerry. Michael was sitting on the couch next to Carly. I looked at him and saw why he wouldn't leave the house. His face was a mess.

'Michael! What the hell happened?' I bent down to look, but he turned his head away. His cheek was red and swollen, his lip split, and there was a deep cut over his left eye. His hair was thick with blood.

'I'm fine. It's no problem.'

'You need to see a doctor. I'm taking you to A&E.' I looked at Carly's mum. 'Has he been sick? Shown any signs of concussion?'

'No.' She was a real Scouser, with a full-on accent. 'He has been drinking tea, though.'

What did tea-drinking have to do with anything?

I gestured to Michael. 'What happened?'

'They jumped me, at the end of the street. Me and Carly had just got off the bus.'

Carly lifted her hand to her mouth. The thick mascara around her eyes was smudged. She'd been crying. 'It was terrible. They were kickin' him. On the floor.'

'What?' I pictured my son, lying on the floor while a bunch of yobs kicked him in the head. It was obscene. Unthinkable. 'Was it those lads, the same ones as last time? I'm calling the police. It can't go on like this.'

'No! Don't you dare, Dad! You'll make it worse.'

'It's ok for now,' Billy said. 'I sorted them out.'

Michael looked at Billy, his expression a mixture of admiration and fear. 'Mr McAndrew came out and stopped them.'

'Still, it can't go on. I'm calling the police.'

'I wouldn't bother,' Billy said. 'They won't do owt.' His face hardened. 'I don't want the cops involved, I don't want any more trouble and I don't want to see Michael round here again. I won't help him out again, it's not my problem. I don't want him seein' Carly no more neither.'

'Dad!' Carly started to cry again. 'Why?'

'Because you don't need the trouble. No arguin'.'

'But I want to see him!'

'Carly, put a sock in it! I don't want to hear no more.'

The room fell silent. I beckoned to Michael. 'Come on. Let's get you to a doctor.' On our way out, Billy put his hand on my shoulder. It felt very heavy.

'Hang on a minute.' He waited for Michael to get into the car then spoke quietly to me outside the front door. 'I don't want them seein' each other,' he said. 'It won't work. It won't go nowhere anyway. He'll go off and do his thing, college or whatever.' Billy let go of my shoulder. 'Carly has to go to school with them lads. She doesn't need the hassle.'

Neither did Michael. I looked at him, watching us from the passenger seat. His face was purpling, the bruises dark in the dim light of the few working streetlamps. I didn't want any more of this. If this was the price of letting him and Carly carry on their relationship, it was better to stop it now, before it went too far. This way it was Billy's idea, so we'd share the blame.

I bit my lip. 'Ok, I'll talk to him.'

Billy nodded and closed the door behind him.

Four hours and nine stitches later, four of them above his eye and five in his scalp, we pulled out of the hospital car park.

'Billy seems a nice bloke,' I said.

'You should have seen him. I was on the floor and he came out of his front door. He shouted something and they stopped, then he grabbed one of them, the one who used to be Carly's boyfriend, and pushed him against the wall. The others legged it. He gave him a right bollocking, then sent him packing. He's well hard.'

'Not like me, then.'

Michael started to speak then stopped himself. 'I didn't mean it like that. It's different. They were totally scared of him.'

Great. Another reason for Michael to look down on me. I wasn't as hard as Billy McAndrew.

I took a deep breath. 'Billy and I agreed that it's for the best if you and Carly don't see each other anymore.'

I felt him stiffen beside me. 'Are you joking?'

'No. You don't need any more trouble with those lads. It's getting out of hand.'

'It's fine! Billy sorted them out! This was your idea, wasn't it? Just because you're sacred of them, doesn't mean every one is. Billy's not. *I'm* not.'

'You can say that now. A few hours ago it was a different story though, wasn't it?'

Why was I trying to prove he was scared? Because I was? Because I wanted him to be in my camp, not Billy's? He was my son. I should be supporting him, but here I was mocking his attempt to be brave. I couldn't help it. I couldn't help but rise to the bait.

'I'd like to have seen you in that situation,' he said quietly. 'At least I tried to do something. At least Billy could help me out. At least he's not a pussy.'

This time I kept quiet. I was the adult; I had to stop this spiralling out of control. He was a teenager; he was just discovering the power of words to hurt and he was trying them out. I had to force myself to remember that this was a child speaking, a child in a young man's body, and that he didn't mean it, not really. If he had known how much it hurt to hear that, he wouldn't have said it. Or would he have been glad, glad to know how much it hurt, glad with the unreflecting sadism of a child?

'Anyway, we agreed. You're not to see Carly. That's the end of it.'

He laughed. 'Ok. I won't see her, honest. I promise.' He paused. 'How are you going to stop me? This is bullshit. You *can't* stop me.'

'Michael!' I shouted. 'That's enough! I'm your father! You're not to see her!'

He fell silent and looked out of the window. Did I know then that it was hopeless? That my ban on him seeing her was as effective as the warnings about illegal downloading of songs or the dangers of smoking? Probably. But it had been a long day, and I didn't want to think about it. It was easier to accept that it was over and done with.

3.

1995: One More Question

I thought about it all day. That first drink, that delicious, eye-opening slug of beer or wine or whisky. In the morning I imagined it. At lunch I thought about how the food would taste better that night when I had something to go with it. In the long afternoon as meetings dragged by I told myself that in a few hours it would be over and I'd be back in the arms of my beloved.

I'd decided I had to control my drinking a few weeks after the funeral. Not stop – that was unthinkable – but control. Find a way of making it work. The grief was no less present, but the intensity of the pain had moved down a notch; no longer searing, too hot to touch – now merely a daily torture. Besides, I could see that my, and Charlotte's, parents, were beginning to wonder whether I was stable enough to carry on looking after Michael. I probably wasn't, but I needed him. He was the only thing that kept me sane.

So, I set some rules. No drinking during the day and no drinking in front of Michael. This was a big mistake.

The problem with rules like those is that, as long as you observe them, the rest of the time you can do whatever else you want. As long as it was evening and Michael was asleep I could drink as much as I wanted. This had two unforeseen consequences.

The first was that I started putting him to bed earlier and earlier. Normally, I got home from work around six, took him from my mum or from Georgina, smiled at them, sober and responsible, then bathed, fed and read to my son. By eight he was asleep, which meant that by seven-thirty I was watching the clock, wishing the seconds away, my mouth moistening with saliva as I anticipated that first long, strong drink. You'd think that five tender minutes holding your sleepy, motherless son would fly by and that you would savour every precious second, trying to hold on to the moment, a moment that would so soon be a memory as he morphed into a boy, then a teenager, in front of your eyes. But no, as the chance of a drink got closer so did the desire to drink it, and I would put him in his crib and shut the door as soon as I thought he'd stay asleep, so I could drink undisturbed. So, gradually, his bedtime crept forward, until he was asleep by seven.

The second unforeseen consequence was that, when I was in the legitimate drinking time, I used it to its full. I guzzled alcohol. I craved drunkenness. Before, when I had imposed no limits, I could drink in a more measured fashion, not worried that I had only a window of drinking opportunity. Now, I had to make the most of every minute. So, by ten, I'd have drunk two or three strong beers and at least half a bottle of wine, and I'd be pouring myself a large whisky on ice and thinking about bed. By eleven-thirty, and two or so whiskies later, I'd be asleep. Sometimes in the night I'd wake up, thirsty, aware of the fact that I needed to re-hydrate, so I'd pour an orange juice – then add just a splash of vodka to help it go down.

I'll tell you something about being a drunk, the key to it all: it's the first drink that counts. However much you drink afterwards, it's the first one that takes your hand and welcomes you across the threshold. When you've had that one drink, you're in a different place. You're home. You're among friends. You're safe, feet up by the fire. When you've not had that drink, you're out in the cold, exposed and nervous.

Every day, more or less, Michael woke up at 6.30 a.m. That was fine by me; I'd had seven hours' sleep. Rubbish, fitful, stuporous sleep, but sleep nonetheless, and I could get out of bed and make his breakfast, sip my tea, get him dressed and hand him over to whichever grandma was on duty that day. That was all I needed to do. It was about survival.

The grandmas. Angels, both of them. I think they'd thought their child-rearing days were over, but there they were, looking after Michael, the pride they felt in the closeness of their relationship with him visibly tinged with sadness at the reason for it. Incredible, selfless devotion. An example I appreciated but which I singularly failed to follow.

Fridays were the worst days. The weekend loomed, long and empty. I dreaded its arrival from Thursday morning, which meant that Thursday was always a heavy night; sometimes I downed the best part of a bottle of Jim Beam or Bell's after the beer and wine. I wanted to drown Fridays in my hangover. One desperate Thursday, I stayed up later than usual, getting beyond the first bottle of whisky and well into another.

The morning after, Georgina let herself in with her key. I was feeding Michael some of my toast.

'Morning.' She was always cheerful, but looking back it must have been an act. If I was feeling bad, how must it have been for her, Charlotte's mother? That's the thing I'm most ashamed of now, my selfishness. We can all succumb to drink or drugs or depression, but the memory of my selfishness still sets my cheeks burning.

'Are you ok? You don't look well.' I didn't. I'd seen myself in the mirror. I was pale, my eyes and face hollow.

'Fine. Maybe some 'flu coming on.' It was hard to speak, hard to concentrate enough to get the words out. When I moved my head the world went out of focus; when I stayed still, it spun.

'Well, take it easy. If you feel bad, come home early and get some sleep.'

I nodded and thanked her, picked up my car keys and kissed Michael goodbye. In the car, I sat behind the wheel, on the verge of throwing up. My hands and legs were shaking and I was sweating profusely.

I forced the key into the ignition and started the engine. The sound seemed distant, somehow unreal. I drove like I was in a dream. At one point, I think I nodded off. I was brought round by the sound of a siren.

The police car behind me was flashing me to pull over. I indicated and slowed to a halt.

The officers put on their hats on they climbed out of the car. I wound down my window and one of them leaned over to look at me.

'Morning, sir.'

'Morning.'

'Have you been drinking, sir? Maybe a heavy night last night? You were driving somewhat erratically.'

I nodded. 'I had a few last night.' There was no point denying it. It was just bad luck, that, of all the days, this was the one they'd seen me, although in truth, I was probably well over the limit every time I stepped into the car.

'Would you mind getting out of the car, sir? We'll have to ask you to take a breathalyser test.'

*

A six-month ban. Not that bad, considering how far over the limit I was, but my lawyer argued special circumstances: clean record, single parent, grief-stricken, and the magistrate was lenient. The firm helped as well, paying for a taxi every day. It was embarrassing, of course, and everybody found out, but I didn't really care. That wasn't high on my list of concerns.

Dad didn't take it well. Drink-driving was proof positive of social irresponsibility. He gave me a lot of grief and little sympathy. *Time to get yourself together, what if you'd hit a child?* I knew all that already. The problem was, none of it meant anything to me. None of it penetrated the carapace of self-pity I had built up around myself.

So, the ban was inconvenient and embarrassing. It wasn't all bad, though. Every cloud has a silver lining and all that. At least it freed me up to have a drink at lunchtime.

Three weeks after the ban I was slumped on the sofa, my feet resting on the coffee table next to an empty bottle of wine. I was deciding whether to open another bottle or switch to whisky when the doorbell went.

I decided not to answer it. Whoever it was could wait. It was nine-thirty and I was already well insulated from the world. I had no intention of letting it in to chill me with its demands.

I heard the sound of a key in the lock, then the front door opening. I sat up as the door to the lounge swung open. Stephen walked in, followed by Dad.

Dad spoke first. 'No surprises here, then,' he said softly. His habitual gruffness was gone, replaced by a sad resignation. 'I was hoping you'd be sober, son. Then we wouldn't have to say what we're about to say.'

Stephen looked at him. 'Do you want me to do it?'

'No,' Dad said. 'He's my son.' He sat in the armchair opposite me, his lip trembling. Stephen stood beside him, his arms folded. 'This is very difficult for me to say to you, for any father to say to his son. Graham – I, we, that is, your mother and I and Stephen and Georgina, Michael's grandparents, we don't think you're . . . we think it would be better if . . . if someone else looked after Michael. At least until you can sort yourself out.'

'What! I'm perfectly capable of looking after him! What's happened to him? Nothing. He's fine! I'd never harm him. You know that.'

'I do. But you're a drunk. You've become an alcoholic. You can't look after a child on your own.'

'I'm not a drunk! That's ridiculous. I don't drink in the day, or in front of Michael. Those are my rules and I stick to them.'

Stephen put his hand on Dad's shoulder. 'Graham, we've been checking on what you drink. Your mum and Georgina have been checking the bottles. It's out of control.'

'Get out,' I said. 'I don't give a fuck what you think! Don't come back! You or your two little spies. What is this, East fucking Germany? Can't a man have a drink without being monitored? Out. Now!'

They didn't move.

'I'm afraid not,' Stephen said. 'We want to make you an offer. You let Michael come and live with us, with Georgina and myself, and, when you're well again, he comes back to you. You get to see him as much as you want, of course.'

'Get to see him? *Get to see* my own son?' I laughed. 'Of course. You sound like you're doing me a favour. Forget it. He's my son. He's staying here. You can't take him against my will.'

'We can. If you don't do what we say, then the social services will take Michael into care. As his grandparents, we'll be most likely to get guardianship of him. And from then on, it'll be on our terms. It'll be much harder to get him back.'

'Graham,' Dad said. 'Listen. We're doing this for you and for Michael. It's for the best. You sort yourself out, then he comes back. There's no need for social services and a court case or any of that. We can keep this in the family.'

'And you? My own so-called father?' I was screaming. 'Get out of my house! Send social fucking services round and see where that gets you, you cunts!'

Stephen slid an envelope onto the table. 'That's got all the details in it,' he said. 'Read it in the morning. When you're sober enough to understand it. We all love you, Graham. Remember that.'

And they were gone. A few days later, Michael joined them. That night, I drank hard, to wash away the betrayal as well as the pain.

4.

2009: The Intimacy of Lovers

Michael stayed in his room the rest of the weekend, save for a few forays into the kitchen to grab food and water. Each time he passed me, he looked away. On Sunday afternoon, I went and knocked on his door and asked if he wanted to talk, maybe go for a walk, or cycle to the Mersey Estuary, but he didn't answer. He wasn't even going to tell me to go away and leave him alone.

Around 6 p.m., I heard him come down the stairs and open the front door. I got up and followed him.

'Where are you going?'

'Out.'

'I can see that. Where, out?'

'Don't worry. I'm not going to Carly's.'

'Then where are you going? Danny's?'

'I told you. Out.'

He turned his back to me and walked down the drive. I called after him, but he ignored me. This was going to be a difficult week.

I sat back down and picked up *The Rotters' Club.* I had barely read a paragraph when I heard the sound of gravel crunching under tyres. I looked out of the window again. The door of a black Golf

GTI opened and Pippa got out. She was holding a bottle of wine and a bunch of flowers. Of course. In all the drama I'd forgotten. I'd invited her over for Sunday dinner.

'Hello,' she said, as I opened the front door. Her hair was down, and she was wearing a knee-length beige skirt and a black blouse. 'Happy Sunday.' She kissed me and handed over the wine and the flowers, a bunch of brightly coloured lilies. The only one I recognized was the stargazer; I had some growing in a pot by the deck.

'Thanks. They're lovely. I'll have to see if we've got a vase. Mike and I aren't that used to having flowers in the house. You look great, by the way.'

She smiled. 'I know it's not normally the woman who gives the man flowers, but I thought, what the hell? Every house can do with some floral decoration.'

'I've got a bit of a confession,' I said. 'I forgot about dinner. We've had quite an eventful weekend. I've not started the chicken. Although at least I bought the damn thing yesterday.'

'Eventful? Anything in particular?' She started to put the flowers into a vase I'd given her.

I paused before I answered, watching her deft, nimble movements. It was a shock to find that I felt better just having her here, the stress and worry replaced by the feeling that, as long as we were together, things would be ok. I put my hand on her forearm and pulled her towards me, wrapping my arms around her. 'It's been bloody awful.'

She pulled her head back and looked at me. 'Really? What happened?'

I told her about the weekend as I prepared the chicken, peeled potatoes, chopped parsnips, made some stuffing. By the time I had finished the story, the chicken was in the oven.

We went into the lounge and she sat on the couch. She patted the seat next to her and I sat down, our hips touching.

'You know they'll see each other anyway,' she said. 'When did teenagers ever listen to their parents about matters of the heart?'

I groaned. 'Don't say that. The last thing I need is another trip to the hospital with a boy who's been beaten up by thugs.'

'You should call the police, definitely. Whatever Michael and Carly do, you can't let those guys go unpunished. It's assault.' She twisted closer to me. I could feel her breast against my side. Was it deliberate when women did that? Did they know, or was it an accident? It must be deliberate, unless she had no feeling in her breasts, which meant she was trying to seduce me, which meant I stopped being able to think of things to say.

She shifted on the couch so that we were touching the length of our bodies, from ankle to shoulder. I smelled her hair, fresh and clean, and slipped my hand down her back to the top of her skirt, resting my fingers just inside the waistband.

'We've got the place to ourselves,' she murmured, her lips against my neck. 'We shouldn't waste it.' She slid her leg over mine and straddled me.

'The chicken,' I stammered. 'It'll be done soon.'

'My, my. I thought you said it'd be ninety minutes. I'm impressed.'

I blushed. 'That's not what I meant. I have to baste it, check the vegetables—'

She put a finger to my lips and unzipped my fly. A few seconds later all thoughts of chickens had vanished from my mind.

I'd had sex with a few girlfriends in the years since Charlotte died, but it had never felt right. I've never had any interest in one-night stands – the few I've had just felt like glorified masturbation, and left me feeling guilty and dirty – or in meaningless, casual relationships, and I'd accepted that I was heading for a life of happy celibacy. I'd forgotten how intimate sex could be, how you could lose yourself in someone so completely.

Afterwards, Pippa lay with her head on my chest as I caressed her back. She lifted her chin and pressed her nose to my cheek, inhaling deeply.

'I'm glad that happened. I was getting sick of waiting for you to make a move.'

I didn't reply for a while. *I* was glad as well; I certainly hadn't been planning anything, but I couldn't say that. In the end, I slid down the bed and kissed her belly.

'Then we'd better make up for lost time,' I said. 'There's still a while until Michael's back.'

We sat at the kitchen table eating takeaway pizza; the chicken was a dry, inedible husk. Pippa pulled the cork out of a wine bottle and poured herself a glass. She took a sip and looked at me, sucking her bottom lip into her mouth. It was a gesture I'd seen her make before, but I hadn't known until today that she also did it when she was having sex; it brought an image of incredible intensity to mind, a picture of her lying on my bed, her eyes fluttering closed as we made love.

Something had changed between us: we had discovered the quiet intimacy of lovers. It's hard to explain the alchemy of sleeping with someone. You share a part of yourself that few others, even your closest family and friends, will ever know, and you can never take it back – you might look back on the experience with disgust or pride or nostalgia, but it will always be between you.

Pippa looked into her wine, swirling the liquid in her glass. When she lifted her head, she looked troubled.

'Are you ok?'

She hesitated. 'There's something I wanted to tell you. I meant to tell you sooner, but there was never an opportunity.'

My stomach shrank.

'Nothing bad?'

'That depends. On your reaction.'

A thousand possibilities flashed across my mind. She had a boyfriend. She'd hated the sex. She used to be a man.

'Go on, then.'

She closed her eyes and kept them shut as she spoke. 'I used to be married. We got divorced.'

The knot in my stomach relaxed. 'Is that it? I mean, it's sad, but it's not that unusual.'

'It's more how it happened.' Her cheeks looked sunken, her eyes faraway. 'We married quite early. I was twenty-three, he was twenty-four. We were at medical school together.'

I sat in silence. Her gaze drifted around the room.

'When I was twenty-nine I was deep into my career, working all hours. I suppose you could say I was a workaholic, but whatever you called it, I put my job first. Then I found out I had ovarian cancer.' She held up a hand. I wanted to take it and hold it to my lips. 'Don't feel bad for me; I was lucky.'

'Doesn't sound that lucky.'

'Oh, it was. Ovarian cancer's nasty. It's deep inside you so normally you don't know you've got it until it's too late. I was lucky; it runs in my family, so I had it checked out. Anyway, they took it out, I had chemo, and it went away.'

'And your husband divorced you because of that? Because you were ill?'

'No. Not because I was ill. He was brilliant, a rock. It was what followed. You see, with ovarian cancer there's always a risk it can come back. The best medical advice – medical, mind – is to have your ovaries removed, which I wanted to do. Pete – my husband – didn't agree. He wanted to try for kids, have a family.'

'But if there was a risk of the cancer coming back you had no choice, surely?'

'We could have had kids, and then I could have had them removed. The risk was not that high.' She was speaking mechanically, quickly, skipping over the words to keep the emotions behind them at bay. 'I panicked; I wanted them out, and I wanted my life to resume. I convinced myself I didn't want kids, that I never would. I had my career, that was enough for me. Kids weren't what I had planned.' She smiled sadly. 'As you'll find out, I'm a planner. So I went ahead and had them taken out. Pete was devastated. We tried to carry on, but the breach between us was too large. He couldn't forgive me. Our relationship never recovered. After the divorce I wanted to avoid the early-thirties dating scene – you know, all the pressure to have kids before the clock stops ticking – and so I threw myself into my work. And here we are.'

I slid my hand over hers. I didn't know what to say. 'That's a sad story, Pippa. But I don't think any differently of you. Any worse.'

She looked up with tears in her eyes. 'That's not the worst of it. The worst is that now I regret it. Not the break up; me and Pete would have broken up anyway, I think, but the decision. I wish I'd tried for children when I had the chance.'

Christ. Now I *really* didn't know what to say. I couldn't imagine how she must be feeling. I ached for her.

'Don't say anything,' she said. 'There's nothing I haven't already thought about. I just wanted you to know. Now that . . . things are getting more serious.'

'Ok. But if you were worried it'd put me off, you were wrong. It doesn't bother me at all.'

She stared through me for a moment then blinked and smiled and poured herself another glass of wine and lifted it to her lips. 'Not even a drop?'

'No. Not for me.'

'It's a shame. It's a good bottle. A Margaux. I can't drink it all myself. I have to drive home.'

'I—' I paused. The reason for my not drinking wasn't something I liked to talk about, but tonight seemed to be the night for confessions. Moreover, she'd asked, and I didn't want to lie. That was one thing you learnt in recovery. Don't lie about it. Concealing the truth about their drinking, whether in the past or in the present, is what alcoholics do. You have to come clean. 'The truth is, I can't drink. I gave it up when Michael was a boy. I was – am, I suppose – an alcoholic. I don't miss it. It's been a long time since I wanted a drink. I'm pretty sure I could have one and be ok, but I don't want to risk it.'

'Good idea.' She squeezed my knee. 'For the record, I don't think any differently about you, either,' she said. 'Although I guess I'd better stop offering you drinks.'

5.

1995–96: My Mummy Loves Me

I'd lost everything. My fiancée, my son, my family, and still I felt I was sinking. I took a week off from work, locked my door and drank. Morning, noon and night.

I slipped into a shadow world, stumbling from room to room in my house, howling at the moon, dribbling sweet, sticky drool, a bottle always in my hand. Time lost meaning, the days blurring into the nights, the television blaring out a succession of meaningless sounds and images. My mind went into overdrive, conjuring up phantoms from the shadows that tormented me, visions that squatted on my chest until I was dizzy. Banshees swept past me, screaming of an impending death. Scenes from my childhood played out in front of my eyes, the happy laughter distorting into cries of terror, the warmth of family turning bitter and cold, the faces of my parents transforming into sinister, threatening masks. I must have slept, but I don't remember it. Perhaps I ate, but I have no recollection of it. I know I masturbated, feverishly, using a pile of magazines I bought from a newsagent and kept hidden in the basement.

Eventually, it ended, and I surrendered to unconsciousness. I was woken by my mother's voice.

'Graham,' she said. Her voice was tense and worried. 'Good God. Wake up, love. Please wake up.'

I cracked open an eye. It was stuck shut by some gluey substance.

'Mum,' I croaked. 'I'm thirsty.'

'Thank God you're alive,' she said. 'What happened? No one's heard from you for days. You've not been answering your phone.'

Slowly, I registered my surroundings. I was lying on my side on the couch, my face pressed into the cushions. The table was strewn with bottles and cigarette butts, crushed directly onto the table top. Cigarette burns covered the carpet. There were tissues and pornographic magazines everywhere.

I looked down at myself. My chest was covered in dried vomit, I had blood all over my legs and arms and I was naked.

My mum was sobbing.

'What's happened, Graham?' she whispered. 'How did it get to this? How did you end up here?'

'I don't know. I don't know what to do.'

'You have to fight it, love. You have to be strong.'

'How? How can I carry on without Charlotte? The pain is too big. What can I do, Mum? I want it to stop, but how?'

'I don't know. The only way is to keep on answering the questions life asks you. One at a time. Life moves on, Graham. You need to – I hope you can – move on with it.'

After Mum had left, I called work and told them I needed to take some leave. I spent the rest of the day cleaning the house and sobering up. I was determined to give up. As I cleaned I kept up a running commentary, describing what I was doing. It was aimed at an imaginary Charlotte. I promised her I wouldn't drink, but when the evening came the craving came back more strongly than ever. I had no way of resisting it; minutes later I was standing by the fridge, drinking from the neck of a bottle of Chardonnay.

The next day I woke up and poured a Bloody Mary, which, because it feels like a legitimate breakfast, is a fantastic morning drink. I mean, apart from the vodka, it's almost a health food.

I switched on the television. A belligerent talk-show host was lecturing a gap-toothed man about his responsibilities to his two children, who were sitting on either side of him. They were in tears; the man just looked bewildered. The host was telling him he had to get himself sorted out; he had to stop drinking before it was too late. He offered the man a session with the on-show counsellor, and told him to go and see his GP. The man nodded silently. He wasn't going to sort himself out, I could tell. All he was thinking about was getting out of there and finding something to drink.

I was relieved to see him. It set my mind at ease. He was much worse than me. *He* was an alcoholic, a ruined tragedy of a man. I was just someone who drank too much, and for a specific reason. I was grieving my dead fiancée. No one could blame me if I drank a bit. I needed it. Once the grief receded, I'd be ok. I just had to wait for that to happen.

'Do you have a problem with drink?' The host's voice said at the end of the show. 'Don't suffer in silence. Get help. See your GP.'

'How can I help you, Graham?' I'd been seeing Doctor Laird for years, although it was a while since I'd been to his surgery.

'I . . . you heard about my fiancée? About Charlotte?'

'I'm sorry to say I did.'

'I'm finding it hard to cope.'

He leaned forward. 'That's perfectly understandable.'

'I . . . I've . . .' It was hard to say the words. Shameful. 'I've been drinking.'

'A lot?'

I nodded. 'But only because of Charlotte. '

'Let's start with you telling me how much you drink?'

I went through it all. The Bloody Marys or Scotch and water in the morning; white wine at lunch; strong lager in the afternoon and Jim Beam at night. He noted it down, impassive.

'And would you say it has had a deleterious effect on your life?'

Apart from my parents-in-law taking my son to live with them? And the driving ban? And not going to work for weeks?

'A bit.' I said. 'Maybe a bit.'

He nodded, tapping his upper lip with his forefinger.

I spoke again to fill the silence. 'But it's only because of Charlotte. If it wasn't for that, I'd be ok.'

'Perhaps. It seems, however, that you're using alcohol, not just enjoying a drink. You're dependent on it. The reason why is, in some sense, irrelevant.'

'But when I stop grieving, I'll stop drinking.'

'Will you? Then why not do it now?'

The implication hung between us. I chewed the inside of my cheek. 'So you think I *am* an alcoholic?'

'I think you are dependent on alcohol, that the dependency is damaging your life, and that you don't know how to stop drinking. So yes, I think you're an alcoholic.'

Alcoholic. The word lingered in the room. I had been expecting some equivocation, some agreement that it was a temporary thing. Not this resounding declaration.

Everything changed with that one word. I couldn't believe it. I'd always looked down on drug or alcohol addicts as weak. I wasn't the kind of person who would succumb to that kind of thing. It was self-inflicted; I was far too strong for that. And yet here I was, not, perhaps, the person I'd thought I was.

And yet the world continued to turn. I looked out of the window. In the morning sun an old man was being helped out of his car by his daughter. My head spun. Perhaps I wouldn't make it to that age. Perhaps Michael would never help me out of a car when I was too old to climb out myself.

'What can I do?' The words came out as a whisper.

Doctor Laird smiled. 'There are some counselling services available on the NHS, or you can try Alcoholics Anonymous. They have a good track record. Here. Take these leaflets. I suggest you arrange something straight away.'

I stood up, clutching the leaflets in my hand. My palms were sweating but I felt cold. As I reached the door Dr Laird got to his feet. I turned to look at him.

'There's help out there, Graham. You're not the first and you won't be the last to go through this. You can do it.'

The AA meeting was in a community centre near Runcorn. A small, balding man in his sixties greeted me with a smile. He wore gold-rimmed glasses and a tweed jacket over a perfectly pressed shirt. He moved very precisely, taking small steps as he accompanied me to a room in which a group of men – and one woman, who was shockingly young – sat in a circle. He motioned for me to take a seat.

I sat between the woman and a man, also in his sixties. The woman was no older than me and very thin, and I tried not to look at her. The man's head was shaven, and he had a lined, unsmiling face. His had intense, staring eyes set deep in his skull. He was wearing a pair of chinos, a white shirt and a badly tied bow-tie.

He contemplated me for a long moment and slid out a hand. 'Welcome. Alban Hiatt. You don't have to tell me your name.'

'That's ok. I'm Graham Melton.' He was very intense. The urge to make conversation overpowered me. 'Have you been coming long?'

He rolled up his sleeve. A date was tattooed on his forearm. *17 March, 1979*. 'Last day I had a drink. Best day of my life. My new life.'

'I had a drink this morning.'

'That's as good as any to be your last one.'

It felt strange to be in this company, to be having these kinds of conversations. I'd never imagined myself at an AA meeting, and I was surprised to find that the main emotion was of overwhelming relief.

The balding man took a seat at the front and led the group through a prayer. Then he looked at me and the girl.

'We have two new members. If you wish, you may introduce yourselves.'

She said her name – Jenny – and told us that she needed help. She wanted to stop drinking but she couldn't do it on her own.

'Then you've come to the right place.' He smiled at me. 'Would you like to introduce yourself?'

My heart was racing and my eyes felt tight. The words were quick to form and hard to say.

'I'm Graham. I'm an alcoholic.'

The meeting lasted forty minutes. Different members of the group spoke about many topics. About how long they'd been sober, about moments of temptation, about how they were rebuilding their lives. It was eye-opening. Many of them seemed normal, respectable people, the kind of people you met all the time but never would have thought had a drink problem. They were not the ragged people I'd imagined. I wondered how many alcoholics I'd met, or worked with, over the years.

After the meeting, Alban Hiatt shook my hand. 'Well done.'

'Thanks.' I felt suddenly empty at the thought it was over.

'You're thinking "what next"?' Alban sat back. 'There's only one thing I can tell you, Graham. When you wake up, just decide not to have a drink that day. Don't worry about tomorrow; that'll take care of itself. You can make a decision for tomorrow, tomorrow. Just focus on today. Make your decision: *today, I'm not having a drink.* The motivation comes from the decision.'

I looked down at the carpet. I wasn't convinced. 'Sounds easy.'

'Doesn't it? But it's the hardest thing you'll ever do. Do you know King Solomon? He had a saying inscribed on his ring. *This too will pass*. Everything does. Remember that.'

That night I tried it. He hadn't been lying about it being hard. My body tried everything to get me to drink. I couldn't sleep, my skin crawled and itched, my stomach rebelled and my bowels seized up. The worst thing was the anxiety, although anxiety doesn't do it justice. It was an all-consuming certainty that I'd fucked my life up, that there was no way I could fix this. I could see no way out, apart from one: just have a drink and I'd feel better.

I didn't, though. *This too will pass*, I repeated, until the words lost their meaning and I fell asleep.

The next day, I went to have dinner at Stephen and Georgina's. I went on the bus. The last time I'd taken the bus to their house I'd been going to see Charlotte. I'd have to get used to these memories.

The world was very different seen through sober eyes. The smells, colours and sounds were so much more vivid. Especially the sounds. I heard everything: the cars, the chatter, the birds.

I knocked on the door. I was clean shaven and dressed in brand new clothes.

Georgina opened the door. She was holding Michael in her arms.

He was wearing a pair of dark blue dungarees and holding a plastic dump truck.

He looked at me quizzically, then smiled. 'Daddy,' he said, and held out his arms. 'Daddy.'

He recognized me. It was the first time I'd felt happy since Charlotte died. I took him and held him close to my chest, kissing his head and smelling his hair. There was a lot more of it, even after a couple of weeks.

'It's nearly bedtime,' Georgina said. 'Bath, then bed.'

'Can I bath him?'

'Of course. He's your son.'

I put in too much bubble bath and the foam overflowed the edges. Michael loved it, standing in the water, then squatting down and disappearing into the bubbles. Every time he did it I pretended not to know where he was and he popped up, laughing at my open-mouthed, cartoon surprise.

I wrapped him in a towel and sat with him on the bed, reading picture books. He loved *The ABC of Animals*, although we didn't get past G; he wanted to stop on the gorilla, which he loved. It was new, this gorilla obsession. I wondered what else I'd missed.

I was putting on his pyjamas when Stephen opened the door.

'Just come to say goodnight.' He leaned over the bed and kissed Michael on the forehead. 'See you downstairs in a minute.'

I took Michael into his room and switched off the light. He gave a little cry when the light went out but settled in my arms, his head heavy against my chest. I rocked him gently, listening to the sound of his breathing. When I was sure he was asleep, I laid him on his bed. I looked at him for a long time.

'I love you. I'll come every night, Michael. I promise.'

*

I woke the next morning and made my decision – today, I won't have a drink – and I clung to it every time my heart rate rose and I started to panic, every time the future seemed impossible, every time the worry threatened to overwhelm me, and I knew that I could end it all with a drink. *This too will pass.*

That was all I could do in the first few weeks. Wake up, decide not to drink, lose myself in work, where, after some awkward moments when I returned from my leave of absence, I was fully re-established. Each day I went to see Michael and put him to bed. Sometimes I ate with Georgina and Stephen; more often I went home. I wanted to prove to myself that I could do it. On the weekends, I took him out or went to my parents. He was happy, and safe.

The pattern stabilized. AA meetings, work, Michael. I got my driving licence back. Over the months, the desire to drink faded. Alban told me that you needed to recognize the signs, the triggers for when it might hit so you could manage them. For me, the urge to drink started with a darkening of the edges of my vision and a smell: the sick smell of a wet dog. Then it would hit me, a terrible, panicked urge to drink. I'd know, with absolute certainty, that the only way to get rid of the smell was to drink, that if I didn't drink I'd be haunted by it forever.

This too will pass. Alban was right. The urges grew fainter and further apart. I started to be annoyed by them, dismissive of them. By the time Michael was nearly two, they had almost gone altogether.

A few days before his second birthday, Stephen came round.

'I wanted to have a chat with you,' he said. 'About Michael.'

'Everything ok?'

'Yes. More than ok. Georgie and I think it's time he came back to you. We think you're ready. If you agree, we'll move him back this weekend.'

I didn't agree. I wasn't convinced I was ready at all. Apart from anything else, we were coming up on a year since Charlotte had died. That was an anniversary I was not looking forward to.

'I don't know,' I said. I reminded him of the upcoming anniversary. 'I don't know how I'll cope. I don't think I will.'

He shook his head. 'I think you will. I trust you. I don't doubt you, not in the slightest. None of us do. If we did, we wouldn't be proposing it.'

'You think I can get through it?'

'I know you can. And if you can get through this you can get through anything. So, do we have a deal?'

He dropped Michael off that Saturday. With my son back in my house, the place felt different, renewed. I had a long way to go, but for the first time I had the feeling – the hope – that I might make it.

That hope became more real on the anniversary of Charlotte's death. Michael and I visited her grave in the morning, then went to the park, then went for dinner with my mum and dad and her parents. Michael had no idea what was going on. That was one of the saddest things about it all. He would have no memories of his mum. I wished more than anything that he would, that somewhere there'd be a smell or a sound or a feeling that he would keep with him, but I doubted it. I tried not to think about it. Every time I did it left me feeling hollow and bitter at what the world had done to us.

I put him to bed and read the newspaper. I wasn't really paying attention to the words; more, I was scanning my feelings for any sign that I wanted a drink. If it was going to happen, today would be the day, but there was nothing.

Not long after, Michael moved into a new bedroom. It was time to put him in a bed, but the one I had was too big for his current room, so one Saturday I began to move his stuff to the larger room.

Michael helped out – which is to say, he threw things around and made a lot of noise – but by the evening, we were finished. After dinner, I sat with him on his new bed.

'Will you be ok in your new room?' I said. 'Don't worry. I'll be nearby.'

He nodded. 'Read a book,' he said.

'Go and choose one and I'll read it to you.' His book chest was still in the other room. He scuttled off. He had this strange stampy way of walking that made an enormous racket. To hear it you would have thought there was a grown man thundering along the landing, not a toddler. When he came back, he was holding a purple and red book that I didn't recognize.

'What's that one?' I said, taking it from him. As I read the title I froze. *My Mummy Loves Me*.

I remembered it. I'd bought it for Charlotte to read to him when he was just an infant. It must have slipped down the side of the bed or another piece of furniture and been unearthed during the move.

He looked at me expectantly. I felt tears come to my eyes. It was ok, I could read it. It was a good test.

'My mummy loves me,' I said, looking at the drawing of a mother gazing at her child. 'My mummy feeds me.' A mother with an infant on her breast. 'My mummy hugs me.' I turned the pages faster and faster, tears running freely. 'My mummy cares for me. My mummy is my best friend. My mummy is always there for me.'

Michael was nestled on my chest, nearly asleep. One arm was around my neck and I gathered him in a tight hug. He protested and wriggled and I put him in his bed, stroking his head while he fell asleep. I picked up the book and crept from the room.

Downstairs, I listened for any sounds coming from his room. He was fast asleep. My vision darkened and my throat constricted. I smelled the rank animal smell I knew so well.

I sat on the couch and picked up the paper. Ignore it, I told myself. Ignore it. *This too will pass.* A vision of Charlotte reading to him swam in front of my eyes. I put the paper down. My hands were shaking. Forget it, I told myself. You've just had a shock. And anyway there's no drink in the house.

But there is in the shop. A two-minute drive. He'll be ok while you go.

I shook the thoughts from my head. All that was behind me. But I couldn't stop them coming. *It's so unfair. Why you? Why your fiancée? It's not your fault you need a drink. If she hadn't died it'd be ok.*

Was it the self-pity that made me drink? Whatever it was, it was stronger than me and I picked up my car keys.

'Hello, there. Been a while since we saw you in here.' The owner of the off-licence smiled at me. He must have missed my regular expenditure. Stupidly, I felt ashamed, as though I'd let him down.

'Been away.' I looked at the beers. Still in the same place. A sense of familiarity comforted me, told me I was doing the right thing, made me feel as if I was coming back to an old club. I picked up a four pack of Special Brew. I didn't like the taste, but it worked; it was what I'd drunk when I wanted to really quieten the voices in my head.

A bottle of wine – make that two, just in case – and a bottle of Jim Beam. I felt good. I was in control here.

'Jack Daniels is on special offer,' the shopkeeper said. 'A pound less than the Jim Beam. I prefer it, if I'm honest.'

'Sure. Why not? A night in with Jack.' A glamorous joke. I'd picked it up from some book or movie.

'Cigarettes?'

I paused. 'Go on then. Make it a night to remember.' I was

babbling, fevered with anticipation. I couldn't pay and get out of there fast enough.

In the car park I ripped open one of the cans of Special Brew and swallowed the contents in one long draught. It tasted bitter and wrong and delicious. By the time I got home, there were two empty cans in the passenger side foot well. A third was about to join them.

As I put the key in the door my heart stopped. Michael. I'd forgotten about him. I listened for any sound from upstairs. Nothing. I crept up and peered into his room. He was fast asleep, his chest moving up and down as he gently snored.

It was a while before I realized where I was. Someone was calling me and there was a child crying. I was deep in a stupor and it was a struggle to wake up. Eventually, I fought to the surface. My mother was shaking me, her face pale, horrified at what she was looking at.

'Graham,' she whispered. 'What are you doing?' She was holding a tearful Michael in her arms. 'He was crying, sitting by his door. It's seven-thirty. God knows how long he'd been awake. I'm going to make him breakfast. We'll talk about this later.'

When Michael was breakfasted and happily playing, she brought me a cup of tea. I was lying on the couch, my head throbbing. 'I thought this was all over,' she said. 'You did so well. I trusted you.'

'It is, Mum, I promise. It was a one-off.'

'How am I supposed to believe that? After last time?'

'You have to believe me. I found a book. It's in the living room, I think. Have a look and you'll understand.'

She came back with the book in her hand. 'Oh, love,' she said. 'I feel for you, I really do. But it can't go on like this, you feeling so sorry for yourself. You're lucky it's me that found you, love. If it had been Georgina . . .'

I hadn't even thought of that the night before. I'd been consumed by whatever had woken in me, so swept aside by the power of its appetite that nothing had mattered beyond feeding it. I shuddered to think what I might have done, what I might have sold or broken or betrayed, and I knew that it was always going to be there, ready to strike in a weak moment.

Mum stroked my head. She was young, only in her early fifties. She was in good shape, walking everywhere. If you glanced at her she looked younger, but up close you saw the marks of age. You could see the strain of the last few years in the lines around her eyes and the corners of her mouth, in the grey hair peppering her temples. She'd been soft and confident and still all my childhood, an oasis whenever I needed reassurance, but now I detected a fluttering in her, an uncertainty born of a loss of trust in the essential goodness of the world. She no longer had the unquestioning belief that things would be ok.

'Mum. It's over. I won't do it again. I promise.'

She continued to stroke my hair. 'I believe you, Graham. Perhaps only a mother would. But I'll be watching you, love. Don't let me down.'

It was then that I realized that it was never going to be over; that I was never going to be free of it. Whenever things went against me, I was going to want to reach for the bottle. Either I was made that way or I'd made myself that way, but there was no point worrying about which. I just couldn't ever drink again. *At least you know now*, I told myself, *at least you've got that on your side*.

6.

2009: Doing the Right Thing

I lowered the paper and watched Michael butter his toast. One day someone will do a study and categorize people by the way they spread their butter; scientists who apply it evenly edge to edge, freestylers who slap it on randomly, minimalists who dab on tiny pats and watch them melt. Michael had a style all of his own: he eschewed the traditional knife in favour of a fork, dug out a great swathe of butter, dumped it on the bread, and flattened it with the prongs. It was an odd way to do it, but I decided not to comment. At that moment, we were not the best of friends.

It was late Saturday morning. The night before Billy had called to tell me that Carly wasn't at home and wasn't answering her phone. He suspected she was with Michael. I'd found them at Danny's, drinking beer in the garden. I was furious when I saw them and even though I knew how much he would hate it, I ordered him into the car. For a second I thought he was going to refuse to come, and I had a horrible feeling of impotence. There was little, after all, that I could have done, but he stood up slowly and, pale and glaring, he sloped to the car. Carly followed him. As she passed she muttered 'sorry', which was the only word I got from either of them on the way to drop her off. I tried to speak to Michael after we left her, but he refused to acknowledge me. As soon as we pulled up in the drive, he leapt out of the car, slammed the door and disappeared into his room. I hadn't seen him until now.

I decided it was time to break the silence. 'Any plans today, Michael?'

He didn't reply. He folded an entire slice of toast into his mouth and began to chew, his cheeks bulging. He swallowed, then looked up at me. 'Never do that again.'

He was so serious. It was clear he'd been planning exactly how he would say those words. 'Do what?'

'Humiliate me like that. And yourself. You have no idea how stupid you looked last night.'

'I can live with it. And I don't think that you're in a position to be laying down the law. You could at least have waited a while before disobeying me and Billy.'

'Didn't want to.' His words were muffled by the second slice of toast, also stuffed into his mouth.

'Doesn't what I say have any impact on you? Or what Billy says?'

He shook his head. 'Not when it's so unfair.'

'But, Michael, it's for the best. Every time you go to Orford you get beaten up. It can't go on. You won't let me call the police, so what can I do?'

'She can come down here.' The toast was gone and he was flattening butter on another piece, crumbs littering the butter where he'd put the fork in to gouge out a new lump. 'Like last night.'

'No. I – and Carly's parents – have forbidden it. It has to stop.' He was indifferent. I could tell that his position was set. It was going to be difficult – if not impossible – to budge him.

'I'm going to see her. If I can't see her in Orford, then why not here? I don't see what the problem is.'

'The problem is that you keep getting beaten up.'

'I told you – I'll see her here. Problem solved.'

'It's not solved. What about Carly? She has to live near those yobs, and go to school with them.'

'Billy will take care of her. They won't mess with his daughter.' He pointed at me. 'See, Dad? There's a solution for all the problems you can think of, apart from the real problem. You think Carly's too common for me.'

'That's ridiculous. Of course I don't.'

'You do. I know what you think. You think that there's no future in it, so what does it matter if we break up now? You're a snob.'

'Michael! That's not true! I like Carly, and your relationship is your business.' I cleared my throat. 'But it happens to be the case that it's unlikely you'll stay together. Not because of Carly's background, but because very few teenage relationships last. There's no point having all this trouble.'

'What about you and Mum? You met when you were young, right?'

'That was different. It was a different time.'

'Why was it different?'

'I didn't get beaten up every time I went to see her.'

'If you had, would you have stopped seeing her?'

I didn't reply; I didn't want to lie to him. Of course I wouldn't have stopped. I would have taken any number of punches to see Charlotte.

He seized on my hesitation. 'Is that what you want me to do? Never see her because of some shitty chavs? Is that the lesson you want me to learn?' He stood up, his eyes bright with anger. 'Tell me. Would you have stopped seeing Mum?'

'It's not about me,' I said. 'It's about you.'

'Answer the question! What would you do? Just tell me. I want to know.'

I shook my head. All I could do was repeat myself. 'It's not about me.' It was feeble. I felt ashamed.

'Is that it? You won't even answer one simple question? You're my dad. You're supposed to be a role model. All you have to tell me is what you would do. I'm not saying I'll do it. I just want to know. Don't I have the right to know what my dad would do if he was in the same shitty situation I'm in?'

'It's not about rights, Michael. Rights come along with obligations, and when you start fulfilling yours, you can talk about rights.' God, I hated myself at that moment. Hated my betrayal. Hated my weakness. My son was crying out for help, and all I could do was seize on some spurious bullshit about rights and obligations so I could get out of answering a reasonable question, a question I didn't want to answer because I knew he was right: I *did* think she was too common for him. I knew I shouldn't – I knew I was hypocritical and wrong – but that was how I felt. It was different to me and Charlotte; just look at the trouble he was in. Nothing like that ever happened to me, although I wondered if that was just luck. There was certainly trouble about when I was his age. I tried again.

'You're not me and your mum.'

'We might be. You don't know that.'

'I do. It's different.'

'Only because it was you who was common and her who was posh. Anyway, it's not up to you. It's my life.'

He may have been right, and to be honest, I didn't know what was right. I just wanted to protect my son, so I fell back on the only thing I had. 'It's not a negotiation, Michael. While you're in this house you'll live by my rules.'

He looked at me, his eyes filmy with disappointment. It was a grimy, sad look. Something ended between us and I felt my heart break. 'Thanks, Dad,' he whispered. 'You've been a great help.'

He grabbed his bag and walked out of the kitchen and into the hall. I heard the front door slam and a wave of guilt swamped me. *Go*, I told myself, *go after him and fix it. Put it right.*

I ran to the front door and flung it open. He was disappearing at the end of the drive.

'Michael! Stop! I want to talk to you!'

He waved his hand dismissively without looking back. 'Forget it, Dad. I've heard enough.'

'Michael! Come back!' He vanished round the corner.

Back in the kitchen I paced up and down. I ached for Charlotte. She would have told him to fight for the girl he loved, like we'd fought for each other. She would have smiled and hugged him and told him she loved him, and that she would speak to Billy and make it work. She'd have given them lifts, let Carly come to our house, kept it all well away from the yobs in Orford. She would have had the courage to tell him to follow his heart, whether it ended badly or not, and to stand behind him while he did so. All I could see was the risk. At times like this, I missed her as much as I ever had.

I was torn with the unfairness of it all, not just to me, but to Michael, who had to put up with one, inadequate, parent. I grabbed my Blackberry and called Pippa.

'I need to talk to you. Can you come?'

'I have to be in work in an hour. I can stop by on my way.'

'Come soon.'

She was there fifteen minutes later. I spilled the story, the words tumbling out in a waterfall, the story about Michael and betrayal and Charlotte all mingling together.

Pippa squeezed my hand. 'How's Michael?'

'Upset. Hating his dad. And I can't blame him. I just thought it would be easier if they broke up. Those lads are trouble. I can't believe they won't just leave him alone. And I can't believe that I can't make them leave him alone.'

'They've nothing better to do. There's a lot of them around. I see them all the time in the hospital. NEETs, they're called. Not in Employment, Education, or Training. They've nothing. No future. God knows what they'll do when they're thirty, forty, fifty.'

'They might have no prospects but I don't need them ruining Michael's.'

'You might have no choice. You know how important things are when you're that age. You love with such intensity. Whatever you do, he's going to see her anyway.'

'I agreed with Billy. He's Carly's dad. He has some say in this.'

'That's your problem, I'm afraid. You've made a commitment to someone that maybe you shouldn't have made. Why should Michael pay for that? You'll have to unmake it.' She kissed me and stood up. 'I have to go to work. But think about this. You're Michael's dad, his biggest supporter, the person he can most rely on. You're a team. I think all he wants is for you to act like one.'

I didn't get home until eight that evening. Michael greeted me with a scowl.

'Don't worry,' he said. 'I've not seen Carly. You'll be glad to know I'm feeling miserable.' I had to fight the urge to laugh. Even when he's angry he can be funny. It's a teenage thing; they're prone to melodrama.

'I know you've not. I've just come from her house.'

He sat up. 'What? What were you doing there? Haven't you interfered enough? God, I wish you'd just leave my life alone.'

'Fine. If you don't want to know what Billy and I discussed, then I won't bother you any more.' I went into the kitchen and opened the fridge, looking for something quick and easy I could eat. He came shuffling in, his jeans trailing behind him. Why kids wore them so low was beyond me; they looked ridiculous. Presumably that was the point. If adults didn't get it, then that was reason enough.

'So? What did you talk about?' It cost him a great effort to ask the question. It was an admission that I might have something he needed.

'You and Carly. I suggested to him that we should let you see each other.' He fought to stop his scowl turning into a grin. 'Go on,' I said. 'Smile. You know you want to.'

He gave in and the grin cracked his face. I loved it when he smiled. I could have lived on that smile for the rest of my life. 'What did he say?'

'He was reluctant, but he agreed. There are some conditions, though.'

His face fell. 'Like what?'

'You only see her at weekends. And you stay round here. I told him I'd pick her up and drop her home.' It was going to be a pain, ferrying them round, but if that was what I had to do, then so be it.

'Really? Dad, that's brilliant!'

'I do listen to you, Michael. When you asked me what I'd have done with your mum, I thought about it and I realized that I would have seen her anyway. In fact, that's kind of what me and your mum did.'

'You? You disobeyed your parents?'

'Not exactly disobeyed. Anyway, why's that such a surprise?'

'You're so straight. You never break any rules. You don't even speed.'

'Christ. Is this the thanks I get? I sort out your love life and you give me an analysis of how boring I am?'

'Sorry, Dad. Back then you might have been cool. I suppose it was different when you were a kid.'

'Right. Back in the dark ages, when dinosaurs roamed the Earth. It wasn't that long ago. Anyway, you can see her on the weekends.' I put my hand on his shoulder and looked him in the eyes. He had a rash of acne on his forehead. 'Weekends only, mind.'

'I can't believe you changed your mind. Thanks, Dad.'

'Thank Pippa. It was her who talked me round.'

'Really? I told you she was cool. I'm glad I set you two up. I'm going to call Carly.'

He shuffled off to his room. I was glad it'd been resolved, but I couldn't help shake the feeling that we – me and Billy and Kerry – had over-reacted in the first place. It couldn't be that bad, surely?

It was bizarre. Did we really live, in the twenty-first century, under the threat of physical violence from a gang of teenagers? Were the authorities unable to sort it out? It seemed so. It seemed the only solution was to keep yourself away from it and hope it didn't find you.

That night, Pippa and I made love. It was becoming a habit. A good habit, but a habit nonetheless. She came over after work, we ate, talked, and went to bed. Sometimes we made love fiercely, sometimes languorously, but always with the melting comfort that comes from being so close to someone you care for. That night, I slipped too far from myself; perhaps it was the sense of family that had grown up between me, Pippa and Michael, but as I moved inside her in the dark, I started to say her name, and the name that came to my lips wasn't hers. She didn't notice; I caught myself before more than the first syllable had slipped out and the 'Ch' became a groan, but for the first time our lovemaking became mechanical and joyless.

I lay beside her. She was a good sleeper, Pippa. She nodded off easily, especially after sex. I thought it was supposed to be me, the male animal, who rolled off his mate and started snoring, but we'd finish, Pippa would cuddle against me, her head on my chest, and the next thing I knew she'd be gently snoring, her mouth parted. She reminded me of a sleeping child.

I stroked her hair. I was shaken by what had happened, shocked both by the thought of how she would have reacted had I called her Charlotte, and by what it meant: I had been falling into this new relationship when perhaps I wasn't ready, even after all these years.

After all, it had never worked in the past. I'd gone on some dates but in the end – when Michael was around four – I'd given up on them, and I'd been happy like that until Michael had interfered with his Dating Harmony escapade. I'd meet the women, and like them, and sometimes have a physical relationship, but it never went further. I could never imagine it going further. It wasn't that Charlotte was present, or that I thought she would have minded, but I always compared them to her, and they never lived up to the mark. I had loved her so much that it was hard to picture how I could ever reach that point with someone else.

But this felt different; it was different, I was sure of it. I loved Pippa, I knew I did. I thought about her all the time. In a way, calling her Charlotte was a compliment: the way I felt about Pippa was the way I remembered feeling about her, back when we were starting out. I doubted Pippa would have seen it like that, though.

She stirred, rolled onto her back and muttered something. I bit my lip, wincing at the love I felt for her. It made me nervous and worried, but there wasn't much I could do about it now. It was already out of my control.

7.

1997: Seamaster

I'd left Michael with my parents for the night so I could go – reluctantly – on a date. He loved staying with them. He was at that age – three, or three and a half, as he was fond of reminding me – when he had figured out that the rules were different with different people. With me he had a strict bedtime and a limit on treats. First he had to eat his meal, then he could have a yogurt, or a piece of fruit, or maybe, sometimes, a cake or meringue. With Grandma and Grandad bedtime was flexible, and he could eat all the cakes he wanted. It was the privilege of being grandparents: they didn't have to raise Michael, they just had to love him.

I scanned the restaurant for Laura. She was a colleague of Pat, Tommy's girlfriend, and we'd been introduced one night at a party at their house. My last girlfriend had broken up with me a few months back, after I'd started finding excuses not to see her, and so I think Pat and Tommy were trying to help. Whether it was a set up or not, Laura had called a few days later and suggested going out to dinner. We'd agreed to meet at Efe's, a Turkish place in town.

She was sitting at a table in the corner. I waved and walked over. She was divorced with two kids – Simon and Mary – and working as a receptionist in a local government agency. It was hard for her to hold her job down and look after the children. She would have been better off on benefits, but she was determined not to go on them.

There was a bottle of red wine on the table, already half gone, but I refused her offer of a glass and ordered a Coke. I could tell from her reaction that she understood I didn't drink, and knew why. Normally, when people found out I didn't drink they were surprised or made some comment – bad hangover, eh? or something like that – but not Laura. She didn't react at all, which led me to think that she was pre-warned. No doubt Pat had filled her in.

Anyway, I didn't mind people knowing. It was what it was: it had happened, it was in the past, and I didn't think about it. I was glad to be free of it all. I enjoyed waking up without a hangover. Once you got used to the social awkwardness, it was really not that big a deal.

Laura took a big swig. She was still pretty, although the strain of her life was creeping in at the edges and the pounds she gained were beginning to be harder to shift. She was wearing quite a lot of make-up, which had the opposite effect to the one she'd planned, serving only to draw attention to the fact she was trying to hide her age.

I didn't think badly of Laura; in fact I liked her. I just didn't find her in the slightest bit attractive. I would happily have been friends with her, helped look after her kids, met for lunch and dinner to keep each other company, but I didn't want to have sex with her, kiss her, touch her at all. It was the same with the, admittedly few, other women I'd gone out with. No matter how good-looking they were, I wasn't interested. I found myself analysing their looks, not appreciating them.

It was no secret why: I was still in love with Charlotte, still grieving for her. I didn't expect it ever to stop, and it got in the way too much. I was happy with life the way I had it. Michael and me and the memories of his mother. I had decided to settle for it. I didn't want anything, or anyone, to disturb what felt like a delicate balance.

'Graham? Are you ok?' Laura patted my hand. 'You seemed miles away.'

'Sorry. I was just thinking about work.'

'What do you do?'

'I'm an accountant, I'm afraid. Very dull.'

'No, it's not. It's . . . it's a great job.' People always tried to tell you it wasn't dull when you told them it was, and they always failed to find something positive to say about it.

'It is. I don't mind. It pays the bills.'

We made small-talk for the rest of the meal. As we left, Laura put her hand in mine. 'Coffee. Can I offer you something, back at mine?'

I let go of her hand and got my car keys out of my pocket. 'Thanks, but I'd better go home. Relieve the babysitter.'

'She can wait a little longer, can't she?' She looked at me with a half-smile and lidded eyes. It was strange how people's body language changed when they thought they were in a sexual situation. You would never do those things normally. It'd be ridiculous.

'I said I'd be back. I don't want to mess her around.'

She leaned forward suddenly and kissed me, her tongue snaking into my mouth. I staggered backwards, coughing.

'What? Don't you like it? Don't you like me?'

I felt my cheeks reddening. I hated this kind of thing. When you were sober it was so embarrassing. 'It's not that at all. It's not you, it's me. I'm not . . . I'm not ready.' Was I really saying this? It was what teenage girls said when they dumped their boyfriends. Was it the best I could do?

'Not ready? It's just a kiss, Graham.' She was becoming defensive. Soon she'd be aggressive, but at least the kissing was over. She shrugged. 'Please yourself.'

'I could give you a lift home, if you want. Save getting a taxi.'

She snorted. 'Forget it. See you round. I won't expect a call. Thanks for dinner. At least I've learned one thing. It's true what they say about accountants. They *are* boring.' She stalked off.

'Cheerio,' I said. 'Good night.'

The next time someone set me up on a date, I refused. It happened more often than you might think; people take a deep interest in the love life of their single friends. It's like a soap opera you can control. Interactive TV, long before the concept was invented. I found myself repeating the same phrase. '*Yes, I'm sure she's lovely. I don't doubt her beauty / intelligence / suitability, but I'm not interested. Thanks, but no thanks.*' Women were off the menu. I knew, just knew, that it wouldn't work. It was sad, and too early, but my loving days were over.

I had to fill the time, so I signed up for an Open University degree in English, which meant that I always had some reading or essay writing to do. I'd never thought of going to university when I was at school. University was a place for drunken yahoos to have a final fling before they inherited the family firm. Years later, I was able to sign up for the English course and discover a world I hadn't suspected existed, the world of Wordsworth's *Prelude*, of Hopkins's sprung rhythm, of Larkin's reluctant embracing of humanity. *What will survive of us is love.* I know, quoting those oh-so-famous words is a cliché, a sign of a beginner, incontrovertible evidence of someone who has only scratched the surface but, nonetheless, when I first read them, late at night, Michael sleeping upstairs, I sat bolt upright in my chair. It was as though Charlotte had walked into the room. *What will survive of us is love.* How I needed that to be true.

The country was coming out of recession and the economy was doing that thing it periodically and dangerously does: heating up.

The firm had received sniffs of interest from a variety of suitors and the owners – Norris and Terry, both now retired from the day-to-day running of the place – were thinking of selling to an American multinational. As a result, my small stake – two and a half percent, to be exact – was also up for grabs. As Finance Director, I was in charge of the negotiations.

Before the first meeting with the potential buyers, Norris and Terry came to my office. I'd done the valuation based on the usual discounted cash flow analysis. I'd made what I thought were pretty safe assumptions about future levels of cash flow. I took them through the analysis.

'So, the model says the business is worth around eighteen million pounds,' I concluded.

'What happens if you bump up the sales growth rate a few percent?' Norris said.

I plugged it into the financial model. The valuation jumped to twenty-five million. They both nodded. 'And what if you assume we get savings from our suppliers because of the additional volume of sales? Say three percent reduction each year?'

The value went up a few more million.

Terry stroked his chin. 'So that puts us at nearly thirty,' he said. 'And then you've got goodwill for all the intangible assets. Innovation pipeline, that kind of thing. I say we ask them for forty million.'

'Hang on,' I said. 'The assumptions you've just made aren't backed up by anything.'

Norris shrugged. 'So? Who knows what will happen in the future? Anyway, we're just naming our price. It's up to them to do their due diligence.'

Terry leaned back in his chair. 'The thing is, once these corporations get involved in this kind of purchase they find it hard to back out. Someone's career depends on doing the acquisition. Their job is to buy it, integrate it and then run it. If the sale falls through, they're out of a job, so unless they've got the balls to let that happen, you can't expect them to act rationally. After all, it's not their money. It's the company's. But it *is* their job.'

'So we'll start at forty and see where we end up.'

The deal closed at thirty-seven million pounds. I got to keep my job, since they needed people who knew the business, and I also got paid out. Nine hundred and twenty-five thousand pounds. I had nothing to spend it on so I paid off the mortgage and invested the rest. I figured I'd retire early and do some more OU degrees.

In May 1997 there was another general election. This one, we couldn't lose. After a succession of national disasters, Major's government felt listless and old-fashioned, a mood at odds with the optimism at large in the country. He was personally even more unpopular, although probably undeservedly so. Anyone dealt his hand would have suffered. Would a Labour government under Kinnock have put us through the ERM debacle? Most likely. But then, so what if he was unlucky? As Napoleon was fond of saying, give me a lucky general over a good general.

Dad came round to watch the election coverage with six cans of mild, his sandwiches and a pack of Benson and Hedges. I made him smoke in the garden, and only when Michael was asleep.

'We'll do it this time,' I said. 'Finally. We'll have a Labour government.'

'Labour?' Dad said. 'Blair's not Labour. He's Maggie's bastard son. He agrees with most of what she said. Privatization, for example. It's a disgrace, what he stands for.'

'You're still stuck on Clause Flour? The times have changed. The government can't own all the industries anymore. It's a new way, a middle way. A third way.'

'It's the wrong bloody way.'

'The old way wasn't working. We couldn't get elected. Even in 1992, when everything was in our favour.'

'The Labour movement – mark that word, son, movement – isn't about power. There are values and principles at stake which are more important than getting elected. It's about how you organize society, about who you prioritize – the many or the few. If you drop all that to get elected, then what have you got? You've not got a Labour government, that's for sure. You can take a box of frogs and stick a label saying "cake" on it, but when you open it you've still got a box of frogs. That's the thing with Blair. He wears a Labour rosette, but inside he's not a Labour man.'

'But not necessarily a bad man.'

'No, but not Labour, Graham. I'm Labour, always have been, always will be, but I'm Old Labour. I believe in the principles of Labour, not the principles of getting elected.'

'So did you vote?'

He shook his head. 'No one to vote for.'

'Dad! You always told me it was my duty to vote! That people had died for the privilege.'

'I know, and I'm ashamed. But who could I vote for? There's no Labour candidate. And it'll get worse, you watch. They'll all follow Blair now, drop their principles for power, even Maggie's lot. Love or hate her, and I hated her, at least she stood for something.'

'If he wins. We've been though this before. We couldn't lose in '92, but the Tories turned it round at the last minute. They always do well in elections. They're like the Germans in the World Cup. However bad they are in between the tournaments, you know that when the finals come round they'll be in the mix at the business end, scraping through to the semis at least.'

We watched as the exit polls came in. They predicted a huge majority for Blair. Then the first results, then more, then a flood. By two in the morning it was clear that it was going to be a landslide.

'He's done it,' I said. 'Blair's done it. We're going to have a Labour government for the first time since 1979! Eighteen years!'

'Aye, although what the real Labour people would say about it, I don't know. You don't remember them. Gaitskell and Bevan, George Brown, Jenkins, the best of all the home secretaries. Foot was the last of them, the last of the true greats.'

'You know, you should do a degree,' I said. I'd been thinking it for a while. He could sign up for the Open University. He had plenty of time. Greenall's had shut down the brewery and he'd been made redundant with a decent enough payout to clear the mortgage. Mum was still nursing part-time, and he had some casual work as a gardener, so they had some income. I would have helped them out, but he still wouldn't accept my money, although most weeks I gave Mum some cash. I think she respected his principles, but she knew that they weren't always much use in practical terms. You couldn't feed a family on them.

He didn't reply. 'You could do Political Philosophy. Or Modern History. You already know most of it.'

'Nah,' he said. 'I'm too old for all that.'

'Rubbish! You're fifty-six. That's nothing. You'll be done in three years.'

'I leave all that to you young 'uns. I don't need a piece of paper. If I want to read summat, I'll read it.'

'It's good to have a teacher, though. Keeps you focused. And you learn more. They point out different things.'

'Give over, Graham. Stop mithering about it.' He hadn't used that tone of voice – a mixture of anger and frustration – since I was a teenager. It brought back painful memories.

'All right,' I said finally. 'It was only an idea. I thought it'd appeal to you.'

He stared silently at the screen. 'I've been meaning to tell you summat. For a few weeks. Not really found the time, but I suppose now is as good as any.' He was pensive and still, seeming not fully present. 'I've been to the doctor. I've got lung cancer.'

I fidgeted in my chair, started to speak, stopped, started again. My thoughts whirled and I couldn't pick one out, couldn't fix on one, so what came out was nonsense. 'Lung cancer? In your lungs?'

'That's where it normally is.'

'Is it bad?'

'Have you got any sensible questions, Graham? 'Course it's bloody bad.'

'How bad?' My mind was clearing the decks, getting ready to deal with the answer.

'Three months. Tops.'

'Three months? Until . . . until . . .' I was like a stuck record. I couldn't move in, couldn't say the words.

'Until I die.' He said it for me. He'd always been braver than me.

'Shit,' I said, after a long pause. 'Fuck. I don't believe it. Fuck.'

'That about sums it up.'

'Does Mum know?'

He nodded. 'I found out a few weeks ago. Told her the next day. Swore her to secrecy.'

'That's why she's not been round much.'

'So there's no point me starting a degree.'

'Come on, Dad. You never know.'

'Sometimes you do. I've been feeling ill for months. Bad cough, and difficulty breathing, but I thought it'd pass. Maybe if I'd gone back then they could have done something about it, but it's too late now.'

It was typical of my father. He was a heavy, life-long smoker, who started suffering from chest pain and lung problems over a prolonged period. What did he do? Nothing. Left it to sort itself out.

'Your mum'll be ok. She's got the house, and I've some money put away.'

And I'll help her, with the money you hate, I thought, *but I won't mention it to you. No point trying to win the argument; just do it. I've learnt that from Mum, at least.*

'Dad, you can't just give up. We can go private, get a second opinion.'

I was desperate or I would never have suggested it. Predictably enough, he looked at me as though I'd just advised him to strip naked and run through the streets in nothing but a clown hat. 'I'll never go private,' he said. 'Don't agree with it.' He took off his watch. 'I want you to have this. Give it to Michael some day.'

I held it in my hand. An Omega Seamaster. It's such an evocative object, a watch. So personal. I'd seen it on his wrist so many times. Having it given to me like this seemed so final. I wasn't sure I wanted to accept it. 'Are you sure?'

'No bloody use to me where I'm going, is it?'

'Where did you get it?' I'd often wondered why he had such a smart watch. Omega was hardly a socialist icon.

'Bought it. Where'd you think?'

'I never thought of you as an Omega man. It's a bit flash for a lefty like you, isn't it?'

'A man needs a good watch. You have to be able to trust it. Don't want to be late for the revolution, do I?'

'All those years you told me – and Mum – not to waste money on materialist rubbish.'

He gave me a half-grin. It looked almost sheepish. 'Don't look at me like that, as though I'm some kind of hypocrite. I bought one for her. It's in a drawer upstairs. She never bloody wears it. She scared of losing the damn thing.'

I slipped it over my wrist. 'Thanks, Dad. I'll take care of it.'

'Make sure you do.'

'So what's next?' I grabbed the cigarettes from the table. He'd already been outside at least five times that evening. 'You can start by giving these up. It's about time.'

'Giving them up now won't make any difference. Should never have bloody started, but it's too late to stop now.'

'It's never too late.'

'Give 'em here. I'm going for a smoke.' I held them away from him. 'Come on, you daft bugger, stop being such a baby. Hand 'em over.'

I put them reluctantly in his hand. I couldn't believe it. He'd just told me he was dying of lung cancer and off he went outside to smoke a fag. I watched through the window as he inhaled, the red tip glowing like a warning sign. On the television, Michael Portillo was losing his seat. In years to come it would become known as 'the Portillo Moment', the defining image of the 1997 election. People would ask 'where were you when Portillo lost his seat?'

I knew where I was. I was watching my dying father shake hands with the thing that killed him.

He died six weeks later, slipping away in a hospital bed with me and Mum by his side. He'd been in hospital for a week; that morning he'd not woken, and we'd called for the doctor. When the doctor saw him he shook his head and gave me the look that comes before someone says they're sorry.

'I'm sorry,' he said. 'He's nearly gone.'

'Will he wake up?' Mum said. 'I'd like to say goodbye.'

'Maybe. Probably not. If he did he'd be in a lot of pain.'

'Can you do anything to wake him up? I didn't get a chance to tell him goodbye.'

'No, I'm afraid not.'

Mum looked down at her husband, lying on a bed with a tube up his nose. The monitor at the head of the bed beeped steadily.

'Ok,' she said finally. 'If there's nothing you can do.'

The doctor gave a strange little bow before leaving; it's the only thing I can remember about him. His face and voice and age have all gone, but I can remember that bow.

'Graham. I'd like some time alone with your father. There are some things I want to say to him.'

I went and got a coffee in the lobby. After half an hour, I went back up. Mum was sitting by the bed reading the newspaper to him. It was an article about Tony Blair and whether he and his family were going to move into 10 Downing Street or not. It was the kind of trivial thing he would have hated. Perhaps she thought that, if he could hear her, he'd be so irate at having this article read to him that he'd come round.

What had she said to him, I wondered? Had she cried and told him she loved him? Called him a selfish idiot for smoking all those years? Kissed him tenderly one last time? If she had, it would be the first time she'd done any of those things for years. Too often we don't say those things when we can, and when we realize we want to it's too late.

I bent down and hugged her. 'I love you,' I said. 'I want you to know that.'

She looked at me as though she was startled, or shocked. 'Thanks,' she said. 'I love you too. And your dad does as well.'

He didn't last much longer. Around tea time, there was a sudden flurry of beeping from the monitor, and then it stopped. A few minutes later the nurse came, and then a doctor, and it was over.

When we got home Mum had a glass of sherry and went to bed. She was wary of drinking in front of me, but I waved away her protests, even though the sweet smell of the alcohol brought a sudden rush of saliva to my mouth.

When she was asleep, I sat on the couch and looked around the living room where I had grown up. It was heavy with memories: the same dark brown couch, the picture above the gas fire of the town centre at the turn of the century, the smell of cigarette smoke. There was an ashtray on the coffee table, empty now, its days of usefulness over. I wanted to smash it against the wall.

Something was digging into my buttock and I felt down the side of the couch. It was Dad's wallet. Opening it felt like snooping, and I nearly put it back in case he came in and found me, but with a sad smile I carried on. A few five pound notes, his Labour Party card, a credit card which he never used and a bank card. And, folded in half and slipped in the coin pouch, two photos. One was of me and Mum in the kitchen at the barn, just after we'd bought it. In it, she was handing me a cup of tea and I was leaning forward to peck her on the cheek. Neither of us knew the camera was on us. The second was a photo of me and Charlotte with Michael when he was a few days old. We were sitting on the brown couch, proud as punch to have our son at his grandparents' house.

I had a lump in my throat. Dad had carried these with him every day and now he was gone, separated from them forever. That was life as a parent: a gradual separation from your kids. For them it's liberation; for you it's almost grief. It was only now I had Michael that I understood, and I dreaded the day it happened to us.

8.

2009: Someone's Home

I stared at my computer screen. The sales report was meaningless. I read the same paragraph twice, but the words wouldn't sink in. I just couldn't concentrate.

It had been like this for days, ever since I'd nearly called Pippa 'Charlotte'. It was an easy mistake to make, and understandable, but I felt dishonest. I'd told her about Charlotte, but only the bare bones. I'd never said how I still missed her, how I would have given anything to have her still alive. If it was going to work for Pippa and me, I needed to get it off my chest.

After work I went to see her at her house. I rang the doorbell dry-mouthed and sweaty-palmed, like a schoolboy about to confess a crime to the headmaster.

She opened the door and beckoned me into the living room. She was cool, and kept her distance. 'You've been quiet the last few days. I was expecting a call.'

'I've been thinking.'

'About us?'

'About us.'

'And?' She looked at me expectantly and picked up a pen from on top of the paper, which she span between her fingers. She'd been doing the crossword.

'And I want to tell you something. I want to tell you that I still think about Charlotte. I still love her.'

She bit the corner of her mouth. 'Do you love me?'

'Yes. Totally and utterly.'

'Then that's enough.'

'You don't mind that I love her?'

'I'm jealous, of course. The man I love loves another woman? That's hard, but honestly, I'd mind more if you *didn't* love her. She was your childhood sweetheart, the mother of your child. If you'd forgotten her I'd wonder what kind of a man you were. It's precisely because you're so loyal that I love you. I'd hope you'd treat me the same.' She shrugged. 'It would have been easier to have fallen for someone else, but it wasn't to be. It's you, I'm afraid.'

I'd been expecting anger, disappointment, a tearful break up. Anything, apart from praise. 'So it's ok?'

'Yes.' She leaned towards me and kissed me. 'We're not the first couple to face this. I— well, I suppose I always knew, and I have thought about it, but if you want to stay together, then so do I. If we love each other, it'll work out well enough.'

The dam burst. We couldn't stay away from each other. I remembered the delicious feeling of safety that being in love could give you, the knowledge that the world couldn't hurt you when you were with your lover. Pippa kept her house, but she started staying over at my place almost every night, even when she was working irregular hours. I loved the nights when she would show up in the small hours and crawl into bed next to me and I'd slump half asleep into her arms.

The house came to life during those months. As summer became autumn and the nights drew in, we'd sit and eat long meals at the big table in the kitchen with Michael and Carly. Gone were the days of Michael and I sitting together, him in sullen silence, me trying to winkle out details of what he was up to. Now, he was a happy, chatty teenager, keen to show Carly what a grown up he was, and thoroughly under the spell of the white witch, Pippa. How she did it, I'll never know.

One Saturday, Pippa and I pulled into the drive. The lights in the back were on, which meant Michael was home. Carly was ill, and he'd been planning to go to Danny's, but obviously that hadn't worked out.

'Someone's home,' she said, running her hand up my thigh. 'Shame. I was looking forward to having the house to ourselves.'

We let ourselves in and walked towards the kitchen, Pippa to get a glass of wine, me a glass of water. As we entered the kitchen, we stopped. There was the sound of raucous laughter coming from the utility room.

The utility room was just beyond the kitchen, separated from it by a wooden door. The door was slightly ajar.

'Look at this one,' Danny said. 'There's nowt to it. I can't believe your dad's bird wears these.'

'I know. Fucking hell. This one's leopard skin.'

'Put it on your head.'

A second later, they collapsed into fits of laughter.

'Oh my God,' I said, as I realized what they were doing. 'I'm sorry. I'll stop them. You wait there.'

She shook her head and put her finger to her lips, her face screwed up to stop herself laughing. 'I'll go,' she whispered.

I crossed the kitchen behind her, treading softly on the stone tiles. She pushed open the utility room door and paused, lifting her hand to her mouth theatrically.

'Oh,' she said. 'I'm sorry. Were you busy?'

Michael and Danny were sitting on the floor by the laundry basket. In his right hand, Danny was holding a lacy black thong; in his left, for some reason, he had one of my socks. Michael was frozen, his face visibly draining of colour. He too had a thong, a leopard-print one, that he was wearing on his head.

Pippa bit her lip. 'Sorry to disturb you boys when you're playing,' she said. 'I was just coming to pick up my washing. Oh, you've already started.'

Neither of them spoke. Michael slowly peeled the thong from his head and held it in his hand, looking from the washing basket to Pippa and back. Finally, his gaze stopped on me. He opened his mouth to speak, but all that came out was a kind of groan.

'See you later, boys,' I said. 'Enjoy yourselves in there.' I grabbed Pippa's hand and pulled her out of the kitchen and into the living room. We collapsed onto the sofa and laughed until we cried.

'Did you see his face?' I said. 'If ever someone wanted the world to swallow them up there and then it was Michael.'

'Do you know how embarrassed they'll feel?' Pippa said. 'I feel a bit sorry for him, really. The poor lad.'

The poor lad indeed. I decided to suggest he wash the car. I thought I could count on him agreeing to additional chores for a while. After all, he wouldn't want Carly finding out what had happened.

A few weeks before Christmas, Pippa and I took Michael and Carly to Tenerife for some winter sun. At first, Billy and Kerry had said no to Carly coming, but the power of teenage persistence had prevailed. Teenagers are like water dripping on a rock; eventually it will wear it away.

One Sunday when I'd gone to drop Carly off, Billy handed me a thick wad of twenty pound notes. I counted it later: there was five hundred pounds.

'For the holiday.'

'It's fine,' I said. 'It's our Christmas present to them, and there's not much extra cost. We've got the villa anyway.'

He thrust it at me. 'It's for the flight. She eats food. We pay our way. Take it.'

I was about to argue. Billy was a young man, and Michael had told me he was struggling for work; it was a lot of money, but if it was important to him to pay, then so be it.

'Thanks,' I said. 'It's very good of you.'

He nodded. 'Make sure she has a good time.'

On the plane, I asked Carly who her dad worked for. 'No one, really. Whoever's got work. He does building, labouring, stuff like that. There's not been much though, since the recession.'

We'd felt it at the factory. In January of 2009, our order book had been forty percent less than January 2008. It had been a tough year, to say the least. We'd offered the workforce two options: redundancies or short-time working, which meant less pay but at least everybody kept their jobs. They'd taken the latter. Things were better now, and we were slowly moving people back to full time. I'd mentioned it to Billy and suggested that he send in an application – we were good payers, with benefits and pension – but he had refused. I didn't understand why.

The weather was marvellous, and we spent most of the week by the pool. The villa had a lot of mirrors, and Michael couldn't stop looking at his reflection: in the last few months he'd been working out with Danny and he was proud of his muscles. I remembered that phase: working on your body, trying to accelerate the transition into manhood. That you could change your body by the things you did was a revelation, and you experimented with it, enjoying the discovery of the latent strength you possessed. Of course, being a teenage boy the focus was on size, and so the bigger your muscles, the better. I smiled inwardly every time I saw Michael checking himself out.

I'd done it differently. I hadn't had access to a gym, like those two, so I'd focused on press-ups and chin-ups. I made a rule: every time I went into a new room in the house, I'd do twenty press ups. Into the kitchen for a drink: down and twenty. Back into the lounge to watch TV: down and twenty. Forgot your biscuit? Back into the kitchen: down and twenty. Return to the lounge: down and twenty. It got to be wearing very quickly, not least for Mum and Dad, who had to watch me falling to the floor every time I entered a room, so I changed it to one hundred every morning and one hundred every night.

I wasn't in bad shape even now, for my age. I walked a lot, went for the occasional run, ate quite healthily. Not drinking made a huge difference. When I looked at other men of my age they often had a kind of flabbiness, a stubborn softness around the edges that started with their swelling bellies. If you think it through, a few beers a night is a lot of extra calories, and over the years it adds up to a considerable amount of extra weight. Not taking them on made it much easier for me to keep trim, which had become important to me since meeting Pippa, in a way that I'd forgotten. I'd always had an abstract interest in staying in shape, but now it was focused around a specific goal: I wanted to look good for her. Just like when I was a sixteen-year-old doing press ups, I wanted my girlfriend to fancy me.

There was another motivation I'd forgotten: sexual jealousy. Whenever we were out, Pippa got a lot of attention from men, young and old. At the same time as making me feel good – the looks I gave the men who were ogling said *I'm the one sleeping with her, pal* – it made me insecure. If she could attract lots of men, what guarantee was there that she'd stay with me? We weren't married, didn't have kids, so she was free to chop and change. I suppose it's the same at the start of most relationships, whether between fifteen-year-olds or eighty-year-olds: you assume that your partner is as attractive to the rest of the world as they are to you and, therefore, everyone is a potential threat. There is no option but to make yourself so attractive to them that they don't look elsewhere, either through the clumsy presents and declarations of love teenagers specialize in, or through the more sophisticated ways that adults like to think they use. In the end, it's the same impulses in the driver's seat: jealousy, lust and fear.

I'd also forgotten how much sex you had with a new girlfriend. With Charlotte we'd done it whenever we had a safe place, and often when we didn't, but I'd assumed that it was a function of being teenagers. I'd accepted that the days of crazed lust were gone. Not so. In Tenerife, I'd catch a glimpse of her getting out of the pool or putting on sun-tan lotion or leaning over her beach chair to pick up a book, and get an instant erection that I had to act on. We learnt to read each other: she'd see me looking at her in a certain way and she'd know what was about to happen; likewise for me with her. She had a way of standing with her legs slightly apart that was a dead giveaway; if she was sitting or lying, her lips went into a pout and her eyes softened. As soon as I could get rid of Michael and Carly on an errand, or with a suggestion they went to the beach, we'd be in the bedroom. That holiday, they took a lot of mid-afternoon trips to buy baguettes, or cheese, or whatever we had a minor shortage of. Sometimes we couldn't wait for them to go. Once, Pippa was in the kitchen in her bikini, a red halter-neck with low cut bottoms, pouring herself a glass of ice tea. I'd seen her going in and been compelled to follow her.

I crept up behind her and put my arms around her stomach, my hand slipping into her bikini bottoms.

'Graham. The kids are still here.' Her protest was half-hearted and she was already pressing against me.

'It's all right. We can see them.' They were in the pool which was overlooked by the kitchen window. She didn't reply, just wriggling her hips to help me push down her bikini. We did it quickly, consumed by need. I kept my eyes on the pool; she looked down, gripping the sink.

What went with all this sex was a deep and growing intimacy. Physical closeness leads to emotional closeness, or at least, it makes it easier. Often we lay together afterwards, murmuring about nothing much but getting closer and closer. I felt myself opening up to her in a way I'd not expected to feel again. I was becoming dependent on her, unable to imagine my life without her in it, or at least, unable to imagine my life as a happy life without her in it.

9.

1999: Fond Goodbyes

'All right, mate.' Tommy walked into the hallway, dripping rain and mud all over the new floor. I'd finished it a few days earlier in time for Michael's fifth birthday. The last thing I needed was Tommy ruining it.

Michael came running out of the kitchen. Now he was growing up, he looked a lot like his mum, but he didn't have her calm. In fact, he wasn't like either of us. He was a lot more mischievous.

'Mikey!' Tommy said, ruffling his hair. 'What's up?'

'I'm doing 'speriments in the kitchen.'

My ears pricked up. The last of his experiments had cost me a perfectly good laptop, although at least Michael could say with certainty that they didn't work underwater.

'What kind of experiment?' I said.

'Cookin'.'

I ran into the kitchen. Fortunately this experiment was nothing more than an attempt to see how many pans he could balance on top of each other. Tommy followed me in. He was dangling Michael upside down and bouncing him gently off the walls. Michael was giggling uncontrollably.

'I've got a problem,' Tommy said. 'Some bird smashed my car and buggered off.' He looked at Michael. 'Sorry, ran off. Don't say that, Mikey.'

'Say what?' Thankfully Michael hadn't heard.

'Buggered off. It's rude.'

I groaned. It was obvious Tommy didn't have kids. Probably a good thing, as well.

'Why's it rude?' Michael said. 'What does buggered off mean?'

'Nothing,' I said. 'Forget it.'

'How can it mean nothing?'

I looked at Tommy and rolled my eyes. *Look what you've started.*

'Never mind, Mikey,' he said. 'I'll tell you later. Graham. I need your help. I want to go and see the bird and get my money back. She's not insured, so she'll have to pay.'

'How do you know who it is, if she went off?'

'I got the reg. Lisa ran it for me.' Lisa was a police officer he knew. 'I've got the address. It's in Bootle.'

Bootle. The roughest place in Liverpool. 'I don't know about this, Tommy. Are you sure it's a good idea?'

'I want my money. It was her fault. She has to pay.'

I sighed. Now he had the idea there was no stopping him.

'Right. I'll see if Mum can have Michael.'

'I was thinking we could take him. There's less likely to be trouble if there's a kid there. Like a kind of human shield.'

I shook my head. His delusions knew no bounds. 'Forget it. He's going to his grandma's.'

Tommy looked disappointed. 'Come on, mate. It'll be all right.'

'No, no, and no. You want me to tell you again? No.'

'All right, mate. Don't get your knickers in a twist. We'll do it without him.'

'Damn right we will.'

I dropped him off at Mum's and we headed off in Tommy's ten-year-old Renault 5 Sport. He'd bought it when the Escort had finally wheezed its last. It had a large dent in one side where the girl, whose name was Lizzie Heyes, had hit it before clearing off.

Fifty minutes later we were standing in the concourse of a housing estate looking up at a sixteen-storey tower block. The entry was next to a flat-roofed concrete pub with blacked-out windows. A shabby teenager emerged and looked at us suspiciously.

'You pleece?' He said. 'You the filth?'

I shook my head.

'Then fuck off.'

He lit a hand-rolled cigarette, jammed it between his lips and walked away, laughing.

'Great,' I said. 'I can see this is going to go well already. For some reason, I don't get the impression that Miss Heyes and her family are going to welcome us in for tea and biscuits and then hand over a wad of cash.'

'It'll be all right. You'll see.' I detected a note of uncertainty in his voice. It must have been bad: even the great optimist was having doubts.

The number of the flat was 7A. The lift, of course, didn't work, so we climbed the dark, piss-soaked stairs to the seventh floor. 7A was the first door on the landing. It was painted a lurid green. I pressed the bell and waited. Nothing happened. Tommy banged on the door, and a dog barked. It sounded like a big dog.

'Shuddup!' A man's voice came from the flat. 'Stop yer fuckin' racket.' The door swung open and a man scowled at us, narrow-eyed. He had a shock of bright orange hair, so bright that it looked like one of the wigs Scottish football fans wore.

''Oo are you? Pigs?' He had no teeth.

'No.' Tommy cleared his throat as though about to declaim from a rostrum. 'Is this where Lizzie Heyes lives?'

'No.' I sensed that this was the man's default answer to any question he was asked.

'Are you Mr Heyes?'

'No.'

'Do you know Lizzie Heyes?'

'No.' He whistled and snapped his fingers. A large, growling shadow appeared behind him and he grabbed its collar in a mottled hand. 'Now, if you ain't the pigs, then I suggest you fuck off.'

'Thanks for your time,' I said. 'It's been a pleasure. You're a gentleman.'

His fist shot out and connected with my left eye. The pain was sudden and intense. No Hollywood fight scene, this: I fell over, sprawling against the low wall of the balcony.

'Don't tek the piss, lad,' he said. He watched us from the doorway, waiting for us to leave.

Tommy didn't move. 'She owes me money,' he said. 'She hit my car. I've got witnesses. If she doesn't pay, I'll involve the police.'

The toothless red-haired psycho laughed. 'Go for it, lad. You think they'll get 'er for that? After all the shit she's done, yer think they'll bother with that?'

'Come on, Tommy,' I said, rubbing my face, the swelling already starting. 'It's obvious he's not got a penny to scratch his arse with. Let's go.'

'Clever lad,' the man said, and slammed the door.

'Well,' I said, when we were back on the stairs. 'That was a fucking disaster.'

'You always give in, you. You've got no balls.'

'Tommy, there's a difference between having balls and being the kind of suicidal idiot who can't recognize a lost cause. You, my friend, are in the latter camp.'

'Oh, well,' he shrugged. Tommy had the gift of being able to cut his losses and move on. He was not a brooder. 'I'll buy you a pint. There's a pub downstairs.'

'Tommy, firstly, I don't drink. As you know. Secondly, even if I did still drink, that pub is probably the one place on the planet that I would have avoided, however desperate the craving for a drink was. We're going home.'

By the time Tommy dropped me off, my eye was nearly closed. As I lay on the couch with a bag of frozen peas on the bruise, the doorbell rang. It was Stephen.

'Hello,' I said. 'I wasn't expecting you.' I took Michael to see Charlotte's parents every week, sometimes on a Wednesday evening, but more often on a Sunday afternoon for lunch. Georgina always made a roast, and it was a tradition I enjoyed.

He looked at my eye. 'Been fighting, Graham?'

'It's a long story.'

'Does it involve Tommy?'

I nodded.

'That's all I need to know. Glad to see he's not changed.'

'Are you coming in?' He sat on the couch and I handed him a mug of tea. 'Everything ok?'

'Yes, fine. There's something I wanted to share. Georgina and I are moving. We're going to live in our place down on the south coast.'

'Oh. Congratulations, I suppose.'

'Aside from you and Michael, there's not that much up here for us anymore,' he said. 'Richard's in the City, with Ginny and the twins, so we decided we may as well live somewhere near them. We don't see them enough.'

I knew he was right, but it still felt like they were abandoning us. Our world was dwindling. With them gone there'd only be Mum left. 'We'll really miss you. Michael loves seeing you.'

'We'll still see you. You're welcome any time. Both of you.'

'When are you going? Not soon, I hope?'

'It'll be a while yet. We've to sell the house in Lymm. That's the other thing I was going to mention. We'd like to do something for Michael. Charlotte would have got something when we died, and we'd like to give that to her son. If you're ok with it, I plan to set up a trust fund for him that he can have when he's twenty-five.' He smiled knowingly. 'I would offer to help with his school fees, but I know where you stand on private education. There's still plenty of your dad in you.'

'Of course it's fine with me. More than fine. I'll make sure he knows where it came from and that he knows everything about his mother. About Charlotte.'

His smile became sad. 'It's hard, isn't it?' he said. 'To keep the memories fresh? They fade so quickly. I struggle to call her face to mind these days, struggle to hear her laugh.'

'I know. I only see her clearly in my dreams.'

'And then you wake and she's gone again. Is that irony? That the only way to see her means you have to lose her all over again.' He stood up, his eyes glistening with tears. 'Make sure you stay in touch, Graham. You're an important part of our lives.'

As they were of mine. But our bond was Charlotte, and she was ever further in the past. With them gone, Michael would have no link to her. He'd see them from time to time, but that wasn't the same as growing up with them round the corner. With them went half of his life; half of what made him what he was came from

Stephen and Georgina. He wouldn't remember his mum, and he'd barely know her parents. I couldn't imagine the sadness that caused me ever going away.

I wanted to hug him, tell him I loved him, for that's how I felt. I suspect he felt the same way, but we're British – English, more precisely, I think the Celts are better at expressing their emotions – so we just gave each other a little wave and he left.

10.

2009–10: Merry Christmas and a Happy New Year?

'*Where's the turkey*?'

'I told you. In the garden.'

Pippa and I had invited Tommy and Pat round for Christmas lunch. Tommy had sworn that he could get the best deal on a turkey – he knew someone who knew someone – so I had left it to him. Now, at 10 a.m. on Christmas morning, I was at his house to pick it up.

'This turkey is dead, isn't it?'

''Course it's dead.'

'Then why's it in the garden?'

He opened the back door and pointed to an old bath tub he had at the end of his yard, where he normally grew onions. 'I put it in the bath.'

The great thing about being friends with Tommy is that he never ceases to amaze you. Amaze and puzzle, but I'd learnt long ago that seemingly meaningless, random things had a logic to them. It was just rarely obvious what it was.

'The bath?'

'The fella who sold it me told me you have to brine 'em before you cook 'em. Which means you leave 'em in salty water overnight. They stay moist. I didn't have anything big enough in the house, so I used the bath.'

He'd covered the bath with a tarpaulin, which we untied. The turkey was half floating, it's pimply skin shockingly white in the grey morning.

'Tommy.' I pointed at the bird. 'It's not been . . . done. The head's on, the feet are on. It's not gutted.' Its black eyes looked up at me. 'It looks like it fell in and drowned.'

'It's plucked, though, and drained.'

'Well, that's all right then. As long as it's plucked. What am I supposed to do with it? I don't know how to butcher a turkey.'

'It can't be that hard. Just chop its head off.'

'If it's not that hard, you do it.'

'Can't. Me and Pat are goin' to me mum's.' Of course. Typical Tommy. A watertight excuse. He looked at his watch, a Casio digital he'd had since the eighties. He been increasingly pleased he'd kept it since Carly had told him it was coming back into fashion. 'We're off in a few minutes.' He picked up the turkey, wrapped the sodden bird in a towel and handed it to me. 'Three o'clock at yours?'

The house was quiet when I got back. Michael had come home late the night before and was still asleep; Pippa was visiting her family and was due shortly. I dumped the turkey in the sink and contemplated it.

I tried to picture what a butchered turkey looked like. Presumably it was something like a chicken: no head, no feet, a kind of hole in the backside for the stuffing. I picked out my sharpest knife and grabbed one of the feet.

The claws dug into my palm as I cut where I thought the ankle was. The knife sliced through the skin immediately, but then caught, snagging on the bone. I needed something with a serrated edge, so I threw it aside and grabbed the bread knife. I sawed hard, twisting and pulling the foot to try and get it loose. There was a gristly snap as something gave and it suddenly came away in my hand. I felt sick.

I sipped some water and grabbed the second foot. With my new experience of cutting off turkey feet, it came away more easily, and I turned my attention to the head. I examined the turkey's neck for a place to cut, trying not to catch its eye. When you grow up away from the countryside you think of meat as something that comes in a packet. I was glad. I wasn't even killing the turkey and already it was nauseating. I felt sorry for it, felt that it deserved better than the indignity it was suffering under my clumsy knife. A bond was growing up between us and I wasn't sure I'd even be able to eat the damn thing later. This was terrible; from now on, it was supermarket meat for me. I didn't want to know what the stuff looked like before it was packaged up in a neat, unthreatening bundle.

'Sorry, mate,' I said, lifting its head and looking at its lifeless eyes. 'Bet you wish you were still running about in the field, eh?'

'Are you feeling a bit lonely, darling? Talking to the turkey?' Pippa walked into the kitchen and kissed me. 'Happy Christmas.'

'Happy Christmas. Don't ask. Tommy can explain later. Although at this rate we won't be eating until Boxing Day. I'm making a right pig's ear of this.'

'Do you want me to help?'

'Thanks, but I might as well finish it, now I've started. I think I've got it figured out.'

She picked up one of the feet and examined the ragged cut around its ankle. 'Did you *gnaw* this off?' She held out her hand for the knife. 'Here. I'll finish it. We did plenty of dissection in anatomy class.'

I puffed out my cheeks in relief. Thank God I'd not had to chop its head off. Now, at least, I had a fighting chance of enjoying my Christmas dinner.

Tommy and Pat showed up at three, and we sat down to watch the Queen's speech.

'Isn't she marvellous?' Pat said. 'She's so dignified.'

'She's the same in person,' Pippa said. 'She came to our hospital.'

'She never?' Pat's eyes lit up. 'You met the Queen?'

'I got to show her round. She was great with the patients, really calm. She was really interested in them. She's very down to earth, considering.'

'The Queen, eh?' Tommy shook his head at me. 'You're out of your depth here, mate. Pippa knows Her Maj.'

'I hardly know her,' Pippa smiled. 'But I agree he's out of his depth.'

'We're all moving up in the world,' Tommy said. 'Look at this that Pat got me.' He was wearing a new jumper. 'It's Tommy Hillfinger.'

'Hilfiger,' I said. 'Tommy Hilfiger.'

'That's what I said. Hillfinger.'

'You said finger, Hillfinger. It's figure. Tommy Hilfiger.'

'Well, whatever it's called, it's a cracking jumper. Isn't it, Michael?' Michael and Carly walked into the lounge. 'Happy Christmas, lad. And to you, Carly.'

'What's that you're wearing, Carly?' Pippa looked at Carly's hand. 'Is that from Michael?'

Carly was wearing an enormous red and green ring. She showed it round the room. 'Mike got me it. It's gorgeous. I love it.'

'Last of the big spenders, eh Mikey?' Tommy said. Michael blushed a deep red.

I checked my watch. 'Turkey time. Kitchen, everyone.' As they stood up and left the room, I put my hand on Michael's shoulder. 'That's a lovely present. Well done. You're a good lad.'

He smiled at me, his eyes sparkling. 'It's good, eh? I think she really likes it.'

'So do I, son. So do I.'

Everyone agreed that brining worked. The turkey was delicious. After Pat and Tommy had left with enough to last them until the New Year, Pippa and I did the washing up. As I stacked the dishwasher she came up behind me and wrapped her arms around my stomach, her chin nestled on my shoulder.

'That was fabulous,' she murmured. 'Thanks for a lovely Christmas. It's the best present you could have given me.'

I turned to face her. 'I'm glad we met. Glad it's worked out. I love you, Pippa.'

The New Year had barely started and already Christmas was a distant memory. We were back to leaving for work in the dark and getting home in the dark. The occasional ten-minute stroll in the sun at lunchtime was a cruel reminder of the glittering days of summer.

I parked in the staff car park of the hospital. 2010 had started with heavy snow, and when we had finally cleared the drive Pippa's car had refused to start. While it was in the garage I was driving her to work and she was getting lifts home, but today I'd finished work early, so I'd come to pick her up. She was supposed to finish at 4.30 p.m., and I thought it would be a nice surprise.

It was bitterly cold so I stayed in the car. The hospital door opened and Pippa appeared, framed in the light. As she glanced into the car park I waved, but she didn't see me in the winter gloom. I was on the point of opening the door and calling to her when she looked back into the hospital and spoke to someone; seconds later a man appeared behind her, linked arms at the elbow and stepped with Pippa – my girlfriend – into the car park.

I shrank down in my seat. Now, being seen was the last thing I wanted. They walked to a black Mercedes sports car, keeping close together against the cold. Pippa laughed at something the man said and he wrapped his arms around her in a hug. It was an impulsive, easy movement, the movement of two people familiar with each other, comfortable with each other. The kind of comfort that only comes from intimacy. The kind of intimacy that only comes from being lovers.

Pippa let go of him to climb in the passenger seat. He paused to take something from the front windscreen – a pale blue flyer – which he stuffed into his pocket. I got a good look at him: tall, angular, dark hair gelled back in a stiff sweep. He wore a long, dark coat over his suit and he was handsome: clean, striking features, and a posture that screamed confidence. He was exactly the type of guy you would have pictured her with. They were a lovely couple.

The Mercedes pulled away, its fat tyres crunching on the snow. I stayed slumped in my seat. How could I have been so stupid? I should have known it would come to this eventually. She'd meet some handsome surgeon and I'd be history, just another internet boyfriend on her path to the perfect marriage. I mean really, how had I thought that she'd stay interested in me, with all my baggage? An alcoholic, one-pace accountant, with a teenage son and a dead partner.

I couldn't even kid myself that she was just getting a lift home. They'd been too close for that. I started the engine and pulled out of the car park.

When I got home the house was dark. She was somewhere with that guy; I pictured them in a Cheshire mansion, reclining in postcoital bliss on a king-size, satin-sheeted bed. The cold seeped through my coat and I shivered.

I waited an hour for her to arrive. She had no reason to hurry; I normally didn't get home until well after seven. I thought of all the other afternoons she'd have spent with him while I was at work, and my skin crawled. I put on my running shoes and dug out a crumpled old tracksuit. I needed to work off the anger before I saw her.

I ran out past the reservoir, keeping close to the hedges on the narrow country roads. The tracksuit was grey, and any cars I encountered wouldn't see me. I soon warmed up, and the rhythm of the running helped me think how I would bring it up. I played out the different ways to start the conversation in my mind. *Do you love me, Pippa? Are you messing around? Pippa, can you look me in the eye and tell me you've never cheated on me?* None of them sounded right. I came across as desperate. I pictured her telling me about her lover, about how she needed more than I could offer. I didn't want to hear it. I didn't want that to be the reason we broke up, didn't want everyone to know, didn't want to have to tell Michael. He'd think I was useless, not good enough for Pippa. He'd probably pity me. God, it was so unfair. She was the one having the affair, but I was the one who would look an idiot in the eyes of the world. They wouldn't be surprised. They'd probably just been waiting for her to dump me anyway.

I turned to go home, my warm breath billowing in the chill air. I should never have let myself get into this. I'd have been better off on my own.

I opened the back door and scraped the mud from my shoes. The kitchen light was on, and I heard the clatter of pans.

Pippa raised an eyebrow when I stepped into the kitchen. 'Been running? In this weather?' She looked clean, freshly scrubbed. Her hair was wet, pulled back from her face.

'Yeah. I wanted to do some thinking. You've had a shower?'

'Wash away the grime. You get so sweaty standing on your feet all day.'

And lying on your back. 'Of course. Right.' I pulled off my tracksuit top. 'I'll have one too, I think. Useful things, showers, aren't they?' My tone was bitter and aggressive and she looked at me with a puzzled frown. I wasn't making the best job of this.

'Graham? Are you ok?'

'Fine. Just fine.'

'You seem annoyed.'

'No. Just been thinking.'

She broke the silence. 'Ok. Well, I'll see you after your shower.'

The hot water coursed over me and I pictured her in here, in my shower, the soap eradicating the smells of sex from her neck, breasts, between her legs. I stayed under the water for a long time, working myself into an ever increasing anger. When I emerged, I was red and hot and ready.

Pippa was eating dinner, picking through her lasagne and salad. 'Sorry. I couldn't wait. I was starving and you were taking your time.'

'You must have worked up quite an appetite, with all that standing up.'

She thumped her fork down on the wooden table. 'Graham, what on earth is wrong with you? I've had a long day and I don't need your cryptic comments.'

How dare she take me for such a fool? She knew damn well what I was getting at, but if she chose to lie, then so be it. I gave her another chance to confess. 'Nothing cryptic about them. Just an observation. Just being honest, Pippa. It's a virtue, you know, honesty.'

She drummed her fingers on the table. 'I've no idea what's got into you, but I don't like it.'

She didn't like it? She obviously thought I was some kind of idiot patsy. She didn't even have the decency to tell me what was going on. I was damned if I was going to keep digging to get it out of her. *Pippa, are you having an affair? How could you do that to me, Pippa?* I hated the thought of having to ask. It was humiliating, like begging.

So why ask? Why bother? Our relationship was over either way. I decided to get out of it with whatever dignity I could. She didn't need to know that I knew about the affair, that it was her fault it was over. She could believe that I just wasn't interested anymore. At least she wouldn't think I was a total doormat that way.

'Pippa. We need to talk.' I stood behind the kitchen counter and looked out of the window.

'Ok.' She held her palms open. 'I'm all ears.'

I wasn't going to be humiliated. If this was going to end, it was going to end on my terms. 'I'm not sure we can carry on seeing each other.'

Pippa looked confused, then shocked. 'What do you mean?'

'I mean I think we should break up.' The words had a strange texture in my mouth.

'Are you being serious? Graham, what's brought this on? It's ridiculous.'

'I don't want a girlfriend anymore.'

'What's happened? It's never been so good between us.'

'I need some time on my own.'

'Graham, tell me what's happened! I don't believe this!'

I reached for the first reason that came to mind. 'It's Charlotte. I can't be with anyone else.'

She clenched her teeth and closed her eyes. 'We talked about this! I don't mind. We can get through it. There's no need for all this nonsense about breaking up.'

I pictured her in the car with her lover. My anger hardened. 'Not this time, Pippa. It's over. Listen to me. I want to be alone.'

She clasped her hands to her mouth. 'You mean it, don't you? You really mean it. Graham, what's happened to cause this? Tell me, please. The truth.'

The truth. How ironic. I shook my head. 'There's nothing to tell.' All she had to do was admit the affair, but she couldn't even be that honest. I was damned if I was going to mention it.

'Do you love me? Tell me that at least.'

I looked away, my back to her. There was no way I could have lied to her, so I said nothing.

She pushed the half-eaten lasagne away from her and stood up. 'I don't know what's going on, Graham, but you can't treat me like this. If you want me to, I'll go. You can call me when you come back to your senses.'

She waited for a reply but I couldn't bear to look at her. I consoled myself with the thought that however much it hurt me, at least I'd have my pride. At least she hadn't humiliated me. As far as she – and the world – would know, it was me that had ended it.

She slammed the kitchen door shut. It reverberated in its frame for a long time.

Tommy and I sat in the lounge in front of the fire. Pippa had left an hour before without another word.

'You sure she was at it with this fella?'

'You should have seen them. They were all over each other. It was disgusting.'

'In the car park? Don't her colleagues know about you? I mean, wouldn't she want to keep it on the QT?'

'I dunno, Tommy. All I know is what I saw.'

He puffed out his cheeks. 'Well, I have to say I didn't see it coming. I didn't have her down for that type. What did she say?'

'Nothing. I didn't ask her.'

Tommy frowned. 'You didn't mention it? Then how did you end up splitting up?'

'I told her it was over.'

'You *what*?' Tommy jerked forward on his chair and spilt his tea. 'Why?'

'I gave her plenty of opportunities to come clean, but she didn't say anything. I didn't want to bring it up. I wasn't going to give her the satisfaction of dumping me.'

'Was that Michael's idea? Because it sounds like something a fucking teenager would do. Graham, we're adults. I thought we were past caring about who dumped who? Why don't you just talk to her?'

'No. She's having an affair, Tommy, so it's over, whether I talk to her or not. If she admits it, it's over, if she doesn't, it's over, both for the affair and for lying about it.' The logic was incontrovertible. Even Tommy would see that.

'This is what you did with Charlotte, you know.'

'No it's not. It's nothing like it. Charlotte wasn't having an affair. Pippa is.'

'It's the same. You always thought she was out of your league and so you always worried she was after other blokes. Same with Pippa. It's self pity, or something. *How could someone like that be interested in boring old accountant Graham*? You're just getting your excuses in early.'

'Whose side are you on here, Tommy?'

'I'm just the mirror of truth, mate.' He shook his head. 'There's a lot of folk who'd be happy with what you've got. You should think on it. You're making a mistake.'

'A mistake? How? If I'm being cheated on, I might as well get out of it with some dignity, right?'

'I'm not sure dignity's the right word, mate. It sounds like a bit of a fucking farce to me.'

'Maybe. But it's better than the alternative.' I switched on the television. 'I'm not prepared to be humiliated. I've suffered enough. Anyway, I've made up my mind. It's over.'

'Michael. I need to talk to you.'

Michael didn't look up from the computer screen. He was perfectly capable of holding a conversation while zapping aliens. 'What?'

'Switch that off. It's important.' He ignored me. I grabbed the controller and snatched it from his hand.

His head snapped round. The computer made a bleeping noise. 'Shit. You've made me lose a life. I was on for a good score.' He leaned over and pressed something and the game paused.

'It's Pippa. We're breaking up.'

'What are you on about? 'Course you're not breaking up.'

'We are. It's already done. It wasn't working out.'

'Dad, you're like a pair of teenagers. Me and Carly laugh about it. You're more lovesick that we are.'

'No we're not. And there's more to it, Michael.' I took a deep breath. 'It's your mum. I feel like I'm betraying her. I can't stop thinking about her.'

'You're not betraying her. I'm her son, and I don't think so. I like Pippa. It's better when she's around. Mum'd be glad about that. And you need a girlfriend. What are you going to do when me and Carly are rich and famous and too cool to hang out with you? You'll be lonely.'

'You don't understand.'

'Did she dump you?'

'No.' I sat on his bed. I felt lost. 'It was my idea.' The words didn't give me as much comfort as I'd hoped.

'Shit, Dad. Pippa's awesome.'

'I know. But sometimes things don't work out how you wanted.'

'Can I still see her?'

'If you want. But it's probably best to leave it for a while.'

He put down his controller and sat next to me on the bed. He gave me an awkward hug. 'I didn't mean that about being too cool to hang out with you. However cool we are, we'll still hang out with you.'

I wasn't sure that sounded like he meant it to, but I hugged him back. 'Thanks. Your mum would have been proud of you.'

We stayed like that for a few seconds, before he returned to his computer game.

My BlackBerry rang. I grabbed it from my coat pocket. It was Friday afternoon, a few days after I'd broken up with Pippa, and I'd been out for a late lunch. Every time it had rung since then I'd found myself wishing it was her.

It was Michael's number. I felt a twinge of guilt at being disappointed to have my son call me.

'Michael?'

'All right, Dad. Where are you?'

'At work. Why?'

'I wondered when you were home. I wanted a lift to a friend's house.'

'I'll be back at six.'

'That's too late. Any chance—'

'No. I have a job. I'm not a taxi service.'

'All right, all right. I'll see you tomorrow afternoon.'

'Tomorrow afternoon? You're not coming home?'

'I'm staying at Danny's.'

'I'm not sure I want you staying out, Michael. And I was thinking we could spend some time together this evening.'

'You want me to stop in with you? Yeah, right. Don't make my life miserable just 'cos you've got nothing to do. See you tomorrow.'

The line went dead. I glanced at my watch. Nearly five o'clock. The weekend seemed awfully empty and awfully long. This was going to be harder than I'd thought it would be.

I missed Pippa, more than I'd imagined. The last few nights she'd had a starring role in my dreams, some of which were frankly pornographic. I hadn't been aware that I knew of some of the practices we got up to in them. God knows where I'd seen them. I hefted my BlackBerry in my hand. Perhaps I should call her, talk it through now the dust had settled. She'd probably be back from work by now. All she had to do was come clean, and then maybe we could work it out. I played out the conversation.

There's something I need to tell you, Graham. I was having an affair, but it's over now.

I know. It's fine. I forgive you. I just needed to hear you tell me the truth.

Really? You forgive me?

I do. I love you. I missed you like crazy.

I missed you too. I'm glad we were apart. It made me realize how much I love you.

Fuck it. What did I have to lose? I found her number in the memory and pressed dial.

The phone rang once, then tripped into voicemail. The sound of her voice was a shock, and I hung up without leaving a message. She'd probably seen my number and rejected the call, but that was ok; I could see why she'd be angry with me. It didn't matter. This was better face to face. I'd pop round on the way home and we could settle our differences.

In the car my mood lightened. There was too much between us just to throw it away. I started humming, a kick of adrenalin heightening the anticipation. As I approached her house, I slowed and indicated left, then came to a shuddering halt, the nose of my car just inside her driveway.

There was a car in Pippa's drive, pulled up close to her front door. A Mercedes sports car. Unless she'd upgraded her car in the last few days then I was pretty sure it was the car I'd seen her getting into at the hospital. Her lover's car.

I reversed out and drove a few yards past Pippa's house. I pulled up, my hands shaking. I shook my head. Perhaps my visit hadn't gone as I'd hoped, but I'd got my answer: our relationship really was over and done with.

In a way I was glad I knew now, before it went any further. I wasn't sure I could survive another relationship as intense as the one I'd had with Charlotte. There was too much at stake, and you could never be sure that it would end well. Even if the other person was a model, loving, faithful partner, there was always the risk that the universe would take them away. There was only one sure way to eliminate the risk: solitude.

11.

2003: Analysing

Michael flopped onto the couch next to me, rubbing his eyes. I put my arm around him and he snuggled close to my chest. He was nine; from time to time I was shocked by how grown up he was becoming, but he was still a little boy, especially early in the morning when he had just woken up.

'What are you watching?'

'It's for my degree.' I was up early, watching the prescribed programmes for my new Open University course. I'd finished the English degree and, full of zeal, started one in Philosophy. It was dragging on much longer than I had expected. The programme was on the question of dualism. I didn't really understand the complexities – still don't. I never took to Philosophy – but, put simply, it's the problem of how mind interacts with body. The thesis runs that mind is a non-physical, ethereal kind of thing – you can't touch it or weigh it or see it – whereas body is something else entirely, the stuff of flesh and bones and piss and sweat. How then do they interact? Where is the link that allows all those thoughts you have floating around in your brain to turn into words or movements or shudders? How does something that has no physical presence manage to move something that does? It's one of those questions that people have been asking for a thousand years and will probably still be asking in another thousand years. I'd probably have forgotten about it altogether, if it hadn't been for Mum.

The day before, Michael and I had been to visit her. She opened the door and kissed me, then grabbed Michael and hugged him.

'How's my darling boy? I've got something for you.'

Mum's treats were invariably of the sweet, baked variety. She handed Michael an enormous gingerbread man, chocolate buttons on his front and thick icing for his hair. She was by no means a great baker, but she knew her audience: the way to success as far as her grandson was concerned was chocolate and icing, and plenty of it. Grandma had never yet failed to deliver.

'Thanks, Grandma.' Michael took a big bite and kissed her, leaving some crumbs on her cheek. I went into the kitchen to put the kettle on, grabbed a mug, then paused.

There was a pile of bottle tops next to the tea-bags.

They were all from different brands of beer. Some were old, some new; some dirty, some clean. I prodded them. It wasn't like her at all. She was a very neat and tidy person.

Mum came into the kitchen. 'Are you making a cuppa? I'd love one.'

'Sure.' I looked at Mum as she opened the fridge door. 'Are you collecting bottle tops now?'

'Sorry?'

'Bottle tops. You've got a pile here.'

She frowned. 'What do you mean, love?'

'Look.'

She covered her mouth with her hand. 'Graham. Did you bring those?'

'No. They were here when I arrived.'

'Give over. Are you playing tricks on me?'

'Of course not, Mum.' She looked grey and ill, and my stomach contracted.

'Michael! Get in here!' Her shout was shockingly loud. I couldn't remember the last time she'd raised her voice. Michael appeared in the doorway. 'Are these yours?'

He shook his head. 'I've not been in the kitchen.'

'It's all right,' I said. 'Go and eat your gingerbread man. Grandma's just made a mistake.'

Mum's face cleared. 'That's right. Sorry, love.' When she looked at me her expression was calm again, but her eyes were the eyes of an animal, trapped and confused. I wondered whether it was the first such mistake she'd made.

A few days later I was due to speak at a meeting of the parish council. A few of the neighbours were protesting about a proposal to build a mobile phone mast in a nearby field. I'd agreed to be the spokesperson. I wasn't that bothered myself, but I'd agreed to go along with it, and Mum had said she would come round and watch Michael in the evening.

I looked at my watch. She was twenty minutes late. I'd said I'd pick her up, but she'd insisted on taking the bus for the exercise. It probably wasn't her fault; the bloody thing was always late, but still. I was due at the meeting in the next fifteen minutes.

After another five minutes, I started to worry. She should have left by now, but on the off chance I called her number and waited while the phone rang.

My mouth dropped open when she answered.

'Mum? What are you doing?'

'Making some dinner. Why?'

'You're supposed to be here. I'm going to a meeting.'

'I don't think so, love. It's not in my diary.'

'Mum. I asked you yesterday. You said you'd come on the bus, remember?'

There was a long pause. 'I'd have remembered that, love. It's important.'

I know, I wanted to say. 'Look. I'm in a hurry. I'll drop Michael at yours and pick him up later. Ok?'

When I picked him up after the meeting, I took Mum into the kitchen. 'Do you think you should see a doctor, Mum?'

'What for?'

'If you've been forgetting things. And the bottle tops. It's a bit strange, that's all.'

'Don't be daft. I'm just getting on a bit. I'm an old lady, Graham. I'm bound to forget the odd thing.'

'You're not that old.' She was a few years into her sixties; hardly a geriatric.

'Look, I'm fine. Honestly.'

'I just think—'

'Graham!' Her tone was shrill and aggressive. 'I don't want to hear any more about it!'

I shut up. It wasn't the aggression in her voice that bothered me, that I could forget. It was the fear. That was much, much worse.

There were many more missed appointments and forgotten conversations over the next few months. I was always uneasy when they occurred but we gradually became accustomed to them – Mum called them her 'little slips' – and we fitted the patterns of our lives around them. If Mum was expected to do something, we called her to remind her; if we told her something we didn't assume she'd remember it; if we found empty cans of coke or old newspapers on the kitchen table we ignored them. Or twigs, or leaves. Or bits of glass. Or bus tickets. So it is that the insidious becomes normal.

On the morning of Michael's tenth birthday party I got up early. The week before was a busy one at work – we'd closed the books for the month – so I'd booked a magician, but had done little else. No balloons blown up, no birthday decorations, no food and no presents for Michael. I left him with the neighbours and went out to run the errands.

I got back at midday and handed him a packet of balloons. 'Here. Blow those up.'

He puffed into a red one. It stretched thinner and pinker until it was as big as his head.

'Not too much. It'll explode.'

My warning came true with a loud bang. Michael grinned at me and started another.

'Come on. Stop messing around. We've a lot to do.'

'And we've got to pick Grandma up.'

Shit. I'd forgotten. I couldn't leave her to take the bus or she'd forget.

'We'll do it now. She can help us get ready.'

When we got to Mum's house I sent Michael to ring the doorbell. He pressed the buzzer and I heard it sound inside the house. He stood outside the door, hands in his pockets.

I wound down the car window. 'Ring it again.'

I opened the door and got out. I still had a key to the house. 'She'll be in the back, or taking a nap.'

It took a few minutes to check the rooms, but I knew as soon as we opened the door that the house was empty. It had the stillness that comes with being unoccupied. Mum had gone out.

'Where is she?' Michael tugged my hand. 'She'll miss the party.'

'She's probably on her way on the bus. We'll see her at home.'

That was the most likely explanation. We'd got our wires crossed, and she thought she had to make her own way there. It was a waste of twenty minutes but it wasn't that bad.

We drove home. Despite her 'little slips', I still expected to see her in the driveway as we pulled up at the barn, but it was empty. A horrible suspicion that she had forgotten the party grew in the pit of my stomach.

Michael frowned. 'Where's Grandma? Isn't she coming?'

'She will,' I said, much more certainly that I felt. 'She will.'

I called her house a few times, but there was no answer. The guests arrived, the magician did his tricks, the children played musical chairs and pass the parcel, the cake was eaten and the presents opened, but Mum didn't come. Michael forgot, caught up in the whirl, but I couldn't put it from my mind.

As the guests started to leave, the phone went.

'Hi, Graham.'

'Mum. Where've you been?'

'Shopping. And I popped in on Rita for a chat. It's been a while since I saw her.' I winced. Rita had been round a few days before for dinner.

'You know, today was Michael's birthday party.'

She froze. All I could hear was her breathing. In that moment I felt the worst I've ever felt about my mother: I pitied her.

'What?' It was a hoarse whisper. 'Oh God. Of course. How could I forget?'

'Mum. Don't worry. We'll come and see you later. I think it's time you saw a doctor.'

I went with her to the doctor and listened to his questions, watched the tests they gave her. I knew what was happening before he said it.

Alzheimer's. I sat with her in the car, holding her hand as she cried. She knew what it meant: a slow, terrifying descent as her mind broke down.

She finally spoke. 'You've enough to put up with, without me to care for.'

'Mum. That's the last thing on my mind.'

'I don't want to be a burden.'

'You won't be. You couldn't be.'

'You say that now, but I know what it means to have this . . . thing. I've seen it enough as a nurse. It's awful and undignified, and I don't want to have it.'

She started crying again and I put my arm around her.

'Don't worry, Mum. I'll take care of you. I promise.'

She sniffed and looked away, staring out of the window. 'Take me home. I want to be by myself.'

It was a few years before she moved into a care home, before the final tragedy of the disease played itself out, and there were plenty of tough moments in those years. But none of them were as bad as the day she found out. On that day she understood that every hope she had for her future, and every memory she had of her past, would be slowly extinguished.

The doctor told me that no one knows why it happens. No doubt they're right, but in Mum's case I had an idea what was behind it. I think in some ways she wanted to forget.

There's only so much a person can take before something has to give. Mum was one of the calmest and steadiest people I'd ever known. She was always smiling, always ready to help, always there with practical solutions: when I was at my lowest point, Michael living with Stephen and Georgina, my dad barely speaking to me, drinking the best part of two bottles of wine and a bottle of Jim Beam a day, Mum always did something to help. Sorted out the washing, tidied the place up, cooked a decent meal. She never judged me or tried to get me to change, she just took care of the practical things in the hope that eventually I'd get through it. She just loved me, quietly and unquestioningly.

But it must have hurt her, deep down. Perhaps not even that deep. Perhaps the hurt was with her always, just below the surface, but she was too proud and too strong to show it. She would never have wanted people to feel they had to help her. She hated to be a burden. She was a carer, a nurse, someone who looked after other people. The last thing she wanted was to have people do things for her. It was an imposition: she was happy to devote her life to other people and, in return, she wanted nothing. It was a way of life I found difficult to understand. Perhaps you need to be a woman; you certainly need to be a better person than I am.

I know she'd wanted more children, but hadn't had them. I've no idea why not; she and Dad never spoke about it, but presumably it wasn't good. What's on the list of possible reasons? Infertility? Miscarriage? Stillbirth? None of those are a walk in the park. Whatever it was must have left its mark.

And then there was Charlotte, who Mum adored. She was beautiful and intelligent and modern. She was everything a daughter could be that a mother would be proud of, and I have no doubt that Mum saw her as a daughter. If I'd ever done anything to harm Charlotte or threaten our marriage – if I'd had an affair, for example – that would have been the one thing Mum would not have been able to forgive me for. When Charlotte died, I was too tied up in my own grief to think about anyone else, but it must have been terrible for Mum. Seeing your son collapse and sink to a point where he nearly lost his child and was in danger of losing his life, all while you are grieving for someone you loved like a daughter: you can't bottle that stuff up forever. There's too much internal pressure.

And finally, Dad. Her husband, the man she'd been with all her life, perhaps the only man she'd ever been with. They were long past the demonstrative stage of their relationship, long past the days when the guiding force of their union was passion, and well into the days when they were companions, two people shaped by each other into matching halves of the same whole. But the loss was no less for that. Yet Mum never asked for anything. Never let anyone see that she needed support. Never leaned on her friends or family to get her through. When someone acts as she did it's easy to assume that they're fine, and move on. The squeaky wheel gets the grease, and Mum never made a noise.

My parents' fate was a bitter irony that I thought about often. Dad's mind was fine; his body let him down. Mum was the opposite. If only they were one person they'd have been fine. Between them, I had one functioning parent. There just weren't enough parts left for them both.

So I think that the pressure built up over the years to the point where it had to come out, but it had nowhere to go. There was no escape valve, no way of bleeding it off the system, so it began to distort and warp the mind that housed it. However strong you are, there's always something stronger. However strong you make the cylinders and pistons of an engine, if you put too much stress on them they'll bend and break and shatter. I think that's what happened with Mum. Her mind couldn't take any more and so it did the only thing it could: it started to forget.

So when we learned about dualism, I always thought of Mum. Are mind and body separate? Are they the same thing? Are they two sides of the same coin? I didn't and don't have answers, but I know this: my mother's body was fine. She was in great physical health. But by the time she was sixty-five, her mind had disappeared, ravaged by itself to protect it from the pain of the memories it housed. It was as though it was a computer that had deleted everything to get rid of the one virus that was polluting it, leaving behind a perfectly functioning piece of hardware with no software to run it. If that's not proof that mind and body are separate then I don't know what is.

12.

2010: Geneva

A volcano. I'd heard some excuses in my time but that took the biscuit.

I was in Geneva airport. I'd come the day before for a meeting, and I was due to fly home that evening. The airport was full of people milling about, looking at the departures board, their faces creased in puzzlement. The boards were covered with an outbreak of red capitals: ANNULÉ. Cancelled.

I finally reached the British Airways desk. Before I could ask the question, the woman shook her head. 'Monsieur . . . there are no other flights. UK airspace is closed. The volcano in Iceland has closed it.'

'So how do I get home?'

'As soon as a seat is available, we'll book you on it.'

'And in the meantime? I just wait here?'

The woman shrugged. I could see in her eyes that she was already sick of this conversation and that she knew she would be even more sick of it in a few hours. 'Go to a hotel. Check with your airline for the latest updates.'

'Thanks,' I said. 'Do you know of any hotels nearby?'

The woman pointed up the concourse towards a large crowd. 'You can ask at information. They'll be able to help you.'

The queue in front of the information desk was already at least twenty deep. A red-faced man with a strong Liverpool accent was arguing loudly with an impassive tourist information-giver, or whatever they're called. I decided to give it a miss. I'd go straight to a hotel and check there, before they all filled up.

As I left the airport my phone rang. Michael had downloaded a new ring tone the night before and put it on my phone. It was the chorus from a song in which the singer declared loudly and at length that she was horny, and horny all night long at that. I had no idea how to change it or how to lower the volume. All day long during the meetings I had kept it in view so I could answer it as quickly as possible. Normally, before the ring-tone went off, the screen lit up, so I could get to it first.

This time it was in my pocket and, by the time I dropped my bag and fumbled for it, it was well into its stride.

A well-dressed woman with stiff hair and pearls looked me up and down in surprise. A young couple laughed as they walked past. The man winked at me. I could feel my cheeks burning. Michael was always doing this kind of thing. A few weeks back I'd been at the doctor for a check-up and the phone had gone off, some loud notes then a voice demanding to know what its owner's motherfuckin' name was.

I managed to pull the phone from my pocket and stop the song. Michael's name was flashing on the screen.

'Michael,' I said. 'How do you change this ring tone? It's bloody embarrassing.'

'I'll do it when you get back, Dad. If you get back, that is. Have you seen the volcano in Iceland? There's going to be no flights for ages. Days, the news said.'

'I know. I'm trying to sort something out. There's still a chance I'll be back tonight.'

'What, have you got a private jet? Don't be daft. There's no flights at all. I checked on the airport's website. You'll be lucky to get home at all this weekend.'

'I'll call you later,' I said. 'Don't have another party at the house. You hear? No party. That means no more than three of you in there.'

'Don't worry, Dad. We're going into town.'

'Where in town? You're not old enough to drink, never mind go to bars in the town centre.' I knew that they bought drink and that they went to pubs; I'd found Michael's fake ID once in his jeans pocket, a student union card for Lancaster University. I'd had one, when I was his age, for Hopwood Hall Tertiary College in Rochdale. Tommy had made it, and, despite the appalling amateurishness of the production, the occasional publican had accepted it. They must have assumed that students did things in that way; either that, or they didn't care. I suspected the latter.

Michael laughed. 'Right. Promise I won't drink. And I won't go to bars. We'll just chat in the street. Maybe we'll go to the park and have a poetry reading.'

'Don't be sarcastic, Michael. It doesn't suit you. Be careful.'

It took a few hours to find a room, at an extortionate rate. The last time there was a commotion in the heavens and no room at the inn, did the innkeepers take advantage of the conditions to jack up prices? Did the manger cost an arm and a leg? The Bible is unclear on the matter, although the harsh commercial reality is probably unchanged between then and now.

I ate a sandwich and lay on my bed. I hated these quiet moments. I always thought of Pippa. It had been three, nearly four months since we'd broken up, and I missed her just as much as I had at the beginning. I was often tempted to call her, but I stopped myself. She hadn't called me, so she couldn't be all that concerned. It was better left alone, now that it was over. It would only end in tears.

I was woken by my phone shouting that it was horny. I glanced at the time. One a.m., midnight in the UK. It was a Warrington number, although I didn't recognize it. Must be bloody Michael. I tried to still the flutter of worry in my stomach. As a parent you always think the worst. You have to force yourself to relax.

'Graham Melton.' My voice was cracked, my throat dry.

'Mr Melton? This is the police. I'm PC Jayce.' A man's voice, young, confident, to the point.

The words shocked me upright. It wasn't Michael, it wasn't Pippa, it wasn't an accidental marketing call from a call centre in India that had got its time zones mixed up. It was the police, calling me at 1 a.m. on a night when Michael was in town.

'Is something wrong?'

'Do you have a son called Michael who was in Warrington town centre this evening?'

'Yes, I do. Is everything ok?' I knew it couldn't be; what I meant was *what the hell's going on*?

'Michael's been involved in an altercation.' He paused. 'You'd better come to the hospital. He's there now.'

The hospital? Not the police station? That meant he was hurt. How badly hurt? Hurt enough not to have called me. Hurt enough for the police to have called me.

Now I said it. 'What the hell's going on?'

'I'd rather wait until you get there to explain. You can speak to the doctor.'

'I'm stuck in Switzerland. Geneva. I can't get there. There's no flights. The volcano.'

His silence gave the words time to sink in. *I can't get there.*

'Mr Melton. I'm afraid . . . It's not good news. He's not conscious. If you can, I suggest you get home as soon as possible.'

My legs felt weak, my mouth was bone dry and my head span. All I could think if was the policeman's word: an altercation.

Was it him, that hooded yob? I didn't even know his name. Michael had never said. I pictured Michael flexing his muscles in the garden, imagined him and Danny in a bar with their chests puffed out, full of beer and swaggering with confidence in their new strength. Was that it? Did he think he was hard now and that he could take on the bane of his life?

I put the phone down and stared at the curtains. I was suddenly aware of how far from home I was. Air travel shortens distances, but when you don't have the option of a plane, a few hundred miles is a long way.

Too long, I thought. Too fucking long.

I threw my belongings into my suitcase and grabbed my wallet and passport. I couldn't just sit here and wait. Even if it was hopeless, I had to try something.

In the sodium glow of the terminal lights a group of four people were haggling with a fat taxi driver with a luxuriant moustache.

'One thousand five hundred francs to Calais,' he was saying, with a shrug. 'That's the price.'

'That's a thousand pounds!' a red-faced man spluttered, his mouth flecked with foam. 'For a ten-hour drive. It's robbery. You should be ashamed, taking advantage of the situation to make money.'

I gestured to the taxi driver. 'I'll take it. One thousand five hundred.' The taxi driver raised an eyebrow. I pushed past the man and climbed into the back seat. 'Let's go. Calais.'

'Hey,' the man said. 'That's our taxi.'

The taxi driver locked the doors and started the engine. The man started banging on the window. Through the darkened glass, his red face looked almost purple.

'You wanker!' he shouted. 'Hope the fucking ferry sinks!'

The taxi pulled into the traffic and the shouting man receded into the background. I saw the taxi driver smile smugly in the mirror. *Don't be so pleased with yourself, mate*, I thought. *Money's more relative that you think. I'd have paid you ten times this to get back home.*

As soon as we were out of the airport I called the hospital. They put me through to a doctor. He sounded reassuring; calm and in control.

'How's Michael? Is he ok?'

'I'm afraid he's still not conscious. We suspect that there's an injury to the brain. It's hard to tell how bad without taking a closer look.'

'Are you going to operate?'

'As soon as he's stable enough, yes. Hopefully in a few hours.'

That was too soon for me to get back. I'd be at Calais 7 a.m., then God alone knew how I'd get across the Channel. I dug my fingernails into my palm to keep myself focused on the conversation. I had to hold it together as well as I could. I rattled off my mobile phone number. 'Keep me posted. Any developments, call me.'

The call ended and I dialled another number.

'Marj? Sorry to wake you up. It's Graham. There's been an accident. Michael's in hospital.' Marj was my secretary. She'd been with me for the last decade, and she knew Michael well. 'I'm on my way to Calais. Can you book me a ferry? I should be there by 7 a.m.'

Ten minutes later she called back. I knew immediately from the tone of her voice that it wasn't good news. All the ferries for the next three days were booked solid and there was no one she could call at this time to explain how badly I needed to get on one.

The feeling that gripped me wasn't panic, exactly. Panic is identifiable, localized. You know what it is, and that you can get through it by breathing deeply, or meditating on the eternal, or whatever. Panic passes. This was much worse: it was the world narrowing to one thought and one thought only. My son is going to die and I'm not there to help him.

I closed my phone and leaned back against the seat. The lights of the French motorway passed in a blur. In the silence Calais seemed a long way away, and England even further. It was unbelievable how fragile the whole system was. One volcano blows up in Iceland and thousands of people are stranded. It makes you realize how vulnerable you are. What if I was in the US, or Australia? The volcano could rumble on for months. We rely on a lot of extraordinary things for our normal existence. Air travel, mobile phones, the internet: to earlier generations these things would have been miracles. To us, they're bread and water. Take them away and we're left exposed, like an unwanted child on a hillside.

This was pointless. I would be just as stuck in Calais as I was here. I wouldn't be home for days. Michael's fate, whatever it was, was out of my hands.

13.

2008: Old Friends

Michael heard the car pulling up in the drive first. He jumped to his feet and looked out of the window. He'd been looking forward to seeing his grandparents for ages and, at fourteen, he was still unself-conscious enough to be enthusiastic about it.

'Grandma!' Michael hugged Georgina. He was nearly as tall as her. He was in year nine, which was equivalent to third year senior when I was at school. Incredibly, he had some of the same teachers as I'd had, but none of them remembered me. I didn't know if that made me feel old or young: young because we shared teachers or old because it was so long ago they'd forgotten me.

'Come in. It's lovely to see you.' I kissed Georgina and shook Stephen's hand. Stephen looked older, gaunt and greying. His new Jag convertible was parked in the driveway. Georgina could have passed for my age, though. Her eyes were bright, her skin smooth and supple. I wondered if she'd had some work done, but it didn't seem like her. Perhaps she was just lucky. It gave me a pang of longing for Charlotte. You know what they say: if you want to know what your wife will look like when they're older, look at the mother. In Georgina, I could see the woman Charlotte would have become.

'Hi, Grandad,' Michael said. 'Cool car. Can we go for a drive later?'

'Of course we can.' Stephen cupped his hand round Michael's face. 'You're looking well.'

'Where's Richard and Ginny?' I said. 'I thought they were with you?'

'They were following us but we lost them. Don't worry, they know the way.'

They'd all been on holiday together somewhere in Scotland and were stopping in on the way home. I'd not seen Richard for years – even though there was no animosity between us since Charlotte's death we were not close and I hardly knew his wife and twin daughters, Molly and Jane. I was looking forward to seeing them all.

A silver Mercedes Estate pulled up behind the Jag. The back doors flew open and two scowling, blond fifteen-year-olds got out.

'I'm taking the train home!' one of them shouted. 'I can't stand another minute in this car!'

'So am I,' the other said. 'I hate going on holiday with you.'

Georgina shrugged. 'Oh, dear,' she said. 'It's been a bit fraught.'

'Hello, girls,' I said. 'It's been a while since I saw you. Do you want to come in?'

They turned and looked at me at the same moment. I've always found twins uncanny, and having them both stare at me with the same searching expression put me on edge.

One of them raised an eyebrow. 'Hello, Uncle Graham.'

The other smiled. 'Do you have Coke?'

'Michael, take the girls inside and get them a drink.' I walked over to the Mercedes. Richard was just getting out. 'Richard. Good to see you. And Ginny. Welcome.'

Ginny stared at me, narrow-eyed. It was obvious that she didn't want to be here. I turned and gestured for them to come inside.

In the kitchen, I put on the kettle. Michael and the twins were upstairs. I could hear the noises of the computer games. 'How was the holiday?'

'Lovely,' Georgina said. 'Absolutely lovely.'

'Apart from the weather.' Ginny didn't look at anyone as she spoke. Her mouth barely moved. It seemed like she was speaking through her nose.

'It wasn't that bad,' Richard said, visibly tensing. It was obviously a sore point. 'You expect a bit of rain in Scotland.'

'A bit, maybe. I felt like Noah. It rained for forty days and forty nights.'

'Stop exaggerating! It was a light drizzle. A persistent drizzle, but we could still get out and about.'

Ginny shrugged. 'We evidently have different standards. I suppose you also enjoyed the food? You would; it was ghastly.'

Richard shook his head and picked up the paper. He muttered something under his breath and Ginny's face darkened. Stephen and Georgina sat expressionless through the exchange. They were obviously used to it.

The kitchen door opened and the twins came in. 'Michael's got an Apple iMac,' one said.

'That's what we want,' the other clarified.

'Well, you can't have it,' Ginny said. 'Daddy's got no money. I told you. That's why we were on holiday in that awful place.'

'You can borrow mine any time you like,' Michael said. 'I think we've got a spare laptop you can have.'

No one replied. I don't think Richard and Ginny were used to offers of charity – but then they'd never needed them. I'd been under the impression that Richard made a fortune in the City, but it seemed that something had changed.

'That's a lovely idea,' I said. I squeezed Michael's shoulder. Why should he be made to feel awkward for his generosity, just because his relatives had some hang ups? 'We'll talk about it later.'

I heard the back door bang open and the noise of someone in the utility room. It sounded like they were putting something in the washing machine. There was only one person it could be, and I braced myself for his entrance.

The utility room door opened and Tommy walked in. I groaned inwardly. He was dressed in his underpants and socks and a scruffy T-shirt that was too small for him so that his belly showed below it. His face opened into a wide grin.

'Fuck me,' he said. 'Stephen and Georgina!' He glanced at Michael and the twins. 'Shit. Sorry, Graham. Don't say that, you three.' He turned back to Charlotte's parents and opened his arms. 'How've you been?'

After an awkward embrace with Stephen and a warm hug from Georgina, he sat at the table. 'Hello, Richard. You must be Ginny. Heard all about you.' Ginny looked like a dog that was having its nose rubbed in its own mess. I almost felt sorry for her.

'So, Tommy,' Stephen said. 'I won't say I'm surprised, since I know you, but I am interested. Where are your clothes?'

'In the washing machine.'

'That I know. What I was really getting at is why aren't you wearing them?'

'Well, they're covered in . . . dirt, and they needed washing, so I brought 'em round here.'

'You didn't want to wash them at home?' I said. 'I don't mind, I'm just curious.'

'It's not, you know, *dirt* dirt. It's dog dirt. I got it on them while I was out. It's the dog-walkin' business. It's not as bloody easy as I reckoned. Bloody things are a pain in the arse. I thought I could just let them run around in the back garden as the cash rolled in, but they dug it up, so now I have to drag them around with me everywhere I go. My missus is sick of washin' me trousers, so I brought them here.'

'I see,' Richard drawled. 'The harsh realities of business can come as a shock, I find.' My hackles rose. I hated that superior tone he used. Hadn't Ginny just been saying he had no money? I was about to ask him about it when Tommy interrupted.

'Is the kettle on? I'm gasping for a brew.'

The tea. I'd forgotten. 'I've just made a pot.' I poured them out. Ginny raised a hand. 'Could I have water? I've a bit of a headache. I think I've a migraine coming on.'

'Of course you bloody have,' Richard muttered. Ginny's head whipped round and she glared at him. In that second I was glad she didn't have a knife in her hand. She looked like she would have used it.

I got a glass from the cupboard and switched on the tap.

'Not tap water,' she said. 'I only drink bottled.'

'Oh.' We didn't have any. 'Can I offer you something else?'

'I'd really like some water.' I got the impression she wanted someone to go and get some for her.

Tommy laughed. 'You want it from a bottle, eh?' I think he thought she was joking, so in the spirit of things he joined in. 'Graham. Pass me the glass over and I'll stick it in a bottle for her.'

Ginny's voice was high and shrill. 'I'm not sure that's what I had in mind.'

Tommy froze. 'You mean you're serious? Give over, love.'

Richard and Ginny left soon afterwards, taking the protesting twins with them. He should have given them the train fare and let them make their own way home.

Tommy's trousers finished in the washing machine and he put them on, dripping wet.

'They'll dry on the way home,' he explained, but I think he wanted to leave me some time with Georgina and Stephen. He wasn't as dumb as he seemed, Tommy. He just had a different approach to life to most people.

Michael took Georgina on a tour of the house. In particular he was keen to show her his bedroom, his school books, the medals he'd won for football. Stephen poured himself a fresh cup of tea. 'Everything well?' he said.

'Great. Michael's doing well at school, business is good. Can't complain. You?'

'Yes. I retired a few months back. Had enough. I'm doing some part-time things now, a few company directorships. Two days a month, that kind of thing. Things I want to do. Georgina's great, lovely as ever.'

'And Richard?'

He sighed. 'It's obvious, I think, that they're having difficulties. He lost his job and since then things hadn't been good between them. Ginny's always on his back to find a new one, and he's trying, but the kind of jobs Richard does don't come up that often. She liked the holidays in Barbados. I always told him when he was making so much money that he should put some aside, but there's so many costs living in London, along with the mortgage, school fees. You have to make a fortune just to break even.'

'He should come and live here.'

'Ginny would never allow it. She can't see beyond the end of her nose. You know, that's something I've come to realize over the years. It's not about money, it's about quality of life. The more you have, the more you want. You can spend a long time counting all the things you've not got. So much that you have no time left to enjoy the things you do have.'

'You're beginning to sound like my old man.'

He laughed. 'Perhaps he was right, in a way. What was that song he used to sing, about the fat man who waters the workers' beer? I rather liked that.'

I started to sing. *I'm the man, the very fat man, who waters the workers' beer / And what do I care if it makes them ill, if it makes them terribly queer / I've got a car and a yacht and an aeroplane and I waters the workers' beer*. 'It's an old trade union song. They used to sing it in the Farmers' Arms.'

We lapsed into silence. It was a comfortable, warm silence, the silence of old friends.

'I'm glad that Michael is doing so well,' he said eventually. 'He seems happy.'

'He is. He's a good lad. I make sure I tell him that a lot.'

'It's funny, isn't it, when you look back at all the kerfuffle we had when you and Charlie were courting, all the nonsense about us being too posh for you. It turns out that all that stuff is irrelevant.' He paused. 'We miss you and Michael, Graham. Georgina and I talk about you a lot. And Charlie. We miss her as well.'

He had tears in his eyes. Even now, the feeling of what might have been was strong enough to cause a physical pain. They could have been visiting the three of us, or four, or five, if we'd had more children. They could have been sharing in our happiness. But it wasn't what had happened. He regretted it, that was etched on his face. As it must have been on mine.

'I miss her too.' The words were weak and inadequate. They didn't cover the range and depth of the feelings, but then they didn't need to. He understood well enough.

The kitchen door opened and Michael led Georgina in.

'Everything ok?' she said. We were standing on opposite sides of the kitchen counter in silence.

'Yes,' Stephen said. 'We were just talking about Charlie.'

'Ah.' She smiled sadly. 'I see.'

'You were talking about Mum?' Michael said. He was ravenously interested in anything to do with Charlotte. He never tired of hearing about her. I didn't mind; I encouraged it. It helped me keep her memory alive. 'Dad told me about when him and Tommy brought a real duck to the duck race the other day.'

'I remember that well,' Stephen said. 'I was very impressed. I have to say I agreed with Tommy. It would have been much more fun if we'd used live ducks.'

'Not for the ducks,' Michael said.

'No, not for the ducks.'

'What did my mum think about it?'

'Oh, I think she was embarrassed,' Georgina said. 'Teenage girls get embarrassed by a lot of things. Once she refused to go out with your dad because he was wearing a head band. He was in a Dire Straits phase, I think.'

'That's right,' I said. 'She preferred Duran Duran and Culture Club. Dire Straits were not on her radar screen at all.'

Georgina glanced at her watch. 'Darling, hadn't we better get going? We've got quite a drive to Dorset.'

'Of course. Thanks for the tea, Graham. And I hope we see you soon.'

'It's a pleasure to have you.'

Georgina hugged me. 'I know you're busy, but we'd love to see you. You're welcome anytime.'

'We'll be there. We'll find a school holiday, or something.'

I watched them drive away. I didn't know it, but the next time Stephen and I met we'd both be wondering if we'd ever see Michael again.

14.

2010: Richard

I called Stephen and Georgina's number, as much to give myself something to do as to keep them informed. Besides, if I wasn't going to be there, and Pippa was no more, it would be good if Michael saw some familiar faces if – *when*, I corrected myself, when – he came round.

The phone rang for a long time before Stephen answered. I interrupted his complaint about how late it was and told him what had happened.

'And you're stuck on the Continent?'

'I'll be in Calais in a few hours, but there's no ferries.'

'Jesus Christ, Graham, that's awful. You must be frantic.'

'Worse.' I paused. 'I feel like it's happening all over again.' I didn't need to say what. 'You and Georgina should head up to Warrington in case I don't make it.'

Stephen paused. 'No, we've got to get you home. I've got an idea. I'll call you right back.'

A few minutes later my phone rang. A number I didn't know. My heart stopped. What if it was the hospital, or the police, with bad news?

'Graham? It's Richard. Dad told me what happened. I'm sorry.'

Brilliant. Just what I needed. Sympathy from Charlotte's brother. I mean, it was welcome, but it was hardly like we were close. It could have waited. 'Richard, thanks. I'll let you know how it turns out, but I'm not even in the country.'

'I know – Dad said. That's why I'm calling.' He sounded excited. 'When you get to Calais go straight to the marina. A friend has a boat. We'll be waiting for you.'

My chest expanded as though I was breathing for the first time. Adrenalin surged through my body. 'What did you say?'

'I said a friend has a boat, a kind of speedboat cruiser thing. We'll meet you at the marina in Calais first thing.'

I started to thank him but he interrupted me.

'Don't. There's no need. You're family.'

I called Carly's mobile. She answered on the first ring. Her voice was thick and tearful.

'Is there any news, Carly?'

'No. He's still in the room.'

'What room? Are they operating?'

'I don't know. I've not seen anyone for ages.'

'Are you on your own? You should go home, get some rest.'

'Dad's here.'

I asked her to put him on. Perhaps he would know a bit more about what was going on.

'All right, mate,' Billy said. 'It's a bit of a shit situation, this.'

'I know. Billy, could you do me a favour? Could you find a doctor and ask for an update? Get as much detail as you can. Better, when you find one, call me and put the doctor on.'

'I will. By the way, don't worry about Connor. I'll make the fucker pay when this is over. However bad Michael is, he'll be twice as worse.'

'Thanks, Billy.' It was a generous offer, after a fashion. Billy was only trying to find a way of helping. 'But you don't need to do that. There has to be a better way of dealing with it. The police, the courts, whatever.'

He didn't reply. I don't think he had much faith in the judicial system, but I did, and I didn't want to get involved in a feud with Connor and his family. I wasn't equipped to deal with it.

'I've got to go. See if you can find a doctor, Billy.'

He either didn't look for one, or couldn't find one, because there was no call back. The not-knowing was terrible. The Spanish Inquisition could not have come up with a more exquisite torture: your only child in a life-or-death situation and you in another country with no sure way of getting home in time. Michael was my life: everything was at stake, but there was no way I could influence the outcome. All I could do was hope.

I stared out of the window and watched the motorway drone by. It grew busier as the sky lightened, and I sat up a little. Dawn was coming, and with it Calais.

We passed the ferry terminal. Crowds were gathered around it, even at this hour of the day. There were a lot of people stranded in France; I realized with a wave of gratitude that without Richard and his friend's help I would have had no chance of getting home for days.

Richard was standing at the entrance to the marina with another man. I unfolded myself out of the taxi, my legs stiff, and shook his hand.

'Thanks.' My lip quivered. 'Thanks for this.'

'Don't mention it. This is Dick.'

I shook Dick's meaty hand. He was tall with a vast stomach and a luxuriant moustache beneath a veined red nose. 'Thank you as well, Dick. It's so good of you to come.'

'It's a pleasure, old man. Like Dunkirk all over again. Bloody brilliant adventure. Wouldn't have missed it for the world. Anyway, let's get on our way.'

Dick's boat was big, the kind of thing you see dotted off the coast in the South of France. He manoeuvred it out of the marina and into the Channel. As soon as we were past the buoys that signified a speed limit he opened the throttle and the boat leapt forward.

It was exhilarating, crashing over the waves. Any other time I would have enjoyed the sensation, but all I could think about was Michael. Now, at least, I knew I would be back in a few hours. I just didn't know whether that would be soon enough to see my son alive.

The crossing took less than an hour, and, with the time going back an hour, we were in Dover at 6.30 a.m. I stood at the bow, watching a misty England come closer. As we approached the harbour, Richard joined me.

'I hope it works out,' he said. 'Keep me posted.'

'I will. Thanks again.'

He paused. 'This probably isn't the best time, but I wanted to let you know that Ginny and I have split up. We're working through the details of a divorce. It's a bloody pain.' He stared into the distance. He looked deflated.

'I'm sorry to hear it.' A silence settled between us. It was broken by Dick calling us to get the fenders ready. I caught his eye. 'Any time you need a bolt-hole you're welcome at our place. Michael would like to get to know his uncle. He loves hearing about Charlotte, and I imagine you could tell him quite a few stories.'

He smiled a thin, weary smile. 'I will. Thanks, Graham.'

Stephen met us off the boat. 'Graham.' His eyes were hollow. 'I'm so glad you're here.'

He ushered me towards the car park and into his Jag. I said goodbye to Richard and Dick and promised to let them know as soon as there was any news, then we got underway.

We pulled onto the road and my phone rang. It was the doctor.

'We're operating,' he said. 'We're going to open up his skull. He's stabilized so we're ready to go.'

'Is he ok?'

The line was silent. 'It's hard to tell at this stage. He's unconscious, Mr Melton, which is . . . never a good sign.'

I winced, something inside me shrinking.

'Where are you?'

'Just left Dover.' That was it; keep focused on practicalities. 'I'll be there in a few hours, depending on traffic.'

Stephen tapped my knee. 'Shouldn't be so bad, on a Saturday morning. And I'll get my foot down. Three hours, max.'

I passed on the message.

'That's great. I have to scrub in. See you soon, Mr Melton. We'll do our best. I promise you.'

Despite the anxiety, I managed to fall into a half-sleep. I was woken by the sensation of the car slowing down.

I opened my eyes. 'Are we there?'

'Not yet. Just south of Birmingham. We've got a problem.' Stephen wound down his window. A policeman leaned down and looked in.

'Morning, sir.' He leant one hand on the roof of the car. 'Do you know what speed you were going?'

'Yes,' Stephen said. 'One hundred and twenty, maybe one twenty-five.'

'You are aware of the speed limit, I take it?'

Stephen nodded. 'Look, officer. Let me explain. His son – and my grandson – is in hospital, with serious head injuries. They're operating now. There's no guarantee he'll make it. If you want to give me a ticket, fine, but I have to get to the hospital in Warrington as soon as possible.'

I stared silently at the police officer. Once more my fate was out of my hands. I wondered whether it always was, but in normal life you had the illusion that you were in control. If so, it was a necessary illusion. The ease with which things could fall apart was an uncomfortable truth; it was better to think that disaster was a long way away than to see how close it was.

'Give me a minute,' the officer said. 'Warrington Hospital, right?'

He went back to the unmarked car on the hard shoulder and spoke to his colleague. A few minutes later he was back at the window.

'On your way,' he said. 'I've radioed ahead and the other motorway cops know the situation.' He looked at me. 'I've got two boys myself. Good luck.'

We pulled into the hospital and Stephen dropped me off outside the main door. At the reception I gave my name and a nurse accompanied me to a waiting area on the third floor. It was empty, apart from one person hunched forward in a plastic chair. It was Carly.

She heard me come in and looked up. She was a mess, the cheap, thick make-up she plastered on herself smudged all over her face by her tears.

'Where is he?' I said. 'What happened?'

'He's in there.' She sniffed and pointed to a set of double doors. 'The doctors have been runnin' in and out.'

'Did they say what was wrong?'

'No. They just go in and out. They look dead serious.' She started to cry again.

'How was Michael? Did you see him?'

'They took me in the ambulance. He was unconscious. He had blood comin' out of his nose.'

He had been in an ambulance, unconscious, bleeding. My heart threatened to beat through the walls of my chest.

'Jesus, Carly. What happened?'

'It was Connor. Him and his mates were in town and they seen Mike.' A sob interrupted her, then another. I put my arm round her.

'Then what, Carly?' She carried on sobbing, out of control. 'Did they get into a fight?'

She nodded. 'I don't know. I was in the Checkers Bar. I only seen him when I came out. Me and 'Chelle seen the ambulance and then someone told me it was Mike.'

'Where's Danny?'

'The cops took him,' she said. 'With Connor and his mates.'

Jesus. I hoped those cops were making sure that they were held in different rooms. I stood up.

'I'm going to find out what's going on.' I pushed open the double doors. There was a long corridor. On either side, green doors led into rooms. I set off. At the far end there was another set of double doors with a red light above them. Next to it was an electronic sign. *Theatre. Operation in Progress.*

I walked towards it, my bowels feeling loose. Michael was in theatre. As I approached, a nurse stepped out of one of the doors, holding a clipboard. She was in her forties, heavy-set with severe eyes and brown hair scraped back in a bun. Her eyes were ringed with dark circles and there were grey flecks in her hair.

'Sir? You're not supposed to be in here.'

'It's my son, Michael. I think he's in there.'

'I'm afraid you still can't go in. It's an operating theatre. It's closed to the public.' Her eyes softened as she spoke. 'Someone will be out as soon as there's any news.'

I went dizzy. I must have swayed, or looked unsteady, as she took my elbow and guided me into the room she'd come from, a small nurses' office, and sat me in a chair. She poured me a cup of coffee and put it in my hands.

'Has he been in there long?'

'A few hours. He should be out soon. Don't worry, you'll be with him shortly.'

I finished my coffee, thanked the nurse and washed the mug, a chipped, red mug with a bull on it and a Spanish flag. A holiday souvenir, no doubt. There were bits of paper on the counter top, rosters stuck to the cabinets, a calendar with pictures of a boy band. I scanned them for Michael's name, but there was nothing, and so I went back to Carly.

She was sitting in the chair, hunched over again, with her face in hands. She looked at me and I saw in her eyes a mirror of my feelings. Bewilderment, fear, shock, love.

'Did you see him?' she said.

'No. He's in . . . they're doing an operation. Someone'll come soon.'

She remained seated; I paced up and down the waiting area, from the door in, past the double doors to the window. Each time I reached the window I looked out over the town and thought: that's where it happened. Out there. Those streets, packed with shoppers in the daytime, change at night into a scrum of drunkenness, a fun-packed circus of bars and clubs, the bright lights and two-for-one offers barely masking the hard-edged danger that lurks beneath them.

It was getting close to ten-thirty when the double doors opened and a doctor came out. At first I didn't recognize her, seeing only the green robes and mask pushed down over her neck. It was when she rubbed the back of her hand against her forehead that I realized who it was. I knew that gesture.

'Graham,' Pippa said. Her face was thinner than I remembered; her cheekbones jutted out and her jaw line was more prominent. It wasn't an improvement. Her bottom lip quivered. 'You're here. Thank God.'

'Pippa? What is it? Is he ok?'

'For now. We fixed him up. He was unconscious when he came in and there was some bleeding in the brain, but there seems to be no lasting damage. The surgeon who operated is the best around.'

'Can I see Michael?'

'Yes. But he's not conscious.'

The double doors opened again and a man came out, dressed in the same surgical clothes, his mask already pushed back. Tall, swept-back dark hair, angular profile; it took me a second to place him. It was the man I'd seen her with, the reason we'd broken up. Even now, I wondered with a stab of jealousy whether they were still seeing each other.

He put his hand on her elbow. It was a gesture that spoke of a deep intimacy and comfort. 'I'll speak to Mr Melton. You go and get changed. It's been a long night.' He turned to me and shook my hand. I barely gripped his fingers. I didn't know what to do: thank him or hit him. 'The operation went well. It might not seem like it now, but Michael has been very lucky. It could have been very different. Had he arrived here an hour later, it might not have been possible to save him.'

Carly was still in her seat, her head in her hands. She hadn't moved from that hard plastic chair. I wondered if she was superstitious, if she thought that it might help Michael.

'How bad is it?' she said.

'We'll see when he wakes up,' the doctor said. 'Are you his sister?'

'I'm his girlfriend.'

The doctor nodded. 'Your boyfriend's had a lucky escape. He could have been killed. Make sure you let him know.' I watched how he talked to her, how he treated her as an adult, and I saw how she must appear to people who didn't know her: a young woman. It was the same for Michael. He was a young man, not a boy anymore. The thought of him facing the world on his own gave me the chills. I wasn't sure he was ready. I wasn't sure *I* was ready.

'Thank you,' I said. 'For what you've done.'

'There's still a long way to go. Michael was lucky. There were some touch-and-go moments in there. I was glad to have Pippa with me. She's a brilliant doctor. We work well together.'

I'll bet you do, I thought. 'I'm glad,' I said.

'I trust her totally. But then, we are family.'

'You're . . . related?' *Family?* Had she *married* him?

'Cousins. Pippa's my cousin.'

I stared at him, feeling as though I was falling forward. I blinked, trying to register what he had said.

'Are you ok, Mr Melton?'

'Did you say cousin? Pippa's your cousin?'

He nodded. So this was the cousin she had told me about, the doctor. The one her father had compared her to. Not her boyfriend. Her cousin. Her bloody cousin. What had I done? Why the hell hadn't I just asked her?

An orderly came to take us to Michael. All thought of Pippa vanished when I saw him. He was lying on his back in a hospital bed, a white bandage encircling his head like a papal cap. Next to him, a monitor recorded blood pressure and heart rate. His eyes were closed; he had one tube coming out of his nose and another, thick like a snorkel, coming from his mouth. I couldn't stop looking at the mouthpiece. It was pulling his lower lip down, and I pointed it out to the nurse.

She adjusted it. 'There we are,' she said. 'That's better.'

I bent over him. He was pale, and there was a bruise under his right eye. How had it come to this? My boy in a hospital bed, unconscious. He should have been at home getting ready for a Saturday with his girlfriend. How could it possibly have changed so quickly?

'He's going to be ok, Carly,' I said. She was staring at him, her face pale and tear-stained. She kissed him on the cheek. 'Go home, get some rest. Your Dad left, right?' She nodded. 'Take a taxi. Here.' I handed her a note. 'I'll call you as soon as there's any news.'

After she left, I looked at Michael in silence, watched the rise and fall of his chest. After a while, the door opened and Pippa came in. She was dressed in jeans and a T-shirt and had recently showered.

'What happened in there?' I asked. The smell of her perfume sent my head into a spin.

'We had to operate to take the pressure off his brain.' She couldn't look me in the eyes.

'Will he be ok?'

She sucked her bottom lip into her mouth. Love and longing surged through me. 'We can't know for sure until he wakes up. From the looks of the injury, he hit something hard. I don't think it was a fist, or a shoe. Probably the kerb, or the road.'

I pictured Michael's head slamming into the kerbside, then a boot or a fist snapping it back, then a doctor bending over him in a dark room. 'Jesus.' A vision of Michael in a permanent coma swam in front of my eyes; worse, a vision of him dead. 'What's going on, Pippa? He just went to town, and this happened. Can't he just go out with Carly in peace? Can't those thugs just leave him alone?'

'Was it them? Is that all still going on?'

'It seems so.' I forced myself to look in her eyes. 'Pippa. I have to tell you something. I've made a mistake. About us. When we broke up, I didn't exactly tell you the truth about why.'

She closed her eyes. 'Graham. Now's not the time.'

'It is. I want to tell you.' I clenched my fists behind my back. 'I thought you were having an affair.'

Her mouth tightened. 'You thought I was having an *affair*?'

'The day we broke up, I saw you with someone. In the hospital car park. I'd come to pick you up at work. I saw you with another man – laughing, linking arms – and I thought you were having an affair. I didn't realize it was – until I saw him now. It was your cousin.'

I was startled to see tears form in her eyes. 'Was that it?' Her voice was raw with emotion. 'Was that why you put me through this? Why didn't you say something?'

'I'm sorry.' Never has an apology so inadequately expressed the depth of the remorse it was intended to convey.

Had we been anywhere other than her workplace she would have hit me, I'm sure of it, but she just gave a precise, quick shake of the head. 'It's too late now. Try and get some rest. I have to go.'

I slept for a few hours, slumped in the chair by Michael's bed. I was woken by sound of the door opening. Stephen and Georgina came in.

'How is he?' Georgina put her hand on my cheek and kissed me.

'Stable. Not changed. A doctor was here a while ago.'

The doctor, a burly red-haired man in glasses, had busied himself around Michael, looking in his eyes, lifting his arm and dropping it, prodding and pinching his neck. I'd watched him with the feeling that he was at a great distance from me, as though he was in a parallel universe. When he'd finished, he'd made some notes on his clipboard and left the room.

We sat in silence for a long time. Georgina held Michael's hand and Stephen stared at him. Eventually he stood up. 'We're staying at the Village Hotel. Call us if there's any news. Or if you need us.'

A few minutes after they left a nurse came in with a cup of tea. 'Mr Davies will be along shortly.'

Mr Davies – Pippa's cousin – came into the room twenty minutes later. He closed the door behind him.

'How are you? I hope you got some rest.'

'Not really. But it's ok. I'm fine.'

He made a smacking sound with his lips. He looked serious. 'I'm afraid I don't have good news for you. It's not bad news, as such, but Michael is not making the progress we expected. 'We're going to have to do some further tests.'

'What do you mean? What kind of tests? You said he'd wake up. You told Carly he'd wake up.' I felt almost disembodied and I could hear the panic in my voice.

His face softened. 'We did all we could last night, but with this kind of trauma to the brain, you never know. I hoped that he would recover quickly, but it's not happening, not yet at any rate. That's not to say it won't.'

'Is he going to be like this for the rest of his life? Like a, a . . .' I searched for the medical term, but I didn't have it. All I could think of was a term I knew wasn't right, but I had to ask the question. 'A vegetable?'

'I don't know. It's possible. We're going to scan Michael's brain to see if we can find out what's going on. I'll make sure you're kept abreast of whatever news we have.'

He left and I turned away to look out of the window, feeling the darkness pressing in at the corner of my vision. I wanted a drink. The worry crippled me; I just wanted it to go away. My mind was tearing under the strain of the gap between the reality I had to accept and the world I wanted. I knew what people meant when they said they were losing their mind. I could feel mine slipping away.

I bent over Michael and wrapped my arms around him, feeling the rise and fall of his chest. Why wouldn't he wake up? His body was working, so why wouldn't he wake up?

'Michael,' I said. 'Michael, I love you. Can you hear me? Please, if you can then do something. Give me a sign.' I kissed his forehead, his eyes, his lips. He didn't respond. I would have rejoiced had he pushed me away, cried tears of joy at his rejection. But he was still. There was nothing there.

I held him close to me until the orderlies came and wheeled him away. It didn't seem real. It was as though I was acting a part in a play that would soon be over, the actors congratulating each other on a convincing performance in the green room. I suppose that's the only way you can get through it. If you thought it was really happening you'd collapse. Sometimes denial is the only protection.

I sat in the chair by the bed and closed my eyes, but sleep was impossible, my mind crowded by a succession of visions: Michael, waking up but brain damaged, unable to speak or care for himself; Michael, in a coma for years, neither dead nor alive; Michael, being carried into a funeral parlour in a coffin. All of them horrified me. I couldn't cope without him, I knew it. I thought about Pippa, about ways I could make it up to her, but I knew, unless he recovered, there was no point. There'd be nothing left of me for her. Without him, I'd come undone. I wasn't strong enough not to.

Then get some help. It's not as if you don't deserve it.

The edges of my vision darkened and the wet, dog-like odour I knew so well filled my nostrils.

Have a drink. What does it matter? You'll be sober when he wakes up. Just one, just to take the edge off.

I looked at Michael. Not now. Not when he still needed me. Please, not now.

I left the hospital and stumbled into the street, crumpled and tired, looking for a bus, or a taxi. The streets were busy: people were walking to work, the traffic was honking, a group of workmen were digging a hole in the road. It was all so normal. The external world was going on as before; inside, I was in turmoil.

A private hire taxi was waiting at a set of traffic lights and I opened the door and fell into the back seat. A man in a suit looked at me in alarm, clutching his briefcase to his chest.

'Eh, mate. Get out. I've got a customer.'

'I'll pay,' I mumbled. 'Drop him off, then take me home.'

'I said get out. Now.' The taxi driver was a fat man with tattooed arms. He unbuckled his seat belt and started to get out of the car.

'It's my son. He's in a coma. I need to get home.' The words sounded meaningless, as though I was just trying them out.

The taxi driver hesitated. 'Jesus. I'm sorry. But it's his taxi, mate.'

'Drop me at the station,' the man said. 'It's not far. This guy needs a lift home.'

I slumped against the door, staring out of the window as the familiar streets of the town centre rolled by. All I could think about was that first drink.

Soon we pulled into the station. The man handed the taxi driver a note and climbed out. 'Keep the change,' he said. 'Put it towards this guy's fare.'

'Stockton Heath, via an off-licence,' I said. 'I need a drink.'

'You sure, mate?' I saw him look at me in the mirror. 'You ok?'

'I need a drink. I've not touched a drop for years, but sometimes you need it, eh?'

'Don't start now, mate. Whatever's wrong, the answer ain't at the bottom of a bottle. Trust me, I've been there.'

'Trust me, so've I, and I need a drink. My son's in a coma and I don't know if he'll wake up.'

He shrugged. 'It's your funeral. Stockton Heath? We can stop at Bargain Booze.'

I bought a bottle of Jim Beam and six cans of Special Brew. The skin on my face tightened and crawled as I paid for them, the burn of the liquor all I could think of. It confirmed my decision: I wasn't even drinking and already all my troubles were at the back of my mind.

In the back of the car I opened the whisky, but the taxi driver raised a hand. 'Not in the car, mate. It's illegal. Wait until you get home.'

He dropped me off at the barn, and I closed the front door. I put the whisky on the kitchen counter. It looked incongruous there. It'd been a long time since there'd been any in the house.

I was salivating, the thought of the drink burning my mind in anticipation of the burn on my throat.

Just one. To get you through the day. When Michael's better – if he's better – then you can stop.

Don't do it, I told myself, but the voice was small and weak. He needs you. You can't let him down. You know what'll happen if you have one drink. You won't be able to stop. There's no such thing as one drink for you.

When he's better, you can stop. If he doesn't recover, then what does it matter?

I reached into the sink and grabbed a glass. It had milk in the bottom; Michael must have had it before he went out, probably to line his stomach. I rinsed it and the world narrowed to the drink I was about to have.

The sound of the whisky pouring into the glass was deafening. The smell invaded my mind, fired long-dormant synapses in my brain. My heart pounded. This was it. This was all I needed. I held it in my hand, watching the liquid swirl and settle. God, it made so much sense. It was so easy; it could have been so easy all along. The answer had been right there.

I licked my lips slowly and raised the glass. I wanted to savour this, make it last. After all, soon I'd be pouring the stuff down my throat. For now, I might as well pretend that there was some element of control.

There was a loud knocking on the back door. I froze, the glass an inch from my lips, and looked out of the kitchen window. Tommy was staring back at me.

He shook his head and rattled the door handle. It was locked. I smiled. He couldn't get in. I, and my drink, were safe. I raised the glass in a cheerful salute.

The back door crashed open. It was shocking how easily a fit bloke could break a lock. Tommy stood in the door frame and shook his head. His face was white, his lips shut tight.

'What the fuck are you doing?'

'Tommy.' My throat was dry. My stomach constricted as I saw the possibility of the drink recede. 'I need it.'

He moved more quickly than I did. That was his greatest strength and his greatest weakness: he didn't think. Tommy just did. By the time I reacted, he had the bottle in his hand and was tipping its contents down the sink.

'No, Tommy, stop.' I watched in despair as the whisky vanished down the plughole.

'Give me that glass.'

I shook my head and held it away from him.

He dropped the bottle and dived at me. His charge dislodged the glass from my hand and it shattered on the slate floor. The whisky darkened the tiles. The smell was intoxicating.

He wrapped me in a bear hug. 'Sorry, mate. But that's all in the past now. I heard about Mikey. How is he?'

I struggled to escape the thought of the whisky. 'Not awake yet. They're doing some tests.'

'What tests?'

'Scans. I dunno.'

'Graham!' He let go of me and grabbed me by my shirt. 'Snap out of it! Stop thinking about the bloody booze. It's gone, but Mikey's still here. He needs you.' He picked up the kettle. 'I'm going to make some tea and something to eat. Go and get yourself showered, then we'll go to the hospital.'

I looked at the sink, the greasy residue of the whisky still visible on the metal. For a second I considered licking it up. Tommy grabbed my upper arm and pushed me towards the stairs. 'Get yourself sorted and we'll go and see that lad of yours.'

I stripped off and got into the shower. I couldn't believe that I'd come so close to drinking. I couldn't even claim that I'd resisted at the last second. I was committed to having that drink. It was only Tommy's arrival that had stopped me.

And I still wanted it.

I had to get a grip. Michael was still alive and, when he came round, he needed a father, not a drunken wreck. And then there was Pippa. I'd made a mistake and I had to fix it. I rinsed the smell of the drink from my mouth and spat the water into the drain. I'd got lucky this time, but you couldn't rely on that forever. Make up your mind; the motivation comes from the decision. I made up my mind, made a bargain with myself: while he's alive, and as long as he's alive, no drinking; but if he dies, then do whatever the hell you want.

Pippa's cousin wasn't there when we returned, but another doctor came to see us, brandishing Michael's file. He looked at Michael, still motionless in the bed, and shook his head.

'I spoke to Mr Davies,' he said. 'The good news is the scans are clear. There's no physical damage to the brain.'

The relief was like stepping into a warm bath when you're cold and dirty.

'The bad news is that we don't know why he's not come round yet.'

The water in the bath drained away. When it comes to your kids, any piece of bad news is one piece too many.

'Is there anything we can do?'

'Just wait here, talk to him. Who knows? I'll be back later to check on him. If anything changes, press this button by the side of the bed to call a nurse.'

Tommy and I sat on either side of the bed, two sentries, silent and unmoving. I yawned. 'I'll go and get some coffees,' I said. 'Milk and sugar?'

'Ask for a strong one,' he said. 'Get a paper as well. Ta.'

I walked down the corridor to the lift. Near the reception there was a newsagent's and coffee shop. A handful of people were clustered around it, sipping their drinks. I wondered what they were thinking, who they were here for. A birth? An ill parent? I flicked through the newspaper. Environmental damage from an oil spill in the Gulf of Mexico, cracks in the new coalition government. It all seemed so remote when you were here, surrounded by all these individual stories. It was hard to see how it all mattered, hard to link it to your own life.

The man behind the counter called me and I grabbed the cardboard cups. I added a packet of sugar to Tommy's, then one to mine. I didn't normally have it, but I'd not eaten much of the breakfast Tommy had made – I couldn't force it down – and I needed some calories. I folded the paper under my arm and set off to the lift.

As I reached the door of Michael's room, I heard the sound of laughter. It sounded like Tommy. I pushed the door open and stepped inside.

'And then,' Tommy said, 'she called out for your dad and he came out from behind his tree. I'd already buggered off. It was embarrassing.'

'He's such a loser.' His voice was a croak, but there was no doubt who it was.

'Michael!' I put the coffees on the table and wrapped my arms around him. 'You're awake! Thank God.' He tried to hug me back, but he was too weak. 'Don't move,' I said. 'Rest. Tommy, did you call a nurse?'

'Ah. Forgot that.' He pressed the button. 'We were too busy having a laugh.'

'What happened?'

'I was telling him all the stupid things you did as a teenager. He must have liked them, because he opened his eyes and laughed. Shame really. I'd only just got started.'

'Will you tell me the rest later?' Michael said.

'When your dad's not around. I don't want him giving you a false version, trying to paint himself in glory.'

'Was he that bad?'

Tommy puffed out his cheeks. 'Worse, Mikey. You wouldn't have believed it. He was lucky I hung around with him. You should have seen some of the clothes he wore. It was the eighties, but still. There was no one else on our street who had such a crap mullet.'

'All right,' I said. 'Enough. I know it's fun, but I don't think this is the time to assassinate my character. And don't believe a word he tells you, Michael. This is the man who tried to use you as a human shield when you were five.'

'It would've worked,' Tommy said. 'Instead, I had to pay for the repairs myself.'

Thankfully, the nurse arrived. She fussed around Michael, looking in his eyes with a light and pinching his skin.

She grinned at us. 'I'll get the doctor.'

Weeks passed. Pippa wouldn't return my calls. I tried her home number, her mobile, her number at the hospital, but she wouldn't talk to me. I tried one more time.

The switchboard at the hospital answered.

'Hello,' I said. 'This is Dr Michael Carly. I work for the *Lancet*. I'm looking for Dr Pippa Davies?'

'Just a minute.'

The line went silent. After a few seconds the receptionist came back on. 'I'll put you through.'

'Pippa Davies. How can I help you?'

Pippa's voice. Her tone was interested, curious to see who this doctor from the *Lancet* was. I hated to let her down.

'Pippa. It's me. Graham.'

There was a long pause. When she spoke her voice was flat. 'What do you want?'

'I want to talk to you. Explain. That's all.'

'I told you it was too late. Stop calling me.'

'Pippa! Please! Just a talk, that's all. There's too much between us to end it like this. You know that.'

I listened to the sound of her breathing. 'All right. I'll meet you after work. At Mediterreaneo.'

Mediterraneo had just opened, the chrome tables outside shining with both newness and the rain that had fallen on them. Cafe culture was going to have to adapt if it was going to take root in the north west.

I took a seat in the corner and waited for Pippa. She was late; when she came in I almost didn't recognize her, shocked by the dark circles under her eyes and by how thin she was.

'You look well,' I grinned. 'It's great to see you.'

'Thanks. You wanted to talk?' She didn't smile back; her face was expressionless.

'I wanted to see you. I just want to see you. I miss you.'

'That's a shame for you. You should have thought about that a few months back.'

'I know. I've never regretted anything as much. But I did what I did, and I can't change it. I can only apologize.'

'I can't believe you thought I was having an affair. That I would do that to you.' She laughed bitterly. 'Oh, well. It doesn't matter now.'

'It does. It matters more than anything. To me at least. I don't know what else to say, Pippa. It was stupid, but it was a mistake. I'm sorry.'

'Some mistakes are worse than others. And sometimes you have to live with the consequences.' She looked away. 'Do you know what you did to me, Graham? Have you any idea what I've been through in the last months? The man I loved, trusted, gave myself to, that man turned round and threw me out of his life without so much as a word of explanation. I've tortured myself looking for a reason, for something I did wrong. I've hardly eaten, hardly slept. And now you tell me it was a mistake? That it could have been avoided if you'd just bothered to tell me what was going on?'

'I didn't want to ask you if you were seeing someone else in case you said yes. Then everyone would know that you'd dumped me.

I was sick of things happening to me. I wanted to be in charge for a change.' Now they were out, the words sounded more pathetic than I had feared.

Pippa shook her head, her mouth slightly parted. 'You're a fucking idiot, Graham. You know that? You ruined what we had because of some stupid, teenage pride.'

The waiter coughed. He was Michael's age, making his way in his first job. 'Now a good time? Or should I come back?'

'Just a coffee.' Pippa glared at me. 'I'm not hungry.'

'Same, thanks.' I was starving, but I wasn't sure how long she'd stay and I didn't fancy munching through a cheap lasagne on my own. I hadn't known she was capable of this much anger.

'Pippa. I've been an idiot, I don't deny it. But it wasn't just teenage pride.' This was it; the only excuse I had. I prayed it would be enough. 'I've thought about it a lot, and I was scared, Pippa. Of losing you. I couldn't go through what happened with Charlotte again so I guess I was looking for a reason to break up. But now that you're gone I realize that, however bad that fear was, it was better than this. Better than being without you.'

She was looking at the ground, motionless.

'I love you. More than anything. I just want you to know that. And if we can get back together, I'll do whatever it takes.'

When she looked up her expression was blank again. 'How's Michael?'

I didn't press the point. She'd heard, and if she wanted to talk about Michael then so be it. At least we were talking. 'He's been reading about Freud. There was a TV programme on him and he was very taken with his ideas. I think it's all the sex. Anyway, he's decided to be a psychoanalyst.'

'That's great. You're always complaining that he doesn't take an interest in his studies.'

'Except that I'm his main patient. Apparently I project my own emotions onto him as a form of defence mechanism.'

'There might be some truth in that. Freud got the odd thing right.'

'I don't think Freud had tidying bedrooms in mind. According to Michael, my requests for him to tidy his room are me projecting my desire for tidiness onto him. Instead, I should be looking at the deeper reasons why I have such a need for other people to be tidy. His initial diagnosis is that I am stuck at the anal stage in my psycho-sexual development.'

'I can see his point. You can be a bit picky.'

'Don't mention that to him. He doesn't need any encouragement. So whenever I ask him to do anything he nods knowingly and asks me whether there were specific things in my childhood that made me this way. It's infuriating.'

The waiter brought our drinks. Pippa stirred her coffee. 'I miss Michael,' she said. 'I'd grown quite fond of him.'

'And he of you.'

'That's why it's such a bloody disappointment that you ruined it. I was so happy. I loved you, Graham.'

I noted the past tense and tried to ignore it. 'We still would be happy. I love you, as much – more – than before. And maybe you still love me, even though I'm an arsehole.'

'Of course I do!' She slammed her spoon onto the table. 'I wish I didn't. I wish I could just forget you. That's the damn problem.'

It was a problem I was glad she had. I kept my face straight. I didn't want to appear triumphant, but inside I was leaping for joy.

I heard the crunch of wheels on gravel and looked out of the window. A panda car pulled up outside the house and two uniformed officers climbed out. I opened the door and shook their hands. One was my age, a slight paunch pressing against his uniform. The other was younger and introduced himself as PC Jayce. It was he who had called me the night of the accident. They asked to talk to Michael. I called him, and we sat at the kitchen table.

The older officer spoke first. 'As you may know, Connor is up on charges of GBH.'

'Good.' I sipped my tea. I just hoped the sentence would be a long one.

'In order to secure a conviction, we need to present the best case possible.' He looked at Michael. 'Which means you testifying about the events of the night itself, but also the other incidents leading up to the assault.'

Michael shook his head. 'No way. He knows who I am.'

PC Jayce nodded. 'We understand that you might be frightened, Michael, but without your testimony we can't be sure of securing a conviction. Connor might walk away.'

'I don't want anything to do with it.' Michael was white. His bandage was off his head now and the scar on his skull was livid against the pale skin of his scalp.

'If Connor is free, this could happen again. If he's locked up, you'll be safe,' the older copper said. 'Think about it.'

'What about his mates? And what about Carly? She lives there. They'll go after her. I don't want to do it.'

He was shaking, and I could see that he was in some distress. I gestured to the police officers to go outside.

'I'll speak to him,' I said, when we were on the drive. 'But I can't promise anything. He's terrified.'

'We get this a lot,' PC Jayce said. 'But we need witnesses to put these people away. Without that, there's no way of punishing them. There's no deterrent.'

'I know, and I agree with the principle. But why should Michael be the one to take the risk?' It's like paying tax. We all agree it's necessary, but none of us want to do it.

'Connor committed a serious assault. He should be punished.'

'Aren't there any other witnesses? CCTV?'

The older officer shook his head. 'The CCTV footage is inconclusive. You can't see what's going on because of the crowd of people gathered around. Everyone we've spoken to has said they were too drunk to remember. They're lying to avoid appearing in court, but there we are. We need Michael's testimony.' He gave me a card. 'You can call me on this number.'

'Ok. I'll talk to him.' I watched them leave. I knew from the way Michael had reacted that this wasn't going to be an easy sell.

15.

2010: Witness

'What do you think?'

Tommy sipped his pint. We were enjoying the afternoon sun on the terrace of the London Bridge pub, Tommy's local, watching the swans glide by on the canal.

'There's two options, mate. Either Mikey goes to court and puts him away or you deal with it yourself.'

'What does that mean?'

He shrugged. 'Sort Connor out.'

'You mean beat him up? I can't. I'm not that kind of person. I wouldn't know where to start.'

'Not you. Pay someone. I know a few lads who'd do it for some cash. They wouldn't have to hurt him. Just give him a warning, like.'

'You think that's an option?'

'It's always an option, mate. Always.'

I didn't want to do it. It seemed so barbaric. I shook my head. 'I'm not doing that.'

'Then it's court. Lock the bastard away. He'll learn his lesson well enough that way. If he went after Mikey again, he'd know what was going to happen: back inside. Don't believe what you read in the

Daily Mail about prison not being tough enough. It's no holiday in there. My uncle could tell you a few stories.'

'Your uncle was inside? I didn't know that.'

'Not doing bird. He was a warder. One night they had a riot and the prisoners got into the sex offenders' wing. He never told me the details, but in the morning they had a corpse on their hands. Death by fork, he said.'

'By fork?' I forced the image from my mind. It wasn't the kind of thing I wanted to dwell on at the moment. 'So you think Michael should testify?'

'Yeah, but if he won't, you have to do something. If you let Connor off scot-free, he'll make Mikey's life a misery. He'll think he's untouchable.'

'Has it really come to this, Tommy? Kids can just go round assaulting each other and there's nothing the cops can do? I mean, what the fuck?'

'It was different for us, eh?' Tommy sipped his pint. 'We couldn't get away with owt. But then we had something to lose.'

Tommy was right. Even in the eighties, Connor would have worked in a factory, with the dual discipline of a shift supervisor who paid his wages and a union rep who kept him on the straight and narrow. Now, he hung around a ruined estate looking for trouble. It was like that in whole swathes of the country, and it seemed that it had become accepted. It was easier to sip oaky Aussie Chardonnay in bars in designer villages and avoid the swamp of the town centres than to do something about it, while a dark morass of near feral teenagers drank cheap, sugary booze and disappeared further from view.

They were second-generation unemployed, these kids. In the eighties there'd been industry all over the north west – in my town alone there were steel works, breweries, tanneries, the wire industry.

Now it was all gone. They'd never seen their fathers go out to work, most of them. The work might have been dirty and low-paid, but you couldn't just take it away without replacing it with something else.

And there was no point blaming the politicians. That was too easy. We were all in it, all of us who'd watched it happen, who'd bought the arguments about free markets and globalization and efficiency, and helped the fat man to water the workers' beer. And worse: it was people like me who had shut the factories. What was it Terry and Norris had told me? *The thing is, Graham, we need someone to manage the transition and we'd like you to do it. You know the business, know the workforce. It'll be better coming from someone like you than some outsider. They trust you.* Dad had warned me about it. You shit on your own doorstep and soon the whole house stinks.

But that didn't justify what Connor had done. And it didn't help Michael.

'There's only one option,' I said. 'We've got to put a stop to it.'

'Then it's court. You'll have to persuade him.'

'Easier said than done. Apart from anything else, he thinks he's putting Carly and her family at risk.'

Tommy snorted. 'Billy McAndrew? Scared of a teenager? Give over. Billy's hard as nails. He knows a thing or two about the inside of a prison, I can tell you.'

'Really? Billy's been in prison?'

'So I hear.'

So that was why he hadn't had a job. I'd never understood it. He was a good worker and a decent bloke, so why wasn't he working? It wasn't supposed to matter if you had a record – if you'd done your time, you'd done your time. Your debt to society was paid. But anyone who believed that was kidding themselves. A record was an albatross round your neck. It also explained why he hadn't applied at our place when I'd offered. He didn't want me to know about his past.

Tommy handed me his pint glass. 'You havin' another pineapple juice? Get me a beer while you're up there, would you?'

I found Michael in the living room, reading a music magazine. It was an article about John Lennon. It was about time they found someone new to write about, but then again, every generation seemed to discover such people and claim them as their own. It wouldn't be long before Slade were making a comeback.

He didn't look up before he spoke. 'I'm not doing it. No way. You can't make me.'

'I'm not going to try and make you. I just want to talk to you about it.'

'There's no point. My mind's made up.' He turned the page; Jimi Hendrix was standing on a stage with his guitar raised above his head, his eyes closed in ecstasy.

'Michael. We have to talk.' I sat down on the floor next to him. Before I could start he jerked away from me and slammed the magazine shut.

'You don't get it, do you?' His eyes were wild, and there was a strident tone in his voice. He looked on the edge of insanity. 'You want me to go to court but you don't get it. Connor's mates will kill me, Dad. They'll actually *kill* me. Do you understand? We're not talking about some kids messing around.'

'I know how you feel. But you have to understand that it's not going to be like that. People don't just go around killing each other.'

'Maybe not in your world. But things are different now. You don't know what it's like.'

'That's what the police are there for. To stop that kind of thing.'

'They don't give a shit about the police! They just deny it, and even if they get put away they don't care.' He shook his head. 'Dad, it's best just to leave it. What happened, happened. I'm all right now. Going to court won't change it.'

'No, but it might stop it happening again. We – you – have a duty. If you don't testify then Connor will be free to do it to the next person who gets on the wrong side of him. And you'll be a party to that. We live in a society, Michael, and that comes with responsibilities.' I could feel my dad looking over my shoulder as I spoke, approving of what I was saying. I could also feel my teenage self rebelling against the memory of when he had told me things like that.

'So this duty – whatever the fuck it is – is more important than your son? Is that what you think? It's bullshit, Dad.' He opened the magazine. 'I'm not doing it. No way.'

I changed tack. 'Look, forget duty. Think of it this way. What's the alternative? You do nothing and then what? He'll know that he's untouchable, that you're scared. He'll keep at you. How will you be able to see Carly? At least if you go to court he'll know that you mean business.'

Michael looked away. 'I don't know what to do.' His voice was breaking. I sat next to him on the floor. 'Whatever I do I'm fucked. If I go to court he'll kill me, if I don't he'll ruin my life.'

'We'll make it work. I promise.'

'How?'

PC Jayce had mentioned a way; he'd known a number of people who had done it. I was very reluctant, but my son had to come first. It was no longer enough to take the path of least resistance. I had to take control and make this work.

'If you testify, and there's a real threat from Connor, then we'll move house. Somewhere out of town. Somewhere far enough away. We'll do whatever it takes.'

It was a wrench just to say it. I loved the barn. It was part of me, almost. It was my first house, the house Charlotte and I had moved into, the house where Michael had been conceived. I'd built most of it with my dad; every brick, every smell, every sound it made was a memory.

'And what about Carly? I want to keep on seeing her. I don't want to move away from her.'

'She can stay over. I'll talk to Billy and Kerry.'

'But if we're a long way away, how will I see her?'

'You could drive. You're nearly old enough. Take lessons, pass your test and I'll buy you a car. Until then, I'll drive you.'

'Really?' He looked up at me and a scowl crossed his face. 'You're not teaching me. No way. I want lessons.'

I almost laughed. 'I don't think that's the key point, but granted. You can have lessons.' This felt uncomfortably like bribery. *Do what I say and I'll buy you a car.* It was different, though. It wasn't a swap of a car for a favour; the car was a solution to a genuine problem.

I saw some hope spark in his face.

'We can do it, Michael. You're my son, and I won't let anything happen to you. Whatever it takes.'

'Ok,' he said. 'I'll think about it.'

16.

2010: New Beginnings

When you want to forgive someone it's easy to do so.

I read the words again. I hadn't called Pippa after our lunch, waiting for her to contact me. When she did, it was by letter. When the envelope dropped onto the mat, the thrill at seeing her writing was physical; the fear of what it might say was paralysing. I looked at it on the kitchen table for over an hour before I pounced on it and tore it open.

The letter explained how hurt she had been when we broke up, how hard she had fought to tell herself that she hated me, that I could never be a good man to be with because of Charlotte; so hard, in fact, that she had convinced herself she was better off without me. And then I had met her cousin and the real reason for the break up had become apparent.

The real reason: a misunderstanding based on my childishness. At first she had hated me more, stung by the triviality of the reason for my behaviour, but the more she reflected, the more she understood. Yes, it was childish, yes it was infuriating, but she understood: having been hurt so badly once before, I was quick to withdraw when the possibility of getting hurt arose again. She wasn't admitting it was justified or reasonable; she was merely saying that she understood.

And then that line. *When you want to forgive someone it's easy to do so.* The joy that swelled inside me as I read those words spilled out as tears. *However hard you try to convince yourself that someone doesn't deserve you, when you love them, that one fact overwhelms all the arguments you can think of. The fact is, I know that I'm happier when we're together. And so, despite myself, I want to try again.*

My fingers danced over the keys of the mobile phone in a familiar pattern – menu, address book, 'P', call – and I lifted it to my ear as it began to ring.

'Hi.' Pippa sounded like she'd been expecting the call.

'I got your letter.' It was hard to stop myself shouting and laughing down the phone. 'I'm so pleased. Whatever you want, Pippa. We'll make it work.'

'Ok.' When she spoke it sounded like she was fighting back tears. 'Just promise . . . promise that you won't do that to me again.'

It was the easiest promise I had ever made.

The trial took place a few weeks later. Pippa and I had seen each other a few times. It was slow-going, but I didn't care. I had Pippa back, I was fighting my son's corner; for the first time since Charlotte died my life was moving forward.

It began with Connor pleading not guilty. My heart sank. If the lawyer representing him had been sure that he would go down then she would surely have told him to admit it and hope for a shorter sentence as a result. The fact she hadn't made me think that the case was far from cut and dried, and I began to worry. A free Connor with a grudge was going to give Michael nightmares.

As PC Jayce had said, the problem was the lack of witnesses. Danny had been in a fight with one of Connor's friends and seen nothing; Carly was in the pub with her friends. Connor's friends and the other people that the police had managed to identify from the CCTV claimed not to remember or not to have seen.

The prosecuting lawyer stood in front of his table, a folder in one hand and his glasses in the other. They seemed to be for effect; he used his glasses as a pointer and only occasionally referred to the folder.

He looked at Connor. 'When you saw Mr Melton in the town centre, what did you do?'

'Nothin'.' Connor refused to look at the lawyer, his eyes fixed on the windows high up at the back of the courtroom. He was shaven-headed, taller than I remembered, and heavier set. His nose was thin and delicate, and he had piercing blue eyes. The acne had cleared up. He was no longer a boy.

'You didn't approach him?'

'No.'

The prosecutor tapped his folder. 'But you did end up in a fight with him?'

Connor nodded. 'Yeah.'

'Then you must have had some initial contact with him. What happened to cause the fight?'

'He started it. He called me.'

'He called you? You mean he called you a name?'

'Yeah.'

'And you reacted? How?'

'I ignored him. Then he called me again and offered me out.'

'By offered you out, you mean he asked you for a fight?' The slang held no mysteries for the lawyer; he had clearly seen a lot of these cases.

'Yeah. So I went over and he hit me.'

'Did you hit him back?'

'No. I pushed him and he fell over.'

'And then?'

'He never got up. He'd banged his head.' Connor looked at the lawyer and threw down his trump card. 'It was self-defence. I never meant to hurt him.'

The prosecutor didn't respond. 'Did you know Mr Melton prior to this event?'

Connor sniffed. 'No.'

'You had never met him?'

'Seen him a few times.'

'Had you had any contact with him? Threatened him? Hit him?'

'No. I knew him because he used to hang round the estate with his bird. But that's it.'

'His bird? You mean Miss Carly McAndrew?'

'Yeah.'

'What was your relationship to Miss McAndrew?'

'None.'

'She wasn't your girlfriend before she met Mr Melton?'

'One of 'em. She was nowt special.' His enjoyment at saying the words was palpable. I wanted to drag him from the dock and shout into his face that Carly was worth ten of him.

'So there was no reason for you to feel bitterness towards Mr Melton?'

'Exactly.' Connor looked confused. His lawyer fiddled with her pen. She suddenly looked a lot less confident; I think she guessed where this was going.

The prosecutor tapped his pen on his yellow pad. 'I see. You had no prior grudge against Mr Melton. Thank you. No more questions.'

The next witness was called. I think I did a double take. It was

Billy. He looked at me and gave a small nod. I had no idea he would be appearing, and I could see from his body language, from the stiffness in his posture, that it was a big step for him. Billy had a natural aversion to the system, the police, the courts. Moreover, he had been brought up in the belief that no one likes a grass. Being known as one could have serious consequences for him.

'Mr McAndrew,' the prosecutor began. 'You are Miss Carly McAndrew's father?'

'Yes.' Billy's hands flicked from the pockets of his suit jacket to the pockets of his trousers, as though he didn't know what to do with them. In the end, he held them by his side, his fingers pointing downwards.

'Were you aware of her relationship with the defendant, Connor James?'

'Yes. They went out for a few months. He was always round ours.'

'Why did the relationship end?'

'Carly told me that he was rude to her.'

The defence counsel leapt up and objected. Billy's testimony was hearsay. The judge agreed, but the point was made.

'We have heard that the defendant had no reason to dislike Michael Melton. Yet, isn't it the case that you intervened in a fight between the defendant and Mr Melton?'

'It wasn't a fight. Connor and his mates had Michael on the ground and were giving him a kicking.'

'Was this the first time this had happened?'

'No. One other time, when him and Carly had just started seeing each other, Michael came to ours with a black eye. He said Connor had done it.'

'Did he give a reason?'

'Because he was seeing Carly. Connor hated him.'

'Thank you. No more questions.'

The judge adjourned the session for lunch. The defence lawyer gathered up her notes quickly and marched out, her face white. It was easy to see why. The prosecution had established that Connor had lied about his relationship with Michael. In a case where it was Michael's word against his, that was important. I was sure that Connor had not shared the incidents with Michael with her; had he done so, she would have seen what was coming. Connor thought he could lie his way through it, but sometimes honesty really is the best policy.

In the afternoon we were shown the CCTV footage. In it, Michael and Danny are pictured coming out of the Red Lion and walking towards another bar. Michael stops and looks round, then raises his middle finger. Seconds later, Connor and a group of four others appear in the shot. They approach him and Danny at speed. One pushes Danny to the side and the others crowd around Michael. When they disperse, Michael is lying on the ground, motionless. There is no way of seeing what happened.

That was my son, lying unconscious on the ground. I felt sick and had to look away.

Michael's testimony began with questions from the defence lawyer. He looked nervous and small on the stand. Connor glared at him, but he looked away, his eyes darting between me and the jury. *Keep calm, son*, I thought. *Tell the truth.*

'Mr Melton, had you been drinking on the night in question?'

'Yes.'

'How much?'

'Not a lot. Two or three pints, and some bottles. Alcopops, you know.' I recognized the signs he made when he was under pressure: the twitching lip, the lowering of his voice. I wanted to jump down from the gallery and wrap my arms around him to protect him from the world.

'Quite a lot, in fact? Enough to make most adults inebriated, I'd say. Would you say you were drunk?'

'I was all right.' It didn't sound convincing. My palms dampened. It was obvious what she was getting at: this was a drunken quarrel that went wrong, related by someone with a memory rendered unreliable by drink.

'Can you take us through the events?'

'Connor called out to me, and I gave him the finger.'

'What did he say?'

'I don't know. Something about battering me.'

'And you decided to antagonize him by giving him the finger? Was that because you had been drinking?'

The prosecuting lawyer objected: it was a leading question. Michael did not have to answer.

'What happened after that?'

'He came over and spat at me.'

'Who did?'

'Connor. Then someone shoved me in the back and I fell forwards onto my knees. Connor kicked me in the face and I fell over. I don't remember anything else.'

'Are you sure it was him?'

'Yes.'

'How? How can you be sure it was not someone else who kicked you? You were drunk, it was dark, you were on the ground.'

'It was him. I watched him do it.'

'But you admit that you could be mistaken?'

Michael shook his head. 'No. I know who it was. It was Connor.'

After a few procedural points, that was it, the trial was over. It was less dramatic than I had expected, drier. I was conditioned by television to expect theatrics in the courtroom, but it wasn't like that. It was just two competing stories, one from a liar, one from a kid who had been drinking. While we waited for the jury to return, I found Michael in an office with a court clerk.

'Well done,' I said. 'You did a great job. I'm proud of you.'

He bit his lip. 'It's not enough. He's going to get off.'

'If he does, then you still did the right thing.'

'I thought it was for sure that he'd get put in gaol.' Michael looked at his shoes. 'If I'd known he might not . . .'

I put my hands on his shoulders. 'Look at me, Michael. Whatever happens, you'll be ok. This is the last you'll see of Connor, ever. I promise you. I won't let him touch you.'

He bit his lip. I could see he didn't believe me, but he didn't need to. I'd make him believe it, in time.

The jury were back about an hour later. 'That was quick,' the clerk said. 'It's usually longer than that.'

Michael's face paled. 'Is that good?'

'Not necessarily. It just means they came to a verdict easily.'

That's bad, I thought. It's a lot easier to set someone free than to send them down.

The foreman of the jury was in his thirties, with a shock of blond hair and a pair of heavy-rimmed glasses. He stood up and looked at the judge.

'Have you reached a verdict?'

'We have.' He had a strong Birmingham accent. 'On the charge of assault causing grievous bodily harm, we find the defendant guilty.'

It took a few seconds to sink in. I looked at Michael. He was staring at Connor, his face expressionless. He turned to me.

'It's over,' I mouthed. 'Let's go.'

*

On the way home I called Pippa and gave her the news. When we got to the barn she was already there, waiting in the drive. She no longer had a key; she'd mailed me hers after the break-up. I made a mental note to get her a new one. After hugging her – for a long time – Michael went upstairs. I put the kettle on.

'Eighteen months,' I said. 'I just wish it was more.'

'How was Michael?'

'Great. I'm proud of him.'

The kitchen door banged open. Michael came in, ripped the ends off a loaf of bread and shoved three-quarters of a packet of cheese between them. It was just about a sandwich; any less refinement and he would have been indistinguishable from an animal eating at a trough.

'We'll go and get your car tomorrow,' I said. 'We can go to that yard at Winsford.'

'It's all right,' Michael said, through a dense mouthful of sandwich. 'Tommy's sorting me one.'

'Tommy?' I tensed. If Tommy was involved, this could not end well. 'Is he a car dealer now?'

'He's going to get me a kit car. We'll build it ourselves.' He looked at me and held up his palms. 'I know you won't think it's safe, but it's a good opportunity to learn.'

I laughed. 'It's fine. Get a kit car. It'll be safe, all right. The safest car around.'

'Really? You don't mind?'

'Of course not. Sounds like a great idea.'

Michael raised an eyebrow. 'Cool. I thought you'd be dead against it. You *have* changed.' He crammed some more bread and cheese into his mouth. Incredibly, it was nearly all gone. Crumbs rained down onto the floor. I'd only mopped it the day before.

'Put that on a plate. You're making a mess.'

'I've nearly finished.' He cupped his hand underneath the sandwich. The crumbs gathered in his palm. He flicked them in the direction of the bin. Very few went in. 'See you later. I'm going to meet Danny.'

He shoved his feet in his trainers and walked out of the back door. Pippa yawned and moved behind me, her mouth against my neck and her arms around my waist. 'Are you really going to let him get a kit car? That doesn't sound like you. Are you sure it'll be safe?'

'It'll be the safest car on the road, because it'll never go anywhere. Tommy knows as much about putting cars on the road as I do about putting rockets in space.'

'Ah. I see. Pick your battles.'

'Anyway, it'll keep him occupied while I sort out the move.'

The move. At first it had seemed impossible. Now though, I was looking forward to it. Giving up the barn had become the means of rescuing my life; the sacrifice proof that I was taking care of my son and that I was serious about beginning a new life with Pippa.

I turned and put my arms around her. 'Can I interest you in some house-hunting?'

She rested her head against my shoulder. 'Any idea where?'

I shrugged. 'Somewhere quiet and safe and beautiful, and not too far from Mum. Most of all, though, with you and Michael. Other than that, I don't care.'

'I've got a few places in mind,' she said.

'Then let's go and look at them,' I said. 'We might as well get started. There's no time like the present.'

'You know, I'm impressed that you're taking this so seriously. I almost can't believe it. Do you think you can do it? Do you think we can do it?'

I thought about the barn, and then I thought of Pippa; of Michael; of my parents; of Charlotte. They were what mattered, living or dead. The barn was just bricks and mortar and memories.

'I think so,' I said. 'I think we'll be all right.'

Acknowledgements

Profound thanks to all those whose interest and support helped to keep me going in the early days: Mum and Dad, Ray, Scott, Adam, Josh, Lisa, Judy, Matt at Books Books Books, Panee (my midnight reader), the Geneva Writers' Group, Helen, Kathryn and Sharon, and Lily and Johnny, for giving me the reason to get started in the first place.

Particular thanks to:

All those I was fortunate enough to have as teachers. To name but a few: Margaret Parker (the first, and yet to be surpassed), James Gibb, Len Rix and the incomparable Paul Ponder.

Sam Copeland, for making it all happen.

Wayne Brookes; he is the ideal editor and I am grateful to have landed on his desk.

Phil and Astrid, for your encouragement and for laughing at the right places in the early drafts.

Jaed, for a thousand pieces of advice on writing, the publishing industry and how to use a Sawzall.

Jon, for your insights into the recovery process (and more besides).

My two boys, who make it all worthwhile.

And Tahnthawan, always and for everything.